Olympic Sacrifice

Olympic Sacrifice

Jack Hocutt, MD

Library of Congress Number:		2004099868
ISBN :	Hardcover	1-4134-7912-X
	Softcover	1-4134-7911-1

This book was printed in the United States of America.

To order additional copies of this book, contact:
Xlibris Corporation
1-888-795-4274
www.Xlibris.com
Orders@Xlibris.com

27150

This book is dedicated to the best gifts I ever received in life, my three daughters. Their love of life, sports, and learning, along with my love for them, inspired this story.

One

Friday, May 9

Fourteen-year-old Wendy Naylor reached the service rear-entrance door of WA Kelly Foundation Hospital (affectionately known as Kelly Hospital) that was labeled "Maintenance Only." She put her palm against a glass monitor to get an access code, and then she looked into the retinal scanner so the electronic door would open. She was tired of feeling like she was sneaking into the hospital for her sports medicine physiology testing and gymnastics workouts, and she wondered why getting inside was so darn secret.

Wendy stepped into the chrome vestibule and waited for the heavy metal door to close behind her. It took the usual 7 seconds to close, followed by the heavy-sounding bolt latching with 3 loud clicks, then a 3-second pause, then another loud click with an echo from the inside door as it began to open automatically. Wendy often wondered what would happen if she slipped and fell in the doorjamb while the door was closing. It was such a heavy door. Would it react to her small frame and stop, or keep on closing? Actually, the door had a safety catch if resistance was met, but that would set off loud alarms and waste another good 20 to 30 minutes of her busy day explaining what happened to whatever security guard was on duty and then she'd have to fill out a very long accident report. She went through this hassle twice in her first week of training. At times she wondered, too, if it was worth being so busy with school and gymnastics. Her training left almost no time for friends and fun, let alone spending any significant time with a boyfriend.

Once inside the forward door, she got on a service elevator and pushed the button marked 3B. All this security was in place to allow her to get on a private elevator that stopped at the interfloors—the floors between the regular hospital floors. These floors were off limits to everyone except a few select members of the hospital maintenance crew and the athletes in Dr. Thompson's training and conditioning study. Most hospitals had suspended ceilings that hid the plumbing and wiring; Kelly Hospital had actual floors between the public floors where all the utilities were easily accessed without crawling around in tight spaces. And the middle interfloor, floor 3B, had 12-foot ceilings, presumably for storage of extra-tall utility equipment. No other hospital in the world had such an extravagant set-up for maintenance and utilities and such plush accoutrements and abundant room throughout its massive structure. No other hospital in the world lived so well off its endowment with no need for patient billing to insure a profit.

After getting off the elevator, Wendy saw Brian Taggart, the security guard, who was just sitting at his fancy electronic desk with 10 large TV monitors, a futuristic computer screen and keyboard, and his small personal TV looking out of place positioned in front of one of the impressive monitors.

"Hi, Brian. It's me again," muttered Wendy. "I'm here for my fitness testing and workout."

"Come right in. It's so good to see you. Right on time as usual," said Brian. Brian had been working as a security guard for the WA Kelly Foundation Hospital on the elite sports medicine center floor ever since he tore the anterior cruciate ligament of his right knee as a freshman football player at the University of Delaware. He dropped out of school after his freshman year when he lost his football scholarship so he could make enough money to finish school. He had been at the Foundation for 3½ years and was having a hard time saving enough money to go back. Brian was hoping the top-security "Sports Medicine Research" division of Kelly Hospital would accept him for training and rehabilitation once the latest research protocols were approved for general population use. His 6'4" stocky frame dwarfed Wendy, but he was as kind and gentle to everyone as if he were a big brother protecting his favorite younger sister. And that was why he was having trouble saving for college. He had a younger sister named Beth who was attending a private school not too far from the hospital who would be devastated if she had to change schools. She was doing well in her studies and in sports and had acquired a good set of friends, and even had excellent rapport with her teachers. Tuition was well above their parents' means ever since their dad had been forced to change jobs, but unbeknownst to her, Brian was paying the freight. Wendy knew that Brian didn't want Beth to know he was paying her tuition because he thought she wouldn't accept the money and he did not want her to be disappointed in their parents if she found out they couldn't afford to pay the tuition.

"Why don't you look your usual happy self today, Wendy? I hear you're making good progress and you'll soon be able to beat me in arm wrestling."

"Oh, it's just annoying that it takes so long to get inside. I could be well into my workout by now and finished that much sooner and get home sooner."

"Does that mean you now have a boyfriend to replace me?" teased Brian.

"Yeah, right, whatever you say, Brian. Now when would I ever have the time or chance to meet a prospective boyfriend? I don't even have time to talk to *you* very often. I train with girls, go to an all girls' school, compete with girls, and have a female chaperone with me whenever I go out of town. I get up at 5:30 every morning, train for 2 hours, go to school till 3 in the afternoon, then come here for another 2 hours of testing and training, and then go home to study and eat dinner. I have to go to sleep before most of my friends even have to be home. Now you tell me where I fit in a boyfriend!"

"Whoa, hold on, I was just teasing. I always thought you were leading a charmed life. You travel all over the world, you're in the newspapers and magazines every other week, you get straight A's in school, and you've got me waiting to go out with you once you're 18."

"For your information, I got a B last marking period. My English teacher didn't like two of my papers. She thinks I'm too rigid in my writing. Now isn't it strange that all my previous English teachers loved my work and told me I'm a natural writer. I'm beginning to think that English is totally subjective and teachers just decide if they like you or not and then give you a grade based more on their comfort with you than your actual work. Since my teacher is overweight and probably never played a minute of sports in her life, I doubt she understands me, let alone likes me."

"She's loaded with her own problems, Wendy. Everyone knows she's not the best teacher in your school. She's been there so long, the principal is afraid of her. You can't get down because of what she's doing to your papers. You have to know it isn't you; it's just her insecurities that make her uneasy with you and your work. Your insight and physical and emotional maturity are way ahead of all your 14-year-old classmates. And the fact that you look like Dorothy Hamill doesn't hurt any. You're usually so pleasant, what's up today? Is your demanding pace getting to you?

"No, I feel fine."

"I guess Dr. Thompson really knows how hard to push your training, since you're doing so well. Just how do you kept getting physically stronger and better without getting tired or worn down? What protects you from over training? Don't you ever have a letdown?"

"Well, I don't get very tired working out, but I sure do sleep soundly. I'd better go now. I'm usually late when I get started talking to you. Dr. Thompson threatened to send me back to Boston every month instead of every third month if I keep showing up late."

Wendy thought it was ridiculous and a waste of time to go back to Boston for 2 days of testing every third month, just to be examined by more sports medicine experts. She was losing valuable training time and wondered why her strength and endurance had to be tested so often. Her strength coach, Michael Ryan, rarely changed her program after her tests; he just kept advancing her weights and pushed her to run harder on the treadmill and pedal faster on the training bike. She was up to 1,000 push-ups twice a day, 250 at a time and didn't want to advance her upper body training because she was starting to look stronger than most boys in her school. She wondered why she wasn't allowed to run or bike outside. Michael said it was too risky. She might twist an ankle or fall if her bike skidded on gravel. Well, what about her mental state—she needed to spend some time with her friends, that is, if she still had any. Physically, after all, she was getting stronger and faster well ahead of schedule. Her strength moves were already the best in Miroslov Tempti's world-famous gymnastics training school in Memphis, Tennessee. Miroslov couldn't believe his favorite little Delaware girl could do a one-handed press to a handstand with such ease. She didn't look quite that strong and didn't have huge bulging muscles or acne that so often comes with being super strong. Sure her shoulders were broad and she had a solid-looking build, but she still looked rather pure and innocent and her skin was smooth and soft.

So why wouldn't they cool all the testing and let her do a few things outdoors? Why did she have to travel to Boston every 3 months and waste a whole weekend indoors testing and training. Why did she have to get her monthly nutrition supplements by injection and not by mouth? Every time she asked, she got the same answer. That's part of the program she agreed to, it was working, and they weren't about to change it for fear something would not go right. They just had to fine tune everything perfectly, get her training nutrition just so, and balance her food nutrients optimally. It just took 20 hours in Boston every 3 months to be sure everything was right.

"Hi, Carrie," said Wendy. "What's on tap for today?"

"Miroslov says we have to practice your double back flips and your kip from a single handstand after pressing to a handstand. Then we finish with strength work for 40 minutes. He's going to teach you single and double twists with your back flips when you go for your next 2-week session in Memphis."

"I have two big tests tomorrow. What do you say we fly through the workout and get me home as soon as possible?"

"We can do that, as long as you hit your flips!"

Wendy warmed up for just 3 minutes and then hit 3 double back flips perfectly with a single speed flip in between.

"You have to be careful doing such a long run, Wendy," begged Carrie.

"But, Carrie, I've got enough space to do 3 normal passes in this top secret gym. I can't hit anything, even if I go off line."

"Yes, but the mat ends just after where you stopped, and if you hit wrong with the 2" drop off to the floor and get injured, you could lose months of preparation and Miroslov would have my head and yours, too!"

"OK, OK, but I just wanted to get done sooner, and I felt so strong I didn't want to stop."

"Well, for safety's sake and to keep your timing for your floor exercise sequence, stop where you're supposed to stop. Save your energy for the double twisting double flip. You'll need more height than you're getting now."

"True, but if I get more height now, I'll overturn the straight flips and land on my butt," said Wendy.

"All right, let's get on with your single hand presses and kips so you can get home."

Wendy realized she was being fussy with Carrie. She was not usually so persnickety when discussing her workouts. She never before worried much about her tests; she always did so well without even studying much. She seemed to learn what she needed to get A's just by going to class. Could this be the first sign of fatigue? Or was she just getting rammy from being sheltered so much and kept away from her peers and the public? She wondered if Carrie believed she was really worried about her tests.

The rest of the workout proceeded in silence, in a businesslike fashion. Wendy didn't complain and didn't seem to get overly tired. Carrie let her go after only one hour, letting her out a full hour early.

"Wow, I won't know what to do with all this time. I might even have 3 hours to study instead of my usual 2. I'll probably get confused with all the new facts I can learn."

"I suggest you study your normal 2 hours and then go to bed early. You seem like you need the rest," said Carrie. "Let me know tomorrow if you have any soreness or if you get more tired than usual tonight."

"You can book it, Carrie," said Wendy.

Wendy took off for home, wasting no time. She hopped on her bike and flew home, barely slowing down for turns—much against the admonition of her sports medicine physician, Dr. Steve Thompson. He was always worried she would skid on her bike and tear up her legs in a fall and ruin all the hard work he had put in making her such a great athlete. Well, she did all the work. Why did Dr. Thompson act like he deserved all the credit for her conditioning? What was so special about overseeing Carrie's workout plans for Wendy? Carrie knew what she was doing. She was extremely knowledgeable not only as an individual trainer, but also as an exercise physiologist and she probably knew more than Dr. Thompson anyway. Wendy didn't like Dr. Thompson much and wondered why her dad paid him so much money to check on her so much. If anyone deserved credit, it was her coach in Tennessee, Miroslov. Why, her dad deserved more credit than Dr. Thompson. He got her started and taught her all the basic gymnastic moves. He was always there to help if she got hurt or was sore or needed help or reassurance. He did encourage her a bit much, but that's what dads are for, thought Wendy.

Wendy sprinted up the driveway and made a hard right turn around the garage and almost ran over her dad who was shooting baskets with Kelly, her younger sister.

"Whoa there, Wendy," he said. "What's the big rush? Can't you wait to hit your history books tonight?"

"Oh, Dad, I just want to get to sleep early and I have to finish studying for two tests tomorrow."

Wendy didn't bother telling her dad and especially her little sister that she wanted to talk to her friend Robbie Coleman for more than a few brief minutes tonight. She had to get some work done fast in order to spend some time on the phone and still get to bed early. Even though she cut her workout short, she was still exhausted doing all those tumbling moves over and over without a break.

She tried not to look so exasperated while she parked her bike and then hurried inside the house. She knew Kelly would know better than to tease her about Robbie. Wendy was a good sister to Kelly, but she could not take teasing about boys without getting all moody and being mean to her little sister.

As soon as Wendy disappeared inside, Kelly said, "Dad, I'll challenge you to a 3-point shooting contest and the winner gets a long back rub—but you have to give me 3 shots."

"OK, as long as we're not playing to 4," replied Mike Naylor. "I'm used to your tricks, Kelly."

Two

Mike Naylor would sacrifice all he had for his daughters. He could bear not seeing Wendy most weekends and nearly all of the summer while she trained with Miroslov in Tennessee because he believed she wanted to be an Olympic gymnast. Even though he was a successful physician he had to mortgage his home for every penny so he could pay Miroslov, a world-class gymnastics coach, his huge fees. Wendy loved the sport so much, it was worth it. Debbie, his wife, worked two jobs to help pay their enormous bills for the kids—private school tuition, Miroslov's coaching fees, and Dr. Steve Thompson's professional fees for supervising Wendy's conditioning and training. Thompson's fees were not covered by insurance.

Mike believed he was incredibly lucky to have run across Steve Thompson two years ago. Mike had heard that Thompson had helped Jennifer Fields, an aspiring track star, who was having difficulty recovering from a few serious injuries. He not only helped her through her rehabilitation, he also dramatically improved her conditioning and her strength. Thompson credited his research conditioning and nutrition program for her success. Mike was especially pleased that Thompson pulled a few strings to get his daughter into one of the eight slots in the preliminary arm of his study.

Mike had taken Wendy to see him against the advice of her coaches who had actually heard of him and didn't like his gruff attitude with athletes. They had heard he was marginal at diagnosing athletes' problems, but they were prejudiced. The coaches also said he had a reputation for ordering way too many tests, but that's what research protocols are all about. It is true he is an orthopedic surgeon and may be quick to operate, but that's what orthopedic surgeons do and are supposed to be good at doing. Besides, Mike was a family physician, Board Certified in family medicine as well as sports medicine, so he should be able to tell if something wasn't quite right.

Thompson had to be a good physician and surgeon if he was in charge of the WA Kelly Foundation Hospital Sports Medicine Department. This hospital had patients coming from all over the world. They had more money than they could spend, so they would only hire the best. The State of Delaware had just successfully sued the Foundation to force them to spend more of their money according to the trusts set up to run the hospital. The State of Delaware won, so the hospital had to double its spending! That was no big deal to the Foundation. They were happy to oblige.

Mike remembered the first time he met Steve Thompson. The appointment was set for 6 PM at the end of office hours for both physicians. Mike made sure his patient visits ended by 4 PM so he could make the appointment on time. Apparently Dr. Thompson didn't have similar concerns. It was almost 8 PM when the two met.

Mike wasn't bothered by the wait. He was excited that he might have found a way to help his daughter. She had just had 3 injuries in a row, and although they were not considered major, he was concerned that the heavy training was taking its toll on the girl and she needed some help or she might have to give up her dream of being a champion gymnast.

Dr. Thompson wasn't particularly friendly or inspiring, but did manage to say a few right things. He told Mike about Jennifer Fields and another athlete named Matt Madison who had started together in his program. They were the first human subjects to try the nutritional supplement after years of study in rabbits and monkeys. They had done exceptionally well in just 6 months and had no apparent side effects or problems. After all, it was just a nutritional supplement—they weren't even considered drugs by the FDA. Dr. Thompson went on to describe the conditioning program and extensive testing that were designed to make sure injury prevention was optimal. Thompson emphasized that that was the main benefit of his program. He had spent years at the University of Michigan perfecting formulas for strength and endurance conditioning, and while none of the formulas were earth shattering, together they represented years of hard work and if followed religiously, they would work beyond the success of the Russian and Chinese athlete nutrition programs.

Mike knew nutritional supplements were not regulated by the FDA and therefore were not particularly risky. If they acted as a drug, they would be highly restricted and controlled because they could potentially have some significant risk. Food supplements, however, were not normally risky. They did have a few drug interactions, but a healthy athlete wouldn't be taking other drugs. Mike conveniently forgot about the steroid effects of many of the supplements weight lifters take.

Anyway, Mike had taken his help as far as he could. He had taught Wendy much of her basic gymnastic knowledge. He had arranged for the best gymnastic coach in the US to take her on, even though he was in Memphis, Tennessee, and not Wilmington, Delaware. He would teach her on weekends, school breaks, and all summer. If she progressed sufficiently, she would eventually have to move to Tennessee and train year round at Miroslov's camp.

But, at that time, she was injured for the third time in 4 months. She was getting discouraged. She needed a boost, or she might give up her main love in life. Mike wanted to believe Dr. Thompson's program was exceptional and he was willing to have his daughter become one of the 8 test subjects in Wilmington along with 8 more in Boston. The program would go through the next Olympics and then if all was going well, be expanded to 50 athletes at each site.

The cost was extremely high—$25,000 every 6 months,

payable in advance. Half was refundable at the end of the first 6 months if athlete and family were not satisfied. After that, there were no refunds. There was no charge for the nutritional supplement—it was included with the testing program. The money all went toward Dr. Thompson's fee; the hospital covered the study expenses in return for the prestige of having such an elite study conducted at their institution.

As soon as Dr. Thompson offered, Mike Naylor agreed on the spot to sign his daughter up. She would be the 7th of his 8 subjects. He bumped her ahead of 3 athletes on the waiting list. Mark McCormack in Boston had another 8 in his group. That was all the Foundation Board would approve until phase two. Gymnastics was a qualified sport for the study, requiring high enough levels of strength and endurance that should be helped by the conditioning and nutritional program.

Mike would explain to his daughter later why he enrolled her in Thompson's program. There were only two spots left and if he missed this opportunity, they would have to wait at least 2 or more years before they could get in.

Wendy started rehabilitating her rhomboid muscle strain the next day. The first injection came at the end of the first session. There was no messing around. They meant business. In only two weeks, Wendy thought she felt much stronger. Mike Naylor thought it was all psychological and that he had made a solid bold decision that was bound to help his daughter in many ways.

He didn't think twice about why "nutritional supplements" were being injected and not taken by mouth. The trainers told him it was given intravenously to be sure it was all getting to the right place and to eliminate the variable of absorption through the GI tract. That made sense; it really was a much more efficient method of administration.

Three

Friday, May 9
World Track Championships
Barcelona, Spain

Barcelona stadium was bristling with energy. Every seat was filled and the overflow crowd was milling around in the aisles and hanging out in front of snack bars and at stairwells. Normally, track meets, even world championship track meets, were less electric because there were usually long periods of time between each event. Today was different. Several records were expected to fall in the brilliant sunlight and comfortably warm and pleasant summer day in the grand and glorious and most beautiful of Spain's cities.

USA's Jennifer Fields checked her watch. It read 10:15 AM. She had just completed her preliminary warm-up and it looked like her event would go off on time in exactly one hour. She felt good, actually, very good. Her slight hamstring pull 3 weeks ago had not been evident for the past 3 days. She was really believing she had timed her training perfectly, even with her injury. She would have hated to train so hard for so many years and then not even get to run because of an injury.

Jennifer thought back to March when she qualified 1st in the 1500-meter run in the USA team trials with a world record time of 4:00.22. Her mom and dad were so proud that she, who had been a pokey 6th-grade basketball player, had worked so hard and had actually become a speed demon—at least at middle distance running. She still couldn't dribble with her left hand, that ended up taking the brunt of her celebration punishment in the pillow fight she and her teammate had had that evening before they went to dinner with her parents. Jennifer broke her thumb when her hand, clutching her favorite pillow, accidentally struck her roommate's hand during the horsing around. Lynn's hand was fine, but Jennifer tore her ulnar collateral ligament at the base of her thumb. Thank God she wasn't on the rowing team. She could run with a bad hand, but not with a bad wheel.

The leg injury came later. She was running outdoors exactly 6 weeks ago during one of her workouts and late in the run, slipped on some ice and strained her hamstring on the left side. Her coach had asked her to stay inside because of the freezing rain, but Jennifer was so bored with running inside on the treadmill, she had to get out. She cried herself to sleep with her leg packed in ice and vowed to do everything her trainer and coach asked to try to get the leg healed enough to win the World Championships in June in Spain. She was fortunate the tear was not very severe and was in the mid muscle area and not at the origin of the hamstring. That meant she could ride a bike to rehab the muscle and maintain her aerobic conditioning. If the tear had been higher, bike riding as well as running would not be tolerated very well and her rehabilitation would be very slow.

"Jennifer, time to get off your feet for 35 minutes now," chirped her cheerful coach Tony.

"OK, I was just getting my Sport Aid before I headed for the lawn chair," said Jennifer. "Coach, have you heard if the rabbit from Germany is still planning to sacrifice her chances in the race by setting a ferocious pace in the start?"

"I'll get the Sport Aid. You sit down. Since Germany has two runners qualified for the mile final, you had better be prepared for one of them to try to run a few of the racers into the ground. Her teammate is used to running with a rabbit, so she can easily stay at her own pace and then at the end of the race only have to beat the few runners who were not messed up by the fast pace. You should be one of the runners who has no problem sticking to her own pace. Your timing will keep you ahead of everyone but the rabbit and Josef, the other German, for the entire race. Just be sure when the rabbit begins to fade that you pass her quickly so you don't get boxed in or bumped or knocked over by the two of them. Josef will fade later about 150 feet from the finish line and will be too tired to box you in. You've done this race well a dozen times this year and no one was able to get in your way. Don't worry, just do it. Pass quickly!"

"OK, Coach, it sounds so easy when you say it. I'll just kick it into overdrive when I need to pass and leave her in my dust."

"You'd be better off downshifting so you can be sure to pass the rabbit on the straightaway if you can."

"I love having these little conversations with you, Coach. It just makes the time pass so quickly and I don't have time to get nervous," said Jennifer.

"Well, you sure don't have the time to get nervous now. You have only a few minutes left for your visual imagery before your massage. I haven't ever seen you get nervous during Barb's magical rubdowns," said Tony. "You'll be all right. Just keep your own pace and pass quickly!"

Jennifer loved having Tony as her coach. He was firm and demanding, but he was very patient. He knew how to get his runners psyched up before their events. He had a brilliant distance-running career and knew all the tricks of psychological warfare in running, including the dirty ones that may be sprung on his runners.

Jennifer was ready. She closed her eyes and concentrated on her hamstring and thumb. They felt fine. Last night's massage made sure of that. Both injuries had seemed to heal exceptionally fast. She then mentally ran her race the standard four times in about double real time—just under 2 minutes each. She wanted to be the first collegiate woman to break the 4-minute 1500-meter record, and she wanted to do it at the World Championships with her parents and her family present.

Dr. Thompson believed in her 2 years ago when she was running in the Delaware State championship meet and severely pulled her groin muscle. He told her he could help her heal better than ever and that he would work with her at the WA Kelly Foundation Hospital Sports Medicine Center. He promised her she would be back to challenge for a US title within 6 months if she worked hard. His injections and intense training program certainly did the trick. She claimed the US title 5 months later after qualifying in the 1500 at her last chance to qualify for Nationals in the Regional tournament. She broke the high school record by 4 seconds! Now she was running for the University of North Carolina and as a sophomore was expected to break her own world collegiate record again and be the first college female to finish the 1500-meter run in less than 4 minutes. And all this was because Dr. Thompson believed in her so much. His support gave her the motivation needed to come back from such a devastating injury.

"Jennifer, get ready. Time for light jogging. Get going," said her coach.

"Right-o, Coach, I'm ready," replied Jennifer.

Jennifer again considered her body. Her muscles felt fine. They felt even stronger while she warmed up with very light jogging. After 3 minutes she headed across the infield in the direction of the starting blocks. Her coach and best friend and roommate Lynn were on each side of her. Lynn was chatting away as always, making sure she was distracted enough not to get nervous. Mental imagery this close to the race was out of the question for her. She was ready.

"OK, guys, you're the best. I'm ready for this. Even though Josef has been so nice to me, she looked too closely at my boyfriend last month so I'm ready to give her a few gravel burns by the end of the race," said Jennifer.

"Wow, Jennifer, I've never heard you be so confident before," said Lynn. "You're usually so quiet and preoccupied. This is great. Go get 'em. I'll get the flag ready."

"Now, Lynn, you know I have to look out for you before my races because you get so worried for me," said Jennifer.

"Enough!" said Tony. "The starter just stepped into his box and that means you're supposed to be behind your blocks within 30 seconds or you'll forfeit the race. Get going. You don't need good luck, you just need to pass swiftly."

"I love you, too, Coach," said Jennifer. "See you in less than 4 minutes. Lynn, please take him away."

Jennifer sauntered slowly behind her starting blocks briskly kicking her legs with each step just like the best runners and swimmers always do. She liked how her muscles felt and the feeling of power she had in her quads, and this habit relaxed her more than anything else she had tried before a race.

The starter gave the signal for the runners to take their marks. She figured she had 12 to 14 seconds to get down in the blocks to not be the first or last to be ready. If she got down too soon, she could get tense and irritated at the others stalling, trying to gain every possible psychological advantage. Generally, the bulk of the field 'went down' between 10 and 12 seconds, and if she went down between 12 and 14, her timing would be perfect. If one or two runners remained standing at 14 seconds, they would start to get nervous that they would not be ready for the start so they would not tarry beyond this time. Getting in position 5 to 7 seconds before the starting gun allowed her muscles to get fired up enough to explode out of the blocks in a reflex response to the gun. She had done this hundreds of times and felt no need to risk a false start to get a great jump. Her legs were street strong. They looked streamlined but not overly muscular, and they were stronger than any other racer in the race.

Bang! They were off. Jennifer's relaxed positioning was just as she had planned. She exploded from the blocks an instant after the gun and in 4 strides was up to pace speed. The rabbit guessed right, anticipating the gun by a few hundredths of a second and had a slight edge on Jennifer. Josef was even with the rabbit, for *her* start was among the few that coaches used as a teaching example. Jennifer had learned Josef 's unique form as well as the master herself who had developed the style a few months prior to setting the collegiate record a year before Jennifer finally broke it at the US trials.

After the first long turn, Jennifer settled in right behind Josef and the rabbit, who was much farther ahead, well ahead of the pack. Jennifer slowed slightly to keep a safe distance from Josef, remembering Mary Slaney's race from Olympics past. She checked her internal clock to be sure she didn't run Josef 's race. She knew she wasn't even going to watch the rabbit, and she'd have to ignore the crowd who would think she was off because she was lagging so far behind in a race she was supposed to win by 8 to 10 strides or more.

Josef was running strong, and Jennifer was pleased. Obviously Josef was running a serious race and did not appear to be playing with Jennifer's timing or mind. Only the rabbit was trying to do that. Jennifer had run against Josef enough times to already have a read on her game plan and her strength for that day.

Josef and Jennifer kept their record pace through the first 3 laps. The rabbit was beginning to fade and Jennifer kept her mind off being winded by planning when she would pass her. If this pace continued, she could just follow Josef by the rabbit in the straightaway. She just hoped the rabbit wouldn't let Josef by on the inside and then cut in front of her. That might allow Josef to start her kick early in an effort to distance herself from Jennifer. Jennifer had to decide whether or not to stay immediately behind Josef to prevent the rabbit from cutting back or hang back enough to be sure there was no contact when she did cut in. Jennifer knew what she would do.

Sure enough, the rabbit pulled wide just as Josef was close. And sure enough, the rabbit cut back just before the last turn to box Jennifer in until the straightaway. She could then slow down enough to give Josef a lead that even Jennifer would have trouble closing.

But Jennifer wasn't about to let this precision teamwork spoil her day. Just as the rabbit cut in front of her, Jennifer burst outside to pass them both on the turn! She didn't care if this was unheard of or against all the traditional racing rules. She had enough wind left and wasn't going to risk getting bumped or dragged down. And, she knew from her coach that the unexpected might take Josef off her concentration as well as give herself an additional psychological boost.

Actually, Jennifer didn't care if Josef slowed or was startled. She didn't want to beat her by disrupting her timing. Jennifer didn't come this far to not be the first college female to break the 4-minute barrier. And she wanted to show all those who supported her that she could break the record in the biggest race of the year.

Her muscles felt strong. She was increasing her speed when everyone else in the race, except for Josef, was slowing. Josef started her kick to try to stay with Jennifer. Jennifer was gaining speed and still hadn't gone to maximum effort. She passed Josef easily on the turn and stayed wide in lane 3 to allow plenty of room for Josef if she somehow had the wheels to catch her. Jennifer wanted to show Josef she wasn't about to resort to boxing out to win a race—even though conventional racing etiquette would say she should cut back to lane one when she was far enough ahead. Such a move would give her insurance against 'hitting the wall' just before the finish line—insurance Jennifer didn't feel she would need.

Jennifer exploded into her sprint immediately after the curve ended and left Josef several strides behind. Josef was still on a recordbreaking pace, but Jennifer was well ahead of even that pace.

Twenty feet from the finish line, Jennifer felt the tearing in her chest. She knew something was terribly wrong. Instinctively, she timed her effort to get beyond the finish line before she collapsed. Jennifer passed out 3 strides beyond the line while still running and having just smashed the collegiate 1500-meter run world record. She fell face first and skidded to a stop on the track as Josef finally caught up to her. Josef knew this wasn't a trick and even slowed before the finish line to be able to stop in time to help her competitor friend. Josef easily broke the world record as well, but Jennifer's collapse was so shocking, Josef didn't even think about the race or how tired she was.

Four

Friday, May 9
Pan American Championships
Toronto, Canada

The Toronto Coliseum was truly magnificent. The eight basketball courts were state of the art for athlete performance and fan enjoyment. The ceiling rose majestically high above the court and stands, giving everyone inside a feeling of vast space and endless room, and yet each court appeared like it was its own separate world. They were separated by large walkways for thousands of fans to have plenty of room to travel quickly from one venue to another. The hallways were large enough to house an infinite variety of vendors for food and drink and souvenirs below a cathedral ceiling. Each venue was its own huge bowl and was sound proofed enough to prevent the roar of fans from an adjacent bowl from disturbing or interrupting the flow of the game in another. In the center and largest hallway, a bi-directional transporter, much like those found in Disney World's EPCOT, carried those who chose to sit and ride along the main corridor separating the two rows of 4 bowls on each side. The huge facility was the equivalent of 8 University of North Carolina Dean Domes arranged 4 to a side with 2 huge aquatic centers housing Olympic-sized swimming pools on each end.

Toronto was proud of its massive indoor stadium designed and built in the hopes of attracting the Olympics in the near future. Each venue was adaptable for basketball, ice hockey, lacrosse, indoor soccer, and field hockey. At each end, two huge swimming pool arenas were built, each with two 12-lane, 50-meter pools separated by a 20-foot wide walkway and crowned with a massive diving pool. The pools were added at each end to maximize efficiency of utility costs. When ice hockey was needed, they were more often set up in either of the two courts at each end. That way, the heat from the cooling systems for the ice arenas could be used to heat the adjacent pools and the cooling from the pools could be used to make ice.

The cost of the state-of-the-art world facility had been kept secret, but easily exceeded two billion dollars. An Internet tycoon donated 80% of the money for the facility in exchange for never having to fill out (or pay) a personal tax return for the Canadian government. Robert Winston, designer and owner of 427 web sites and their companies, was glad to give such a large sum of money to keep the government out of his business and to guarantee his name would be forever favorably remembered not only in the city of Toronto, but also throughout the world. Ever since news of the deal broke, several large cities had been trying to negotiate a similar deal for upfront money with their richest citizens. The oppressive tax structure in Canada gave their cities an advantage over most US cities in working out such a deal.

Matt Madison didn't care about how much it cost to build the Coliseum or the original tax deal Robert Winston had worked out. Right now he wondered why such a futuristic facility was so hot. If they could afford two billion dollars for a fancy gym facility, why couldn't they afford to keep it at a comfortable temperature? Matt was playing in his fourth basketball game in 3 days, and he needed to be on the court the entire game to keep his Canadian team in the game against the United States. The US had many professional players who were big and strong and very experienced, and all of them could wear down his teammates. Matt, on the other hand, was deceptively strong and had incredible endurance. No one player could consistently stop his scoring or rebounding.

Matt had resurrected his basketball career after an injury-prone sophomore season at Temple University by rehabbing at the WA Kelly Foundation Hospital in Wilmington, Delaware. He thought his career was over with no chance of making the NBA, until Dr. Thompson approached him after a Temple—U Mass game in which he was hurt in the first 5 minutes for the third time early in the season. Matt was willing to try almost anything, and when Dr. Thompson, who knew Matt's father from medical school, virtually guaranteed him a rapid recovery and future success, he decided to try Thompson's program. Matt was lucky his college coach loved to have early morning practices so he could head south for an hour on Interstate 95 to Wilmington to train in the evenings. Team managers took turns driving him most days so he could study in the car and not waste the 2-hour round trip.

Matt weighed in at 244 pounds without an ounce of fat and stood 6'9". His muscles were so well developed and so streamlined, he looked more like a weight lifter than a star basketball player. He had a 32" vertical leap from standing still. The nutritional supplements the Kelly Foundation supplied gave him such incredible endurance that he could play 3 games a day under good conditions without slowing down at all. His ability as a player was extremely good, almost exceptional. His strength made him nearly impossible to contain. His conditioning made him immune even to a rotating system of players covering him. He ran them all into the ground in just a few minutes of game time. He hated timeouts because it gave his defenders a chance to rest, helping them stay with him for the next minute or two.

Matt got along great with most of his Canadian teammates. He was humble enough from all his previous injury problems to appreciate what it was like not to be a star or team leader. Only one player, Tyrone Biggs, constantly irritated him. Tyrone was the shooting guard and did not like all the fuss over Matt and did not like giving him the ball inside as much as Team Canada had to do to win the tougher games. Matt believed that Tyrone also felt Matt would deliberately give him super hard kick-out passes trying to make him look bad handing the pass or hurting a finger in the catch. Matt felt Tyrone constantly threw the ball at his feet trying to make him look like a klutz. Fortunately, both players wanted to win, so at least in the second half, they tried to work together.

Coach Jerry Washington, a retired NBA player, with aspirations of coaching in the NBA after demonstrating his coaching talents with the Canadian team, knew his team didn't have to win the game against the US to do well in the games. They did, however, have to put on a good showing for his players' confidence and to intimidate the other teams in the World Championships just prior to the Olympics. Not only were seedings very important, psychological edges could mean the difference between a medal for Canada and a disappointing finish in the lower half of the standings.

Matt was getting very tired. He was so hot. He hadn't felt this overheated or worn down since last November when he was getting injured all the time. Coach Washington told him two of the massive HVAC units for their venue were not working and the back-up units for some unknown reason weren't kicking in. He told him the heat should be to Matt's advantage because he was so much better conditioned than any of the other players. And besides, it wasn't all that hot. After all, the units for the massive corridors and other venues were still working.

Matt decided he had to step things up. He had to keep his team close so the NBA scouts would increase his projected value in the next draft. And, he did want to show the world his Canadian team could beat all non-US teams so his teammates would have the confidence to win the remaining games to insure pool play outside of the United States' pool in the Olympics. That way they would have the best track for the silver medal. Matt figured a silver medal could be cashed in for about 7 million a year in the next NBA draft. Then he could move his parents out of their row home in Philadelphia. He never understood why his father, an anatomy professor at Temple Medical School, didn't make enough money to afford a better home for his family of 6. Dr. Thompson was cool, but why did he make enough to have a huge home with a heated pool and his father, who also knew so much, could only afford a small, boring home in one of the run-down neighborhoods surrounding Temple.

"Matt, box out next time," said Coach Washington. "Tyrone can't get his 3-pointers off if you just turn around. His player is doubling down on you, so you need to step into a screen to clear a shot for Tyrone after you pass and then clear out for the rebound." "OK, Coach," said Matt. "Brian, be sure to come across more quickly to screen for me just above the box. And be ready—if I can't shake loose for the shot, I'll draw the double and get you the ball back."

"Matt, are you OK?" asked Coach Washington. "You look drained. Is Shaq working you over too much? Do you want to come out for a minute?" Actually Shaq was working him over quite nicely, and they were both getting exhausted.

"No way, Coach. I'll be fine. Just tell the refs he's punching me in the kidneys every time I turn around."

"It looks clean to me, Matt," said Coach Washington. "The refs are letting you both go at it inside. That should favor you. You can't afford to get fouls. Shaq can. They have 2 other big centers to replace him. We don't have anyone. If he's really punching you, that must mean he's getting tired and frustrated so don't take it personally, just use him."

"Right, Coach, I'll take care of it."

OK, just wear him down, thought Matt. Shaquille O'Neal, the strongest NBA player in the league. He gets to rest and I don't. I'm hot as the dickens and tired and sweating more than I've ever sweated in my life. I'm sweating so much, the floor is slippery, and the refs keep stopping the game to wipe the court and that gives Shaq time to rest so he stays in the game longer. I'd at least like to try working on someone else.

"Hey, Matt, you're not going to wimp out on me now are you?" bellowed Tyrone. "Just get me the ball quickly enough and

I'll rip the nets for you so you can rest. You won't even have to fight for the offensive rebound if I put it in for you."

"Just be sure you get back on D, Tyrone," said Matt. "We can't afford to give them open shots. We need you working both ends of the floor."

"OK, good buddy. I'll cover for you."

Casey King, their point guard from Minnesota, had one of the best entry passes for post players. His bounce passes were crisp and hit the hands just below the waist. They were hard to block or intercept and quite easy to catch, especially if you had good hands like Matt. He wasn't much of an outside shooter, but he could penetrate well and either draw a foul, hit the lay-up or 6 footer, or better yet, dump it off to Matt just before the double team swallowed him up. He was patient enough to move the ball around and wait for a good opportunity to either penetrate or make a good entry pass. He had to be patient since he wasn't known for his long shot.

Two minutes and seventeen seconds to go, and Canada was down by 3 points. Casey had the ball. Canada was in its half court offense. Casey headed right, drawing his defender with him who was expecting a wrap-around right-handed bounce pass inside to Matt. Casey saw the overplay and instantly threw a gorgeous behind-the-back bounce pass to Matt, who was starting to cut in the same direction. The pass was perfect for Matt to reverse direction on Shaq, spin to his right, and lay the ball in with his left hand while drawing an obvious but to no avail foul from Shaq, his fifth. Matt spun as set up by Casey, laid the ball off the glass, and took a ferocious hit by Shaq who slipped on Matt's sweat on the floor.

Matt didn't know why he was so dizzy with just a hard body hit on his side. He'd taken many of them in other games and even in this game without being fazed. He was perplexed about why he should be so weak, and all he could do was just stand still with his hands on his knees and his head down. Suddenly, his legs gave out. He dropped to his knees and then over to his left side, while barely catching himself with his hands as he fell. He was so tired, and the room was spinning. He just had to lie down on the floor until he could catch his breath.

Casey grabbed him and shook him and then asked, "You OK, man? Did you get hit in the head?"

Matt looked at Casey and started to speak, but then passed out completely. The trainer, who had started walking over to the scene, broke into a sprint to get to Matt, felt his pulse and then immediately called for the team physician, the defibrillator, and 911. The trainer and physician started CPR while the paramedics on site hooked Matt up to the defibrillator. Three shocks were required to restore normal cardiac rhythm. He was rushed to Toronto General Hospital 3 blocks away. He was pronounced dead in the Emergency Room after 30 minutes of high-level resuscitation failed.

Five

Saturday, May 10
Wilmington, Delaware

The headlines in the morning paper read, "Two Star Kelly Foundation Hospital Athletes Stricken during Major Competition." Mike Naylor had a sudden feeling of panic deep in his chest and immediately felt guilty and extremely worried. He had always felt a background concern that enrolling Wendy in Dr. Thompson's program might be a double-edged sword. He certainly saw the results of her training and how happy his daughter was in her sport, but after all, the nutritional portion of the training program was research. And with research, things could go wrong. Was this a coincidence, two of the 8 athletes in the Delaware arm of the program were "stricken?"

> ***Wilmington, Delaware, Delaware Morning News.*** Two WA Kelly Foundation Hospital athletes suffered serious cardiac events yesterday during strenuous competition. Jennifer Fields is hospitalized in critical condition in Barcelona, Spain, after winning the women's 1500-meter run in collegiate world record time. She collapsed at the finish line with severe sudden chest pain and was taken

unconscious to the cardiac care unit of Menendez Memorial Hospital in Barcelona.

Doctors at the world-famous hospital say Jennifer is recovering as expected after thrombolytic or clot-buster therapy for an acute heart attack but remains in critical condition. They further report she had no signs of cardiac disease or any hardening of the arteries. They stated it was extremely unusual for a world-class athlete with no obvious heart defect or hardening of the arteries to suffer a heart attack. Normally, an athlete overexerting herself would suffer heat exhaustion or just collapse from excessive fatigue.

Jennifer is presently conscious and is now pain-free, but she is being monitored closely and undergoing extensive testing to determine why she had an apparent heart attack. One condition being considered is a protein C or S deficiency that may lead to excessive clotting in small arteries. Other conditions under consideration include a congenital defect of her coronary arteries (which preliminary results from her heart catheterization make unlikely), pericarditis (infection of the membrane around the heart), and cardiomyopathy.

Cardiac catheterization revealed normal coronary arteries on preliminary review, making a congenital abnormality very unlikely. The total size of the heart was quite large, but contraction of the heart musculature was extremely strong and efficient, with an ejection fraction of 72%, making cardiomyopathy very unlikely.

Matt Madison, star sophomore basketball player for the Temple University, collapsed during a very competitive basketball game between the Canadian national team and the US Dream Team 3. Madison, also known as the "Iron Man" for his superb conditioning and playing strong without ever resting during basketball games, collapsed while guarding Shaquille O'Neal late in the second half of a surprisingly hard-fought game between the US and Canada. The US team was heavily favored, but the heroics of Matt Madison kept the game close the entire way.

Madison was resuscitated on the court, but remained unconscious during transport to Toronto General Hospital, where he was pronounced dead in the emergency room shortly after arrival.

Doctors at the Toronto Hospital said Madison had no known medical problems or heart defects. Cause of death was unknown, and autopsy results are pending.

Matt Madison led his Temple University Owls team to conference titles the past 2 years. He was credited with single-handedly elevating the play of his team and saving the job of his college coach who had come under fire the two years before Matt's arrival as a player. NBA interest in Matt had been high since he led his unheralded team to the Final Four this past college season. His performance to date in the Pan Am Games had been called spectacular, and many scouts believe he was planning to leave school early to turn professional if he and his Canadian team performed well in this pre-Olympic competition.

Matt led his Temple team in both points and rebounds his freshman and sophomore years. He also led his Canadian team in both categories and was on track to set a Pan Am record for rebounds, previously held only by Americans.

Hospital spokesperson Josephine Williams promised more information tomorrow, when she expected to release preliminary autopsy findings.

Dr. Steven Thompson, Director of Sports Medicine at the Kelly Institute in Wilmington, Delaware, was unavailable for comment yesterday and today, but his office issued the following statement: "We are saddened by the misfortune that has befallen two of our beloved athletes. We wish Jennifer Fields godspeed in her recovery, and we give our most sincere condolences to the family of Matt Madison. They have suffered an infinite loss that words cannot soften. Matt was admired and loved by everyone in our sports medicine facility."

What in the world was going on? Was there something risky in the nutritional arm of the study? Mike decided he needed to talk to Dr. Thompson immediately. He had to find out if a problem existed that could affect his daughter, because if it did, he would leave no stone unturned in trying to fix it. He owed that to his daughter for getting her involved.

Six

Monday, May 12
7:30 AM

"*Good morning, Dr. Naylor,*" said Amy, Dr. Thompson's receptionist. "To what do we owe this visit?" Amy was always pleasant and made patients and doctors alike feel good. Dr. Thompson, on the other hand, was usually too serious and often made people feel ill at ease. He was never rude; he just didn't inspire good feelings in most people. Amy was the perfect foil for him.

"Good morning to you, too, Amy," said Mike. "I'd like to talk with Dr. Thompson as soon as possible about my daughter. Do you know where I might find him?"

"He was here earlier for a few minutes and asked Sally to move some files and then he left in a hurry. He said he had an emergency and to page him only if absolutely necessary. I think he is quite upset about Jennifer and Matt. I guess you heard what happened."

"Yes, I sure did. And that's why I need to talk to your boss. I want to be sure Wendy isn't training too hard and also make sure she has been tested for any cardiac defects. It's just too much of a coincidence for two athletes in the program to be stricken like that—I just have to be sure when my own daughter is involved."

"I sure can understand your concern, Dr. Naylor. Wendy is such a good girl. But don't you think all the testing we do for this study would pick up any heart problem?"

"Most likely it would, Amy, but with this new information, I'd like to reassess where we are and what we should do now to be sure. Is Dr. Thompson expected back to see patients or is he in the Sports Medicine Clinic today?"

"He asked that I clear all patients for the morning, but he should be back by 2 this afternoon. Do you want to see him then?"

"That would be great. It should be OK to wait that long. I'll just extend my lunchtime, and I'll get here a little before 2. See you then."

Mike left the Sports Medicine Clinic reception area and figured he'd call his office from the car to shuffle patients around a bit. He didn't like changing appointments on such short notice, but he had to get started on figuring out what was happening and how that might affect his daughter. Mike had learned long ago in medical school that researchers didn't always volunteer details about what was being tested and how. He hoped that his trust in Dr. Thompson was justified and that his daughter would be all right. He would have a long talk with Wendy to be sure she was still thrilled to be working this hard. He had to be sure she still wanted to give up her normal childhood life to be a world-class gymnast.

As he headed toward the door to the hallway from the clinic waiting room, he bumped into Sally. He noticed she had a pile of charts in her hands and he had to help her with the door. The top chart was Wendy's—he knew it was hers because it had the big Tigger sticker on it that her younger sister Kelly had insisted Dr. Thompson put on the chart a few months ago when Kelly went with Wendy to her 6-month check-up. Dr. Thompson even showed a rare display of humor when he commented that the sticker was appropriate for Wendy since she could jump just like Tigger in her gymnastics. Wendy sure could bounce through her floor routines.

"Sally, let me hold the door for you," said Mike. "Where are you going with all those charts?"

"Thank you, Dr. Naylor," said Sally. "I'm headed to our

interfloor office where we keep all our research data. Dr. Thompson wanted me to take the charts there personally and not use the hospital train system. He was afraid they'd get misplaced. He's so particular about paper work. Anyway, at least he trusts me to care for them."

"Isn't that where Wendy works out?" asked Mike.

"Yes, of course. That office and training area are even nicer than our main office here on the first floor. I'm still not sure why we have two training areas. It would make more sense to have one large one and all our offices located in one place."

Mike scratched his ear. *Now why was Wendy's chart being moved to the private, more secure office? Why was the chart in the main office in the first place? And why was Dr. Thompson thinking about having these charts moved when he was obviously preoccupied with an emergency?* Sally seemed to think it was so important that she was instructed to hand-carry the charts upstairs.

Physicians are taught many scientific principles in medical school, and one of the most basic and important is to be very suspicious. Feelings of suspicion did not make people feel good, but they often worked to the benefit of patients, helping doctors figure out just what was causing a patient's problem. Mike remembered a favorite medical school professor teaching him that spouses of doctors just have to put up with their husband or wife always questioning things. Mike's wife was really glad he was not a psychiatrist, because they had to be the most annoying, always questioning motives behind every behavior.

Mike could not accept there was no significance to the charts being moved in a hurry right after two of the athletes in Dr. Thompson's program were "stricken." He hoped Dr. Thompson was just being thorough, making sure Wendy and the others had been completely tested for pre-existing problems before they started in the study. Mike decided he would have to see if there was an inconspicuous way of seeing Wendy's chart. After all, it wasn't unusual for doctors to look at charts. He remembered a story his non-physician father told him about going to a nursing station to ask for information about a patient he was visiting and because he had a suit on, the nurse just handed him a chart before he could say what he wanted. So if he could just get to the chart rack at the right time, he could easily peruse her chart without causing a stir. Hopefully, the private sports medicine workout area had enough patients to have a chart rack.

Mike hurried to his car. He was already late, and he had to stay on time to get back to the hospital before 2. He had to catch Dr. Thompson before he started to see patients, or their discussion would be too brief.

Seven

Saturday, May 10

Kent and Patti Nash were an interesting couple. Kent was an introvert and a brilliant researcher. He loved to work endless hours at a time in his lab not only finding possible answers to questions posed by his research grants, but also changing the questions to deeper levels of mystery with more significance so he could have a broader area more difficult to conquer.

Patti was the outgoing distaff side. She was athletic and a little hyper. She was always pleasant and could usually lighten her quiet, more serious husband. Fortunately, she was naturally independent, because Kent's long hours of work would have made her lonely if she wasn't. She was also very loyal and quite attached to Kent ever since they navigated the highly emotional experience of college and grad school together. He was a Scorpio; he felt the same way about her. His horoscope said he was destined to love only once. He was quite content to believe that was his destiny, even though astrology wasn't exactly based on scientific principles.

Kent Nash had just turned 50, and his wife of 20 years had essentially tricked him into going rock and mountain climbing at Mt. McKinley near Fairbanks, Alaska. Why his wife had picked the highest mountain in North America in such a vast, remote area was beyond his understanding. It all started with the climbing wall his lawyer friend donated to the local community center. Kent was invited to the inaugural dedication and to honor his friend, he decided to go. He took his 10-year-old daughter, and she, of course, was invited to try to climb the wall. And naturally, she was not about to turn the offer down. After she sped up the toughest part of the climbing wall like a kid bounding up museum steps, she begged her daddy to give it a try.

Kent had been a good athlete in college, but had not kept up with athletic endeavors since leaving school. He preferred to read materials relevant to his research rather than breaking a sweat exerting himself, but he wasn't going to disappoint his daughter Stephanie on a semi-reasonable request. Maybe it was a macho thing, but what the heck. He should be able to handle this. He did make it up the easy side of the wall without difficulty, and it was worth the effort when he saw his daughter looking so proud of her daddy who wasn't so old and fuddy-duddy that he wouldn't try neat things.

After he jumped off the wall and saw his happy daughter, he realized two things. First he felt the muscles tighten in his forearms almost immediately. Second, he began to wonder if his wife had set him up to go to the dedication with his daughter. She seemed too enthusiastic that he take Stephanie. She even offered to make him his favorite dessert while they were at the ceremony. He wondered, too, if his attorney friend was in on it with his wife by donating the wall and inviting him to come to the dedication. Then he realized he was being too paranoid—about his friend anyway.

Looking back now, he discovered he had been right about his wife. It was planned, and she had planted a seed of thought in his daughter by asking her while they were getting ready to go to the dedication if she thought her dad could or would even try to climb the wall. Her mother had suggested ever so subtly that she try the wall first and then ask her dad to try it. She did, she asked him, he tried it, and now he was headed to the remote wilds of Alaska for a month-long expedition with another very athletic couple, the Donovans, and their own hired professional guide.

How his wife got him to agree to this, he still didn't know. He was supposed to be exceptionally smart, but how in the world did his wife talk him into wild adventures like this? He didn't like leaving the kids either, but they were already committed to camps for the entire duration of the trip. He tried to say he shouldn't go because he shouldn't leave his research for so long, but his team was months behind running the tests for all his ideas on the project. And, he hadn't taken a vacation for 8 years—his staff certainly needed a break—from him. His last reason against going was he didn't want to risk leaving their kids without parents if something happened. Patti was ready for this one with two answers. He (and they) needed adventure in their life and no one had died or sustained a serious injury in 20 years on this expedition. Besides, she had already paid for it and they could only get 50% of their money back if they cancelled. That was enough to convince him. Even though he was well paid as a researcher and received 6 figures a year in royalties from his patents, he did not like to waste money.

"Patti, what time does our plane depart from Philly?" asked Kent. "We leave at 9:10 this morning and arrive in Fairbanks at 6:05 their time. We spend the first 3 days in Fairbanks with the Donovans. Then we catch the amphibious plane at 12:45 in the afternoon for the 2-hour flight south." She was so organized, and she had a memory that rivaled Kent's—especially for remembering practical things. "Remember, we're packing light. The guide will have ample supplies and gear for us. Your work clothes won't cut it in the wild."

"Right. Can I take my computer? I've got a few formulas to review so I'm ready when we get back," said Kent. He still wasn't completely adjusted for a full month away from civilization.

"You can use your computer on the flight to Calgary, and maybe in the amphibious plane, but you'll have to leave it at the base camp from there," patiently answered Patti. Kent knew she was wondering if he would be OK without his books and beakers and computers for an entire month. This could be a real test of their marriage.

"How about my cell phone? Should I take that?" he asked.

"Same answer, my man. There are no towers where we're going. You'll just have to talk to me, old buddy. I fully realize I will have to keep you occupied enough to stay sane." The agency she had hired had successfully taken all kinds of geeks on this expedition, and most of them came back more well rounded and quite happy with the experience. However, none were quite like Kent.

"All right, I'm done packing, my email is set up for auto reply, my secretary knows how to find us, I've written 10 letters for each of our delightful kids, which my secretary will mail every third day, and I've got my new StarSAT phone ready and tested," he stated to whoever was listening. "Let's get going, the North Pole is waiting."

"Great job, Nash! I'm really proud of you. I knew you could pack for yourself," she replied. "But I wouldn't keep telling people we're going to the North Pole. It's not quite that cold where we're going."

Eight

Saturday, May 10

Delta Flight 828 powered down runway 27 at Philadelphia International Airport, pressing its passengers back into their seats. The liftoff was smooth, and the climb out was strong at 3,000 feet per minute. Kent Nash already had his computer in his lap, and as soon as the aircraft lifted off the ground, he opened it and powered it up for liftoff as well.

"Wow, what great graphics! What's that operating system?" asked the passenger sitting to Kent's right. Bob Towson was a graduate student at Washington State University and had just finished visiting his grandparents back East. He was headed to Calgary for a summer job at the University in Calgary in the Physics Department.

Kent turned to him. "It's Windows XP with a little modification from one of my research assistants. It's a combination of a fireworks show at Disney World and the latest Flight Blaster game from Egenda.net." Kent Nash had a lot of kid left in him.

Even though money was not a large concern, the Nashes usually flew coach class. They were reasonably frugal, did not drink alcohol on airplanes, and actually thought the middle of the aircraft was safer than the very front. The limited space was the only concern, and maybe crying babies was another. First class was also completely booked on this flight because they had changed their booking three times with Kent's reluctance to go away. Their friends, Tom and Marsha Donovan, took the last 2 first-class seats with Patti's blessing.

Patti Nash could sleep in any vehicle moving at a different rate of speed than the earth itself. She had been the perfect baby as far as settling down. There was no need to put her in a car and drive around when she was a baby; just rock her in your arms or a swing and she was out. The Mardi Gras could be going on all around her and she wouldn't wake up until her carriage stopped. And put her in front of a TV or movie, bye, bye. If she rode in a van with a TV, you'd probably need cardioversion to get life back. Patti's charm was not evident in a moving vehicle. She sat next to the window, not for the view, but to avoid offending someone sitting next to her. Snoring was not out of the question. Kent took the middle seat and, if appropriate, would talk to the person in the aisle seat for a few minutes before he got lost in his computer.

"Are those data about gene therapy that I've heard so much about?" asked Bob Towson. Kent sensed his seat neighbor was determined to be curious and not let the man sitting next to him get immersed in his work. He appeared quite nervous about flying and acted as if he just wanted Kent to entertain him so the flight would pass much more easily.

Kent Nash was the guru of gene therapy in the Western Hemisphere, and the Western Hemisphere was the only part of the globe that knew very much about gene therapy.

"Yes, it is. How did you know?" asked Kent, intrigued. He introduced himself. Bob introduced himself, told Kent about his summer job, and said, "I saw the term, 'transfection' and figured it had to be related. I don't know anywhere else that word is used. Are you doing research on protein vectors?"

"Yes, we've designed both viral and plasmid, or protein, vectors," said Kent. "Viral vectors have been the best penetrators of cells taking the DNA coding we want inside the cell, but they seem to cause problems once they mingle too closely with the nuclear DNA. They don't seem to want to stay attenuated. They sometimes wake up and get into some sort of ruckus with the DNA strands and then change something important. Protein vectors, on the other hand, don't get inside very well, but stay out of trouble once in there. I've seen viral vectors propagate the good gene we've sent inside so much it becomes uncontrolled in some way, and well, you know what happens when you get too much of a good thing."

"This is all pretty much new to me. Could you start over and simplify this gene therapy thing for me?" asked Bob. "Suppose I wanted to impress my girlfriend, or even understand one of my professors, what's this gene therapy all about?"

"Well, basically, gene therapy takes genes that code for the production of something we deem desirable and gets them into the nucleus of the proper cells in our body with a vector," answered Kent. "Once inside the cell's nucleus, the gene joins with the DNA code of that cell, causing it to make the protein that causes the cellular or chemical reaction we wish to induce."

"Two of the biggest problems science has had to overcome for gene therapy to be of clinical use are getting the gene inside the proper cell and controlling the extent of the reaction the inserted gene produces. If the gene is properly coded, it will respond to feedback systems and shut down or slow down when its effect is getting overwhelming."

"Our group developed an excellent plasmid vector for the various muscle cells in the body about 3 years ago. We can direct genes to heart muscle, skeletal muscle, bowel muscle, virtually any specific muscle group in the body. That's pretty well perfected. We presented that information at the 2004 North American Conference for Gene Therapy in Dallas, Texas. We finished that work just weeks ahead of two other groups."

"What has kept us stymied, maybe until now, is how to control the reaction we start. I'm working on the coding that tells the inserted gene to shut down or deactivate itself after a fixed period of time. I've arranged several possibilities that are being tested this very moment back in my lab at the WA Kelly Foundation Hospital in Wilmington, Delaware. I believe we've got a side chain that's easily attached that will limit new protein production to all factors of 2 squared."

"For example, the shortest limit would be 2 cycles, then 4, then 8, then 16 and so on. If this side chain works well, the next step would be to have protein production merely slow down to a pre-determined level once a unit of time passed or, better yet, once a certain amount of the protein is produced. The best side chain coding would be one that responds to feedback from levels of what is produced and makes only enough of the protein we want to keep at the new desired level. The absolute gold standard would be to program when the cell should function at baseline level and know exactly when the cell should step up production to meet specific demands placed on the cell. That type of control is years away because the variables are virtually endless and no one has even listed half of the key situations in which we'd need control."

"A good compromise would be to somehow tie control to codes already in the cell with a simple instruction like increase production by 20% more than 'x' whenever output is told to increase to 'x.' That is doable, but we have to decipher an area of gene coding we haven't spent much time on yet."

"How does that sound? Will that explanation get you in good with your girlfriend?"

Kent had had to explain gene therapy many times before to all kinds of people. His "simple" explanation was sometimes troubling to listeners because those with imagination extrapolate that gene therapy could be abused and potentially control or convert humans into a different animal or even species. They envision a warrior growing a new arm seconds after it was shot off. Or, they imagine super strength or armor-like skin or robot-like behavior for some reason, or some project that gene therapy could be used in to control the minds of innocent people or even be used to take over a country without firing a shot or declaring war. Kent just wished he could harbor the energy of these people's imaginations.

"Well, it sounds easy, Dr. Nash. Is it true it's already being used to grow new anterior cruciate knee ligaments without surgery?"

"Currently, it's being tested to help repair partially torn ACLs to prevent surgery in several studies around the US! And that's exactly the type of application gene therapy should be most useful for. I'm glad you didn't ask me about robots."

"Robots? What do you mean robots?" asked Bob.

"Oh nothing," said Kent. "It's just a question people who have seen too many sci-fi flicks ask."

"Thanks for the lecture, Doc. I feel like I've just sat through another of Professor Apson's 8 AM classes. I've got so much to think about, I'm ready to fall asleep. Hey, would you mind giving me one of your cards so I could call your department if I had any questions or if I found any one at my school working on this stuff and I could help you two get together?" asked Bob.

"I didn't bring any cards, but you could just ask Dr. Fred Jeffries at your university if you wanted to communicate with my department. He's working on a viral vector because he believes he can control it and it would be less expensive to mass produce."

"OK, fine. I will. I guess it was silly of me to try to help you out. You probably already know all the researchers in gene therapy around the world."

"I know most of them, but it can't hurt to have another spy keeping me informed. Here's my email address. Let me know if you discover something you think I ought to know."

Patti stirred. "What are you doing, Kent? Where are we? How much longer?" Kent's talking would wake her, even in a moving vehicle, because she wasn't used to hearing him say much. He would usually get immersed in a deep level of concentration and just peck on his computer. Her sixth sense woke her up after 20 minutes of oration. She also could ask how much longer in a nonannoying way.

"We're only ½ hour into our flight, and I've been explaining gene therapy to Bob here. And, I've just recruited him as a sort of corporate spy for us. I bet that will teach him to be careful asking so many questions," said Kent. "I'll be quiet so you can sleep now." Kent knew it wasn't the volume level of his talking that awakened her because she could sleep through almost any noise. It was his actual talking that rallied her.

"Thanks," whispered Bob. "I'm ready to sleep, too."

Kent figured he only needed an hour or so to do more checking of the control formulas he left behind to be tested while he was away. He was sure they would work, but testing would yield much in the way of fine-tuning. He was also sure his team had enough to do to keep them busy day and night for the whole month he was gone. He gave them a schedule so they did the most important testing first. He was actually planning to enjoy this adventure with his wife and two friends.

Nine

Monday, May 12
Myrtle Beach, South Carolina

To the west, the sun was partially eclipsed by the fresh evergreens lining the championship golf course at Myrtle Beach, South Carolina. To the east was the calm tranquility of the Atlantic Ocean, with gentle waves cascading in along the beach. South Myrtle Beach was private and therefore was nearly always quiet and peaceful—especially in the early evening. A lone ship in the distance was headed north a mile off the coast. The homes in this stretch along the beach were all 7 figures in value, and their architecture ranged from Victorian to contemporary to traditional. Whatever their design, they all had private circular driveways with 3- or 4-car garages, usually detached. Tennis courts and enclosed courtyards adjoined many.

Jessica Miller was ambitious. She grew up in one of the tougher neighborhoods of Atlanta, Georgia. Her father was a schoolteacher who was promoted to principal of a large regional high school. Two years into his new position, he became the innocent victim of a School Board scandal and was fired so Board members wouldn't lose their jobs. One Board member had pulled some strings to obtain some sorely needed equipment for her dad's school and failed to go through the proper bidding process to get them. He, of course, had not told Mr. Miller how he had arranged for their purchase. An auditor with political aspirations called the *Atlanta Centennial* first, rather than handling the situation in house. By the time the reporters were through whipping up the story, her dad and the Board member were classified as crooks and embezzlers.

Jessica was determined nothing like this would happen to her or her family. She would be financially secure and improve the standard of life for her kids and her parents, who were now living in a row home on the outskirts of Atlanta. Her dad was almost 65 and working as a truck driver trying to save money for retirement since his career as a teacher never paid much above minimal level and his retirement fund was quite anemic. His entire savings were wiped out in legal fees, which fortunately did manage to keep him out of jail.

Jessica had two kids from her previous marriage. They were living with their dad because she was always on the road catering to her professional sports clients. She had managed to collect eleven clients, most of whom were professional football hopefuls. Two were minor league baseball players and one was a verbal commitment from a player still playing basketball for Georgia Tech. She had met five of these players in gyms in Atlanta, where she had excelled as a female weight lifter, winning numerous competitions. The other 6 clients were contacts through the first five.

She had managed to win most of her weight-lifting competitions without having to use steroids. Her coach firmly believed her anger from her father's hard times was fuel enough to drive her to unbelievable levels of training. Fortunately, she had a lean and slender build that hid most of her strength as street strength. In spite of her world-class level strength, however, she remained very attractive in a natural, wholesome way. Her long, natural blond hair helped considerably.

Jessica's best attribute was her intelligence. Being the daughter of a Physics teacher father and a mother who was #1 in her high school class, she had a top-quality genetic background for having a high IQ. Her worst attribute was her anger and her temper, which frequently got her into trouble. However, she used her anger as a motivator for her success in weight lifting competition and in the business world as an agent for the upcoming Southern Sports Agency. Jessica Miller was already the second busiest agent in SSA, right after the owner and founder John Getty, a former professional football player for the Atlanta Falcons who had several big-time football players in his fold.

Jessica's temper cost her her marriage. After she retired from competition at age 30, she found herself in bars far too often. She could be hard enough to live with when she was sober because of her rigid, demanding nature, but with a few shots of alcohol in her, she became the proverbial mean drunk. And maybe the steroids she resorted to in her late 20s to try to maintain her competition level wiped out enough of her liver to make her more susceptible to alcohol. Either way, after 4 bar fights and 3 DUIs and multiple arguments in front of the kids, her husband of 8 years moved out with the kids.

Randy was confident enough to marry a strong, bright female, but when she refused to get help together after their many episodes of discord, he was also strong enough to leave before the kids were too affected. Once they were living apart, Jessica woke up enough to stop drinking and to focus her anger on working 18 hours a day. She was not about to place her agent/client relationships in jeopardy, so the high-risk situation of meeting her athlete clients in bars or restaurants did not pose enough of a risk to get her drinking. She remembered her drive to produce for her kids and her dad so she kept her act together. She frequently visited her kids at home and actually maintained a cordial relationship with her ex-husband. They were together whenever she was in town, so she managed to avoid being lonely.

She was also angry because she was a woman competing in a man's domain. Less than 2% of sports agents with any significant business were women. True, she managed to obtain 11 clients with her hard efforts, but they were all hopefuls, none were big time or had large contracts. She attracted the underdog, the one who had never had a sizable professional contract. Consequently, she had not made it yet. Her spot on the beach today was courtesy of her boss. He invited her to stay in his beach home while she worked 3 of the firm's clients. Two belonged to her boss, and they needed personal attention to keep them happy. One was a hopeful who had signed with her a year ago.

Jessica knew how she was going to make it big. She had the perfect clientele for her plan. Joe Reilly knew that also. He knew Jessica from high school, lost touch with her when he went to law school, and renewed contact with her when he learned through his one client that she had become a sports agent also. He was working with the prestigious Brey Agency in Boston. His one big client came to him because his father was a close friend of his client's father. Herb Reilly had actually saved the client's life on a fishing trip, and in return, Herb's friend insisted Herb's son at the Brey Agency manage his son. Joe lucked into a very high-profile professional football player who commanded $6 million a year. Thus, Joe did well with only one client. Very few people knew, however, that the Brey Agency had been founded and was now run with mob money.

Joe's client suffered a series of four injuries in 5 weeks, and his career was being threatened before his prime. Joe heard Dr. Thompson speak at the Annual American College of Sports Medicine Conference and figured he might be able to help his injured client. He took him to the WA Kelly Foundation Hospital in Delaware and enrolled him in Dr. Thompson's program on the basis that Dr. Thompson had helped 2 athletes come back from extensive injuries. Joe convinced his boss it was a worthwhile thing to do after Joe had deduced that Dr. Thompson had not told his first 2 test subjects everything about the nutritional supplement he was using on them. Doctors could be such easy targets. And if they were dishonest, they were extremely easy.

Joe Reilly was smart enough to know he could control Dr. Thompson with the threat of disclosure and the likely potential reward of huge money. Nothing worked as well as positive and negative reinforcement together. Thompson could get his study of

16 athletes published on his conditioning techniques, barely mentioning his nutritional supplement in order to avoid scrutiny of the real reason for the athletes' success. The Brey Agency would then sell the untraceable chemical to hungry, aspiring athletes with little chance of making the big time. The wonder drug would give many of them the huge advantage they needed to score big.

Reilly would make it big on two fronts. He'd take 50% of Thompson's fees up front, and he'd score huge on the back end once his clients landed gigantic professional contracts. The Agency thought Reilly's business plan was well thought out and had little risk. Their clients could not admit they were using an illegal substance or whatever they had won would be revoked and they would be banned from the sport and ostracized forever. And at the right moment in their climb up the success ladder, the Agency informed them how unhealthy it would be for them to discuss their working plan with anyone. What risk existed, the Agency was well used to handling. When in doubt, they responded actively. They did not wait to be sure.

Jessica had nearly a dozen fertile prospects. They were all very hungry for a chance at making it big in sports, and they all needed help. Her boss didn't have to know how her clients made it big. And she had Reilly's henchmen to enforce her role and remove anyone who got in the way. Once she groomed a few of these hopefuls to the big time, she'd have all the clients she wanted. Then she'd buy her daddy a retirement he deserved, right after she bought her own Myrtle Beach ocean-front estate.

Ten

Monday, May 12
Wilmington, Delaware
8 AM

Kristin and Lindsey were both on the phone when Mike blew into his office. He waved to both and headed for his office. On the way, he saw charts on three doors and the door to a fourth room was closed with no chart in the box. He figured Nikki Mantu, his nurse practitioner, was in that room with a patient. He grabbed his stethoscope and prescription pad and headed for the room marked "Sequence 1."

Most doctors' office staff have to "cover" for their physician or physicians at one time or another. Mike Naylor's staff considered themselves lucky because their physician's main weakness was his kids, something relatively easy to handle. He didn't play golf or skip out for a commodities broker or drink too much. He just had to get to all his kids' school games and plays. Most early departures were able to be scheduled weeks in advance, but come playoff time, they had to move quickly and think creatively. And once or twice a week, actual emergencies occurred, and they had to change schedules on the run. Most patients understood and appreciated the time they received in Naylor's office. His partner, Bill Owens, also spent time with patients, but too often stayed too long with some older patients who liked to talk a lot. He didn't have the heart to cut them off if they were describing their multiple woes. Mike thought that was fine. Bill attracted the talkers, and Mike was more at home with the "get to the bottom line" folks. It was a good relationship. Fortunately, even though the space and equipment were shared, the staffs were separate. Nikki had tendencies to be overly entertained by elderly patients, too. God forbid how far behind they'd be if Nikki and Bill worked together.

When the schedule was behind, Nikki could ramp up to a higher speed. Being a nurse practitioner, she could also see patients by herself and save Mike the visit. Nikki could sense when patients were satisfied and didn't have to see Mike that day. Fortunately, many patients knew when things were behind and offered to move things along. Either way, patients got an honest effort at improving their main reason for coming. Naylor and Owens did not run an assembly line, even if behind schedule.

In high-efficiency mode, Mike saw all his morning patients by 1:30. He didn't get to talk in person to Kristin and Lindsey, but he would do that tomorrow. He had to get back to Kelly Hospital before 2.

He left before his last patient finished checking out. Mike sailed down the steps in his building three at a time. He was in his car in less than 30 seconds and headed toward the hospital, only 5 minutes away.

The WA Kelly Foundation Hospital was 12 years old. The Kelly family over the years had placed millions in trust funds to help medically deprived patients in the Delaware Valley, where they had made their fortune three generations ago. The trust funds were managed by investors who were not only good, they were very lucky. They went years without a weak investment, and the huge Bull market of the 80's coupled with real estate values skyrocketing in the area meant the trust funds broke through the billion dollar level several times over. At the same time, there was so much money available to the state's needy because the state and federal government had programs already helping the medically indigent. This meant expenditures for the Kelly Hospital were limited—there was actually a problem deciding where to spend foundation money. The State of Delaware, at the request of the Kelly Foundation trustees, sued the trust funds to open up their spending. The State won and the trustees suddenly felt safe spending money. One of the big expenditures was the $2 billion dollar WA Kelly Foundation Hospital—paid for in cash.

The hospital was obviously quite modern and state of the art. Money was essentially no object, so the architects tried several new ideas, including installing a computerized train system connecting offices and nursing stations on all floors, allowing for the automated delivery of objects as big as a small kid. Furniture had to be moved the old-fashioned way, but nearly all supplies and medicines went by train.

The trains ran in the interfloors. The interfloors were service floors between hospital floors. Most people didn't know the floors were there—the public elevators didn't stop at them or even have buttons for them. The architect with an unlimited budget thought he would save money by building huge service floors between the regular hospital floors. Most of them had short 7-foot ceilings, representing a small effort at being frugal, at least in the long term. One interfloor, where the secured sports medicine training area was located, had a 12-foot ceiling. The only way to get to them was through the 8 pairs of service elevators spaced around the huge facility, or through one of the 4 systems of trap doors with rail ladders located in utility rooms on the floors.

The Kelly Hospital had a patient capacity of 550 inpatients, each with a luxury room. It was situated on the former Kelly family estate, a gorgeous 210-acre manor with extensive gardens, an historic bell tower, fountains, and several guest homes. Outpatient facilities were so extensive that patients with disabilities felt intimidated by the time it took to get from one office to another. The accommodations were so plush and expansive that most patients had great difficulty believing they weren't going to have to pay dearly for the service they received. As it turns out, patients were almost never charged. Their insurance companies were, but patients were not. The hospital was never more than half full. They were looking for patients, but primarily for patients who would fit into one of their research protocols.

Dr. Nash and his reputation and staff commanded an entire floor of this gargantuan facility. He had multiple research protocols going at the same time. His gene therapy held huge promise, and private and public grant money sought him out. Most came with strings and tried to return controls and copyrights back to the grant bequestors, but a huge amount of unrestricted money was still available because Nash had proven he could produce.

Dr. Thompson was recruited to the Foundation to run the sports medicine facility. He was supposed to initiate meaningful medical studies as well and attract grant money to pay for the excess staff and cover the lack of patient billing. The hospital was an excellent example of how readily those with money just made more money.

Thompson had only two studies under way so far. Drug studies get most researchers going because that's were the money is. He managed to lasso one company which wanted to prove their new Cox 2 inhibitor anti-inflammatory agent was effective in sports injuries and not just degenerative arthritis. The lure of the hospital's reputation helped snare that large study. The idea the company liked was that opening their drug up to "sports injuries" would expand the drug's permitted use in HMOs by millions of prescriptions every day. The Cox 2 study was very large and literally saved Thompson from being hassled by the administration. His "conditioning" study was small and only meant to be a preliminary study that, if very successful, would attract significant grant money in phase 2. His idea to spice it up with a "nutritional supplement" was meant to guarantee positive results, but he would be sure to ascribe the success in the study conditioning techniques.

Thompson wasn't quite sure how he was going to handle phase 2 when the grant money came in. He didn't want the nutritional part to get much credit, or he might be found out.

Eleven

Monday, May 12
1:35 PM

The entrance gate to the WA Kelly Foundation Hospital reminded the visitor of Buckingham Palace. The gates opened to a wide divided 2-lane driveway with plush gardens on each side and cypress trees majestically hanging over the road. The gates had thick, black, ornate rungs with gold spear-like bars at the top. The outline of the gates curved gracefully and peaked at each end and in the middle. They were attached to a 10' high stone wall, which completely encompassed the entire 210-acre manor. The center pillar of the gates was stone, 6 feet wide, and crowned with the Kelly family seal. Bright floodlights illuminated the colorful seal at night and provided extensive backlighting to the gate and gardens.

The hospital was built on the former Kelly family estate, and the driveway and grounds looked like Colonial Williamsburg. The Kelly family donated the 210 acres to house the showpiece hospital built with Kelly Foundation funds. The family understood they could economically do almost as well by donating the estate with its gardens, historic bell tower, and guest homes as compared to selling the land, but the monument to their family name was more than worth any difference in money the donation would cost. And, the family truly did strive to return something to the community that had been very good to them for several generations.

The hospital was so large that it was easy to park near an entrance—there were several. The problem was, no matter what entrance you chose, you had a long walk to wherever you were going inside. If the building were any larger, a tram would be needed. As it was, golf carts were used to move many of the patients around. The inside of the hospital appeared in many ways like the inside of a space station.

Mike knew a relatively direct route to Dr. Thompson's office. He got to the waiting area by 1:45 and approached the large reception counter.

"Dr. Naylor, you made it!" Amy cheerily said. "I made sure Dr. Thompson was here on time for you. Come right in, he wants to talk to you before his patients start at 2."

"Thank you, Amy."

Mike went through the double entrance doors from the waiting room to the suite and headed directly to Thompson's office. Steve Thompson was sitting behind a large colonial desk turned to the side facing his computer. He seemed lost in thought studying data on the screen.

"Hello, Professor Thompson," said Mike. He wanted to keep the tone light.

"Hi to you, Dr. Mike," answered Thompson turning around. "I'm sure you are here, as you should be, about your daughter. The tragedy with Jenn and Matt is extremely unfortunate and totally unpredictable. Neither one had any medical concerns to even hint that something adverse might happen. I know you knew them both and I'm sure you're very upset for the families."

Dr. Thompson was exceptionally cordial.

"I'm reassured to hear you say that about Jenn and Matt," said Mike. "I know you and your staff would have thoroughly checked them and on a regular basis. Do you have any idea what might have happened? Could this really have been a coincidence? Is there any way the nutritional supplements could have sparked an idiosyncratic reaction and led to these events?"

"They had been checked by me and Mark McCormack in Boston and repeatedly checked by several of our residents," Thompson said. "They had been examined and tested thoroughly for 20 hours every 3 months. There was no indication of any problem at all. They were doing great. There is no reason for this. The nutritional supplements are harmless. There has to be something outside of our program or they both had unfortunate accidents." Thompson appeared very concerned, a little more than Mike expected from past experience. He also seemed sincere. Mike just could not figure out why the nagging concern in the back of his mind still gnawed at him. He decided not to bring up the chart transfer issue. It was probably nothing, but he'd look into that on his own later.

"Well, I know you have patients waiting, so I'll get out of your way," said Mike. "Are you going to the meeting tonight and to Matt's funeral on Wednesday?"

"I'm going to both. I'm glad the funeral is in the afternoon. I'd hate to have to try to see patients afterward if it was in the morning."

"I'll probably see you tonight, Steve," said Mike. "If you hear anything or if something comes up, please let me know."

"You, too, Mike. See you tonight."

Mike left Steve sitting at his desk looking quite depressed. Maybe Dr. Thompson really *did* care about his patients. Mike thought that if something had gone wrong, Dr. Thompson would have been more annoyed than depressed, but Mike decided he would stay true to his training. He would remain suspicious and check things out as much as he could. He had to make sure his daughter would be OK and he had to reassure himself he hadn't made a bad unilateral decision for her. He then called his office.

"Hi, Kristin," said Mike. "How's the schedule?"

"We're OK," said Kristin. "Nikki is seeing a patient now. We have three more scheduled for her, and she should be able to see anyone else who calls. So you're free to finish up where you are. Your wife called. No rush. Call her on the cellular when you have a minute."

"Sounds like you have everything covered, Kristin. Page me if you need me to come in or if you get any messages I should answer this afternoon. Thanks for your help."

"Right-o, boss. See you tomorrow."

Mike remembered how good it was to work with people who took pride in what they did. Since he had time, a rare happening in his life, he figured he should case out how he might get into the interlevel sports medicine facility in the evening. He headed to the maintenance elevator in the west wing, got on, and punched 3B. Nothing happened. He then noticed key locks by each "B" floor on the elevator controls. He needed a key to get the maintenance elevator to stop at an interlevel floor. Unbelievable. Was this the Pentagon or what?

"Hey, Doc, what are you doing here in my neck of the woods?" asked Hugh Winston. Hugh was a patient of Mike's and at only 29 was the head of maintenance at Kelly Hospital. Hugh saw Mike as he was walking by the elevator.

"Hi, Hugh. I'm trying to get to the sports medicine training facility. My daughter thinks she left her jacket there. I told her I'd pick it up if I had time." Mike was glad he'd figured out a reason for going there before he got on the elevator and didn't wait until he was outside the entrance.

"Hey, no problem, Doc. I'll go with you and show you around. Have you seen our train transport system yet?"

Mike realized he was going to have great difficulty sneaking into the center after hours. He might end up having to confide in Hugh and ask for help. But, the more he could find out about the hospital, the better. So, he decided to go look around and accept the offer of a tour. He'd feel Hugh out, and if getting in was going to be impossible, he'd decide if he thought Hugh would help him before he risked confiding in him.

"Are the elevators the only way to get to the interfloors? What happens if the power is out?"

"That's an interesting question, Doc. Technically any floor with public access must have multiple stairwells in case the elevators go on the fritz. The interfloors were originally designed only as service access floors, so they were built with locked elevator access only through the maintenance elevators to keep everyone out for safety reasons. The patient elevators do not even have the floors marked on the panels. There are 4 emergency large trap doors in stairwells, 1 in each of the 4 wings, with steel ladders in utility rooms spread around this fortress. We created a secure outside entrance for the athletes with direct access to an express maintenance elevator that only stops at 3B after palm and retinal analysis of the arriving person. And that entrance is closely monitored by TV cameras."

"Now, next you're going to ask how come we have the sports training facility on 3B. We decided to use it because it was such a perfect space for a gym-type facility with 12-foot ceilings and long passages between the service equipment. The architects designed the middle service floor with 12-foot ceilings for storage of oversized equipment. We managed to get a waiver to use the space for non-handicap patients only—a perfect fit for our elite athletes. That way, we do rehab for our everyday patients on the ground level and our elite sports medicine training and research studies are done in our secure facility on 3B—which is really the 6th floor. About the only sport we can't train there is basketball; 12-foot ceilings are not quite high enough for shooting."

"Let's go see if I can find my daughter's jacket before we go on the tour. Is that OK with you?"

"That's cool. I'll show you around the sports facility before the tour, if the trainers don't have the time. There won't be many people there for another hour or so."

At 2:20 in the afternoon, the training facility was mostly empty. Kids weren't out of school for the day yet, and there were only two adult athletes going through their paces. One employee athletic trainer was working out, but the 30 or so expected high school athletes wouldn't arrive for another hour or so. Another 6 or 7 would come in the early evening.

Mike's arrival in the training facility with Hugh didn't draw any attention. Brian Taggart let them in through the heavy metal doors without even asking who was with Hugh. Evidently, there was no concern with an unknown person going through the facility if he was with Hugh.

Hugh showed Mike the long floor exercise courses where his daughter Wendy trained. They saw the walk-in whirlpools with multiple adjustable jets. The long row of electronic equipment for working out all extremities at variable speeds was quite impressive. Each piece of equipment cost $75,000 rather than $3,000 or $4,000 like those at health clubs. The artwork on the walls and ceiling was impressive. Massive sketches of all types of athletes performing their sport brightened the room. Large-screen TVs were effectively positioned so that everyone could see a screen from every piece of exercise equipment. The sound was impressive—a stereo effect was evident almost no matter where people were in the 50,000 square foot plush sports medicine center. This facility would have made the most elite and expensive health clubs in New York City proud. If the local health and fitness centers had to compete with Kelly Hospital for members, they would all be in trouble.

Mike took the time to walk all the way down the main section of the training suite. He noticed a large utility room next to the massive equipment closet at the far end. Maybe that would be his way inside. He tried the door. It was unlocked, from both sides. He quickly looked inside and noticed a large bilco door on the floor towards the back of the large room. A wide steel ladder heading to the ceiling was built into the wall next to the bilco door.

"Boy, Doc, do you have to see everything?" queried Hugh. "It's just a utility closet. We'll be here all day if I have to show you all the janitor closets, too."

"I just wanted to see the trap doors you talked about. They sound so mysterious."

"We consider them a goof by the architect. Why build all those trap doors? No one ever uses them. The State of Delaware forces us to keep them unlocked in case of an emergency to maintain our waiver to use this floor for our elite athletes. It kind of kills effective security. It's a good thing people don't know about them. I bet the staff doesn't even know about them. I put a piece of scotch tape at the top of each bilco door and check it every now and again to see if anyone ever opened the doors. No one ever has. Now there's so much dust around them I could probably tell just by the dust marks. But anyway, how likely is it that all the elevators will go out and stay out at the same time? The smart thing the architect did was put the large windows on each floor on top hinges so we could bring in heavy or large equipment or furniture quickly and easily with a crane. He also made the hallways extremely wide, which helps a lot. And the service floors are real handy, especially for my back. I'd hate crawling around for as often as we have to get to all the utilities, wiring, and most importantly, the trains."

"Were those tracks for the train transport center that came out of the wall to the left of the entrance counter?" asked Mike.

"Yes, sir," said Hugh, "but you have to look behind the false wall on this floor to see the layout because we've pretty much made this floor look like a real hospital interior. Over by the charting area, there's a door to enter the service area on this floor. We can get in there if you like. Then I'll take you to the loading dock master control room where you can see an electronic map of the train system with lights identifying all stops and all moving trains."

Hugh and Mike walked back to the other end of the training facility to the charting area located just inside the large reception work area.

"Where do all those doors behind the charting area lead?" asked Mike.

"They are offices for Dr. Thompson, the residents, the chief therapist, and the head athletic trainer. All the others sit at a station in the large circular counter to chart or dictate."

As soon as he heard Dr. Thompson had a private office here, Mike grabbed a Post-it from a pack on the counter and began to fold it together over and over.

"All the charts are kept here in the main chart rack for the 80 or so actively training athletes," offered Hugh. "At least they are supposed to be here. Looks like several are missing."

"Do you have a minute before we leave here? I need to write Dr. Thompson a personal note," said Mike.

"Take your time, Doc. I'm here till 6 tonight."

Mike found some notepaper in the massive charting area and wrote a note he didn't intend for Dr. Thompson to get. However, he made the note innocent and interesting enough to leave if necessary. He wrote, "Steve, when you get a chance, give me a call. I have an interesting prospect for your study I'd like to tell you about. Cordially, Mike." Mike knew Dr. Thompson was already looking for candidates for phase 2 of his study and would probably be interested in a basketball player Mike was coaching this AAU season.

"Hugh, could you put this note on Dr. Thompson's desk for me?" asked Mike. "I'd like to be sure he gets it by tomorrow."

"Absolutely," answered Hugh. He pulled out his master key for the sports facility, opened Dr. Thompson's office, and walked across the large room to place the envelope on the desk. When his back was turned, Mike quickly wedged the folded Post-it in the latch of the door so it wouldn't lock when they shut the door. All the hospital doors, except hallway doors, were auto lock doors so Hugh wouldn't have to lock the door shut with a key. Mike knew Dr. Thompson had patients until late in his first floor office and then he was supposed to go to the quarterly staff dinner meeting at the Kelly Country Club by 7 PM. Dr. Thompson rarely skipped these quarterly meetings. He wanted to be sure he didn't miss any of the hospital politics. Mike stood by the door so he could shut it when Hugh came out. Hugh didn't seem to notice only a single click instead of a double when the door was shut. Mike clearing his throat as he closed the door was probably unnecessary. Mike decided he'd just have to take the unlikely risk that Steve would come to this office before going to the dinner meeting.

Immediately out of Dr. Thompson's office, Mike didn't waste any time grabbing Hugh and heading for the exit to go see the loading dock.

"Let's see the loading dock and master control area," said Mike. "I've got to get back to work real soon, so let's hurry."

"No problem, Doc," replied Hugh. "We can take the maintenance elevator directly to the loading dock."

The two men waved to Brian who let them through the exit doors and they then boarded the maintenance elevator large enough for a small car. Hugh inserted his control key in the space marked "Loading Dock" and the elevator came to life. It was exceptionally smooth and quiet and fast for a maintenance elevator.

"How come these elevators are so quiet, Hugh?" asked Mike.

"It's a hospital, Doc. And money is no object in this hospital."

"Right, I forgot."

The loading dock looked like the regional warehouse for Wal-Mart. The ceiling had to be 30 feet high, and there were 6 massive loading docks to receive supplies from the largest of trucks. Inside there were 3 or 4 dozen steel erector shelves lining each bay. Three forklifts were evident, unoccupied, and left more or less between the bays. Two computer terminals were at the end of each receiving bay—apparently one was a back-up for each bay. The 6 loading bays opened up to a huge storage area. In the center of the storage area was a small train station. Hugh headed toward the station.

"Doc, here's where we load the trains and punch in the codes to tell the train where to go. Kinda neat, huh? It's the biggest train set I've ever seen. We have the largest of its kind in the world, but there are 4 others like it. They stopped making the system after 5 were sold because there was so little demand." Mike was beginning to see why. The system had to cost a fortune, and it had to cost a fortune to keep it running and in good repair. The company probably switched over to making life-size replicas for amusement parks.

Hugh opened one side of a large double door behind the main train loading area. "And inside here is the master control room."

Mike followed Hugh into a large room and saw the huge complex electronic map high up on the wall opposite the entrance.

"That's amazing," said Mike. "It looks like an electronic map of Disney World. I can't believe I've come to this hospital a hundred times and never even thought to check out the interfloors and loading dock. How come nobody talks about all this?"

"If we did, we'd be giving tours all the time and never getting our work done. We just tell everyone the interfloors are service areas with a bunch of wires and heating ducts, and no one gives it a second thought."

"Well, how come you told me about this?"

"You're my doctor, I want you to know what I do. And besides, I know you can keep it quiet. You don't even tell my wife when I come to see you—unless she tells you first that she knew I was there."

"That's just a good habit I try to follow, Hugh. Technically I'm not supposed to discuss even the fact that a patient came to see me unless it's medically important or legally mandated or instructed by the patient."

"Well, Doc, I know you've got to go. Come back any time. I'll be glad to show you more."

"Thanks, Hugh. I'll have a bunch of questions next time I see you in the office."

As soon as Mike left Hugh, he started to get nervous. He wasn't used to breaking the law like he was planning to do tonight. Oh, he would drive his car too fast regularly, but he wasn't experienced in breaking and entering. As a physician, he was permitted to go nearly everywhere in the medical world, and he never really had time to go places he wasn't permitted. But tonight would be different.

Twelve

Saturday, May 10
Fairbanks, Alaska

Delta Flight 828 touched down on runway 32 at Fairbanks, Alaska, moments before the sun set. The landing was smooth and right on the numbers for the 3-mile long runway. Both Patti and Kent had slept the last 2 hours of the flight, only to be awakened with the please fasten your seat belt announcement.

"What a good way to start our adventure," Kent said to Patti. "I trust our landing is a good omen."

"You think almost everything is a good omen," Patti said.

"A positive attitude is incredibly helpful. And what are you talking about, Patti? You're so positive all the time you don't even bother with omens!"

"Did you get the control formulas checked OK?"

"They seem fine to me. It only took 45 minutes. I hope my staff has fun testing them while I'm playing with you in the North Country."

"At least you're saying North Country now instead of North Pole. Who knows, you may never want to go back. You just might embrace your college vow to retire early and become a forest ranger."

"I said that before I found out forest rangers don't have heated tents with dish TVs and crews to do all the cooking, cleaning, and carrying of heavy loads. If I could return home to a resort type of cabin with a high-speed computer connection to Wilmington, I could be happy here—that is if you stay, too."

"That's a thought. I'll have to consider that offer. I wonder how much vacation forest rangers get?"

"Moving right along, what's booked for tonight. I'm sure Ms. Organization has the restaurant reserved and the entertainment arranged."

"Well, first we find our hotel, the Regal Alaska Hotel. It's just 2 miles north of the airport. Tonight we have a reservation at the Crow's Nest Restaurant in downtown Fairbanks in the Hotel Captain Cook. They have a panoramic rooftop view of the city. We're supposed to try the Beluga caviar and sea beans. The other two nights in Fairbanks, we get to try the Marx Brothers Café and Simon and Seaforts. We also have the option to go to Sullivan's Steakhouse. Calgary beef is supposed to be the best in the world."

"After 3 days in Fairbanks, we catch the bush amphibious plane at 12:45 in the afternoon for the 2-hour flight south, to the Denali National Park and Mt. McKinley. We base out of Denali Grizzly Bear Cabins and Campgrounds and take several guided tours into the wild unknown! We spend 2 weeks exploring the park and Mt McKinley, mostly on foot! Later in our dream month, we squeeze in a trip to Moose Pass, North Pole, which is just south of Fairbanks, and Crooked Creek State Park."

"Isn't Mt. McKinley rather high? I mean half the mountain is in the clouds. How are we going to see where to land? And isn't the wind rather tricky around regular mountains, let alone record capable tall mountains?"

"Yes, McKinley is tall. It's 20,320 feet high—the highest land point in North America. And I suppose the winds are tricky around the mountain peaks, but we aren't going to land anywhere near the top. We get to the top by climbing!"

"Dear wife, I know you've lost it now. We, especially me, are not experienced climbers. I know you realize we are not going to climb that mountain. It's covered with ice and snow and glaciers and wolves and lions and tigers and bears. Even our base camp is named after bears. Do you have a dog team to pull me up, because I'm not climbing a class 5 climb on my third try?"

"There are several base camps and climb stations within reach of the novice. That's where we'll go. You're supposed to be athletic, and you carry on like a tough guy. I thought you'd be more up for the challenge. Your research award covers several private 2- and 3-day private excursions into the wilds. There will be no one around. We travel mostly by bush amphibious plane and our guides help us pitch our tent and they even cook for us. They say the fishing is unbelievable. The salmon jump into your boat and taste incredible."

"What about the bears?"

"No problem, they don't like boats."

"Are we planning to camp on the water?"

"No, we brought a sign that says, 'No bears allowed.'"

"Great, now all we'll get are the illiterate bears attacking us rather than the civilized ones."

"Don't worry, I'm told the guides have all that figured out."

"Do they carry snake antivenin?"

"My word, where were all these questions before we picked this trip? You really are worried, aren't you?"

"I was too busy before we left to get into the details. I came just to take care of you, my love. I knew you most likely didn't consider the dangers—you just go off exploring when the urge hits you and deal with whatever comes up."

"I'm so glad I've got you to watch out for me. I know you'll be brave when you need to be. But these trips are supposed to be easy enough for novices. They couldn't afford the insurance for real danger."

"I'm not so sure Alaska operates like the East Coast. I heard there are only a half dozen or so lawyers in Alaska so insurance rates are incredibly low. I hear all kinds of city slickers never make it home from Mt. McKinley. I heard the natives call it Mt. Finale."

"Oh, brother, what an imagination. A comedian on TV said that. He couldn't camp out without his own chef, a refrigerator, big screen TV, and Japanese carriage for transportation. We really ought to be a little more informed from more reliable sources before we choose to worry. Only 11 people died exploring in Alaska and the Yukon last year."

"What did you say?! Doesn't 11 sound rather high, dear wife?"

"So what's your point?"

"So where did you get that number?"

"I checked out the Alaska Mountain Rescue Group reports. It's right on the Internet. They've been saving people for several years. I thought we ought to have their number, just in case."

"Just in case? Now I'm really getting worried. You never consider that angle. We must be going into a war zone."

"Well, Murphy's Law says that if you prepare for something untoward to happen, that's the best insurance for it not to happen. Anyway, I registered our planned excursions away from civilization with them just in case we miss one of our call-in checkpoints. I figure the worst that can happen is our transportation breaks down and we're stranded somewhere. AMRG can get us out if they know where we are."

"My, you are thorough. What made you consider we may need help?"

"Our kids, Daddio, our kids. We'll be gone a month. That's unheard of in the realm of parenting. I thought we should take extra precautions, that's all."

"You know, Patti, you and I need to talk. I'm beginning to realize just how much you do for and with the kids that I don't even know about. You do tell me the important stuff, don't you?"

"You're on a need-to-know basis, oh great husband . . . Actually, I do tell you the key information. And, I put the major events on your calendar. As busy as you are saving the world with medical research, you're doing OK showing up for about half of them."

"How do the kids handle my .500 batting average?"

"You tend to save yourself on the weekends. And your backrubs and bedtime talks keep you in the game. Actually, they're doing just fine, and they aren't even annoyed at you. I, on the other hand, have to schedule far-out adventurous trips like this to get you alone. Well, not quite, I do exaggerate some."

"So you planned this trip because you're jealous of the 15 minutes I spend with our kids each night."

"Not! You wish."

"Well, honey, I'm looking forward to being alone with you in a tent, high up on Mt. McKinley, in the remote wilderness, with the wind whipping all around, and having that heater you said will make the tent room temperature. I just hope room service is prompt."

"No problem. They've already delivered the K rations."

"Well, since we're spending one of our last few days in a real hotel, what do you have planned for tonight?"

"We can go to the Alaska Heritage Aviation Museum before dinner if you like. After dinner, I thought I'd take you to the hotel's sports bar for a short while before we spend some more time alone, without the kids."

"You've planned well, Patti. I'll make one call when we get to the hotel, and I'm all yours."

"You've got a deal, my man."

Thirteen

Sunday, May 11

"Patti, wake up, babe. It's 9:30 already. We're going to miss breakfast with the Donovans at 10 if we don't rally soon," said Kent in a husky, sleepy voice.

"I thought there was no problem with jet lag flying west."

"There usually isn't, except when we have an abundance of wine and stay out until 2 in the morning. Then it gets a little heavy."

"I didn't know I could sleep this late. We haven't done this for a couple of years."

"I don't really figure 7 hours of sleep is sleeping late, even though it's a little more than our usual. I guess we'll have to shower together to save time."

"I thought showering together was for saving water, not time."

"Whatever works to my advantage, Patti babe. Quotes are made to inspire and help people get the most out of life."

"I never heard that one before. Where's it from?"

"It's from the orientation manual for our college fraternity. I should show it to you sometime; it's full of original perspectives on the mysteries of life. Yogi Berra and Will Rogers gave us the most material. I can't tell you how much these quotes and thoughts ring true today. And some are pertinent to our safari adventure. Like . . .

'***Even if you're on the right track, you'll get run over if you just sit there.***' Will Rogers said that. And, '***If you don't know where you're going, you will probably end up somewhere else.***' Laurence Peter came up with that one—he's the fellow who wrote about the Peter Principle—the precursor of Dilbert. Ernest Hemingway said, '***Courage is grace under pressure.***' I sure hope we don't need that one on this voyage into the deep, dark unknown."

"The guides even give massages, dear wimpy husband of mine. I sincerely doubt we'll be close to roughing it. But **my** favorite quote is, '***Before I got married I had six theories about bringing up children; now I have six children and no theories.***' John Wilmiot, the Earl of Rochester, uttered those sage words way back in the 1600's."

"'***I hear and I forget. I see and I remember. I do and I understand.***' I believe that's an old Chinese proverb. Is that why we're actually going to risk our lives in this snow-covered North Country mountainous terrain?"

"My, but you do have a tendency to exaggerate. Are you looking to be a hero in our kids eyes when we return?"

"Speaking of heroes, Will Rogers had a clever notion. '***We can't all be heroes because somebody has to sit on the curb and clap as they go by.***' And he also said, '***This thing of being a hero, about the main thing to it is to know when to die.***' Gee, I sure hope that doesn't apply either."

"I'm astounded that you're this worried. You probably can't stand to be away from your computer—it just makes you too anxious!"

"In what century does that happen? Certainly not on this trip, I hope."

"Well, dear, you can pack you own backpack. And if there's room for your computer, feel free. Just remember, you'll have to carry the weight."

"Who's carrying the refrigerator?"

"The same person who's carrying that heavy StarSAT satellite phone you hope to bring. It's just that he hasn't arrived yet. Arnold Schwarzenegger doesn't rent himself out very often as a pack mule." "The phone is light, and it's a safety feature. I'm sure our guides have one."

"A communication system yes, a SAT phone I doubt. I bet you'll be the first to introduce them to satellite phones. Now, you've quoted Will Rogers, what could Yogi Berra have said that was so prophetic?"

"My two favorites were '***If the people don't want to come to the park, nobody's going to stop 'em.***' And '***You can obser ve a lot just by watching.***'"

"I guess that's deep. I bet Yogi never heard Laurence Coughlin's famous words, ***'Don't talk unless you can improve the silence.***'"

"That's a little too intellectual for Yogi. But my favorite of all time is Robert Frost's shortest poem. He said, ***'Oh, Lord, forgive the little jokes that I have played on thee and I'll forgive the great big one that you have played on me.***'"

"That sure makes you think! And now we **have** to shower together, we've only got 20 minutes left to meet them for breakfast!"

Kent and Patti made it to the breakfast buffet 2 minutes early. Tom and Marsha were already waiting.

"Hi, Tom! Hi Marsha!" said Kent. "What's up for today?"

"I negotiated a man's dream deal," answered Tom. "We get to go fishing in Eagle River while Patti and Marsha tour the city. Now that's the way to start off an expedition into the wilds and avoid the life-and-death dangers of shopping at the same time!"

"That does sound good," said Kent. "Patti tells me we'll spend a few days together in the big city here before we each go on our separate tours. Patti and I, the adventurous ones, catch an amphibious plane at 12:45 in the afternoon on Tuesday for a 4-hour flight north to Mt. McKinley, and don't you two head off for that dude ranch for 2 weeks before we meet up and then head out together for some camping?"

"That's right," said Marsha. "I can't wait to see Tom in cowboy boots and a ten-gallon hat."

"And I can't wait to see you in cowgirl boots with tassels!" said Tom.

"So, Patti, why did you plan the 2-week survival trek first in the trip? Weren't you afraid you'd wear Kent out?"

"Wearing him out wasn't my concern," said Patti. "I was afraid he'd be called back to work. The government is all over his gene therapy research and if anything is even remotely not perfect, they act like he's building an atomic bomb and Kent's the only one who can fix it. The government is pretty touchy about secrecy. They're afraid someone will use it to build King Kong or a master race."

"They're also worried about all the protestors and the *X Files* type drama," added Kent. "The Cold War is over, but the CIA thinks Saddam Hussein of all people is trying to get a hold of what we're doing for obvious reasons. They claim they've caught two of his spies on the grounds of Kelly Hospital already! They weren't working for the hospital. They had infiltrated a supply company and were working as their deliverymen and casing out the lab when they brought supplies in. They caught them when a small camera fell out of one of the worker's overalls."

"Now aren't you glad to be out of there for a month, Kent?" asked Patti.

"Actually, the timing for a break seems quite good right now. Once the sequences are tested for the control messengers, the research gets quite hairy in preparation for human trials. That will be pressure-packed, so I'm glad to have a break now, and to be here with my adventuresome wife and my good friends. I couldn't ask for more fun and excitement. I'll be totally refreshed, and we'll have memories galore and tons of stories to bore our kids with."

"Now you know why I planned the longest part first. Kelly Hospital Research will start to get antsy if the team finishes the testing early."

"Patti honey, I promise you they won't finish for at least 3 weeks."

"That's still early!"

"Well, they can wait one more week. What could be the rush? How important can one week be?"

"OK, Livingstone, I'll hold you to your promise," said Patti. "Tom, you just be sure your rear isn't too sore from riding horses so you can keep up with us when we return!"

"Who said anything about riding horses?" said Tom. "I was planning to get a massage and sleep late every day, and then watch all the East Coast sports at a decent hour."

"Patti, where did we ever find two such non-macho men?" said Marsha.

"You got me, Marsha. They must be fast talkers."

Fourteen

Monday, May 12
Wilmington, Delaware
4 PM

Debbie and Kelly Naylor pulled into the driveway and were surprised to see Wendy's bike. She should be at the Kelly Hospital for her training. Debbie stopped the SUV to turn around, and Kelly hopped out of the car before her mother could say something to stop her.

"Kelly!" Debbie called, but Kelly was already running inside.

Kelly ran up the stairs to Wendy's room and rushed into the room, even though the door was shut. "Why are you home? Are you all right?" asked Kelly.

"Why do you always ignore my bedroom door when it's closed?" asked Wendy. "There's no privacy here!"

"I just wanted to see if you're OK. You don't need to be so mean."

"I'm fine. I'm just taking a break from my training. I have two tests tomorrow, and after the two I just took, I'm really beat."

Wendy had just hung up with Robbie Coleman, her friend from school. It was a good thing he had to head back to practice and had already hung up or she'd be taking teasing from Kelly.

Debbie Naylor finally made it to her daughter's room. "Wendy, is everything OK?"

"Yes, Mom. I'm just a little tired, and I have two tests again tomorrow. Miroslov says I can take 2 extra days off training each month—whenever I need to let my body recover."

"Well, I'm glad you're fine. Just be sure to tell your dad when he comes home. He'll want to check you out. He worries about you." "I'll definitely tell him. But, oh, does he worry too much. It's funny, you know—he lets me do just about anything, but if I don't act 100% energetic, he gets all fussy."

"That's why you have two parents. Our concerns overlap so you don't get away with anything," said Debbie half teasing as she left the room to finish unloading the car. As she left, Wendy surprised Kelly by tackling her. Kelly started laughing and Wendy, pretending to be mad, told Kelly she had better knock before coming in next time. After being released, Kelly said, "No way! You should just consider yourself lucky that I don't listen to your phone calls with Robbie the hunk."

"He's not a hunk," exclaimed Wendy. "Oh, you are such a brat. He's a nice guy, and we're just friends. He doesn't barge into my room or scare me."

"When he gets to know you better he will," stated Kelly. "And besides, a hunk is a good thing. Hey, since you're just fine, can you help me with my jump shot for awhile, please?"

"Your jump shot is solid. Why do you want my help?"

"I'd tell you, but I don't want you to get a big head."

"OK, 10 minutes. And then I've got to get back to studying."

"Thanks, big sister! Let's go."

Kelly and Wendy headed for the driveway with their dog, Sandy, a frisky poodle, right on their heels. Sandy was disappointed they didn't really get into wrestling this time, but maybe they'd play with him outside. He'd make sure he brought them his favorite ball to chase while they were busy with the big ball.

"Kelly, you shoot some to warm up while I feed you," said Wendy. "Then I'll show you a trick that really helped me develop my shot."

Kelly put considerable energy into her shooting, figuring she would only have the maestro for 10 minutes, stretchable to 20 max. Dad was sometimes easier; he could be extended to a full half hour before he realized what was going on. After 5 minutes of positive reinforcement and reminding Kelly to keep her release high, Wendy brought out the mini trampoline they got for Christmas.

"Now if this doesn't work, I'll put you on the full-size trampoline, but you don't get to shoot at a basket on that one," said Wendy. "Hold the ball at your waist like you're protecting the ball in a game, and with each bounce, bring the ball up above your head and look at the basket from underneath the ball. Every fourth bounce or so, shoot. We'll start in real close and gradually move the trampoline away from the basket. The trampoline will give you more time in the air to practice timing your shot. When you finally learn to jump, you'll already have a jump shot!"

"You had to get that last dig in about the jumping, didn't you?!"

"I had to say something to get you fired up. Now show me you can jump and shoot as well!"

Mike Naylor pulled over to the side of the road behind his home to watch the scene unfolding in the driveway. He noticed what looked like basketball activity, and when he got the car stopped, he could see Kelly and Wendy bouncing around and laughing. When he saw these two together, he couldn't help thinking how lucky he was that they got along so well . . . most of the time. The scene was worth watching from afar. If he drove up, it would probably change or stop. Then he realized, what was Wendy doing home? She was supposed to be at the Sports Medicine facility working out. Mike promptly headed up the driveway.

As he pulled into the driveway, his daughters waved, quite surprised to see him home so soon. They stepped aside to allow his car to go in the garage and not tie up valuable driveway space, and Kelly ran to greet him. The youngest child's role was to show affection. She could get away with an open display of emotion.

Wendy could hug her parents and still be cool as long as she didn't act too excited.

"Hi, Daddy!" exclaimed Kelly. "What are you doing home so early? Can you play basketball with me? Wendy has to study."

"I'd be honored, Kelly. Is it OK if I change my clothes first?"

"I'll wait. Wendy and I have to finish first."

"Hello there, Wendy," said Mike. "Are you skipping practice?"
"Yes, Dad. But you'll be proud of me. I was home studying and just took a break to teach your younger daughter how to shoot a jump shot the right way."

"Well that's good! I'll go change and relieve you soon. But please tell me what to say to her so I don't interfere with a real coach."

"I don't think that will be a problem, Dad. You kinda know the John Wooden type who taught me." Wendy was referring to her Dad as her instructor.

The little Tigger on the trampoline resumed her lesson while Mike went inside.

"Howdy, Debbie," said Mike. "How about we're all home before 5 o'clock? That's a first!"

"That's for sure, Mike," said Debbie. "Isn't it funny that we all long for a day like this and when it finally occurs our first thought is that there must be something wrong? I hope there isn't, but I'd feel better if you talk to Wendy after dinner. She says she's just a little tired and overloaded with homework and is just taking one of her free days, but she rarely chooses to miss practice. And remember, we need to have an early dinner tonight so I can get over to Marshall's to work on the Wine-Tasting Benefit with him."

"That's fine. I'll check her out after dinner. Hey, have you seen my dark wool cap?"

"Yes, it's in the second hall closet with the gloves and winter coats. What do you want a wool cap for? It's summer."

"It gets cold at night, especially after water skiing. I'd like to keep it in my car in case I need it."

Mike changed his clothes and headed to the driveway to coach Kelly. He usually only got to coach her on Tuesdays and Thursdays at AAU practice, so an extra session on a Monday was a treat. He'd be sure to keep it fun. After dinner, he planned to have a talk with Wendy, finish a few medical reports he was working on, and then head to the hospital for a little undercover work.

Fifteen

Monday, May 12
6:30 PM

"*Debbie, you had better get going to Marshall's,*" said Mike. "I don't know when you'll be back, but I have to head over to the hospital later. I'll have my pager on for either you or the kids in case one of you needs me."

"I'll probably be very late," answered Debbie. "Are you jealous?"

"Hadn't really thought about it. Should I be?" said Mike. "After all, Marshall is president of a fund-raising firm. Would you ever trust a man who just kept asking for money?"

"Only if he kept getting large amounts of it!" retorted Debbie. "I guess it would take quite a lot to make you jealous."

"I figure, if you want me to be jealous, you'll pretty much tell me. You normally don't do things that make me jealous. However, just why **do** you usually have evening meetings with him instead of daytime meetings in his office?"

"Now, I know I've told you this before. Marshall's the president of the fund-raising firm for all our charitable projects for the Medical Society and for the Society itself. He prefers to meet off hours when he's donating his time, which he does for our charitable projects. And he prefers to meet at his home because of his two young kids—especially on a school night. His wife died in an auto accident 3 years ago, so he needs to do these things at home so he can take care of his kids. Tonight, we have to finish the planning for the Wine-Tasting Benefit. His firm has to print the program and make the final contacts by Friday this week. Since I'm president of the auxiliary, I get stuck, I mean I get the honor of making the final detail decisions. He promised to have dessert tonight while we work. It probably won't take much more than an hour or so."

"Oh, is he a cook, too?"

"Now that I don't know," said Debbie. "He'll probably have ice cream sandwiches, but I'll have to let you know."

"OK, m'lady. I'm going to have my little talk with Wendy now. I'll see you later. Have fun! Be good!"

"Oh! You're incorrigible! Pretending to be jealous, just for me. Bye!"

Mike headed upstairs to Wendy's room thinking that it made perfect sense to actually use her two free days a month; that's why the coach gave them to her. He just wanted to be sure she might not be having any ill effects from the "nutritional supplements" Dr. Thompson had been giving her.

"Hi, Wendy! Your mom thought I ought to check you out. What do you think?"

"I think you both worry too much. It's very nice of you two, but sometimes I feel like I have two mothers."

"I guess that's a compliment, for a father to be called a mother."

"I'm just trying to make a point. I know you'll always be there for me, but you do sometimes get carried away with your imagination. Is that because you're a physician and you know all the bad things that can happen?"

"You're a wise girl for 14 years old to ask that question, and that is part of it. Thank God I don't know everything bad that can happen."

"Dad, you seem so confident because you let me do and try so many things, but you still worry so much when I'm not all full of energy and acting real peppy. You know, I'm getting much older now, and I don't plan to be bouncing around all the time anymore."

"Ha, ha. You're still cute. I'll try to remember you're aging fast. But seriously, do you feel OK? Do you have any specific symptoms?"

"I feel pretty good. I just had two tests Friday, a paper due today and two more tests tomorrow. I thought it would be good timing to take a few hours off and actually study."

"And talk on the phone a little?"

"Yes, that would be nice. Tell me, Dad, is that something teenagers tend to do more than once every week or so? Do teenage girls actually talk to boys, too? Or do they need to be much older, as you keep suggesting?"

"I suppose some do at your early age. And you are precocious. So I bet you could. Once every other week or so, that is. Who do you have in mind?"

"I'll tell Robbie you were asking for him. Do you have any other messages you'd like for me to relay to him?" Wendy suddenly got a little serious. "When's the last time you talked to him, now that we're on the subject?"

"I talk to him only when he's with you, which isn't very often because of your schedule, and when he's in the office as a patient, which isn't very often either. But, now that you mention it, we should probably do lunch sometime."

"Oh, Dad!"

"Don't worry, I won't cook for him. But, really, please tell me if you get any symptoms, even if they are weird or brief. I want to be especially careful after what happened to Jenn and Matt."

"What do you think happened to them, Dad?"

"I don't really know, but it concerns me that both of them had a major problem within hours of each other and they started in the same program you're in at about the same time. The field of medicine doesn't believe in coincidences. Happenings like that are related until proven otherwise. I just hope it's not related to the nutritional injections you all are getting."

"Do you know what's in them?"

"No, I don't. I should. Dr. Thompson says they're harmless, but he hasn't told anyone what's in them. He says it just part of his special blend of food supplements that are supposed to be safe and just act as nutritional support."

"Then why does he inject them?"

"He says that way he knows exactly what each athlete is getting and can document it for his study. It is logical to do it that way. Compliance is nearly 100% and GI factors, including absorption, are eliminated as variables. But just the same, I'm going to look into it myself. I'm not sure how, so don't tip Dr. Thompson off just yet, OK?"

"Should I stop taking the injections, Dad?"

"I wouldn't stop just yet. If he's right, they are harmless and stopping wouldn't help you and could slow down your progress. And if he's wrong, it may be harmful to suddenly stop taking them without tapering off. When I get more information, we'll decide then."

"OK, Dad. I'll tell Robbie 'Hi' for you."

"You do that. I'm going to check on Kelly now. I have to go in to the hospital later, but I hope your Mom will be back by then. If not, I'll have the pager."

Mike left the room feeling slightly better, but also a little more guilty. He knew that Wendy trusted Dr. Thompson only because he had encouraged her to enter the program. The fact that Wendy was doing so well didn't affect Wendy's impression of Dr. Thompson very much. She thought her trainer and coach were the reason for her success, not Dr. Thompson. Mike probably should not have trusted Dr. Thompson so much that he didn't bother to get more information on the injections. Not where his daughter was concerned. He read somewhere that many athletes would give up their long-term health for Olympic-level success, but Mike would never knowingly decide that for his family. Now he had to find out if his daughter's success so far was artificially assisted.

Mike went to look for his dark wool cap, even though he figured the best way for him to get into the hospital late at night was to just be a doctor. Maybe he'd need it if he had to sneak out.

Sixteen

Monday, May 12
7:30 PM

Debbie Naylor pulled into Marshall Keller's driveway and noticed very few lights were on in the Keller home. The driveway lights and front porch light were shining, but the house looked too quiet for two young kids to be active inside. She parked in the double driveway and headed for the front door. As she approached, the door opened.

"I see you're on time as usual," said Marshall. "Thanks for coming. Come right in."

"Where are John and Megan?" asked Debbie. "They're usually the first to greet me."

"They're at their grandmother's house. They don't have school tomorrow. Fordam School has parent conferences tomorrow so their grandmother claimed them for the night. They'll miss seeing you, but we can get more done in peace."

Debbie headed into the combination family room and kitchen and saw the paperwork for the benefit on the main kitchen island. A large fragrance candle was burning and soft music was in the background.

"Brother, when your kids are away the whole mood in this house changes from controlled chaos to mellow calmness with soft lighting and scented candles."

"Both atmospheres are good, and it's especially good to intersperse one with the other."

"I'd say that's a good idea. Where do we start?"

With no interruptions, Debbie and Marshall made quick work with finishing the planning for the Wine-Tasting Benefit that was 4½ weeks away.

"Since you were so good, I've prepared a special dessert as a reward," said Marshall. "It's my own version of chocolate mousse. It's an old family recipe."

"It looks like it's individually wrapped to me," said Debbie.

"Or did you have the caterer do that after you prepared a whole batch?"

"Actually, they are store bought. I don't really cook. We eat a lot of spaghetti and steak here. The kids are still into macaroni and cheese. I usually get Chinese when they eat kids' meals."

"Since you have a 6-year-old and an 8-year-old, you must have either Hershey Bars or Hershey Kisses around here. Let me show you how to spice this up a little. I'll need a carrot peeler to make this happen."

Marshall found the Hershey Bars and carrot peeler, and Debbie placed Hershey shavings on their mousse dessert. Marshall just watched admiringly and came closer.

"Before you start eating, I have something to say to you."

Marshall put his hand on Debbie's waist, looked at her eyes and then her lips, and then slowly and gently kissed her while holding her waist with both hands. He held the kiss for several seconds, and Debbie responded, placing her hand on his arm. Debbie was surprised, but felt excited with the kiss and did not pull away. After a few seconds, Marshall pulled back just enough to see her eyes.

"I've been wanting to kiss you ever since I met you," said Marshall. "It just never felt like the right opportunity until now." He then put his arms gently around her. Debbie responded with a soft hug. With her head on his shoulder, Debbie's thoughts were racing. Marshall was very special to her, but she had never thought of him as someone to kiss. She was attracted to him and he was good looking, but she cared for him as a generous person who did an exceptional amount of charity work. She felt sorry for him as a widower, and she admired him for spending so much time with his kids. But now she could start to think after the completely unexpected kiss had moved into a hug. She rallied, held him by the waist as she pulled back a little, and said, "You know, Marshall, that was really nice, but I need to keep you as a good friend and not complicate my life right now."

"Debbie, you have a kind way with words. You've just very politely told me no in a way that makes it easy for us to talk. I didn't know how you'd react if I ever kissed you, but at least I tried. You do kiss very well, by the way."

"You do, too, but let's keep it our last. I do love my husband. We have two great kids, and he still laughs at my jokes."

"Thanks, Debbie. I'll remember your wishes."

"*Now*, can I eat dessert?" asked Debbie, half kidding.

"Of course. What would you like to drink?"

They ate in silence for a brief period, and then Marshall asked, "How is Wendy doing? How is she handling the tragedy with Jenn and Matt?"

"We haven't talked much about it yet, but as far as I can tell, she seems OK. She did take today off from training, but Mike was going to talk to her tonight to see how she felt. She is planning to go to Matt's funeral Wednesday evening."

"Boy, that is unbelievable, and both kids from this area are in the same conditioning program. Does Mike have any concern about the study?"

"I don't believe so. He said the conditioning is somewhat rapid, but not excessive considering how Wendy is responding. The nutritional supplement should be safe, so I don't believe Mike has any real concern. I'll have to talk with him about that, though. That's a good thought. Thanks, Marshall. You're always thinking."

"Yeah, maybe too much."

"Now don't start that. We're moving on from here, right, Marshall?"

"Onward and upward, Debbie. If there is anything I can do or if you want me to talk to Dr. Thompson, let me know. His sports medicine program and the Kelly Hospital are both clients of mine."

"Thanks, Marshall, I'll remember that. Now I'd better get home, Mike has to go back to the hospital when I return. I'll let you know every few days how the registration is going. Thanks again for your help on this project."

Debbie stood up and headed slowly for the front door. She thanked him again and departed as Marshall held the door, but kept a safe distance away.

Seventeen

Monday, May 12
10:30 PM

Debbie Naylor pulled into her driveway and noticed Mike's car was still there. She hoped all went well with Wendy and Mike's little "talk." As she headed inside, she saw Mike in his study.

"Howdy, Mike. How's our Wendy?"

"Well, partner, she's doing OK. She's in the middle of a huge crunch at school, and in spite of how smart she is, she really does have to study on occasion. She's just taking one of her 2 free days per month. I don't detect any real problem, physical or otherwise."

"Thank goodness for that. Hey, I thought you had to go in to the hospital tonight."

"I do. I was trying to finish these medical reports first. They keep getting postponed."

"I hope your patient or patients have insomnia with you coming in so late."

"I suppose you're right. I should get going soon. But 11 PM is the change of shift, and no patient is allowed to sleep through that. Besides, making rounds late in the evening tends to catch patients when they are sleepy and less likely to talk as long. They only tell you what's really important, and rounds go much quicker. I'll head out as soon as I finish this page."

"OK. Hurry home."

Debbie headed for Kelly's room, and Mike thought about his strategy one more time. He'd head over to the hospital to do his normal rounds. He'd stop at his patient's room on 3A, write a quick note on the chart, and while the nurses and staff were busy during the change of shift, he'd slip into the utility closet and climb up to the next floor through the trap door to the interfloor where the sports medicine training center was. All staff should be out of there by 10 PM or so, and Dr. Thompson would be at his staff meeting. If he heard any noise, he'd just stay in the utility room until it was completely quiet and the lights were out. He would use his small aviation white- and red-light flashlight to see to get around, using a red light to keep his eyes from losing their night vision. Getting out of the sports center and back on a patient floor should be relatively easy if he was careful exiting the utility closet. He always had the option of exiting the trap doors on the 1st or 2nd floor as well.

Mike grabbed his cell phone, dark ski hat, small flashlight, and pocketknife and stuffed them in his sport jacket pockets. He also took 4 surgical gloves, putting 2 in each front pocket of his pants. He thought it would be good to have a kit to pick locks, but he didn't have one and he wouldn't even know how to use it. He was getting nervous already.

Once on the patients' floor, he headed right for a patient's room, figuring the fewer who saw him the better.

"I didn't think I would get to see you again today Dr. Naylor," said Mr. Hawkins.

"I thought I'd check on you just in case you were recovering enough to be discharged tomorrow. So far, your cultures are still negative, your fever is coming down, and your lungs are clearing. If your infectious disease doctor agrees, I should be able to send you home in the morning on the same antibiotic you are on in the hospital. If you continue to get better, you can take Levaquin by mouth and head for home. So, keep your fever down all night, and in the morning I'll try to get you out of here."

"That's a deal, Dr. Mike."

Mike Naylor finished his chart note in the patient's room and headed for the nurses' station to replace the chart. The entire staff was in the back room discussing the patients for the change of shift and didn't notice a physician visiting their domain. Nurses seemed to have a knack for sensing when a guest was on the floor, but evidently they had gotten so good at ignoring physicians, they often didn't even know when one was around. Mike then headed down to the end of the hall to the utility room and, after a furtive glance around, quickly slipped inside. He located the metal stair rungs on the wall with his flashlight. He put on a pair of surgical gloves and climbed up to the trap door in the ceiling and positioned himself to push them open. They wouldn't budge! He thought they must be rusted shut. How could that be? What was happening to his plan? He climbed up one more rung for a better position, pulled out his flashlight, and pushed again while studying the trap doors. They weren't rusted shut, they were locked! Now that was a violation of the fire code! Mike saw there was virtually no way he could break the lock, especially quietly, nor did he want to leave evidence of a break-in.

He climbed down and sat on a chair by a table in the maintenance room to think. He really wanted to get to his daughter's chart. He just had to know what he'd gotten his daughter into. His cause was noble, so he had to continue. Should he get bolt cutters? They would probably work, but they would be so big he'd have trouble sneaking them inside the hospital. And he would be leaving evidence of a break-in if he did cut the lock. Maybe he could just take the cut-up lock with him, making it look like it just wasn't locked in the first place. There had to be another way! Wait, if he could climb up, why couldn't he climb down? The door on the 4th floor might not be locked. Hugh hadn't seemed to indicate that the doors would be locked, but then again, he hadn't indicated that any of the trap doors would be locked shut.

Mike took his gloves off. He'd need a third pair for backup, just in case. He could get some at the supply cabinet in the back of the procedure room behind the nurses' station. At this hour, no one should be in there, so he should be able to go in unnoticed. He stood quietly next to the utility closet door, listening carefully for any activity. He took his time, making sure a nurse wasn't charting a medication on the medicine cart in the hallway. He waited for 5 minutes to be sure. It was perfectly quiet. He figured most crooks got caught by being careless and not paying attention to the details. Even the slowest nurse would be done charting and on to the next patient by now, so he figured no one should be in the hallway since he hadn't heard any noise at all. Mike carefully and slowly opened the door. What would he say if someone saw him? He figured he could say he went in the utility room to wipe a smudge off his pants. Luckily, no one was there! He quickly slipped into the hallway and quietly shut the door. He headed to the procedure room.

He was right—the procedure room was empty. No one would be doing any procedures at this hour, and the nurses had it cleaned hours ago. He discarded his used gloves and grabbed two more pairs. He then boldly walked out the door into the hallway and headed for the elevators. Mike knew the stairs would be unlocked, but they would only let people out on the ground floor. They were an emergency exit. All doors were locked heading inside, but would open on the floors to get inside the stairwell.

Inside the elevator, he pressed 4. He didn't know the nurses on 4A very well, and he didn't have a patient on that floor, but he'd handle that when he got there. He remembered they had a great lounge on that floor with snacks for the house staff and a large-screen TV with unlimited 24-hour cable access. He'd say he was looking for a resident. And the nurses would think he was possibly doing that or more likely looking for a snack. Either would be OK with the nurses.

The hallway was quiet. No one appeared to care that the elevator opened. He stepped off and headed down the long hall, avoiding the nurses' station. Evidently, the nurses had finished their rounds, and the patients were all tucked in. The nurses probably thought the person getting off the elevator was an IV nurse on rounds or a phlebotomist preparing to stick someone for an every-2-hour blood sugar. Or, they just figured the elevator opened and no one got off. More likely, they just weren't paying any attention to the elevator. Anyway, he was glad they didn't feel the need to act like a police force.

He darted by the door to the residents' lounge. He didn't want to go inside and have someone see him unless it was absolutely necessary. He certainly didn't want to arouse any suspicion. He located the door to the utility room and quickly slipped inside. He was already getting better at sneaking around. He immediately took out his flashlight and directed the white light to the ceiling. No, he wanted to go down a floor, not up. He then looked for the trap door in the floor. He did not see a lock, but he remembered the door on 3 was locked on the ceiling side. He looked up again and saw there wasn't a lock on the ceiling door. Hopefully, that meant the floor trap door was unlocked as well.

Mike put on a pair of surgical gloves and carefully inspected the trap door. Details, remember the details. He carefully pulled on the door. It was stuck. It wasn't moving at all. Could it be rusted shut? Where was the state inspection team when you needed them? The door wasn't moving. It didn't look like it was locked. It was just stuck. He looked more carefully around the trap door. He noticed the leg of a heavy metal shelving unit on the edge of the door. He'd have to move the shelf before he could even hope to budge the door. Be careful, he thought, empty the shelf before moving it. With his gloves on, he emptied the shelving of all the heavy and mobile objects. He then slid the shelving unit a few inches back off the door. He made sure it was clear and any opening of the door would not knock the shelf over. He replaced the objects on the shelf and dusted the skid marks from the shelving legs. He then braced himself by the trap door and pulled hard on the door handle. It gave suddenly and he fell to his butt, but he kept hold of the door so it didn't slam shut. He was lucky he held on! And the door wasn't locked! Great!

Mike made sure the room was back to normal before he stepped down onto the wall rungs. He very carefully held the trap door open and slowly let it close above him as he headed down. As soon as the door was shut, he took his flashlight out again and looked around. This utility room was much more crowded. It contained all sorts of equipment, and there was a desk over the trap door right below him.

Mike looked at his gloved hands. They were quite dirty. He knew he would be knocking some dirt onto the desk by stepping on the rungs while climbing down, so he would have to check the desk before he returned. He should probably clean the ladder before leaving the floor so he wouldn't leave evidence of someone using the trap door on his way out. He was glad he brought an extra pair of gloves. He'd need at least two more to finish his work. Mike very slowly and carefully stepped off the ladder, avoiding the desk and chair that were both in his way. Mike wondered who would work out of a desk in a dingy utility room. He thought the maintenance staff had much better digs to locker their belongings and take a break. Maybe this was a substation for them.

He removed his gloves and placed them inside out in his pocket. He again stood by the door for a few minutes to be sure there was no activity in the hallway. There shouldn't be anyone on the floor. This should be easier than getting in! It was quiet. He stepped outside, stood very still, and listened. Nothing! He headed down the hall. He was surprised at how squeaky his shoes were. They must have just waxed the floor. He stepped more up and down to cut out the noise his shoes were making. The high stepping was much quieter.

Now he had to hope his folded paper was in place in Thompson's office door. It should be, unless the cleaning staff had gone into the room. But they usually wouldn't be on the floor so late. They didn't clean while patients were using the facility, and patients were around until 10 PM. The cleaning team shouldn't be on this floor until early morning. Anyway, he couldn't help it if they had already been here.

He slipped carefully around the corner where the security counter was near the elevator. He knew a security camera was there along with a relatively bright night-light. Fortunately, it had been very dark around the utility room. But here, he had to be careful. He studied the camera from the side for several minutes. It looked like he could just walk under the camera hugging the wall and get to Thompson's office without being seen. So far, so good.

He paused again at the door to Thompson's secondary office. He figured security wouldn't be so tight up here because Thompson wouldn't ordinarily keep sensitive papers in this office. Plus, it was supposedly secure just gaining entrance, so little additional security would be necessary. He listened and looked around. He kept close to the wall. Mike then put gloves on again and then spun around close, facing the wall and door. He grabbed the doorknob, carefully turned the handle and pushed on the door. It opened! And he heard no alarm. He didn't expect he would, but he thought Thompson might be paranoid enough to have one. He stepped inside and carefully shut the door. He looked for another camera. He saw none. He went to the desk and saw a pile of charts on the side. He ran his index finger down the pile reading the names. There it was! Wendy Naylor, Sports Medicine study participant # 221-22-3085.

Mike looked around some more and then removed Wendy's chart from the pile. He pulled his flashlight out, and slid down to the floor behind the desk to read the chart. He had some note paper and a pen in his shirt pocket, but he thought he could remember anything important that he saw.

The problem list inside the chart was short—the hamstring and groin injuries were the only entries. There were no medical conditions or problems. The family history section on the problem list was empty, but the immunizations were up to date. Thompson's staff was thorough.

He lifted up the problem list and saw the medication list underneath. The only entries were the nutritional supplements. And they were coded so he wouldn't know what they were. He figured he should write them down. There were 3 entries, and he noticed that when one was discontinued, another was started. Mike thought that meant they were changing the dose. Changing the dose—why should Thompson have to change the dose? That usually meant a person had to get used to a small amount of a drug before taking more. That meant the supplement should be acting more like a potent drug than a vitamin or nutritional supplement. Food supplements weren't usually given in increasing increments. Occasionally supplements would be cycled, like changing the concentrations before and after a heavy competition, but not stop one and advance on to another without going back. Mike didn't like what he was thinking. He wrote the 3 coded numbers on his small pad and moved on to the body of the chart.

Noting Wendy's visits with Thompson, he did check off numerous normal findings, but he wrote very little for each visit. He did write "progressing well" and "npws" on nearly every visit. Mike wondered if the latter meant no problem with supplements, since it was similar to his group's shorthand for no problem with meds, npwm. It was good if it did, except that it meant Thompson was concerned enough to ask at each visit about the supplements, so there must be something risky about them.

After the progress notes, he saw some notes marked "Family." Mike read this section and noticed Thompson was writing about Mike. He found the first entry.

"Mike Naylor, family physician, on staff at Kelly. Anxious to help daughter with recovery from injury and progress to champion athlete. Not overly concerned with risk to daughter. Good candidate."

What! Not overly concerned with risk to daughter! Incredible. Mike was quite annoyed at that assessment! Then he thought some more. Maybe he had acted like he wasn't too concerned. After all, he had never asked Thompson for details about the supplements. He had just assumed and trusted Thompson that they were indeed supplements and wouldn't be harmful. Now he knew for sure that they were much more than supplements!

He paged through some more notes from the athletic trainers and found the printed study protocol. Numbers similar to the 3 on the medication list were sequenced in 6 sections under protocol options. A male and female branch each had 3 arms. Wendy's chart had a star at the second female section. The sequences each had 7 drug numbers. Wendy had apparently skipped the first and was on drug/nutritional supplement section 4. The numbers all began with GTO. Mike then noticed the footer at the bottom of the page. It read, "Sports Medicine Gene Therapy Study Protocol, draft 4A." Whoa! Gene therapy. That was too much. Mike knew what gene therapy could do. He also imagined how risky it could be. Sending codes inside cells to alter instructions to cellular DNA was extremely advanced and extremely experimental. That could be great if it worked under control, but he knew the research was too young to be sure of the specificity of the messages. It could be like asking for a little protein to help with healing and getting too much of the wrong protein so massive clotting could start. He quickly returned to the medication list and saw GTO was in front of each drug/nutritional supplement Wendy had received.

Mike thought some more. Where had he seen GTO before? He remembered it was the initials for a car from the 50's, but where else? That's it! He remembered Kent Nash, the worldrenowned gene therapy specialist, had told him a little secret. He used GTO as a prefix for all his original gene therapy drugs. He told his staff it stood for gene therapy option when it really stood for his favorite car from his teenage years. Kent had more of a sense of humor than his staff and loved keeping little secrets like that from them. So if these were all GTO drugs, then they had to come from Kent Nash's lab. Well that should be OK. Kent wouldn't let his drugs be used on people unless they were proven safe. But that didn't add up either. Kent had told Mike 2 months ago that it would be at least 6 to 12 months before they were ready for human trials and the hospital was pressuring him to move the date up or at least stay on the 6-month pace. Kent was adamant about not moving the date up; he had a conscience. And Kent wouldn't say something like that to Mike kidding around; they were good friends. If Mike really shouldn't know something, Kent just wouldn't mention it.

Mike thought some more. If these drugs were gene therapy drugs and they were from Kent's lab, they either had to be stolen or were being used without Kent's knowledge. Or, Kent was lying to him and must be in some trouble and being forced to advance the study ahead of schedule. The trouble part Mike seriously doubted. Kent seemed happy as ever, and he wouldn't head to Alaska for a month if he were in any kind of difficult situation at home. He certainly wouldn't leave his lab if he were in trouble!

Mike remembered part of what Kent was working on with gene therapy was speeding up healing of musculoskeletal injuries with ligament—and muscle-growing protein messages. Maybe that was what had helped Wendy. Maybe these proteins were being produced out of control as the dose was increased and causing cardiac events in the two athletes who had had problems! Maybe Thompson, with or without the hospital's knowledge, was fieldtesting Kent's work without Kent's knowledge! Mike knew that Kent Nash wouldn't risk Wendy's health or life for anything in the world. She had babysat his kids countless times and spent much of her precious few free hours at their house. Mike had to get to Kent to find out what was in these drugs and if Kent knew what Thompson was doing. He'd call Kent as soon as he got home. It didn't matter what time it was in Alaska.

Mike carefully placed Wendy's chart in the pile exactly as he found it. He looked around the room to see if he had moved anything else. Everything was in order. He headed for the door and stood quietly by the door for 3 minutes. He knew that was unnecessary, but he wanted to be careful. He quietly opened the door and slowly edged out of the door while gently closing it. He bent over to pick up the folded piece of paper he almost forgot. He turned to hug the wall and BUMPED INTO SOMEONE! He turned quickly and sprung into a defensive stance. He couldn't believe his eyes. It was Hugh!

"Easy, Doc, you're going to have a heart attack," said Hugh. "What are the gloves for, Doc? It ain't that dirty up here."

"My God, you scared me, Hugh," said Mike. "What are you doing here? You should have been home hours ago."

"Well, I thought I'd come back to help you out. I saw you put the folded paper in Thompson's door earlier today, and I figured you needed something from him and you'd be back. Thompson's a bit of a jerk, so I figured he had been messing with you. I knew you had to come tonight because in the morning, all kinds of people would be going through that door. So I put 2 and 2 together after all your questions about the trap doors and guessed you'd get here around 1 or 2 in the morning. You're a bit early, aren't you?"

"Why didn't you say something when we were together?"

"You've been my doctor for quite a few years, and we've been through a lot. You kept me out of trouble my junior year of high school, and you stuck by my mother during a difficult time. I wanted to help you, but I figured you weren't ready to ask for or accept help. You looked a little bewildered. So I thought I'd come by to help you get in. I pushed the paper in better so you could open the door if you beat me here. And you did. If you don't want to tell me now, that's OK. I owe you, and I'll help without knowing why. I'm pretty sure you're not doing anything illegal."

"No, Hugh, I'm not. Well, technically I am by sneaking in, but I'm just trying to help my daughter. You know those 2 athletes, one died and the other had a heart attack?"

"Yeah, what about them."

"I'm afraid their problems may be related to something Thompson's doing in his study. My daughter's in that study, and I want to be sure she'll be OK."

"Why don't you ask Thompson?"

"I did. He reassured me as if I were a layman. That worried me enough to sneak in to see if he was hiding anything from me."

"Was he? Do we need to go back in there? I have a key."

"I saw enough. I just have to check with Dr. Nash to see what Thompson's up to. I'm going to call him as soon as I get home. Hugh, I really would appreciate your help. I'm not too good at breaking and entering. You discovered what I was planning to do seconds after I planned it. We may need to get into his other lab, and I'll definitely need your help with that. But first, I have to talk to Kent Nash. Can I call you at home after I talk to him?"

"Doc, call me anytime. It will be fun working espionage with you. I don't know much about breaking and entering either, but I do know every nook and cranny of Kelly Hospital. I worked here while this castle was being built. I know all the secret passages. Oh, by the way, I checked lost and found, your daughter's jacket wasn't there."

"OK, Hugh, you got me again. I'll call you later. Now how do we get out of here? I hope we don't have to use the trap doors."

"We don't. We take the elevators as soon as you take off your gloves. I disabled these 2 cameras. Maintenance thinks I'm working on them."

"You mean I didn't have to worry about them?"

"That's right, Doc. I'll take care of you. Oh, did you take anything out of Thompson's office? Do we have to cover your tracks?"

"No, everything is exactly as it was, even the trash can I almost knocked over."

"OK, Doc, we're outahere. Give me your gloves."

Eighteen

Tuesday, May 13
12:30 AM

Mike Naylor was pleased he could leave Kelly Hospital without sneaking through trap doors, but he was quite concerned about what he had just learned. He was not reassured at all about his daughter as he learned more information. As a matter of fact, he was slowly realizing the dream he thought he bought for Wendy just might have been too good to be true. What was that old adage? If it seems too good to be true, it probably is. How many times had he told patients that? How many times had he discovered that to be true in his own life? All the good things he had, he had worked to get. He had taken his time and gone through the normal hassles and effort required to achieve what was worthwhile. Most of the time when he tried to take a short cut, the results just weren't the same. And now it was turning out that even though his intentions were pristine and his efforts were unselfish, the outcome of his plan for Wendy just might be too good to be true. He felt sick thinking that something he had planned could harm his daughter. He wanted so much for her to have every opportunity in life, and to think that he possibly put her life in jeopardy made him feel even sicker.

He jumped in his car and sped home. He prayed he would be in time. Now he had to depend on his wife and a good friend to help undo a wrong he did. He had to try to salvage what he could of a bad situation he had created with good intentions, even though he knew enough to advise his patients to avoid a similar temptation. He had jumped in without using his knowledge and medical training to thoroughly check out potential risks for his daughter. Wendy had trusted him to tell her if it was all right for her to trust Dr. Thompson. Wendy had trusted and still did trust him to tell her when the path was safe.

Mike decided he should stop berating himself. He was too upset to be objective, and it was wasted energy. No matter what he had done, no matter how much he might have let his daughter down, he needed to use all of his energy and effort to make the best of the situation that existed now. And he couldn't create much of a recovery if he kept beating himself up.

What should he do next? He knew he should call Kent Nash; that was obvious. But should he enlist Debbie's help as well? She obviously could be trusted, but as Wendy's mother would she be able to think clearly? Would she focus too much anger on his mistake? Would she be too upset to be helpful? Would she require too much attention just to dampen her worry for Wendy? Or would she recognize that the real culprit here was Dr. Thompson?

Mike thought hard on the way home. He didn't have long since the hospital was conveniently close, and for once he wished he lived farther away. He figured Debbie deserved to know. He would have a hard time understanding why he'd been left out of the loop if the tables were turned. So, he would tell her. If she lost it, he'd just have to make her understand as much as possible and move on. Mike realized Debbie would do just about anything for her daughters, so she should be able to control her fears to get Wendy the help she probably needed.

As Mike approached the house, he was glad to see several lights on. Debbie was apparently still up. He sped into the garage, bolted from the car, and sprinted inside. He rushed through the hallway and turned the corner into the foyer, ready to take the stairs three at a time. As he turned the corner, he collided with Debbie and they both fell to the floor.

"Whoa, Mike! Couldn't wait to see me, eh?"

"Debbie, we need to talk."

"Sure, Mike, no problem. Do we need to talk on the floor, or can we go into the family room?"

"Oh, yeah, right. The family room is better."

As they headed through the kitchen into the family room, Debbie was fully alerted to a problem.

"Mike, what's wrong? Are you all right?"

"I'm fine. I'm just worried about Wendy."

"Wendy said she felt great tonight after you left. She's asleep now and seems fine to me. What are you worried about?"

"I went to talk to Dr. Thompson this morning because of what happened to Jennifer and Matt, and I felt he was giving me the run-around. Then I discovered he was moving charts around and that seemed suspicious to me, so I decided I had to find out what was going on with Wendy and the study. So I snuck into his office and read her chart and saw that he was using gene therapy drugs instead of nutritional supplements! I think he has been using her as a guinea pig for a gene therapy study. Or at least I'm pretty sure he is. And we need to move quickly to find out what is going on. If I'm right, he's been lying to us all along."

"What does this mean for Wendy?" cried Debbie. "Could she die?"

"I don't know if anything is wrong with her. She might be just fine. She probably is OK for a time, but if we only have a few days or weeks before something happens, I don't want to waste any time figuring out what's going on."

"OK, Mike, what do you think we need to do?"

"First, we need to get hold of Kent and see what he knows about this. He should be able to figure out what's going on. I think it's too much of a coincidence that Dr. Thompson is into gene therapy at the same institution without Kent knowing about it. If Kent doesn't know, then Thompson is most certainly up to no good and may be testing Kent's drugs without his consent."

"Well, let's think this through first. Before we call him, can we trust Kent?"

"Of course we can, Debbie. He's Wendy's godfather. But you know, that's a good idea. We should think this through before we call anyway, because we may need to be prepared for an angle we hadn't considered. Debbie, I thought you might be too emotional with all this suddenly thrown your way, but you surprised me. You're pretty smart at 1 in the morning."

"What if Kent is involved in the study in some way? What if Kent is in trouble and is being bribed or threatened for some reason?"

"Deb, I think that is extremely unlikely, and even if he's involved somehow, I just can't believe he would place Wendy's life in jeopardy. He just has to want to help."

"You're probably right. I can't see Kent risking harm for Wendy. He's been there for her all her life. He's too attached to her."

"And who else can help us with gene therapy? Who else can understand the science and probably fix the problem if something has gone wrong? We have no choice. We have to call him and get his help."

"What time is it in Alaska now? Can we call now?"

"Alaska is 7 hours earlier, but I don't care what time it is there. This is urgent, and we can't wait. Who knows how much time we have?"

"Patti gave me the telephone number of the hotel in Fairbanks where they're staying for the first few days. I'll get it."

Mike dialed the number, figuring it was 6 PM their time.

"Regal Alaska Hotel. How may I help you?"

"This is an emergency call for Dr. Kent Nash from Dr. Michael Naylor," said Mike. "Please get him as soon as possible. Thank you."

"One moment please. I'll ring his room right away."

Seconds went by that seemed like minutes.

"He's not answering. I'll page him if you like, or would you like his voice mail?"

"Yes to both thank you. Please page him, and if you can't find him, I'll take his voice mail."

"Oh, I'm sorry. I now see he checked out early. He was supposed to be here until tomorrow, but apparently he had a change of plans. Is there anything else I might do for you?"

"Do you know where he went?"

"No, but I do see he has a reservation to return in 2 weeks. I'm sorry I can't be of more help."

"Thank you, ma'am. Oh, what is your name please?"

"My name is Laura Connor, sir."

"Thank you very much for trying, Laura. Please let me leave my number in case you see him again soon. Ask him to call right away if you do. It's a real emergency. Oh, and by the way, do you have any rooms available?"

"I believe we're sold out for the summer . . . oh, no, now I see we just had a cancellation of a block of 6 rooms. Probably because of the weather we're supposed to get tomorrow."

"What weather is that?"

"We're expecting a major tropical storm. The chinook is playing tricks with us, and we've been told to expect flooding in Fairbanks and over 2 more feet of snow in the surrounding mountains. Would you like a room, sir?"

"Yes. Please reserve a non-smoking room for tomorrow night for 2 nights. Here's my credit card number."

Mike pulled out his credit card and read the number off.

Debbie just shook her head at Mike, grinned, and mumbled something about not giving her notice for road trips, and said, "Do you really think we have to go to Alaska to talk to him? Won't he just come right home anyway?"

"Quite probably yes. However, if we go in person, there will be no doubt about how much danger Wendy is in. He'll know how serious this is right away if we show up. And, even more important, if he's involved in any way, we'll know by his reaction when we talk to him in person. So, it's probably better that we couldn't reach him by phone."

"What if he left Alaska? What if he's on his way home?"

"I'm positive he's left for his mountain climbing. He would not disappoint Patti by not going mountain climbing with her unless it was an emergency involving family. And we're family. He would call his sister and us instantly for any significant change of plan. He always has in the past."

"OK, we'll go. I'll start packing and call my sister to watch the kids."

"I guess I'll have to tell the details to Bill Owens. He should know what's up in case something happens to Wendy while we're gone. I'll call the airlines first so I'll know when we can leave. Hey, don't you want to let me talk you into going first?"

"Go ahead, I'm listening," said Debbie. "Just be quick about it. We've got a lot to do before we leave."

"You take all the fun out of it when you talk like that. You could at least let me think I was clever enough to convince you."

"I'll do my best. Maybe we can talk some more after we're on our way."

"I'm going to call Hugh Winston. He helped me tonight at the hospital and already knows my concerns about the study. He seemed very anxious to help. He was even willing to unlock Thompson's door for me. He can keep an eye on Thompson for us."

"OK, Mike, we're making arrangements to go to Alaska. Let's think for a moment first. Is this the best way?"

"Deb, their itinerary says they're at the Regal until tomorrow and then they head out for a 2-week expedition away from civilization. Now, I figure they changed hotels, or they left early for the expedition because of the weather. Either way, we need to go in person to convince them to interrupt their vacation of a lifetime and come home to save Wendy."

"I'm sure Kent will come home immediately for Wendy, or you or me for that matter, whether we ask by phone or in person. However, I agree with you, I'd feel better asking him in person.

He'll know how serious this is right away if we both show up. And if he's not at a hotel in town, we're going to be better able to track him down by being there. My partner Bill will take care of our daughter medically until we get back, if that becomes necessary. If she starts to have any problem, one of us can come home."

"And maybe your sister will start calling Fairbanks hotels for us while we're en route. She's pretty good at finding people."

"I'm sure she will. Let's see when we can get a flight because we may have time to start calling if we can't get a flight soon."

"Good idea. I guess we can pack light, but warm."

"I'll be sure to pack your matching snowsuit and boots!" Debbie said jokingly

"Right. I'll call the airlines, Deb."

Nineteen

Tuesday, May 13
Pan American Championships
Toronto, Canada

The Toronto Coliseum was still abuzz over the death of Matt Madison four days earlier. The grandeur of the world-class facility was not enough to make the spectators forget the tragedy that had taken the life of one of Canada's heroes of these American Continent Championship games. The background hum of the crowd was noticeably less throughout the massive walkways between venues as well as during competitions. Important as elite-level sports is for many people, a feeling of spiritual loss seemed to pervade the air even in the heat of competition. The athletes felt the tragedy as well. Most remained focused on what they came to do, but a few actually lost their edge. Only the most rabid and self-centered competitors were unaffected.

Kim Taylor stood in the waist-deep water at the end of her lane with her thoughts 500 miles away on her life in Media, Pennsylvania. She had grown up in a western suburb of Philadelphia, where she could enjoy the benefits of a big city nearby along with the room and comforts of a small, close-knit community. She had spent more than 10 years dedicating her life to swimming and being as close as family with four other team buddies who had stuck together through school and a collective two hundred thousand miles of swimming workouts.

In his interview before the Pan Am Games, their coach had remarked that he was sure nowhere else in the world had five youngsters from the same relatively small town been together half as long with so much success in an individual sport like swimming. Normally, individuals from all different parts of the country are matched together for training for a year or two at a time. The burnout of competitors is high, and the nomadic nature of coaches and swimmers alike leads to very short teammate spans. Coach Cooper believed the extremely close long-term relationships among these five swimmers had nurtured their development so much that they were able to achieve far more than they would have without each other's support.

Kim realized how lucky she was to have such good friends and her family with her at all her competitions. She wondered what Matt Madison's life had been like and if he had even had some of the pleasures she had enjoyed in her 16 years. She couldn't imagine losing one of her "fab five" buddies. Kim had known Matt from the Kelly Sports Institute in Delaware, where she had spent some time recovering from her chronic shoulder tendinitis. For the past 2 years, the fab five had moved their training together to Boston, where Coach Cooper had a national training facility and a world-class reputation for producing champion swimmers. The five teammates lived together in a large townhouse with their mothers rotating as chaperones. All five attended the same private school and focused their athletic and social life on swimming seven days a week.

Dr. Mark McCormack, Director of the Boston Elite Sports Medicine Center, supervised Kim's conditioning and training on referral from Dr. Thompson in Delaware. Kim had seen Dr. Thompson just before moving to Boston to see if he could help with her recurrent shoulder pain. MRI scans of her shoulder indicated chronic tendinitis with no joint damage or laxity, and fortunately Dr. Thompson had an associate in Boston who could carry on the same program he had to heal chronic major problems in elite athletes. The other four swimmers occasionally needed the services of the renowned center in Boston, but only Erin Bradley joined Kim for conditioning at Dr. McCormack's center. Kim remained with Dr. McCormack's program because of the quick success she had getting over her long-term shoulder tendinitis and because she didn't want her problem to return. She was afraid the haunting pain would return if she weren't faithful to the detailed training program Dr. McCormack offered. Her more than 3 years of shoulder pain were hard to forget. She was happy at least one of her friends joined her at the center for the intense one-on-one conditioning.

Kim thought back to her first days of swimming at 3 years old, when she would jump off the side of the pool into her father's arms and swim for hours at a time. She loved the water and couldn't get enough of jumping in and burrowing under water until her little lungs were about to burst. She remembered never having difficulty getting enough air, even while under water. She thought about the long hours of training and how she kept her mind occupied while her muscles ached from fatigue and relentless work. She could detach her thoughts from her body and, in a trance-like state, daydream for hours at a time while her body was directed to keep pushing ahead. She remembered her first race when she thought she was not ready to swim against others. She had finished so far ahead that she looked like a dolphin swimming against humans.

"Kim, are you going to finish your warm-up?" asked Coach Cooper. "You only have 3 minutes left."

"Oh yeah, right, Coach. I was just thinking," said Kim.

"You are a unique little fish, Kim. Most swimmers do their thinking while working out. You seem to be in a far-off world just before and during the race. How do you keep your concentration going to time your pace?"

"You're asking me such a heavy question now, right before a major race? You're my coach. You're supposed to have all this down a year ago."

"Actually, I was admiring your unique ability, Kim. I'm amazed at how naturally you swim workouts and races. You don't seem to ever waiver from your timing, even when the other swimmers are starting too fast or too slow. I've just never had to work out a method with you for keeping your pace. I've always wondered what your internal clock control is."

"Thanks for the compliment, Coach. I just separate my mind and my body and tell my body to be strong while my mind goes off until the last lap. Then I check back in just in case I need to change my stroke for the last 50 meters. But I usually do just fine on autopilot, even for the last lap."

"Kim, let's talk later. You have 2 minutes left to warm up."

"OK, Coach, three quarters speed up and back and I'm ready."

"Do me a favor and check out your flip turn at each end. The markings are a little deeper in this pool, especially with the higher water level they're running for this competition."

"I already did, Coach. Be right back." Kim cruised up the first length feeling quite comfortable and just before the wall noticed the different perspective with the markings on the flip turn now that her coach pointed them out to her. That's what the coaches get paid the big bucks for, she thought. You just never know how such a little piece of information might save a race. On the 50-meter lap coming back, Kim decided she was just going to stay focused on swimming strong the whole race and not save a lot for the sprint. She was heavily favored, so she shouldn't have much of a problem. Psychologically, it would be better for her to get way ahead, so that the other swimmers would feel it would be hopeless to try to catch her. Once she got through this event, she'd head quickly to the pool at the other end of the complex to see her friend Erin Bradley compete in her qualifying heat. Erin wasn't feeling well, and everyone thought that if she could just get through today's race and qualify for the finals, she would have 3 days to rest before the finals competition. She would most likely be much stronger then, especially if her problem was indeed a viral infection. Kim figured the more moral support Erin had, the more likely she would do well.

As Kim came to the wall at the end of her second lap, she stroked for a flip turn once more, adjusting her timing for a slightly earlier rotation because of the higher water line. This time she over-allowed and nearly missed the wall for the push off. She stopped after three strokes and headed back for one more try. This time she had a better estimate of the distance needed and flipped near the middle of the sweet zone for a strong push-off. She thought she was really glad she didn't do that in the race. She wouldn't want to spend the energy making up that loss of time.

As she got out of the water, her coach was ready with a beach towel. They both then headed for the team area so she could put on her headset and tune out until 10 minutes before the race, when she would start her mental imagery. After 5 minutes of mentally swimming her race, she and her coach would head over to the staging area. Even Kim didn't want to get to the ready area too soon. Nerves are overstimulated there, and much energy could be wasted. Occasionally swimmers are psyched out by another swimmer's innocent or sometimes purposeful comment. Kim always kept her headset on, and the other swimmers knew it was useless to try to talk to her when her stereo was on just before a race. Her coach made sure she ran the songs together so there was no silence on the tape allowing her to hear a word or two that just might distract or worry her. Kim was constantly amazed at how many little details the coaches and other swimmers worried about. But in a world where a hundredth of a second could be the difference in a medal and gold medals were often the nidus for large future earnings, she certainly understood all the fuss. Anyway, she thanked God for her ability to tune out and still get her body to perform so hard.

Finally, the time came for her race. When her coach started rubbing her shoulders, it meant she had to start paying attention to get on the starting block. The 200-meter freestyle was one of her favorite races, one in which she felt very comfortable. She took inventory of her arms, then her legs, then her stomach. Her arms and legs felt strong and raring to go. Her stomach was neutral, only minimal butterflies. She was primed enough to do well without getting too nervous. As she took her position, she waited for the gun and exploded off the starting block near the head of the pack. She didn't like to risk a false start and usually avoided diving in if one was called. She preferred to save her energy for the first 10 to 12 strokes to be sure she could pull ahead. Then she'd lock into cruise control at a hair slower than her initial sprint and get ready for the first turn.

Kim's breathing was so natural, her mouth was only one third out of the water exactly long enough to get her normal tidal volume. She chose to breathe every 2½ strokes so she could observe her progress compared with swimmers on both sides. Kim had a half conscious way to watch for an unusual pace and didn't really register any active thought about where she was in the race unless someone was closer to her than she expected. She had swum so many races against the world's best swimmers that she had developed a very precise warning signal. Today, she was a little ahead of schedule, so she didn't have to bring her mind back from its detachment. She just poured on the speed, steadily improving her lead with each length.

She had a lead of two body lengths going into her last flip turn. Wait for right view of the markings and then kick, she thought. She nailed her last turn and gained another half-length on the turn alone. She had to be near world-record time, and she felt like she had plenty of energy left. Her mind came back into focus. As she took her breaths, she checked each side of the pool and saw no activity near her on either side. She felt strong and increased the tempo to be sure she discouraged someone from trying to catch her. Kim wanted to convince the other swimmers to forget about her and save their energy to sprint against each other, and not take a chance on catching her. Her strategy seemed to be working. She pulled out to a four-length lead and still felt strong. Now she just had to finish without letting up, hop out of the pool, and rush to other swimming pavilion. Her coach could get her times and splits and discuss them later.

Kim chuckled as she approached the finish. She figured she might as well sprint even harder so she could get to Erin's race sooner. She thought it was funny that she was more worried about getting to Erin's race 1 second sooner rather that whether or not she broke a record. What the heck she thought, go for it. She sprinted the last few strokes hard and hit the wall full speed. She then immediately grabbed the top of the deck and quickly pulled herself out of the pool. She grabbed the beach towel from her coach and quickly turned to leave the venue. She knew her coach knew what was up, and he planned to explain to the other swimmers why she had left so quickly. However, that was not to be.

As Kim turned the corner at the end of the pool, she saw sparkles at the edge of her vision. She felt light-headed and sick to her stomach. She stopped and placed her hands on her knees while bending over, her head down. She felt sweaty and had a chill, which was unusual after just finishing a race. Then her legs felt rubbery, her vision went black, and she fainted. Her head hit the deck as she fell in a crumpled heap. One arm was under her side; she lay motionless.

Kim's coach watched her the whole way and was already heading for her when she stopped. He just missed catching her as she fell, and as he got to her, he immediately felt for her pulse as he pulled her eyes open and spoke to her.

"Kim, what happened? Can you hear me?"

There was no response, and he could not feel a pulse. He moved his hand from her wrist to her neck and still could not feel a pulse. By now, the site athletic trainer arrived and with one look at Coach Cooper, who returned the gaze, in effect telling him there was no heartbeat, he started CPR.

"I've already called for assistance," said the trainer. "You breathe, and I'll pump on the chest. The code blue team will be here in less than 3 minutes with a defibrillator."

Twenty

Tuesday, May 13
Wilmington, Delaware

Debbie leaned over to wake Mike after 3 hours' sleep. "Time to rally, number one husband. Our plane leaves Philly at 7:45, and we have to finish packing."

Mike awakened with a jump. "I'm awake . . . or getting there anyway. What time is your sister coming for the kids?"

"She'll be here by 7. She has to do a few things at home before she leaves her family."

Mike and Debbie packed light, except for some extra warm clothes. They grabbed some juice and a few bites of cereal and headed for the car.

"Hey, Deb, will we need our passports?"

"We shouldn't, but who knows where this could end up. Let's take them so we won't need them."

Mike went back inside for the passports, just in case, while Debbie finished loading the bags. Then, Mike and Deb headed out for the airport, riding in silence for a few minutes. Both were thinking about Wendy, and both were tired.

"Besides Bill Owens, can you think of anyone else we need to tell what's up?" asked Mike.

"No, we're good for now," said Deb. "My sister will handle our kids for as long as we need her help. We can explain to her later. Bill Owens has to know in case something happens to Wendy. And we'll need him to cover the practice. I know he'll do it. The kids are busy enough; we can explain to them later. Your sister could be very helpful, but we can enlist her aid over the phone if we need to. She'll rally quickly even if in the dark. My parents will figure we're just heading to another medical conference. Nope, we need tell no one else right now. So, why don't you start telling me how your first day in a life of crime went?"

Mike told Debbie the whole story about visiting Dr. Thompson, seeing the charts leave the office, and running into Hugh and getting him to conduct a tour of the training facility on the interfloor. He told her about the flash of brilliance with the folded paper in Thompson's office door, except for Hugh seeing his handiwork. He described the "Mission Impossible" entry through the trap doors and under the security cameras, reading the chart, and then bumping into Hugh, and how his heart had raced. He also described how nervous he felt leaving Kelly Hospital the normal way and almost running a red light with a police officer right at the light.

"And then I headed home for the brains of the outfit to figure out what to do."

"Flattery will achieve little," said Debbie, "but feel free to continue."

"OK, maybe later. We've got some thinking to do. What's the name of the outfitters the Nashes hired for the first part of their trip?"

"The itinerary says, 'Denali Grizzly Bear Cabins and Campgrounds.' That sounds more like a scout camp facility than a hard-core guided tour expedition outfit."

"I bet they subcontract out the guided tour business. They most likely just maintain the base camps, most of which are probably more like vacation or tourist areas, and not true base camps. Hey, we're almost at the airport. How about I let you off with the bags, park the car, and meet you at the gate?"

"That's fine. It should be easy today. It's not very crowded."

There were no direct flights from Philadelphia to Fairbanks. The best they could do was a flight to Los Angeles with a 4-hour layover. At least they had time for a meal in LA. They chose Rose's Seafood Sensation inside the LAX airport and settled in a large booth so they could spread out the maps and information about Fairbanks and Mt. McKinley that Deb had found on the Internet that morning. The food was rather good, most likely as a result of their being very hungry and the recent nationwide effort to make airports a place to visit for shopping and dining. The service was fast, considering that almost everyone in the airport was in a hurry, and TVs with CNN or ESPN were positioned so that folks could catch up on what was hot in the world while they ate what was hot in LA.

After the main course, Debbie was focused on her maps, and Mike was listening to CNN. The commentator highlighted the story about the market recovering from a tech dip, then rambled on about a protest against unequal free trade, and then raised the level of attention of her listeners with the overused phrase "this just in." The next words grabbed Mike out of his half-listening mode and had him shush his wife to be sure she heard the TV personality.

> *"A second athlete has died today in the Pan American Games in Toronto. Jus t after wining the 200-meter freestyl race in record time, USA's Kim Taylor rushed out of the pool and collapsed a few feet away. Resuscitation was not successful, and after an extended effort, she was pronounced dead at the scene by the medical staff of the Toronto Coliseum. Kim Taylor's death follows by four days the death of Matt Madison, star basketball player for Team Canada. This is the first time in modern history that two apparently healthy athletes competing in separate sports have died during the same international competition. The cause of*

death is presently unknown. An autopsy is planned. The Pan American Games' Committee has declared a temporary halt to competition until the medical staffs from Canada and the participating countries can determine if some at present unknown health hazard could be affecting the athletes. Unconfirmed sources have indicated that the Games are likely to resume after a day's delay unless something unexpected is discovered. We'll be back after this."

Debbie looked at Mike, who appeared hypnotized by the TV. Tears flowed from his eyes. He looked scared. Debbie just reached across the table to hold his hands, looked him in the eye, and waited for him to speak.

"I don't believe this can be happening. That's the third in Thompson's program, out of only 16. What is that Frankenstein doing to these kids? How can he treat them like laboratory mice?"

"What do you mean third?" asked Debbie. "Are you counting Kim Taylor? She's not in Thompson's group. Didn't she move to Boston 2 years ago?"

"Yes, she did. And that's where Thompson's study associate is. He's at the Boston Elite Sports Medicine Center. She's probably on the same or similar protocol that Wendy is on. Her progress has been rather meteoric, like Wendy's."

"Mike, I don't understand. If Thompson is giving these athletes drugs, why haven't they shown up on drug testing?"

"If it's gene therapy, it won't show, ever. It's just proteins and attenuated viruses that have been coded to change cell activity. It's not really in a drug category that current testing covers. It won't even show up as an elevated serum protein because the amounts are too low to bump up the overall amount of protein in the blood. We should check with Kent to be sure my understanding about drug testing is right. I haven't read much on gene therapy yet, but Kent tells me it's 6 months away from human trials for helping with sports injuries. I'm calling your sister to make sure Wendy doesn't exert herself until we figure out what's going on. I sure hope Wendy isn't so affected that she can't even hold on for 6 months for this problem to be worked out. I wonder if Kent even knows about this problem. It could take years if it's something he hasn't addressed yet."

"Whoa, slow down, Mike. You always tell patients you don't want to play the 'what if' game with them. Let's take this one step at a time. I agree we should call my sister and tone down Wendy's activity. My sister will make that happen, even if Wendy doesn't understand. That's not a problem. But let's not be so pessimistic. Remember, gene therapy is not your specialty, and we're still not 100% sure gene therapy is what's involved here. How about we call this Grizzly Bear Jamboree outfit to start tracking down Kent and Patti?"

"That's a good idea, Deb. Do me a favor—you do the talking. I'm going to call Bill Owens."

Twenty-One

Tuesday, May 13
Boston, Massachusetts

Dean Carter and Dan Dellose were not happy. They liked control, and they liked things to go enough according to plan that only a little redirected pressure here or there would reroute developments toward the outcome they had arranged. Dean was the business brains behind the Brey Agency who managed many high-profile professional athletes in seven different sports—football, baseball, ice hockey, basketball, lacrosse, bowling, and golf. Dean knew many professional athletes were in dire need of continued parenting, and he was especially sharp at understanding how different personalities needed different approaches and varying levels of oversight to achieve anywhere near their maximum potential on the field. In many ways, his agency provided the chaperone service many professional teams never even considered. Such lack of oversight cost many professional sports teams millions of dollars each year. Fortunately, the Brey Agency was able to keep most of their athletes inside a safe operating zone that minimized their problems with drugs, sex, crime, and violence. Such "control" saved their professional teams a fortune in athlete investments, but it was a shame that many of the teams did not even know what their silent benefactor was doing for them.

Dan Dellose handled the mob connections and the undercover work. He directed the chaperones and matched up the appropriate person or persons to act as a bodyguard for each athlete under input from Dean. Some of the less-disciplined athletes quickly learned their bodyguard was more than a safety or service type employee. Once in a while, a client would test the resolve of a bodyguard and not follow instructions about his behavior. Dan could handle that with either subtlety or magnum force, depending on which was more appropriate.

Very few clients ever left the Brey Agency. They learned it was probably not a healthy thing to do, and after all, they were well cared for in many ways. Most contract negotiations were high-pressured but fair, and thus productive for all parties involved. The Brey Agency did not generate income by having its athletes sitting out or missing games. Dan and Dean rightfully believed they were performing a very much-needed service neglected by family, society, and the teams that spent millions on their athlete investments.

Dan and Dean stayed on top of their business. They had to, because there was always the threat of unlawful activity being discovered and of unauthorized unlawful activity being done by employees who misunderstood instructions or felt they could improvise without consulting their bosses. Dan and Dean knew Thompson and McCormack's operations quite well. Both were research and development areas that were projected within 2 years to produce huge economic gain in a brand new, millennium-type business. The thought of actually molding merely good athletes into superstars had huge potential for their firm. Their level of control over the athlete and team would soar, and they estimated that within 5 years, they could take over control of at least three of the professional sports on which they concentrated. They admired the visionary foresight of Joe Reilly, who saw and recognized a revolutionary opportunity and had the wisdom to bring the whole deal straight to them. Reilly would be rewarded well, and the plan was that he would eventually run that arm of the business once he proved he had the business experience and, most importantly, that he was loyal until death.

"When the hell will Hugh Winston get here?" asked Dan.

"Our corporate jet left Wilmington about an hour ago," said Dean. He should be here in 30 minutes. Thompson will arrive by 7 tonight. The same crew will pick him up at 5:30 after dropping Hugh back off 2 hours earlier. They know to be sure Thompson does not know Hugh was here. Now what was it you heard Hugh discovered?"

"He caught that nosey Dr. Naylor, Wendy's dad, sneaking into Thompson's office. He said we would want to hear what he discovered in person. We should probably take his word for that. He's been a decent employee and seems to have good judgment as far as knowing when to talk to us in person. Let's hope he's right this time."

"Christ! We could use a break here. I don't like two athletes in our program dying in major competition. It's bad for business. It will make recruiting more difficult. I'm beginning to wonder if this Thompson fellow is capable of running such a large part of our operation."

"Right! He's not really running anything. Our men meet with him three times a week and direct his activity. We supervise everything he does. Hugh keeps a very close eye on him and reviews his charts on a daily basis. Until the deaths, everything was running very smoothly, and he was very happy with his outside income. He's been looking forward to huge bonuses he believes will come once we open up to the general market. And, he's been behaving as if he really was loyal."

"Well, maybe so. But, death is not smooth, especially when we haven't ordered it. If Thompson was any kind of a good doc, he should have detected a problem long before healthy world-class jocks cash in their chips in the middle of competition, dammit!"

"You may be right, but let's see what Hugh and the good Doctor Thompson have to say. Joe's waited long enough. Let's hear what Hugh says is so important."

"Yeah, I'm ready. I hope our employees are."

Dean and Dan headed for the executive conference room across and down the hall from their offices. Their entire building was secure and swept for bugs or listening devices three times a day with three different crews. Each conference room had three secure phone lines, but both men preferred that sensitive discussions be held face to face. They both knew how to read people, and they were rarely misunderstood by their audience. As they walked in the room, Joe Reilly and Hugh Winston were serving themselves from the brunch buffet, anticipating a wait and or a long meeting.

Dean spoke first. "Hello, gentlemen. I'm glad you're both here promptly and safely. Hugh, tell me what you know, and it better be good."

Hugh told the three bosses about his tour of Kelly Hospital with Mike Naylor and his discovery of Mike's break-in. He went into great detail about his decision to allow the break-in so he could win Naylor's trust.

"Dr. Naylor bought the line that he helped me when I was in high school," said Hugh. "Actually, he almost got me kicked out of private school. I certainly had a significant black mark on my record because of him, and that's what kept me out of college. I had to go to a junior college just because he made me confess to stealing an exam. He did help my mother when she was sick, but that's his job. Anyway, he thinks I'll help him break into Thompson's office whenever he needs to get in. I know he trusts me because after he got home, he called me at 2 in the morning and said he was going to Alaska to find Dr. Nash and bring him back to help his daughter. I thought you would want to know that."

Dean and Dan knew the real history between Hugh and Dr. Naylor. Mike Naylor had encouraged Hugh to take the best route out of a rough situation. Hugh had already been caught, so his confession was indeed the most practical way to minimize his punishment. It was only a matter of time before Hugh would have been expelled from school had he not confessed before the headmaster found out what he had done. Naylor most certainly gave him good, practical advice. Dean and Dan would have advised the same action. However, they saw no need to discuss Hugh's resentment of Dr. Naylor at this time. Hugh's feelings would help keep him loyal to the Agency, and they apparently could be controlled enough for Hugh to make good judgments. They didn't know about Hugh's religious and monetary connection to the Middle East. Hugh had converted to the Muslim religion 4 years ago after his Arabian mother died. She should have stayed Muslim. It was such a logical and kind religion. If the people in the United States could only get together under one religion, the real religion, people wouldn't get hassled like he had been. And the Catholics and Jews arguing all the time over Jesus, what he did, and when he came or will come. What's the difference? He's just a prophet; he's human. Why do they fight wars over such silly differences? Well, he was going to be sure he was rewarded on Judgment Day. Abdul Khan introduced him into the Delaware cell that was going to provide the biggest contribution to Allah that had ever come from the West. Once this gene therapy was perfected, the soldiers of Al-Qaeda would be made superhuman and have no trouble squashing the infidels in the West. Then they would back off supporting Israel and leave the Middle East to its own destiny.

"La ilaha illa Allah, Muhammadur rasodu Allah" was so easy and so logical and so right. There is no true god but God (Allah), and Mohammad is the Messenger (Prophet) of God. Hugh said that oath 4 years ago, and it was the smartest thing he ever did in his life. He was not only going to be truly rewarded after life, he was going to get a seat of honor with Allah for single-handedly making the Muslim warriors invincible.

"Hugh, you made a good decision. It's OK right now for Naylor to know what Thompson's been doing. He suspected something wasn't right anyway. He's going to have to keep this quiet and try to work secretly with Nash to correct the problem in the gene therapy that Thompson is using. Thompson isn't going to figure it out on his own since he's just stealing the drugs from Nash's lab. You know, you may have stumbled on to the best scenario for us. Naylor's going to bring Nash back to fix the problem. Nash will be highly motivated to save his friend's daughter, assuming she's in danger. Naylor won't want to go public with what's happening because that will tarnish his daughter's career. Nor will he want to go public right now for fear that that would slow any resolution or antidote to what has killed two athletes and might be endangering his daughter. He will have to be watched carefully, though, because he may try to make a deal with the authorities after his daughter is OK in order to shut down Thompson. He could claim he didn't know what Thompson was doing, which is actually true. And if his daughter dies, he most certainly will go to the police claiming Thompson killed her."

Dean continued, "Hugh, you know what to do. We need level-four monitoring on Naylor and Nash and their entire families. I want every room and every phone line bugged. I want to know where everyone of them is 24-7. I want a mike on Naylor's belt and his shoes. Most men use the same belt every day, so you probably only have to bug one. I want to know what their habits are and how we can predict where they will be in addition to knowing where they are at all times. I want to know when this man goes to the bathroom. This is a potential billion-dollar enterprise, gentlemen. We can't miss anything. There is no room for error. Dan, send three of your best men to Fairbanks. Have them make sure both Nash and Naylor get back to Delaware safely immediately. We need Nash in his lab as soon as possible working on this."

Dean turned to Hugh and said, "Hugh, continue keeping an eye on Thompson. Make sure he doesn't get in the way. Be ready to help Naylor if he calls you. Stay on his trusted side. We'll get you some information about Thompson to give Naylor so he learns to depend on you even more. Call me every night on a secure line. We'll have the monitoring team keep you up to date. We've got to be sure Nash has what he needs to straighten this gene therapy out. We need both of them alive and well and devoted to helping Naylor's daughter."

"What do I do if Naylor goes to the authorities?" asked Hugh.

"We'll know before you know, and probably before he knows. I doubt he will bother unless something happens to his daughter or he feels he needs their resources to help his daughter. He's probably smart enough to know that they would only slow him and Nash down. He's not going to risk that. Now, once he and Nash believe his daughter is OK, we'll have to watch him very closely. But for now, he should do what we need without our having to persuade him. If he tries to go over the line, Naylor is expendable; Nash is not right now. Whatever happens, Nash must be kept alive and well. We can always improve his motivation, should that be necessary, but he's the only one who can fix our plan right now. Any other questions?"

"What if he tells others what's going on?"

"It looks like he's already told his wife, and that's OK for now. Let's hope they are smart enough to keep this to themselves. We'll be sure to monitor for that. If he or his wife decides to tell others, we may have to persuade them to be more discreet. If either starts to do so on a phone line, we'll terminate the call and decide what to do. If they tell the wrong person, we may have to take active control of their lives. We'll let you know."

"What about Thompson?"

"Thompson knows to keep his mouth shut. We've made that clear to him. We'll straighten him out tonight. He shouldn't be a problem. He wants this to work as well. He gains nothing by talking to anyone but us. For now, we still need him to run phase two of this project. He just better get smarter about detecting problems early with his athletes."

Dean didn't bother to tell Hugh that Thompson was being closely monitored already. He had been watched ever since the project had started. Thompson had no real close friends and wasn't about to tell his wife what he was doing. The Brey Agency was not worried about his loyalty and had relaxed his observation. However, during this time of uncertainty, he was again being watched very closely. Hugh had been told his phone line was recorded, and it was clear to him that he was a lifetime employee of Brey. Only the agency could determine when he could retire. Even then, he would remain silent. To do otherwise would bring about a premature death. Hugh would see about that. Al-Qaeda might have something to say as well.

Twenty-Two

Tuesday, May 13
Boston, Massachusetts

Dean Carter and Dan Dellose sat quietly for a moment after Hugh and Joe Reilly left. Dan spoke first. "I'll have both homes wired today. It should be easy with the families out of town. I'll send the 3 former Special Forces guys to Alaska. They work together well, they know how to keep quiet, and their training may come in handy in the wild. I still can't believe the military treated them so poorly. They are much more efficient than the other men we have, and they have to be among the best the military had. Giving them ten times their former pay rate has made them very loyal to us. I guess peacetime didn't give them enough to do. What a waste of taxpayers' money for all that training."

"Use our other jet," said Dean. "I want those guys there immediately. I don't trust doctors and their wives climbing around mountains. They think they can do anything and they don't need any training. Damn doctors get too confident about their abilities. They don't even know half the dangers they luck through. Our three musketeers will probably have to save their asses and the doctors won't even know it. They don't belong in the wilderness;

they should stick to hospitals and pay attention to their patients. If they paid more attention to their business, they might know when their patients were having a problem long before it kills them!"

"My, my, are you through with the soap box, my man?" asked Dan. "Don't worry so much. I'll get Lewis and Clark home where they belong. Anything else you want? How about I get them some educational tapes for their airplane ride home?"

"Just get them back to productive work soon. We don't need any more problems with our athletes. We can't let this get any more out of control."

"OK, fine," said Dan. "I'll meet you here at 6:30 tonight, a half hour before Thompson arrives. I'll update you then."

"Oh, and Dan, find out why our men monitoring Hugh's phone didn't bother to tell us Naylor headed to Alaska this morning."

"I already did. They said they didn't know it was important. They knew Hugh was coming to meet us and Naylor's surveillance was coded white so they felt there was no need to report the doctor's vacation plans other than in the daily report."

"Well, be sure he's coded red now. I want to know any unusual movement, any travel, and any meetings with people other than patients and pure social activity."

"His code has been red for the past 3 hours. The Special Forces crew knows how to handle information transmission."

"Fine. Let's hope they catch up with him before all four of our city slickers are loose in the wild!"

"Our men will find them. We know they want to get back home right away. They'll make sure our foursome doesn't miss their flight home. They know how to delay a flight, among other useful tricks."

"It's a shame we can't fly them back to Delaware on one of our jets."

"I already told our men to keep that in mind as an option. Who knows? They're clever."

At 6:15 PM, Dan reappeared in Dean's office.

"The terrific trio has arrived in Alaska," reported Dan. "They were a little surprised at the short notice for their assignment, but they responded quickly. That military training is exactly what more of our men need."

"It sure would be nice to have an inside man in the military sending us the right men already trained. See if you can find someone our guys know who might be able to do that for us. I bet there are a few military men who wouldn't mind two paychecks. And technically they wouldn't be doing anything wrong. They would just have to be a good judge of character. We have a more pressing concern now, though. A third athlete has gone down at the Pan Am Games. This one is McCormack's."

"Do we have any other athletes at the games?" asked Dan.

"Actually we have 3 others. But they've already competed. Thank God, because we can't say anything to our athletes or they would become suspicious and one might try to go to the Feds. We don't want to eliminate any of our athletes to prevent that; another death would not be good right now. It's beyond blaming it on an accident. We've got to keep saying it ain't our program, it must be something at the games, and we've got to get Nash back here to fix the problem. The hold on competition should help deflect blame from us."

"What do you want me to do with McCormack?"

"Just have him review all the testing data to see if there's any clue why these athletes are going down. Make sure they both do an up-to-the-minute literature search on gene therapy so they know what the latest concerns are. They have to be completely up to speed so they know how to interpret Nash's team's work. Good God, it's only a multi-billion-dollar project. Don't we have another doctor somewhere who can make sure these guys know what they're doing?"

"We have no one else in research. But how about Honeycutt in North Carolina? He's clinically very sharp, and he's on the up and up. We could have him review the data on both Thompson and McCormack to see if they're missing something."

"Yeah, but if he finds something, then we have to kill him to keep him quiet," Dean said. "We'll save him for legitimate examinations of our prospective clients. He does a good job there. We've got to limit the killing—we may have to do more soon. We're drawing too much attention to ourselves. That's another thing. Doctors are too damn independent. They don't know how to sell their services."

"We have no one else. We could probably retain a good research doc for a half mil a year; we just don't have that much for him to do to keep him on the payroll."

"OK, we'll just have to have Nash figure it out for us. Hopefully, he'll uncover why Thompson missed any warning signs. And we won't have to pay him."

Dean's intercom beeped. His secretary came on the line. "Reilly has Thompson downstairs. He's bringing him up now."

"That's fine. Send them right in when they get upstairs."

Three minutes later, Thompson and Reilly walked through the double mahogany doors to Dean's expansive office.

"Sit down, gentlemen," said Dean. "Anything to drink? Dr. Thompson, I trust your flight was OK."

"Smooth and on schedule," said Thompson. "Thank you. I had dinner on the plane, so I'm fine for now."

"Well, this project is not 'smooth and on schedule,' Dr. Thompson," declared Dean. Tell me what's going wrong and what you suggest we do about it."

"Well, we somehow need to get the word to Nash that his gene therapy treatment is out of control," stammered Thompson. The sternly directed command startled Steve Thompson, who knew that Dean and Dan were not patient men. When they were upset, people who worked for them had better be on their toes and had better remain very respectful. "I've reviewed all his notes on the project, and there is no mention of any serious side effects. Well, at least I've reviewed all the notes Hugh has gotten for me. I assume they are all the notes."

"And how do you suggest we tell Nash his gene therapy on humans is out of control?" asked Dean. "He doesn't know it's being used on humans. Shall we just tell him you've been stealing samples from his batches and giving it to innocent athletes? Shall we tell him we need it fixed soon so we can use his research to make us a fortune? Do you think he will join us? I think not. You've read his work. Why hasn't he used it on humans yet? What is he concerned about?"

Thompson thought carefully before he spoke. He realized Dean was not happy that 3 of 16 athletes in his study, almost 20%, were either stricken or dead. "I saw no concern. He is just going by the book. He must complete a series of animal studies, document the safety and effectiveness, and then apply for permission to proceed with human testing. He wrote of no concerns. The animals are all doing well."

"And how long were the animals getting the drugs," asked Dean.

"Each round of the study used 6-month periods."

"Doesn't that tell you something?" asked Dean. "You've been giving this to humans for 2 years—four times as long! It sounds to me like it's too much or you should have decreased the dose or something. These athletes are all going down suddenly. That usually means the heart. Why couldn't you pick up something that might be going wrong with their hearts?"

Thompson respectfully replied, "Their treadmill scores were all excellent, and each subsequent one was better than the previous one. There was no problem in any of them."

"**There sure was in 3 of them**! You had better get back to Wilmington and figure out what it is. If we have any more tragedies, we'll never get athletes to sign up with our agency."

"I'll start tonight," said Thompson. "Could you please have Hugh go in to check the research logs tonight and get me the latest write-ups? I'd like to see what they're doing to prepare for human trials. I heard that the protocols were drafted last week."

"Yes, you will start tonight. You and McCormack will meet at his Sports Medicine Center and work all night if you have to until you're both up on the latest thoughts on gene therapy. Then once you both have a plan you agree on, you'll be flown back to Wilmington to review Hugh's intelligence and start testing your athletes—the ones who are still alive anyway. You'll have a crew of

4 to help you. They'll get whatever information you need. Two of them are Internet whizzes and two are nurses. One of the nurses works on Nash's team, so include her in your plans. She has an inside track on where they're going, and she should be able to get you answers you can't figure out by reading the logs. Dan, Dr. Thompson has already eaten dinner. Please be sure he gets right over to McCormack's center. Dr. Thompson, any more questions?"

"No, I'll get started."

Joe Reilly walked Thompson out of the office and headed right for the elevator. Neither one spoke. Joe knew to wait downstairs in the lobby for Dan.

Back inside Dean's office, Dean spoke to Dan. "Once you're confident our two physician professors have a workable plan, send two of the four research crew with Thompson and keep two with McCormack."

"Right. When do you want to tell Thompson that Naylor plans to tell Nash that Thompson stole his work?"

"When it's to our advantage. Right now I don't want Thompson waiting for that to happen. I want him under pressure to figure out what's affecting our athletes. We might not have time for Nash to get home before another one bites the dust."

"I'll keep you posted, Dean."

"I know you will, I know you will. Be ready to go to Alaska. We may need you there next. And get ready to take Ken Turner, the father of one of McCormack's athletes, with you. I have a plan for him."

"My thoughts exactly," said Dan.

Twenty-Three

Tuesday, May 13
Fairbanks, Alaska

Patti and Kent climbed on board the 4-seat amphibious airplane as Tom and Marsha waved. The Grizzly Bear Campground folks had everything packed and ready for them, even on short notice when their trek into the wilderness was moved up one day because of the approaching storm. Apparently they were used to novices bringing too much. They handed them each their backpack with a big piece of foam inside and wouldn't let them take it out. Their instructions were: "Feel free to take whatever you can fit in the pack, ***with the foam inside as well***, and then take everything out and repack only those items without the foam." Just to be sure, the campground crew repacked the backpacks anyway. Kent had little room left after he squeezed the StarSAT phone in the bottom.

"Patti, do you really think this is such a good idea? I mean, isn't it just a little counterintuitive to fly right into a storm, not away from it?"

"It made sense to me, Kent. They said they'd take us above the storm 10,000 feet up the mountain. It's supposed to be calm and peaceful up there. Just think how much hiking you're avoiding. They said if we waited, it could be 10 days before we could go again. They said Camp Tenderfoot at 10,000 feet is a full-service lodge. Why do you think they call it Tenderfoot?"

"I'd say because your feet must hurt to climb that high."

"Wave goodbye to your friends. I get you alone in the wilderness for two full weeks."

"Two weeks and one day. I bet you planned the early start, too."

The bush pilot taxied to the end of the grass runway and started his run-up. The plane shook as the pilot advanced the throttle to full with the brakes locked in place. With the run-up complete, he checked his passengers' seat belts and said, "We're off" as he pushed the throttle full speed ahead again. While the small plane was bouncing down the irregular grass strip, he calmly started giving them a narrative of the flight plan. His relaxed nature helped everyone settle down.

The pilot told them that once they were airborne, he would call to get an IFR, or instrument flight rules clearance, to go into the clouds to climb above the forming storm. He had reliable weather reports that above 9,000 feet, it would be "VFR on top," or visual flight rules above the clouds. In other words, it should be clear above 9,000 feet, with smooth sailing to the small lake in the side of the mountain where they would land at 10,000 feet—right next to Mid Camp Tenderfoot.

What the pilot didn't say was that flight service weather reports weren't completely reliable, especially when big mountains were involved. The temperature had dropped much faster than predicted, and even though it was the warmest part of the day in early afternoon, it was quite cold at 6,000 feet. The pilot was still giving a Cook's tour narrative to his two passengers and didn't get around to checking the outside air temperature. If he had, he would have put his carburetor heat on. He left it off with the understanding it would be much warmer and to turn it on unnecessarily would slightly decrease the climbing ability of the old amphibious airplane. At 9,000 feet, the engine began to sputter just as they were beginning to clear a few of the clouds. By the time the pilot realized he had carburetor ice, the engine quit, and their brief glimpse of sunlight and the beautiful but imposing mountain gave way to solid instrument conditions. The silence was impressive. The view was solid blur.

No one spoke, and with the engine quiet, the fierce power of the wind outside became hypnotic. After a few seconds, the pilot regained his composure and decided to turn away from the mountain he couldn't see and attempt to glide to a reasonably safe landing spot he would figure out in the next several seconds.

He didn't have more than a few seconds. By turning away from the mountain in record gusty conditions, he hit a major microburst of wind shear, and suddenly the plane dropped like a rock. The nose of the plane dropped first, and in 3 seconds, the plane was in a dive. As the plane picked up speed, the pilot pulled back on the yoke with all his strength. The speed started to recreate lift, and the small plane, shaking beyond its tested G force tolerance, started to fly again. Still headed down, but beginning to slow, the pilot finally yelled.

"We hit wind shear. I, I think we're starting to come out of our dive. We should be OK in a minute or so. Grab your backpacks and put them in your laps."

Once again, he didn't have the time he wanted. The small plane hit the ground at over 100 knots nose first and skidded on an ice- and snow-covered downward slope on the side of Mt. McKinley. The nose section crumpled, driving the yoke deep into the chest of the pilot. He could speak no more.

For some reason, the pilot had installed double H-harness seat belts in all 4 seats. And fortunately, Kent and Patti had chosen to sit in the back together. Holding on to the backpacks in their laps with the H harness holding them in their seats saved their lives. Another passenger in the front would have met instant death along with the pilot.

The plane skidded over the rough icy and rocky terrain and hit a 3-foot high rock, which spun it sideways. In the turn, the high wings braced the plane as it spun sideways, keeping it from tumbling. When the plane finally stopped, Kent and Patti were pinned in their seats by the front seats and the crumpled side walls of the plane. Kent was dazed; his head hurt and his vision was blurry. He smelled smoke and started to feel warm—the engine was on fire, illuminating the cabin! His chest hurt, and his right ankle was throbbing and trapped twisted under the front seat. He tried to pull it out, but it was pinned tight; he winced in agony as he tried to move.

As smoke started to fill the cockpit, he realized where he was. He looked at Patti. Her head was slumped to her left. She was unconscious, but held upright by the front seat that was driven against her chest. He freed his right arm and held her head. She was breathing OK. He felt her pulse. That was strong. Kent then set out to free his left arm so he could move the backpack and get his leg free.

He started coughing as the smoke became thicker. He unlatched the door and kicked it open with his left foot. It took some effort, but he finally succeeded. He threw his backpack out the door and slid to the side, changing the angle where his foot was pinned. He forced it free, but tore the skin getting it out. He fell out of the plane onto the snow-covered, icy ground.

Kent's ankle was swollen, but he could stand. He realized he had to get Patti free before the fire, smoke, and noxious fumes overcame her. He climbed into the plane and knelt on his crumpled seat. He had very little room to work. He tried to pull her backpack out, but it was trapped by the front seat that had caved in at the middle from the yoke. He tried harder to pull the backpack free. It wouldn't budge. He tried one more time, wedging his left foot against the side of her seat. After a few seconds his hand slipped, forcing him back hard against the opened side door, and he once again fell out of the plane. He hit his head against the top of the doorway, stunning himself once again. He was lying in the snow, dazed as he fought for control. He remembered he had to get Patti out. The crackling fire was getting brighter and bigger.

He quickly climbed into his seat again and studied the backpack, trying to figure how he'd get it free. Then it dawned on him. Empty the damn thing. What a good idea the backpack was; it undoubtedly saved Patti's life. Now he just needed to get her out before the fumes suffocated her or the plane exploded. He emptied the pack, throwing the first few articles in the back of the plane before he realized he should throw them out of the plane so they wouldn't burn up. Once he freed the backpack, Patti fell toward him. She was out cold and dead-weight heavy. He tried pulling her toward his door, but both her legs were trapped.

Kent decided then to go to her door. He opened it from inside and then went out his door. He ran around the rear of the plane slipping twice and falling. The high wings made her door accessible. He could see from this new angle that the front seat had been forced back off its track up onto her legs. Panting with the effort he needed to push the seat off of her, he finally got her free. The smoke was not giving him much time—he had to get her out of the plane now. He wondered if her legs were broken.

He pushed hard and couldn't get the seat to budge. Red-faced, he tried again and again. He thought for a moment, realizing that brute force was not working and that he had to be clever. He looked around. He saw a strut from the wing hanging free. He grabbed it, twisted it, and ran to the side to break it free. He then wedged that under the seat and pushed the strut up. Suddenly, the seat broke free, completely off its track. He pushed further getting the seat up out of the way and sending the top of the seat through the broken windshield. The seat shielded them from the fire, but as the seat caught fire, the smell was nasty.

Kent's eyes were burning! He could barely see, and he was coughing so hard he couldn't catch his breath. He turned to face outside the plane. Fortunately, the wind was strong and blowing into the plane from Patti's side. His eyes cleared, and he slowed his coughing. He turned back facing Patti and felt her legs. They were free, but the left leg was bleeding below the knee and he felt sharp bone sticking through broken skin. She had a fractured tibia. He looked at her face, and she fell on him like a rag doll. He shuffled his position and with all his strength put one arm around her mid back and another under her thighs as he sat on the edge of the doorway. He slid her toward him carefully, checking her legs as he pulled. He finally got her on his lap, and he reached down with his right leg. It hurt to put weight on his ankle, but he had no choice. He pulled hard and, holding her close to his body, slowly turned to his left and slid off the doorway bottom so his left foot touched the ground. He was leaning against the plane now with both feet on the ground and with the wind in his face and the flames close behind. He rocked forward holding Patti in his arms and staggered away from the plane.

He got about 15 feet away and sat down from exhaustion. He sat still for a moment, happy to be alive and happy to have Patti in his arms still breathing. Then he realized he'd better get what he could out of the plane before the fire destroyed everything they would need to keep warm and protect themselves until help arrived. He carefully placed Patti over to his side and gently laid her head down into the snow. He now noticed the snow was rather heavy. He looked at her broken bone. He needed to get some cloth to wrap the leg to limit the bleeding.

He scrambled up and headed to the plane, remembering to approach from Patti's door with the wind at his back. He reached in the back for one of the suitcases and was trying to work it free when an explosion knocked him backward against the door that had swung loosely closed. His sleeve was on fire, and he dove out of the plane to smother it in the snow as another explosion rocked his world. He crawled away and went back to Patti. He picked her up to a sitting position, even though his medical training told him to make her comfortable lying down. He held her in a sitting, hugging position while he thought. Their bodies kept each other warm.

Kent was so tired, and he felt helpless. He was used to always knowing the best next thing to do. He took off his glove to feel for Patti's pulse. It was strong, and her breathing was essentially normal. He shivered from the cold for the first time and hugged Patti in his lap.

He sat there for 10 minutes gathering his thoughts and strength. The plane was burning, but the explosions had stopped.

He once again placed Patti lying down and headed to the other side of the plane—this time to get his backpack and the loose items from Patti's backpack. He didn't know his own strength. He'd thrown them quite a distance from the plane, so they hadn't caught fire. He found Patti's coat, some clothes, her toiletry kit, and the emergency survival food the Grizzly Campground's staff had packed.

He checked his backpack. His clothes and extra jacket were OK, as was his toiletry kit and survival food. His StarSAT phone was crushed and obviously had no chance of working. The phone looked like it had received a karate chop in the middle, crushing the metal cover and folding the rectangular device at a 20° angle. The phone had definitely saved his life! Actually, the StarSAT phone had saved both their lives. Because the device protected him from so much of the force from the crash, he remained conscious and was able to get both himself and Patti out of the plane before the fumes and explosions did them in. He'd be sure to remind Patti of his wise decision to bring the phone.

It was starting to get dark, and the temperature was dropping. Kent decided he needed to determine where they were going to spend the night.

Twenty-Four

Tuesday, May 13
Fairbanks, Alaska

Debbie and Mike boarded flight #722 for Fairbanks both deep in thought. Debbie got through to the Grizzly Campground organization and was advised that Kent and Patti Nash had departed that afternoon for Mid Camp Tenderfoot at 10,000 feet, almost halfway up Mt. McKinley. The pilot, who was their guide, was expected to check in upon arrival at Tenderfoot and Grizzly would advise him that the Naylors were en route and needed to talk to the Nashes as soon as possible regarding a family emergency. Debbie had asked that they arrange radio contact at approximately 10 PM local time. She believed they should be at the hotel well before 10.

Mike had called his partner Bill Owens and asked that he go by Debbie's sister's home and check on Wendy. He asked him to arrange for an ECG and echocardiogram with Doppler to be sure Thompson wasn't hiding something obviously wrong with Wendy. Bill was extremely understanding and reassured Mike that he would keep Wendy under extremely close scrutiny and would not let her exert herself to any major degree. He promised to call the Regal Alaska Hotel with any information of significance. Otherwise, Mike would call him every night at home. Bill said he had already talked with Wendy that evening and she sounded fine. They had arranged to meet tomorrow.

Mike spoke first. "You know, Deb, we should have called the hotel and left a message for the Donovans. They were staying at the Regal also and would probably still be there. I bet they know the latest on this storm situation and how to contact Kent and Patti."

"We can call from the airport in Fairbanks and leave a message," said Debbie. "You're right, but we should be talking to Kent and Patti in just a few hours. I told Grizzly I wanted to arrange an urgent radio contact at 10 tonight."

"Where are they?"

"They're on their way to Mid Camp Tenderfoot, 10,000 feet up the mountain. Evidently, there's a small lake nestled on the side of the mountain there where small amphibious planes can land, so it's easy to get in and out. They have a large cabin on the lake with a fireplace for heat. It even has a radio line installed for easy communication. They don't have power, but they just plug their battery-powered radio into the antenna wire, which connects directly to Base Camp Grizzly at the foot of the mountain. That way they get good reception even during storms."

"I guess they don't have conference calling," joked Mike.

"Nor do they have a fax line," said Debbie. "But they do have the plane parked by the cabin, and it's a short trip back down if there's an emergency."

"How did you, calling as a complete stranger, get all this information from one short phone call?"

"Simple. I just told the kind lady that my daughter was sick with a rare disease and Kent was the only physician in the world who had the expertise to help her and that since he was her godfather, he'd like to know about the problem. She got on board halfway through the conversation. She even tried contacting the plane by radio, but couldn't get through. She said that's not unusual in the mountains, especially with a storm, but said as soon as they checked in, she'd arrange for them to talk to us. She thought about sending another pilot, but with the storm coming she thought that might not be such a good idea. And then, she told me about her daughter being sick for two months and how she got better. If all Alaskans are like her, they sure are friendly and down to earth. She was very helpful."

"We can sure use help right now," said Mike. "I'm glad you established rapport with the Grizzly folks. Since you have such a good way with words, how about you call the Donovans when we land and I'll get the bags."

"Better yet, I'll call from the air. We can see how good these flight phones are."

As soon as the Naylors' plane got to altitude, Deb called the Regal Alaska Hotel in Fairbanks to try to reach the Donovans. They did not answer in their room, so she left a voice mail message.

"Mike, I got through while you were in the rest room. The reception was fine, but the Donovans weren't in. I left a message telling them we'd be in tonight and we needed to talk to them."

"Sounds good. After we land, I'll get the bags while you check out transportation to the hotel. OK?"

"I'll have our ride waiting."

Even though it seemed like an hour, the bags appeared quickly, and Mike and Debbie were promptly headed into town for the Regal Alaska Hotel. The rustic scenery went unnoticed as they both were concentrating on what they should do next. As the car pulled into the circle entrance for the hotel, Mike was out of the car before it was completely stopped. Debbie figured that she was elected to wait for the bags and tip the driver while Mike darted inside to secure the room and get on the phone.

As they headed upstairs in the elevator, Mike suggested, "I reckon we should call Grizzly Campgrounds first. The Donovans are still not answering their room phone, and Grizzly left us a message to call."

"Did they say what they were calling for?" asked Deb.

"No, they just left their number and a message to call as soon as possible. Here's the message with the number. Deb, you should probably call since you're bosom buddies with the Grizzly lady."

"She was very helpful, and her name is Barb Thomas, not Grizzly lady. You say that in front of her and she might be offended."

"Of course she would, but I only said it to you, and you know I was kidding. I was just trying to lighten things up and in a round-about way compliment you on your people skills."

"OK, you got out of that one. Here goes."

Deb dialed the number, and Barb answered after the first ring. "Grizzly Bear Campgrounds. Barb speaking."

"Hey, Barb, this is Debbie Naylor. We're finally in Fairbanks at the Regal."

"Hi, Debbie. Welcome to our frontier city!" said Barb Thomas. "I called to tell you we still haven't heard from our pilot. He's 2 hours overdue to call in. We've contacted the Alaska Mountain Rescue Group. They have the authority to handle all search and rescue missions in Alaska and the Yukon."

"What?!" exclaimed Debbie. "Rescue mission? What do you mean 'rescue mission'? Why do you think they need rescuing? Just because they didn't call in yet? Maybe they forgot. My kids forget to call all the time."

"You're right, Debbie. It is possible he just forgot to call. It's also possible the wire from Mid Camp Tenderfoot is broken. That happened 3 years ago. But the wire is in PVC piping now and well . . . our pilot knows it's mandatory for him to call. It's absolute company procedure."

"How about the radio? Maybe the radio is not working."

"That's just not possible. There are 4 back-up radios in the cabin plus the one in the plane plus the portable one our pilot carries. And he has 3 back-up batteries in the plane plus the plane's battery if all else fails. If the wire is broken, he should have been able to contact an airliner flying overhead by now. That's how we made contact 3 years ago. It took less than an hour to reach us through air traffic control."

"Can you contact him?"

"No. He has to turn on the radio. We can't leave them on because they are battery-powered . . . maybe you should come out here. The rescue team would like to talk to you about the Nashes to learn what they can about them. The Donovans are here already. I'm sure they'd like to see you. I'll call the hotel and have them bring you here so you won't have to worry about directions. Just go on downstairs to the concierge, OK?"

"We'll go right down. Thanks . . ."

"Mike, you . . ."

"I heard, Deb. Dress warmly and let's go."

Twenty-Five

Tuesday, May 13
Boston, Massachusetts

"M*r. Carter, a Mr. Frank Vinton is on the secure line* calling from Fairbanks, Alaska. He says it's urgent."

"Thank you, Megan. Please transfer the call to me."

"Mr. Carter, this is Frank Vinton. Operation Lewis & Clark, calling from Fairbanks. I assume I'm still on a secure line."

"Yes, you are, Frank. Have you found our city slicker doctors?"

"We've located the Naylors, but our reports indicate the Nashes are en route to Mid Base Camp Tenderfoot, approximately halfway up Mt. McKinley, and may have encountered some difficulty reaching their destination, sir."

"What difficulty, Frank? We must have Nash healthy and back in Delaware as soon as possible. What's going on?"

"Sir, the Alaska Mountain Rescue Group has been called in to search for their plane. It's now 3 hours overdue for what should have been a 30-minute flight. Flight service is getting a transponder position report to the Rescue Group. They have to review tapes to get a more precise location, but air traffic control is unable to track small planes in that section of mountainous terrain. Their last contact with the plane was at 5,200 feet before it passed out of radar range behind the mountain. There was no radio transmission closing the IFR flight plan as expected 15 minutes later. Air traffic control contacted Base Camp Grizzly to inform them of the failure to close the flight plan, although Base Camp Grizzly normally closes the flight plan after hearing from the pilot. Grizzly continued to attempt to contact the plane and waited another hour to hear from the pilot. When no word was received from the pilot by 2 hours after takeoff, Grizzly then notified the Rescue Group, sir."

"So, Frank, who is the Alaska Mountain Rescue Group and what's being done to locate the Nashes?"

"Sir, AMRG, as they are called, is a top-notch organization with the authority to perform all rescue missions in Alaska and much of the Yukon. They are already on site at the base camp, sir. They are organizing snowmobile teams to search along the flight path, with a planned start in less than 1 hour. They are organizing their radio contact and supply network and are planning sequential antennae stations along the way so no one will be out of contact. Air search and rescue is out of the question because of the weather, especially at night. Do you have any instructions for us, sir?"

"Will they let you help them in the search and rescue?"

"Well, sir, it appears they may. Ted Duffy knows the assistant chief of operations. They were in training for Special Forces together and were good friends. He told them we were hired by a medical foundation to protect the Nashes in a clandestine manner. We Special Forces types love that kind of operation, and the assistant chief said to tell him no more. He said he would use Ted Duffy and Rob Glenn as one search team if they agreed to take absolute orders from his team. We, of course, agreed. I plan to stay in the background at Grizzly and will keep you posted, sir."

"What do you plan to tell the Nashes if and when they're found?"

"Sir, we will fade into the background once they are safe. If we're directly involved in the rescue, my men do not give out information; they only collect it. They will remain silent and speak only to give directions."

"Right. I forgot they are military trained."

"Yes, sir!"

"OK, OK, Frank. Just get them back safe, pronto. I'm working on arranging their own private jet ride home. It's beginning to look like they need permanent bodyguards."

"I'll call you every 4 hours to update. I'll call sooner if critical information is learned."

"Tell you what, Frank. Page me every 4 hours with your number. I don't know where I'll be, and I want to be on a secure phone."

"Yes, sir. Out."

Twenty-Six

Tuesday, May 13
Base Camp Grizzly, Mt. McKinley, Alaska

Mike and Debbie Naylor arrived at Base Camp Grizzly in the Regal Alaska Hotel limousine, their eyes wide at all the activity. The place looked like a military base, albeit one from the 1950's. The camp had a wooden rail fence around the compound and a 10,000-square-foot log-cabin building marked "Headquarters." To the right of the building was a large garage with 8 storage bays and 4 service bays, with the doors open on them all. Inside were various snowmobiles and all-terrain vehicles. Sport utility vehicles were parked in 3 of the bays. In front of the garage building were several SUVs with trailers for snowmobiles, which were being unloaded. Twenty-five or 30 military-looking men and women were busily preparing backpacks and equipment and loading them into the snowmobiles. The garage office and country store were spacious and had racks for life preservers, cold-weather clothing, boots, radios, backpacks, and all types of survival gear. To the left of the headquarters building was a western-style hotel/saloon and restaurant. The style of the building was rustic but with the obvious comfort and class of a first-rate hotel in the old Wild West. There was even a large flagpole with the US flag flying high in the large entrance circle. There was enough street lighting to make the scene look like a large movie set. The snow was clean and well packed and added to the wholesome atmosphere. All that was missing were the ski rental facilities.

"Good night! I wonder if the President of the United States would attract this much attention?" Mike asked Debbie. The limousine driver answered for her. "Alaska Rescue is extremely well run, and in addition to their permanent professional staff, they never lack for experienced volunteers to perform a rescue mission. This is routine for every rescue mission. You don't have to be the President to get this service."

"Thanks for the ride," said Mike. "Where will we find Barb?"

"She's inside the headquarters building in the main office on the left as you enter. Good luck finding your friends."

"Thanks. We'll need all the luck we can get."

Mike and Debbie headed inside to get the latest information from Barb. As they walked in the office, a pleasant, slightly stocky blond-haired woman rushed over to greet them.

"You must be Dr. and Mrs. Naylor. I'm Barb Thomas. Welcome to Grizzly."

"Thank you," said Debbie. "Boy, this doesn't look like your typical campground. Your facilities are quite impressive."

"Thank you," said Barb. "We serve as the headquarters for Denali National Park and the entrance way to a very serious mountain. Mt. McKinley is the tallest peak in North America, and thousands of visitors come here to see her splendors every year. We have to be up to speed to prevent people from getting in over their heads, because the elements can be ferocious year round here. Most people have no idea how rough it can get."

"Anyway," she continued, "we still have no word from your friends and our pilot. That is highly irregular. Our pilot is required to call in to cancel his flight plan. It's strict company policy, and he has never neglected it. So we're proceeding as if they have had difficulty. The storm is limiting our search capabilities to snowmobile teams, but Alaska Rescue is planning 12 teams with

4 radio antennae stations starting in about half an hour. They are mapping sectors for the search teams as we speak."

Mike responded, "I have four questions first. One, how long can they survive in these elements? Second, how long will it take to get to the Mid Camp Tenderfoot by snowmobile? Third, what medical staff do you have? And fourth, are there any dangerous wild animals they could have to defend themselves against?"

"How about I introduce you to the operations commander for Alaska Rescue so he can answer those questions? He's in the camp store setting up an operations center there. He's used our facilities before, and we've created a little command post for the rescue team there."

Barb, Mike, and Debbie walked over to the command center to meet the operations chief. As they entered the camp store, Barb addressed Bill Smith.

"Smitty, do have a moment to meet Mike and Debbie Naylor, two of the Nashes' close friends?"

Mike and Debbie saw the Donovans sitting next to Smitty's desk and immediately extended their hands and arms for hugs.

"Hello, folks," Smitty said to the Naylors. "How many more friends do the Nashes have in Alaska? I just briefed Tom and Marsha here who told me the Nashes have no medical problems and are inexperienced mountain climbers, but let me summarize our rescue plans again. Our rescue group actually likes to include friends and family in the mission. That way we have the most information about the people we're looking for. And we can show everyone how serious we are in our mission. We normally do not have a problem with people getting in the way, especially when we organize their efforts under our direction. So feel free to help us, but you have to agree to follow orders first."

"Yes, sir," said Debbie. "Let's get started."

"Right, ma'am. We have 12 snowmobile teams of 2 rescuers each and 4 radio antennae supply station teams of 2 each. The antennae station teams will set up temporary 12-foot antennas and supply stations for our mission. We expect to screen the area covered by the flight plan in 24 hours and more thoroughly search the area within 3 days. We start now because an injured person without proper warm clothing could die during the night. We have 3 emergency medical technicians spread out among the 12 snowmobile teams. All of our staff are trained in survival techniques and basic first aid. We're in real-time contact with Fairbanks Hospital for medical care and instructions, but if you two physicians are up to it, we'll use you to advise us medically if necessary, either remotely or on site."

"We'll do whatever is needed," said Mike. "How long will it take for you to get rescuers to Tenderfoot by snowmobile?"

"Approximately 8 hours at nighttime. Approximately 5 hours during daylight and non-storm conditions. It will take longer during storm conditions."

"What about wild animals?" asked Mike.

"There are mountain lions and bears. They normally avoid people."

"Normally?" asked Mike again.

"If the animals feel threatened or sense a bleeding injured person, they have been known to say hello. Otherwise, they should not be a factor."

"What should we do now?" asked Tom.

"All four of you should get rooms at the base hotel and prepare your cold weather garb for quick dressing. Call me with your room numbers, get plenty of rest, and feel free to come to our main briefings every 6 hours—midnight, 6 AM, noon, and 6 PM. If you leave the area, we'll give you a radio that will work between here and Fairbanks and inside the city. Write your questions down for the briefings, and if you have any ideas or information that you feel is important and probably shouldn't wait, come here and talk to me or whoever is the officer on duty. Questions?"

Debbie's face was grim. "You're very clear. We'll arrange our rooms and let you know."

"Thank you," said Smitty. "But I have done this before a few times. Now, please excuse me, I have to go over the route plans and get these guys going."

Twenty-Seven

Tuesday, May 13
Mt. McKinley, Alaska

Ted Duffy and Rob Glenn were not intimidated by the perils of search and rescue when no one was shooting at them. The subzero temperatures and howling wind were mellow compared with the spartan conditions under which they had trained. Even the mountain lions and bears were no concern, because they were without fear and the animals sensed that and would leave them alone. They were also smart enough to not leave food out to attract them.

Both Ted and Rob were concerned with proving to Dean Carter and Dan Dellose that they were worth the large sums of money they were being paid to do undercover work for the Brey Agency. They wanted to quickly complete this mission to gain the respect of their bosses so that they would get the best and most challenging jobs. They loved the money, but more importantly, they loved the adventure. They did not particularly like taking orders from less experienced men, but the two Alaska Rescue team leaders were both ex-military and the assistant was ex-Special Forces. They were qualified. Ted and Rob would stay in radio contact, but they weren't about to cycle in all the breaks scheduled for each crew. They would gas up and go, but they didn't need to take a break for more than 2 hours' sleep twice a day. They were assigned to Mobile 4, sector 9. They picked up their sector map and a few extra supplies they were to leave for antennae station #3 and headed for their snowmobile.

* * *

Kent took a quick look around using the flashlight from his backpack. Luckily enough, the most level place was right where he had placed Patti. The ground was covered with snow and ice where they were, and he didn't believe he could move her very far, so he decided he'd set up as best he could against a cut in the mountain about 10 feet away. He put Patti's coat on her—something that took an enormous amount of energy while holding her neck straight. He rested for 3 or 4 minutes and then picked her up to move her 10 feet where he had placed the blanket against the large rock. He pushed snow around to make a semi-protected area against the cut in the mountain and the big rock to one side. He padded the gap with snow and packed as much as he could to build up a wall on the rock side. It was snowing heavily and the wind was strong, but nestling in against the wall and rock seemed to provide protection for them from most of the wind and snow.

Kent rested again for a few minutes and then headed back to the plane to look around once more for anything useful. He noticed the door to his side had been almost blown off and the fire was almost out. Kent envisioned that the door would reinforce the wall to their "fort," so he started testing how strongly it was attached to the plane. The lone remaining hinge had only one bolt connected to the airplane so he climbed up on the wing strut and wedged his feet against the frame of the door and started pulling the top of the door. The hinge bent some, but seemed strong. The plane rocked with his movement. Kent repositioned himself on the ground and pushed up on the door. Back and forth movements should eventually break the hinge. He repeated the sequence 3 times and rested for a moment. He then climbed back up on the door frame, grabbed the door from the top with two hands and pulled with all his might. Suddenly the door broke free in the middle of the pull, effectively launching Kent with the door backwards onto to the icy ground. He broke through the icy surface into a crevice, hitting his head on a large chunk of ice. At the same time, a big gust of wind got under the opposite side wing that was high in the air and started to spin the plane in Kent's direction, now that it was jostled loose from where it had been stuck.

Kent was dazed from hitting his head, but saw the fuselage of the plane sliding toward him. He was already mostly under ice in a small crevice, but he tried to work free. He quickly realized he would not have time to get out of the way so he ducked and balled up tight in his hole. The body of the plane slid over top of his hole, pivoting around the large rock that had stopped the plane's slide, and fell over a precipice just a few feet away!

The plane must have dropped quite a long way because Kent did not hear it hit ground. What else would happen? Kent took off a glove and felt the back of his head. He felt a large lump and dried frozen blood. He put his glove back on and began to feel around where he had fallen to decide how he was going to get up. He was in a small crevice in the dark. He remembered crevices could be huge and drop down many feet deep. He decided to move very slowly and carefully. He felt around the edge of the ice he had just fallen through. He felt hard metal—the door was still there! It appeared to be wedged into the ice surface. He started to pull on the recessed area of the door latch and slowly pulled himself up and then toward the door. He slowly rolled out of the hole and onto the door. With his newfound respect for where he was, he treated the area like he was on a frozen lake and had just fallen through a crack in the ice.

Kent slowly slid off the door away from where the plane had fallen. He worked to free the door that had wedged itself into the ice and then pushed it across the ice toward Patti. After he had moved about 10 feet, he felt it would be safe enough to stand and take what remained of the airplane back to their fort. He paused for a moment. He then slowly slid to his knees. He felt the cold, harsh wind biting his face. He was sweating from all his hard work, but he was starting to feel very cold anyway. His legs were dead weight, barely movable. He rested again and then slowly stood up, picked up the door, and headed toward Patti. He had lost his flashlight, but he had evidently traded it for an improved windward wall for his snow fort. He was glad he hadn't traded his life. After a few more minutes of rest, he sculptured the door in place with snow for a third wall, put on his extra jacket, and huddled closely with Patti against the walls of the fort. He opened some food rations and began to eat. At least, he thought, there would be no problem with the food spoiling—it was cold enough. He would stay close to Patti during the night and find a better place to stay in the morning. He noticed her leg had stopped bleeding; the blood was frozen on her leg mixed in with the torn pants leg.

* * *

According to the maps, Ted and Rob figured there would be only a small risk of a crevice large enough to fall through until they got up to around 8,000 feet or so. Consequently, they tore up the mountain with abandon in their snowmobile. They reached the location for antennae station #3 at 6,000 feet in 2 hours—a full 2 hours ahead of the planned time for the antennae crew carrying supplies for the station. They unloaded their stock for the station and placed 3 battery-powered lights on poles around the equipment they were leaving. They then headed up the mountain to get to their assigned sector and begin their search.

They spent the next 4 hours searching their sector with no luck. They figured the station crew would be looking for them to return, so they called in reporting their search coordinates, no contact with the missing, and that they were headed back to refuel and rest.

On their way back to antennae station #3, they heard Mobile 7 report sighting the wrecked airplane. They copied the coordinates, checked their fuel, and headed toward the wreckage.

Twenty-Eight

Wednesday, May 14, early morning
Mt. McKinley, Alaska

Ted and Rob were the first mobile unit to join Mobile 7 at the wreckage of the bush plane. The two rescuers in Mobile 7 had just finished scouting the terrain, checking for crevices or faults in the snow and ice-covered ground. Their preliminary impression was that the aircraft was on secure footing and the risk of a cave-in was low. With that in mind, they had started digging toward the wrecked plane with the hope of finding survivors. They were experienced rescuers and knew the realities of a 12-hour-old airplane crash, but because the plane had landed in a large snowdrift, they dug with the hope of finding someone alive.

Ted and Rob unloaded their shovels to join in the digging. In just 10 minutes the foursome had cleared enough snow to get to the left side of the aircraft. The missing left rear door had allowed the inside of the 4-seat aircraft to be packed with blown snow. The Mobile 7 rescuers continued digging with their hands while Ted and Rob stepped back to see if they could determine how the plane came down.

It took just two minutes to clear the left rear seat and start on the right. Finding no one in the rear of the plane, they started working on the front. In just 3 more minutes, they found the pilot's frozen corpse. Further digging soon made it clear that no other bodies were in the plane. The fire damage quickly became obvious, and more digging revealed the curious finding of the front seat ripped *forward* off its track.

"The plane could not have burned buried in the middle of that snow drift," commented Rob. "And why was the seat ripped forward in the crash? That shouldn't be."

"You're right," said Ted. "That means the plane crashed somewhere else and fell to this spot. Someone had to be alive to rip up the seat like that, and since there are no other bodies in the plane, he must have been able to get out alive."

Both Ted and Rob looked at each other, and then looked up. They saw the ledge 800 feet above them and realized what had to have happened. They sprinted to their snowmobile, and Rob pulled out his radio. "Mobile 4 to Base. Mobile 4 to Base."

"This is Base. Go ahead Mobile 4."

"Base, the plane wreckage is at 7,000 feet with one body on board. There's evidence of extensive fire as well as inside survivor activity. There may be survivors on the ledge 800 feet or so above the wreck. We're headed there now. Mobile 7 is with the plane."

"That's a roger, Mobile 4. Mobile 8 is near that location. I'll alert them to your findings and have them meet you in the area. Be careful of crevices and ice slides or chutes. If the airplane slid off, you could, too."

"Understood, Base. We'll report in when we get to the ledge. Mobile 4 out."

Smitty, who was still on the job as the chief of search operations, was directing the operations at the base. It was he who sent Mobile 8 to the ledge to join Mobile 4. Upon learning the wreckage was found at approximately 7,000 feet of elevation and that survivor activity was suspected at 7,800 feet, he shifted the remainder of his mobile team coverage areas, concentrating 8 of the 12 mobile units between 6,000 and 10,000 feet elevation. He left 2 units patrolling below 6,000 feet and had Mobile 11 cover above 9,000 feet, with Mobile 12 continuing on to Mid Camp Tenderfoot at 10,000 feet, expecting to arrive there within the hour. Smitty revised the sectors to have 2 mobile units cover each of the 1,000 feet of elevation from 6,000 to 9,000 below and along the flight path to Tenderfoot. He sent Mobile 8 to join Mobile 4 at the ledge area at 7,800 feet elevation. He had to continue to cover the entire mountain because no one was sure yet exactly what had happened. He knew multiple scenarios were possible. The plane could have wrecked even higher and eventually fallen to the drift at 7,000 feet. He trusted the experienced judgment of Ted and Rob that the plane probably fell from the ledge at 7,800 feet, but the ledge could still have been an intermediate point in the plane's downward slide, with the survivors getting out of the plane at a point even higher. He also knew that if there were survivors, they could have started down the mountain on their own. In either case, he still didn't know where they were, and he had to find them soon. He wasn't about to send all his mobile units to the same spot like 6-year-olds herding around the ball in a soccer game.

Smitty knew any survivors couldn't last much longer in such frigid conditions. If they had been injured, they were probably already dead. Finding the wreckage before dawn meant there was now some hope, but there was little time left.

* * *

As dawn slowly appeared under low, overcast skies, the gently falling snow cast a peaceful hue over the surroundings. The snow fort had functioned relatively well for having only three walls. The drifting had not come over the windward side of the fort, and the open fourth side proved handy for pushing away what snow blew in and fell on them. Thank God they were sheltered from the howling wind all night. Now it was calm. Kent felt only mildly cold with Patti snuggled close to him. He wondered if she was cold. He was glad he was able to find her extra clothes, especially a coat and gloves.

Patti's breathing had been regular all night. On occasion, she would stir, and she even moaned for a few seconds every now and again. Kent figured she was in a light enough coma for her body to still be able to sense so she should shift positions periodically to protect her circulation. Kent welcomed the light, even if it was snowing and overcast. At least now he could see where they were, and rescuers would be much more likely to find them. Kent decided he should get up to look around, and anyway, he couldn't wait much longer to relieve himself.

Kent shifted Patti from her side leaning against him to her back while holding her head. Patti sensed the movement and lightly resisted. She groaned and then started to mumble something. Kent was excited with the signs of life and rocked her back into his embrace. "Patti! Wake up, Patti! Say something." Patti continued to mumble and then suddenly, opened her eyes. She stopped talking and tried to focus on Kent. "Patti, it's me, Kent. Look at me! Wake up!"

Patti tried hard to focus on the blurry face in front of hers. Finally, she recognized her husband's face. "Kent, what happened? . . . Where are we?"

"Oh, Patti, thank God you're coming back. Our airplane crashed, but we're OK. Take it easy. Now that you're awake, I'm going to get us out of here. Are you cold?"

Patti faded back into her sleepy state. Kent shook her gently and implored her to speak again. "I'm so sleepy, Kent. Where are we?"

Kent could see she was still quite dazed, but he was thrilled at her return. He checked her pupils and was happy to see they were 4 to 5 mm in size, and even though there wasn't much light, they each seemed to constrict when he pulled the eyelids open.

Kent again gently rolled her over on her back so he could get up. He then returned her to her side and placed a knapsack under her head for a pillow.

"Patti, I'm going to look around. I'll be right back."

Kent noticed the cold as he left their fort. The mild wind, from which the fort had shielded them, was enough to send chills through his body. At least he wasn't hungry, and he could feel all his fingers and toes. Since they didn't have the airplane wreckage to identify their location to rescuers, he figured he should make a large sign in the snow. After that, he wasn't sure what to do. He knew he couldn't carry Patti very far, and she wouldn't be walking, even if she did wake up more. At least they had food for a few more meals. Maybe he could make a better fort. But first, he had to empty his bladder.

Kent looked for an appropriate spot. Since he figured he'd probably be staying put for a day or two, he didn't want to contaminate a spot he may need. He didn't know if any animals would be around in all this ice and snow, but he thought he didn't want to leave such a strong scent tract so close to their shelter. So he chose a place off to the side out of the way where he thought they might be headed once Patti felt strong enough to move with improvised crutches.

Opening his pants enough to go really made him feel cold. But once he started urinating, he felt instant relief. He was concentrating so much on feeling relief that the snowmobile was almost next to him before he realized something was there. He turned suddenly while closing his pants and fell backwards. He gasped while falling down, but quickly scrambled back up on his feet. Rob and Ted laughed at the obviously healthy but clumsy survivor.

"It's a good thing we weren't a bear," said Rob. "Did the plane crash damage your hearing?"

"How did you find me?" asked Kent.

"We found the airplane wreckage, and when we saw what you did to the seat and door, we figured you had gotten out. Since the drift was too big for you to escape, you had to have gotten out before the plane got there. So we looked up. Are there any other survivors?"

"Yes, my wife! She's got a head injury, but she's just starting to wake up. How soon can you get her down the mountain?"

"We'll start now. Let's go. Where is she?"

"Right over there, against the cut in the mountain."

Rob helped Kent get out of the deep snow, and Ted drove the snowmobile over to the fort. Ted found Patti in the shelter and checked her pulse and lifted her eyelids to see her pupils. Kent and Rob were not far behind. Patti again mumbled in response to being handled and started to open her eyes.

"Kent, Kent . . ."

"Take it easy, Mrs. Nash," said Ted. "We're going to get you out of here. We'll have to check you over first, but then we'll put you on the snowmobile and head down."

Kent spoke. "She's got a fractured left tibia and fibula. It broke the skin, but the bleeding seemed to stop, and I wrapped it tight with a T-shirt and it seems to be OK now. Pulses distal to the break are strong. Her neck seems to be OK as well. Her pulse has been strong all night, and her breathing was regular. She just started to wake up a few minutes ago."

"We've got some adjustable splints in the bag," said Rob. "If she wakes up any more and her ankle pulse is OK, we'll be able to take both of you down on the snowmobile while one of us stays behind. Did she move all four extremities when she woke up before?"

"Yes, she did, and she's been moving her whole body a bit off and on throughout the night. I pushed all over her neck, and she didn't seem to flinch. It doesn't seem to be hurt." Rob retrieved the splints, while Ted got the radio.

"Base, this is Mobile 4. Come in, Base."

"Mobile 4, this is Base. You're breaking up. Come back."

"Base, we've located two survivors at seventy eight hundred. Dr. Nash appears well, and his wife has sustained a concussion and tibia/fibula fracture. She is beginning to wake up. Over."

"Is she transportable? Over?"

"Possibly. Will let you know in 10. Over."

"OK, Mobile 4. Mobile 8 should arrive shortly. I'm sending 9 there as well. The two survivors account for all souls on board. There should be no one else to find. You'll have to get her down on your snowmobile if possible. Aircraft extraction of any kind is still impossible and is likely to remain so for days. Be sure her neck is stable first. Over."

"Roger that. I'll call back in 10. Over and out."

* * *

Smitty smiled. He knew how lucky his team was. They found the two survivors in 13 hours, and only one person died in the crash. And none of the rescuers were injured, at least so far. He dialed the Naylors' hotel room.

"Dr. Naylor, we've found Dr. and Mrs. Nash. Dr. Nash appears OK, but his wife is coming out of a coma with a broken leg. We're stabilizing her right now, and once we get her warm, we'll start to bring her down. It should take 3 or 4 hours to get her to base. You're welcome to come here if you like."

"That's wonderful, Smitty. We'll be out soon."

"Take your time. It will be at least 3 hours before she gets to base, and it could be a lot longer depending on how she tolerates the trip down."

"Thanks for calling. I'll tell the Donovans, and the four of us will be there in 2 hours."

Twenty-Nine

Wednesday, May 14, 10:35 AM
Mt. McKinley, Alaska

Mobiles 4 and 8 arrived at the base camp together with the two survivors. The ambulance was waiting with its engine running and the cabin warm. A second ambulance was ready and waiting, too, but everyone already knew that Kent Nash was not leaving his wife for separate ambulance rides to Fairbanks Hospital. The 3 ½-hour ride down the mountain was painstakingly slow in an effort to jostle Patti Nash's brain as little as possible. She seemed to tolerate the ride rather well, but the movement obviously aggravated her situation because she settled back into a light coma shortly after starting the trek and had not made any conscious conversation since. Stops every 15 minutes proved her vital signs remained stable and her pupils, reflexes, and muscle movements remained normal.

Kent Nash refused medical evaluation, hoping to keep things moving for his wife. The rescue team knew he needed observation because of all the physical and emotional stress. The Donovans and Naylors watched quietly while Patti was loaded into the ambulance. They saw Kent helping with the loading and rejoiced to see him acting so normally. They did not speak in order to allow this stage of the rescue to continue as efficiently as possible. Once the ambulance was loaded and had started toward town, they jumped into their rented Montero Sport and followed.

Hospitals in the wilderness are much more informal than in big cities, although they are often quite efficient. The need for security is minimal, and the staff and patients alike rarely let concerns for safety slow down the need to deliver prompt urgent care. The Donovans and Naylors were led back to Patti Nash's cubicle while she was being examined. Kent was paying very close attention to the emergency physician's technique.

"Thank God you're all right!" said Mike.

Kent turned to face the voice and his visitors. "My goodness!" said Kent. "What in the world are you doing here? How did you get here so quickly?"

"We have a problem back home," said Mike. "Your family is fine, don't worry. But we need to talk as soon as we know Patti is OK."

"Her vital signs are perfect, she has purposeful movement in all four extremities, and she's beginning to respond verbally to being annoyed," announced the ER physician. "There are no focal signs, her pulse distal to the fracture is strong, and there are no signs of frostbite yet—although that may take a day or two to start showing. Basically, I bet she's going to be OK. We'll x-ray the leg and neck, get a CT scan of her brain, and get her up to ICU as soon as possible. Why don't you talk to your friends while we send her to x-ray?"

The ER physician turned to the visitors. "Your buddy here has just been through an ordeal. He is tired and dehydrated and could go into shock at any time. He could also have a panic attack or huge emotional let-down. He's refusing care, so I'll leave it to you folks to talk him into getting checked and observed for 24 hours. If he still refuses, don't let him out of your sight for 2 days. He should consume no alcohol or drugs, and wake the stubborn dude every 2 hours to be sure he doesn't have a subdural hematoma. He's probably OK. You usually have to have a significant degree of central nervous system function remaining to be so obstinate after just having your life saved. He'd fit in well with most of the other people around here. They're all nice as hell, but they don't like being fussed over."

"I'm not so stubborn. I'm just saving the HMO money," kidded Kent. "They will probably hassle us both before paying the bill. But really, I don't want to be in another room away from my wife getting checked when I feel fine. I just want to be here with Patti so I'm informed of her progress in real time. I'd like to be around when she wakes up to reassure her."

"Whatever you say, Doc. We'll be here if you need us."

Kent spoke to his friends. "It's so good of you to come. I'm really glad you're here. What a nightmare. What's going on back home that's so important you'd come all the way to Alaska to talk to me?"

The Donovans, Naylors, and Kent took turns hugging each other. Kent seemed fine to everyone.

"So . . . what's going on at home? Are your kids OK?"

"We're really worried about Wendy, Kent," said Debbie. "We're afraid she's in line to have a catastrophe like three other athletes in Thompson's study group of 16."

"That's right, Kent," said Mike. "I believe Thompson's been stealing your gene therapy test drugs and using them on his athletes without their knowledge. Two athletes have died, and one has serious heart damage. I broke into his office and discovered Wendy's protocol is similar to those of two of the three athletes."

"You're going to have to go just a little slower, Mike," said Kent. "I thought I was thinking clearly, but now I'm not so sure."

"I'll give you the details later, Kent," said Mike. "But we came to Alaska to bring you home as soon as possible to see what you thought about what Thompson was doing. We especially need to know if you think Wendy is at risk for a heart attack or stroke. We figured you would be the only person in the world who might be able to fix whatever problem the gene therapy was creating. We didn't expect to find you crashed on a mountain with your wife unconscious."

"Nor did I," said Kent. "But, start over, give me the details slowly, and maybe I can get something started remotely. I'll leave with you as soon as I know Patti will be OK. She would want me to go help Wendy. Wendy is my only godchild and is very special to both of us, so if I can help in any way, I'm there. You two are important, too, but . . . damn, you know what I mean. I'll go once Patti is stable. I couldn't go any sooner because I wouldn't be of any use anyway."

"Wendy should be OK for a few days," said Mike. "Let's get Patti stable, and while we're waiting, we'll get you up to speed on the dirty tricks back home."

A nurse stuck her head inside the room. "Mr. Nash, you have a visitor. He says it's urgent. Do you wish to speak with him now, or shall I ask him to wait?"

"Good night! Am I being followed? Who else knows I'm in the Emergency Room of Fairbanks Hospital after surviving an airplane crash halfway up Mt. McKinley?"

The nurse took the whole scene in stride. "I don't know, but you're either popular or important, because everyone seems to know what you're doing and where you are. Shall I send him in?"

"Why not? Please do."

The nurse turned and spoke to the visitor. "Mr. Turner, he said you can come in."

A tall, athletic-looking man in his late 40's or early 50's, impeccably dressed, entered the room. He appeared confident and spoke in a friendly, calm manner.

"Dr. Nash, I'm terribly sorry you've had such a rough time. My name is Ken Turner, and I have a son who's an athlete in Mark McCormack's Boston study arm of the Kelly Hospital gene therapy study. I understand you are the person most able to help figure out what's going wrong with our athletes and therefore help my son. I have my personal jet with a top-notch crew standing by at the airport to take you and your friends back to Delaware. I'll send the plane back here fitted for air ambulance to get your wife once she's stable enough for transfer. My interest is in saving my son from what happened to the other three athletes."

Silence overtook the room as Kent just stared at Ken Turner wondering what surreal world he was in. Maybe he hadn't been saved on the mountain. Maybe he was dead already and he just had to have some time to get used to the new reality he was in. "How did you know I was here? How did you know I was in the Emergency Room? How did you know the study was using gene therapy? I'm just finding this out at this very moment. Do you have any other revelations to tell me right now? I didn't even know there was a human gene therapy study going on until 5 minutes ago."

"I'll let these folks tell you what they know, but first, let me quickly answer your questions. I was offered to put my son in a top-secret gene therapy study for athletes if I was willing to make a large donation. My son has dreamed of becoming a professional football player ever since he was 2 years old. I thought I could buy my son an improved chance of achieving his dream. I know better now, but 4 million dollars later I'm here with you trying to get you involved to correct what Thompson and McCormack did not know. To his credit, Dr. McCormack said I should contact you and that I should tell you we all want to figure out what went wrong and fix the problem. He strongly advised against going to the police just yet because their paperwork and politics would definitely slow us down and interfere with your work. So I called your office, said I'd like to make a large contribution to your work, but I needed to talk with you right away. After much encouragement, your office reluctantly gave me your phone number and your itinerary."

"I see."

"Well, I hope you'll take me up on using my plane. I'd hate to see any further delay, except for caring for your wife."

"Is your jet safe? The last plane I flew in crashed."

"I've got the best crew around, my head mechanic travels with me everywhere we go, and the plane seats 22 with room to spare. It's quite comfortable. Again, money is not my concern. My son is."

"OK, I appreciate the offer. Will you be around? Where will I find you to let you know?"

"I'll check in with you twice a day if that's OK. I'm at the Regal Alaska Hotel in Fairbanks, and I'm not going anywhere until I take you back to Delaware."

Thirty

Wednesday, May 14
Boston, Massachusetts

"*Talk to me, Vinton.* What's happening in Fairbanks?" asked Dean Carter.

"We're making progress, sir," said Frank Vinton. "So far, everything is on script and on schedule. The Alaska Rescue Group is an efficient and competent organization, and we were able to help them. Kent Nash is OK. He's off the mountain after his airplane crash and overnight camping escapade in Arctic conditions. He did rather well for a city slicker. His wife wasn't so lucky, but she's slowly coming out of her coma and it appears she will recover, probably completely. She's in the ER getting a CT scan of her head, and he's there as a visitor, not a patient, talking to his buddies about getting home ASAP. We were able to place receivers on both the Naylors' and Donovans' clothes and shoes. We'll have to get Nash later. He was out of our reach for several hours building a snow fort on the mountain. Oh, and our man Ken Turner just finished meeting the group of them and apparently was well received. It sounds like Nash will probably take him up on the offer of a plane ride home. However, the bad news is that the Donovans now know about Thompson."

"How soon do you think Nash will come to Delaware?"

"He says he'll leave as soon as he's sure his wife is stable. But I'm sure having Turner's private jet on standby in Delaware to return to Alaska if necessary will help get him to go home sooner. That was a brilliant idea you had, sir."

"Make sure those doctors know what they're doing. I don't want any unnecessary delay getting Nash to Delaware. It will go much better if he thinks it's his idea to investigate this problem and not ours. Do they have a good neurosurgeon in that hospital?"

"I'll check and get right back to you."

"Let me know in an hour. If they need a good one, we can get Turner to fly one in. It seems such a waste to spend so much effort getting her better when we'll probably have to quiet her forever very soon."

"I guess it's the cost of doing business, sir. Collateral damage is a necessary evil."

"Oh, before I forget, get Turner to have one of his men buy Kent Nash some clothes before Nash does, so you can 'tailor' them without having to risk breaking into his hotel room. It could be even more tricky if he tries to stay in the hospital."

"Turner already thought of that, sir. It's under way."

"Fine. Get back to me in an hour."

"Will do, sir."

Kelly Hospital, Floor 3B
Wilmington, Delaware

"Wendy, do you feel that?" asked Dr. Thompson.

"Feel what?" she asked.

Suddenly, Wendy felt dizzy. Her cardiac rhythm had converted to ventricular fibrillation while she was being monitored during a stress test on the treadmill. Dr. Thompson broke her fall, picked her up in his arms, and turned to place her lying down on the examination table next to the treadmill. He gave her a firm thump in the center of her chest.

"Hey, why did you do that?" asked Wendy.

"Your heart went off," said Dr. Thompson. "But I think it's coming back now."

Thompson turned to his assistant. "Get phlebotomy up here stat! And I want the portable Doppler here stat as well. Tell them it's an emergency."

Wendy's rhythm returned to a regular sinus pattern after the chest thump. Wendy felt better, and her dizziness passed.

"What happened, Dr. Thompson?" asked Wendy.

"Your heart started beating irregularly, but you're OK now."

"Why would that happen? I thought I was in great shape. Is something wrong?"

"I sure hope not," said Thompson. "I don't know what could be wrong, but I don't like your heart beating like that, even for a few seconds."

"Will it happen again?"

"Let's hope not. I'm going to keep you in the hospital tonight, Wendy, just to be sure. Where are your parents?"

"They're out of town for a few days. My aunt is looking after Kelly and me. But you can call Bill Owens. He's my dad's partner, and he checks on me twice a day. He would want to know about any medical things."

"I'll call him right away. Once you get to the unit, I'll have a nurse bring you a phone so you can call your aunt and your sister. Don't worry, Wendy. I'm not going to let anything happen to you."

"Dr. Thompson, is this what happened to Jennifer, Kim, and Matt? Am I getting affected, too?"

"Wendy, I promise when I know what's happening, I'll tell you everything I know before I talk to anyone else."

Thompson left the bedside with Wendy still connected to the portable monitor. He figured he had better call Dean Carter immediately. Thompson didn't know that Carter already knew what was going on. Hugh Winston patched Dean Carter in on his monitoring bug right after Thompson started giving stat orders.

Thirty-One

Thursday, May 15, 2 AM
Fairbanks Memorial Hospital, Fairbanks, Alaska

The lighting was evening-light status, and for once the ICU was exceptionally quiet and peaceful. Hospitals make a sincere effort to achieve a quiet atmosphere, but they usually succeed only in subduing excessive noise. They usually maintain the background clatter level of Grand Central Station with all their technology and respirators and electronic devices.

Kent was nestled in the recliner next to Patti's bed. Everything had caught up to him, and he was deep in a sound sleep. The nurses and hospital staff wanted him to remain with his wife, and because he was calm enough not to interfere with her care, he was accepted like the mother of a frightened 4-year-old would be. He did not make waves, and he would certainly be a beacon for Patti, leading her back to reality with his voice and his support when she started to wake up. He would be a comforting connection to conscious thought as Patti struggled to get her bearings as she slowly emerged from her coma.

Or so it appeared. Suddenly Patti's random brain activity all came together while the ICU was idling through the early morning hours. She opened her eyes and focused on her surroundings. No one was aware of her return, so nobody got excited and pestered her to start talking to see if she was all right. Her thoughts began with simple concepts. She figured she was in a bed and likely in a hospital because of the equipment on the wall and the IV poles next to her. She noticed the tubes running into her arm. She saw her husband sleeping in the chair to her left. She stared at him for a few minutes, trying to figure what he was doing and what time it might be. She wondered what hospital she might be in and then decided she would like to have some questions answered.

"Kent, where are we?"

Kent was out. One soft sentence was not enough to restore conscious thought in the deep level of sleep he was in. Patti tried again, speaking more loudly.

"Kent, wake up. I need to talk to you."

Kent woke up with a start! "Patti, you're awake! Thank God." He reached over, held her hand, and kissed her on the cheek.

"Kent, please answer me. Where are we?"

"Oh, Patti, thank God you're OK. Let me get the nurse! I'll be right back."

Patti reached for Kent's arm leaning on the side of the bed. "Fine, get the nurse, but first, tell me where we are!"

"Oh, right . . . we're in Fairbanks Memorial Hospital's Intensive Care Unit. You were unconscious for a day and a half after our airplane crashed, and thank God you're back. Can you see OK? Do you hurt anywhere?"

"I just feel so confused. What time is it?"

Patti's nurse came to the bed after hearing a conversation coming from the glass-enclosed room. "She's talking already? That's pretty fast. I had better call Dr. Marlton. He'll want to know right away. Usually it takes them a few minutes to start talking when they wake up."

Patti dozed off once the nurse started talking. The nurse gently shook her arm, and Patti returned to the conversation.

"Can you move your arms and legs?" asked Kent. Kent's look

was intense as he studied her. Patti moved purposely and then winced when she moved her fractured left leg.

"Whoa, what's on my leg?" asked Patti. "Why is it so heavy?"

"Patti, your leg is broken, and it has a cast on it. It got trapped under the seat in the airplane. But it's going to be OK. The fracture was easily set, and the alignment is good. Just take it easy. We've got plenty of time for you to get better."

Patti's recovery was incredibly fast. The trip down from the mountain had to have been extremely rough on her concussed brain. The steroids helped dramatically with the swelling, but it would be normal to take 3 or 4 days for Patti to begin to wake up. Waking up 12 hours after coming off the mountain was an incredible blessing.

"Patti, save your energy. You're going to be fine. Go back to sleep and rest." Kent watched her for a few minutes and then fell asleep as well.

Once the 7-to-3 shift arrived for work, the activity and noise level ramped up threefold. Kent couldn't sleep in the middle of the bustle, so he got up and headed for a shower. The medical residents showed him where to go and where to get clean scrubs. As Kent was leaving ICU, Ken Turner appeared. "How is she?"

"Much better, thank you. She's talking and making complete sense."

"All right. That's what we want to hear. Is she awake now? I'd like to meet her if it wouldn't be too much strain on her."

"I'd suggest you just look in her room and watch her for a few moments. She needs to talk a little at a time until she gets her bearings."

* * *

Patti spent the day taking naps after short periods of being completely lucid. She became oriented to her surroundings quickly and listened intently while Kent gave her a detailed run-down of their overnight adventure. She was alert enough to know she was very lucky.

Dr. Marlton visited three times during the day and explained to Patti and Kent that the CT scan of Patti's brain showed only very mild swelling. There was no sign of any bleeding in the brain or spinal cord. Her cervical spine was normal as well. Patti was free to sit up in a chair for as long as she could tolerate it, and he would remove the nasogastric tube when appropriate, hopefully soon. Late in the afternoon, Ken Turner stopped in for a visit along with Mike and Debbie. The Donovans waited outside for their turn to keep the crowd down around Patti's bed.

"You're an amazing woman, Mrs. Nash," said Ken. "You must be in great shape to endure all the trauma and frigid temperatures and be so awake the next day."

"Yes, you're right," said Kent. "We were also very lucky."

"We were incredibly lucky," said Patti. "It's time to move on, though. When am I going to get out of here?"

"Kent, she sure doesn't sound like a very passive patient," said Ken. "You've got your hands full."

"That's why I married her! I don't have a dull life, and she takes good care of all of us. Ken, it's time we talked. Let's go to the waiting room so we can give Patti a break."

Kent told Patti he would be right back, and then he and Ken headed for the waiting room. The waiting room was deserted, and the two sat across from each other in comfortable padded chairs.

"Why did you tell me about McCormack and Thompson in front of everyone yesterday," asked Kent.

"I overheard Dr. Naylor telling all of you, so I thought it was OK, that everyone already knew. I figured they were your trusted friends and you would want them to know. Was I wrong?"

"No, you were right. But as I begin to understand this whole situation, I'm concerned that it may be quite dangerous for anyone to know. What do you know about Thompson and McCormack? Who's behind all this? Just how big is this operation?"

"I'm afraid I don't know very much about who is behind McCormack and Thompson. Like your friend Dr. Naylor, I just wanted to do something to help my son Josh in his quest to be a star football player. I checked out Dr. McCormack in Boston and found out that he had an excellent reputation and had helped many top-level athletes in the Boston area for years. I trusted him when he promised me the gene therapy study was absolutely safe and the worst-case scenario would be that Josh wouldn't get any benefit from the injections. He would, however, benefit from being in the same program that had already helped numerous athletes, and the upside potential was huge if the gene therapy worked as it had in animal studies—which, he pointed out, exhibited no measurable side effects."

"You put your son in a first-generation medical study? Does he know what's going on?"

"He does not know about gene therapy. I did what I thought was best for him. His dream is so important to him. Being the best in football has given him so much confidence in everything else he does. He is admired by his friends, and he is so good to them and helps them in so many ways. He excels in school with straight A's and is the president of a 3,000-member student body. He has worked so hard and asks for so little. Money is no object to me, so I thought I could buy him an improved chance to achieve his dream. I didn't tell him because I didn't want him to ever doubt that it was his natural talent and drive that enabled him to achieve his goal. I was wrong in two ways. I should have checked further. Lord knows, I have the means to do so. Second, I should have discussed this up front with Josh. He's mature enough to have made this decision with me."

"I guess your success in life hurt you in this situation. You must have been so used to making decisions for people, you made a big one for your son."

"Yes, I did. And I can't change what I did. All I can do is move forward and do the best I can from here on out. Who was it who said, 'Don't ever look back'? Well, the success I've achieved is largely based on learning from my mistakes and then going forward with my best effort. I believe that's what we all must do now. Are you willing to help us figure out what's going wrong with this study?"

"There is no doubt I am. My godchild is involved. My best friend is involved. I'd just like to know what I'm getting into."

"That, Dr. Nash, is a good question. And I believe all of us should meet together as soon as possible to plan our strategy. We need to be very careful who we tell about this, because I'm afraid you're correct—it may be dangerous."

Both men thought about Ken's last sentence for a few moments. "How is your wife doing, medically speaking?" asked Ken. "She appears quite stable. Her testing shows she has an excellent chance to recover fully. There is almost no risk for a cerebral bleed. And I guess you'd like to know when I'd be able to get started."

"Yes, of course. But I don't expect you to leave here until you are ready. My offer stands. I'll take you and your friends back to Wilmington on my personal jet whenever you are ready, and I'll come back for your wife when she's stable enough to travel. I will bring you with me for the air ambulance ride for your wife if you wish, and I will bring you back here to visit whenever you wish if she can't travel. I want to help my son, and I understand you are the best person to help me. I will do whatever it takes. Cost is not a concern."

"What does that mean? What will you do if I don't agree to help?"

"I'll have to approach other gene therapy experts, perhaps at the University of Washington or Texas. But I figured you would be most interested since your program is involved and now I know your godchild and best friend are involved."

"If I don't help, does that mean I'm expendable?"

"Look, I'm a victim here. I'm not behind this scheme, if that's what you're thinking. But the five of us do need to talk, whether you are going to help or not. You already knew enough to be involved. I just asked for your help. I guess we had all better prepare for being in danger."

"OK, let's talk. I hope you understand I had to ask you some pressing questions. I had to be sure you're not part of the problem."

"I understand and appreciate your foresight. Remember, my son is my motivation. I hope that helps you trust me."

* * *

"Dean, this is Ken Turner. I'm on a secure line Mr. Vinton arranged for me. Did you hear my conversation with Dr. Nash live?"

"Yes, it was forwarded here. Our crew in Alaska is very efficient. They are keeping me informed up to the minute and transmitting live whenever it seems appropriate. And things are happening quickly there. When are you meeting with everyone to plan your strategy?"

"We plan to meet at 7 tonight. Dr. Nash is having a meeting with the neurosurgeon, Dr. Marlton, at 6. I expect Nash to agree to help, and since his wife is doing so well, I figure he'll agree to go to Wilmington by tomorrow. He could delay a day or so to wait for his wife if she is cleared to travel very soon."

"Well, make sure those overconfident doctors understand why they should keep this secret and stop telling everyone about Thompson's illegal study. It's getting out of control, and I don't want to have to eliminate half of Wilmington to keep things quiet."

"I believe Nash has figured that out already. We should be safe for now. I don't anticipate a problem until Wendy is cured or she dies."

"Right. Call me back after the meeting. I'll be in the office until I hear from you."

Thirty-Two

Thursday, May 15
Fairbanks Memorial Hospital, Fairbanks, Alaska

Kent Nash walked into the patient conference room and saw his friends and Ken Turner waiting patiently. Tom and Marsha Donovan were on a couch sitting next to Ken Turner, and Mike and Debbie Naylor were seated across from them. Kent stood arms akimbo facing all five.

"How's Patti?" asked Mike. "What did Marlton say?"

"He says Patti is doing remarkably well. I told him we have an emergency at home and asked how soon we could take her home. He said she's stable enough to be transferred to another ICU via air ambulance if we need to leave the area. It would be ideal for her to stay put for another day or two, but if she's on a high rate of flow of oxygen, the risks of an air ambulance move are low. She needs to keep her activity to a minimum for several days because of her extended loss of consciousness. I agreed to wait until tomorrow to take her home, but only if she continues to do well overnight. That should give Mr. Turner here time to outfit his plane as an air ambulance and make any necessary arrangements."

"My jet has served as an air ambulance before. I already have most of what we need on board. I'll instruct my crew to prepare immediately and coordinate with Dr. Marlton. The jet holds 22 people comfortably, so we shouldn't have a problem with space. I already checked the weather over our flight path. Once we get out of the Fairbanks area, we should have no problem in the next 24 hours."

"Thank you for your help, Ken," said Kent. "I am anxious to get back to start figuring out what's been going on with the pirating of my gene therapy study, especially since my godchild, Mike and Debbie's daughter, is involved. I appreciate the fact that your son is also involved, and I hope I can help him, too. Let's pray that Patti continues to do well so we can get her home where she can heal in familiar surroundings. But I understand we need to set up a strategy, not only to figure out what might be going wrong, but also to protect ourselves from a possible mob-type involvement. Ken, just what information do you have for us? Earlier, you said our being involved may be dangerous."

"First, let me tell everyone here, as I've told Kent, that I'm not behind what's going on with Thompson and McCormack's study. I made a large tax-deductible donation to the Boston Elite Sports Medicine Foundation to get my son enrolled so he might benefit from cutting-edge technology. I may not have made the best decision, but I value my son and my family more than anything in life, so I'm prepared to spend whatever it takes to protect him. My motivation here is to save my son and keep him healthy. Since I'm used to working in big business, I've learned to be appropriately paranoid, or cautious—whichever phrase you wish to use. Since I knew human gene therapy experimentation was involved from the start and did not yet have legal approvals, I knew big bucks were being invested and I thought the extremely large size of the investment would insure the success of the study. I also knew that technically, this study was not legal. Clearance had not yet been obtained from the notoriously slow FDA. Now that things aren't going well, I figure that whoever is behind all this is most certainly devious enough to protect themselves from the law. I am concerned that the 'investors' may be willing to use force to keep us from going to the authorities."

"Do you know any of the principals involved?" asked Mike.

"I dealt directly with Dr. McCormack. Obviously, he did not tell me names."

"Yes, but he told you it was a gene therapy study without FDA approval," said Debbie. "Didn't you ask any more questions?"

"Not about who was running the show. McCormack said he had authority over the study. I did not want to know who was behind him at that time. I thought I was better off not knowing. I was just told my son would be accepted into the last spot of a 4-year study if I made a sizable contribution to the Foundation."

"What recourse did you think you had if something were to go wrong?" asked Tom.

"I didn't plan on anything going wrong. There was big money behind this, and things rarely go wrong when that much money is involved. Dr. McCormack's reputation and practice were at stake, so I though the risk was very low. But, folks, regardless of the mistake I made, we must move forward. Things appear to be going wrong, and we have to correct the problem with the study. I brought all this up, not to be tormented by your questions, but to speculate on our strategy. I suggest it may be critical for us to keep our mouths shut to anyone not involved. If mob-type money is involved, birds who sing are silenced. Since we are involved with our families, we may be able to strike a deal to remain silent since 'they' may trust that we do not want to risk hurting our families or the careers or names of those athletes in the study who died. I'm sure we'll be contacted sooner or later. Certainly our bargaining position is enhanced by finding the problem with the study. 'They' are much more likely to trust us if our kids are still involved and spilling the beans would adversely affect our families."

Silence followed Ken's words. Tom and Marsha's emotions went from concern for their friends to absolute fear for their lives. They didn't have any kids involved—they were most likely already expendable for what they knew! Mike and Debbie were anguishing over their family's involvement and how they would have any energy left to defend themselves when it was all they could do to try to figure out how to help Wendy. Debbie finally broke the pensive silence.

"So! We've got a lot to do. We've got to get Kent back to his lab. We've got to talk Hugh into getting us all of Thompson's information, including the autopsy report on Matt Madison. We've got to somehow lean on McCormack for the autopsy report on Kim Taylor, his fallen athlete. Then Kent not only has to figure out how to cure Wendy and Josh, but he also has to do it in just a few days, when the process would normally take a year or two. And, we have to do this while we are looking over our shoulders for hit men while we're continuing to work and pretend we're leading normal lives. Guys, we need more than strategy, we need a miracle."

"We need a string of miracles," said Mike. "Medical school and residency didn't include a course on espionage."

"A trip of 1,000 miles begins with one step," said Ken. "Shall we break Debbie's excellent summary up into individual tasks and then put them together for a plan?"

"We should do that," answered Tom. "But selfishly, I'd like to discuss the concerns Marsha and I have for our lives. Assuming what you say is true, that the people behind all this may have mob ties, what reason is there for us to be kept alive, both now and in the future? As I see it, we are expendable already, and our deaths could serve as a warning to the rest of you to keep quiet forever."

"You sound pessimistic, but very realistic," replied Ken. "I would suggest that you two stay out of this starting immediately. You shouldn't come back with us on the plane—you should stay here and act as if you know nothing. I can't believe the group behind this scheme knows what's going on out here. If you stay here for the remainder of your vacation, you should appear completely uninvolved. Do you have any expertise in gene therapy that we might need to solve this riddle?"

"No. Marsha and I are attorneys. Most people consider attorneys expendable anyway. My wife and I know only slightly more than the average lay person about gene therapy, and that's only because of Kent. We might be a little useful in the espionage area, but we have no marketable talent in the medical field."

"Then I would suggest that we go our separate ways immediately and that we break off all communication to keep you out of harm's way. Mike, Debbie, Kent, what do you think?"

Kent spoke first. "I've never had to think in such a dimension. This doesn't seem real. It's like we're all in a John Grisham novel. Are we going to be watched by undercover types? Are our phones going to be tapped? Will we be followed? And for how long?"

"Kent, I'm sorry to put you and Patti in the middle of this mess," said Mike, "but with Wendy's life at stake, I had to ask. I didn't consider that you would be risking your lives, but even if I did, I still would have asked for your help. I hope you understand."

"Yes, of course. I'd do the same if one of my kids needed your help. I don't see that we have much choice. We just have to hope the 'mob' understands that we understand our silence is something we would agree to in exchange for our families' lives."

"Well, even if they don't, they have to understand that, at least for now, the five of us are more valuable to them alive than dead," said Ken. "That is how business cutthroats think, and the mob understands business better than most."

"OK," said Mike. "As Debbie said, we must pretend to be carrying on normal lives and keeping totally silent as we help Kent determine if Wendy and Josh have a problem. Ken, it seems obvious that you should be the one to ask for the autopsy report on Kim Taylor. Will McCormack do that for you? And can you find out who might be behind McCormack in Boston—that is, without risking your life?"

"McCormack knows I'm here. He welcomes Kent's help. I don't believe he's into killing, and he would have had to kill me to keep me from coming for your help. And besides, he'd like to keep his other athletes out of harm's way. He thinks there is still time to salvage his study. He will definitely give me the autopsy report. It's accessible to others anyway. However, I doubt he would tell me who his benefactors are, especially if they aren't clean. And if they are sponsoring unapproved human trials, they can't be clean.

Kent, he urged me to discuss your helping with no one except the Naylors. I understood I would be putting a death sentence on anyone else I told about this problem. He doesn't know about Tom and Marsha, and we'd better keep it that way."

"It sure does sound like the mob is in charge of this project," said Debbie. "But, Ken, if you believe McCormack trusts you, you could at least *broach* the topic of who's behind this. You might learn something of value."

"I'll be as subtle as possible. It can't hurt to sniff around—unless I probe too deeply. Well, my assignment is clear. Let's get on with the easier duties now."

"Easier?" asked Kent. "No problem. I'll just write it all down on a chalkboard, connect a few arrows, and the computer will have the answer ready by morning."

"Whoa, hold on, Kent. I'm just kidding. My job can be done over the phone in just a few minutes. Yours will take considerably longer. We may not have more than a few days, so if you can get started now, we'd be most appreciative."

"OK," said Mike. "Tom and Marsha, it's time for you to leave. You really shouldn't hear any more. It's agreed you will not be in touch. If you discover something critical, contact me only in person. Since you're both my patients, get an appointment to see me if we must talk. Otherwise, enjoy your trip. We'll see you at your law firm's annual fall crab bake."

"You know, Kent, we came on this trip because of Patti, oh, and you," kidded Tom. "And now we're the ones who will have to pretend we're having fun hiking in six feet of snow instead of watching the big games on TV with a few drinking buddies or playing a civilized sport like golf. And you get to go home where all the excitement is."

"You could use this opportunity to hit a few dream courses on your way back East. You could play that course with the island green in the Midwest, I believe it is Coeur d'Alene. And how about Pebble Beach? This would be a good time to extend your vacation."

"That course is booked over a year in advance. We'd never get in on such short notice."

"Why don't you call your travel agent and tack on a golf package after your Alaska adventure?" said Debbie. "Your firm owes you both months of vacation. Have you ever taken any until this trip? I bet your agent could get you on a waiting list for Pebble Beach and at least find you a dream package. Now, get going, before someone sees you with us. We'll see you in September. Don't call. Just go have fun."

Tom and Marsha looked at each other for a moment; long enough for each to know they agreed with leaving. They'd be no more than a liability if they tried to help. And their lives would be in serious jeopardy if they stayed. They each silently hugged their friends as well as their new friend and then left the meeting room. They didn't even try to look in the ICU for one more peek at Patti. Neither one planned to head back up the mountain. They each knew their good health wasn't likely to thrive there either. They would stay in Fairbanks at their hotel until their agent booked a long, comfortable vacation far from their home. As they left the room, Mike heard Marsha say something about the golf courses Down Under and satisfying each of their vacation goals.

Once again, the room was silent. The low-grade hum of the heating system was hypnotizing and relaxing. The tension remained in the room. Ken spoke first this time. "It sure is nice of this hospital to give us our own private conference room."

Just then, a nurse appeared. "Dr. Nash, your wife would like to see you."

"Ken, let's plan a 9 AM departure," said Kent. "That should get us in Wilmington by 3 PM. I'll work on Marlton to have Patti ready to leave the ICU by 8. Can your pilots have everything ready by tomorrow morning?"

"We'll be ready. And I'll have them prepared to remain on standby in case there is any delay."

"Sounds good," said Mike. "I'll talk to Hugh as soon as we get home. I'd rather talk in person. Talking over the phone might get him ready sooner, but I may misinterpret his reaction."

"We should talk every day morning and evening," said Ken. "How about 7 AM and 7 PM. We could all talk together with a conference call. We should avoid cell phones for now—they're too easy for folks to listen in. Give me your phone numbers and a schedule, and I'll set up the first call. We can confirm the next call during our first."

Mike and Debbie knew this was just the beginning of a rough next few days. They were exhausted, and they hadn't even spent the night wrecked on the side of a frozen mountain. How much more could they take?

Thirty-Three

Friday, May 16, 4 PM
Kent Nash's Lab, Wilmington, Delaware

The flight to Delaware was smooth. The tailwind enabled them to cross the continent in under 3 hours. Patti slept through the entire trip; it seemed that the relative lower oxygen concentration at altitude helped her stay asleep without her even noticing she missed the whole trip.

Kent Nash turned to Mike Naylor and asked, "What do you think the likelihood is that you could get hold of Matt Madison's autopsy report?"

"Hugh will help me with that," Mike replied. "I'll be sure Hugh gets us everything on Jennifer as well."

"I sure would like to see his autopsy slides," said Kent. "I doubt the pathologist looked at the cardiovascular system from a gene therapy viewpoint. I just hope he did enough stains on enough samples."

"Yeah, let's hope. I doubt we'll be able to dig up Matt's body to do our own autopsy."

* * *

"Hugh, I need to talk to you right away," said Mike. "It's urgent."

"No problem, Doc," said Hugh. "I'm listening."

"No, I mean we need to talk privately, in person."

"Are you in the hospital?"

"Yes, I'm on the 5th floor, in Dr. Nash's lab."

"Shall I come there?"

"That would be fine. See you in a few minutes?"

"I'll be there in 15 minutes. I have to finish verifying a shipment of medical supplies, and I'll be right up."

* * *

Hugh immediately called Dean Carter at the Brey Agency in Boston with his SAT phone. He knew better than to use a hospital line. The agency would not want the long-distance charges to be investigated, allowing establishment of any kind of link with the Brey Agency and Kelly Hospital.

"Mr. Carter, you may want to listen in live when I talk to Naylor. He's with Nash now, and he has asked me to come to Nash's lab to talk to him. I'm betting he wants me to talk with both of them. It should be interesting."

"Dan's here. We'll both listen in. Thanks for the alert. Be sure to play along, but make it believable."

* * *

Hugh walked into Nash's expansive lab and noticed it was deserted. He wondered what was going on. Mike heard Hugh enter the lab and watched him in the reflection in Kent's glass door. He studied Hugh for a moment before he spoke.

"Hi, Hugh. I'm in here, in Kent's office. Come on in."

Hugh sat down in front of Kent's desk and waited for Mike to speak. He looked tense; his eyes darted. The lab was eerily quiet, in marked contrast to its normal bustling level of activity.

"Kent will be back soon, but I wanted to talk to you privately before he returned. I need your help. And I need Kent's help to interpret what is happening with Thompson's gene therapy study. So I had to tell Kent what I know; I saw no way to avoid that. I know I can trust him, but I need to know how you want to be involved. You said you'd help me get information from Thompson, but is it OK for Kent to know you're the one getting me the information?"

"Can Dr. Nash keep his mouth shut?"

"I'd trust him with my life, so I'd say so."

"Will he tell his wife?"

"Well, first of all, his wife is in the ICU recovering from a severe concussion. So he's not going to tell her in the near future. Secondly, he most likely will not ever tell her in order to protect her. If you need to know, I can feel him out. But I'm not sure how to absolutely know unless I ask him directly."

"What do you mean, 'protect her'?"

"Hugh, we believe a mob-type organization may be behind this illegal gene therapy study. Whoever it is, we believe we should be very careful because they may decide to use force to quiet anyone who knows about their scheme. So, you may not want anyone to know that you know anything about this."

"Boy, Doc, this sure is getting exciting. Do you really think this is a large operation?"

"I really doubt Dr. Thompson would risk his career over a small study with only 10 participants unless big money was involved."

"Good point. But, Doc, what would you tell Dr. Nash about how you're getting Thompson's information if you don't tell him about me?"

"I could suggest I had an informant in Thompson's office. He would probably surmise one of Thompson's staff was helping me. Two of them are patients of mine, and he would most likely figure that was my source. He wouldn't push if I told him my source wanted to remain anonymous."

"Then let's leave me out of the loop for now. What do you need?"

"I need the autopsy report on Matt Madison, current testing on Jennifer Fields, and all other medical records on both of them.

Later, I will need copies of all the records on every study participant. You had better get going now. Dr. Nash is in the back with his staff, and he could return in just a few minutes. We shouldn't be seen together. Call me on my cell phone, pretend to be my brother, and tell me when you will meet me for a beer, or whatever, depending on the time of day."

"I didn't know you had a brother."

"I don't."

"Oh. OK, I understand. I'll call you tonight."

* * *

Hugh left, knowing the information Mike wanted was already being prepared. He returned to his office and called Dean.

"Mr. Carter, any instructions?"

"Yes, call him right after work, and get him the information he wants early this evening. We need them to get started without any more delay. And good job telling Naylor you didn't want Nash to know about you. It sounds more believable. We can always have you change your mind later if we need to."

Hugh smiled knowing he was doing a great acting job not only on Mike Naylor, but also on Dean Carter. All he had to do was ride this gene therapy gig with the Brey Agency through until the field testing was completed on the human athlete guinea pigs and then he would pirate the know-how away for Al-Qaeda. Then not only would he become a physically supreme warrior and a hero for Islam, he could begin to make all those pay for the difficult time and unfair treatment 'they' had given him. He would be judge and jury for the pathetic lazy American infidels who had ruined his mother's life and his inside track for a political future here in America.

Mike left for Thompson's office. Wendy had appeared fine when they returned and had been out of the hospital since Thursday morning. Dr. Thompson had an event monitor on her 24 hours a day and was checking it before and after school. He ran into Thompson in the hall near his office.

"Mike, I'm glad I caught you. Welcome home. I need to tell you about Wendy."

"That's why I'm here. Let's go into this conference room."

"Wendy had multifocal atrial and ventricular beats during stress testing on Wednesday at a moderately high level of exertion. Of course, for Wendy, it was really not a very high level of exertion, so I am concerned. I've told her that she is not to exert herself in any way and that I will check her ambulatory cardiac monitor twice a day. So far, she has had no abnormal rhythms. None of my testing so far has shown a reason for her cardiac excitability. Her lab work and echocardiogram are perfect. I'd like to send her to Boston for electrophysiologic testing. One of the world's best, Dr. Williams, is at Mass General, and he has agreed to see her any time. And he'll avoid the press, which I'm sure you'd prefer."

"I've already arranged for her to see Dr. Dorland in Philadelphia at Jefferson. She also has an excellent reputation, and she's much closer. Wendy and I would feel more comfortable close to home. Besides, Dorland's agreed to see her here tonight as a favor to me, and then she can go to her lab tomorrow in Philadelphia. They can do extensive testing on her on Saturday since they don't usually schedule patients on weekends. Dorland trained with Williams, so maybe they can confer, and we'd have the best of both worlds helping Wendy."

"Dorland is fine. I'll call her. When is she seeing Wendy? I'd like to be there if she's coming to Wilmington to see Wendy."

"That's fine. I'm glad you're willing to work with her. She was going to see Wendy in my office around 6 tonight. Do you think she could do her examination in your lab, in case she needs any of your equipment?"

"I'll set it up."

"Great. I'll see you tonight at 6."

* * *

Mike then headed for Kent's lab. His partner was covering patients, and it looked like he'd have to do so for several days.

When Mike walked into Kent's office, he saw three of his staff huddled around Kent's desk deeply immersed in charts.

"Hi, Mike," said Kent. "Come on in. We're planning a 48-channel ECG instead of the usual 12 channels to see if we can refine our investigation of Wendy tonight. Maybe you could get Dorland to see Wendy in our lab."

"I just arranged for the use of Thompson's lab at 6 tonight, but I'm sure we could use whichever lab is better."

"Thompson has much more refined cardiac equipment than we do. And I'm sure Dorland will know how to use it better than we do. I'm really glad she's coming tonight. I don't feel comfortable waiting any longer to get started with Wendy's testing. I just wish we had the autopsy reports for review now."

"Ken Turner faxed me Kim Taylor's autopsy report at home this morning. Here it is. It shows widespread cardiac infarction, most likely from a dysrhythmia. But take a look at the description of the myocardium."

Kent read the cardiac section out loud. "Diffuse nonfocal necrosis most likely secondary to refractory cardiac dysrhythmia. Mild cardiomegaly compatible with high-level athletic conditioning. Diffuse amyloid-like protein deposition throughout the myocardium, most pronounced at the sinus nodal and AV nodal areas."

Kent looked up. "It sure sounds like excess protein accumulated in the heart and especially around the conducting system. I read that something like that happened in the first large-series dog study, which I believe was done at the University of Washington. They had excellent healing of induced fractures, but some of the dogs died from heart attacks. I thought staying away from the 17-sulfa side chains eliminated that problem. I'll have to call Dr. Gebhart out there. Sara, would you please . . ."

"I'm on it," interrupted Sara. "I'll have their articles on your desk in 20 minutes."

"Mike, I met a graduate student named Bob Towson, from Gebhart's program, on the plane to Alaska. Maybe I should call him, too. He sounded gung-ho. He may be willing to help Gebhart as well. It can't hurt to ask. I'll ask Gebhart about Towson when I call. He'll probably think he's a spy for me, but we'll take all the help we can get right now. You know, Mike, if Matt's autopsy shows a similar finding, we may have identified the problem. That will help us in figuring out how to correct the problem sooner, but that could still take weeks or months. Has Wendy stopped taking the supplements?"

"No. I told her to continue taking them because I didn't know if stopping them suddenly would be more harmful than continuing them."

"I'd say she should stop for now in light of Kim's autopsy. Those supplements, the gene therapy stimulants, may be causing this protein deposition, and we don't want any more to accumulate. We should have Matt's autopsy report soon, and we can rethink our decision as soon as we see the report."

"All right. I'll tell Dorland we're concerned about a medication or disease process depositing excess protein and we suggest all medications and supplements be stopped for now. I'm sure Dorland will agree, especially since Wendy is supposed to be so healthy and doesn't need nutritional supplements."

"That should be a tactful way to work with Thompson. I'll call him to coordinate our examination tonight. I'm sure he'll be pleased we're all coming to his lab."

"See you tonight. Call me on my cell phone if you need me. Pretend you're my brother and talk figuratively. I'll figure out what you want. Remember, we have to be careful in case someone is listening."

"I'll do my best. See you tonight."

Thirty-Four

Friday, May 16, 5 PM
Kelly Hospital, Wilmington, Delaware

The monitor showed a classic R-on-T phenomenon and resultant ventricular tachycardia. The cardiac monitor blared its alarm and the words ***"Ventricular tachycardia! Check patient and check leads!"*** appeared in bright red letters at the top of the screen. Wendy simultaneously said to Susan Larson, the exercise physiologist running the test, "I don't feel so good. I have to stop. I feel dizzy . . ." Susan immediately hit the stop control on the treadmill and reached to grab Wendy, holding her up as her knees buckled and she passed out. Susan cradled her in her arms and set her down on the carpeted floor next to the exercise treadmill.

Dr. Thompson was panic-stricken. His face was ashen, and he stared at the monitor in disbelief. Susan's voice brought him back to reality. "Dr. Thompson, we've got to shock her now! Get the paddles ready. Go!"

"All right," replied Thompson. "I'm getting them ready. 300?"

Normally, the first shock is given at 200 joules for witnessed ventricular fibrillation in a patient Wendy's size, but Susan wasn't so sure that Dr. Thompson was going to be able to think clearly during this emergency. Where did he come up with 300?

"360 is fine. Let's do it now," said Susan, as calmly as possible.

"Clear," said Thompson. "I'm going to shock on 3."

"Do it on one," said Susan. "I'm clear, and we're the only ones here! Hit it."

Thompson pressed lightly on the paddles and simultaneously hit the discharge buttons on both paddles. Wendy suddenly stiffened and arched her back as the jolt hit. The wavy chaotic line of ventricular fibrillation changed to a flat line for 3 seconds and then a normal sinus beat appeared. Thompson continued to stare at the monitor. He didn't speak, and he seemed unfazed by the return of a normal rhythm.

Susan felt for a pulse. It was strong, and Wendy's breathing became normal. Wendy started to stir, although she was not aware of what was happening.

"Damn," said Thompson. "She was only walking and then she went into V tach! This must mean she's getting worse."

"What do you mean, 'getting worse'?" asked Susan. "I thought she was in great shape. What's going on to cause such a serious arrhythmia?"

"Yeah, right, she is in good shape, but for some reason, she's developed an extreme conductive system sensitivity to exertion. I wish the Doppler echo and MRI would show me what's causing this. Now we have to hope the electrophysiologic studies tonight will explain why she's so prone to V tach. I'm going to order a Cardiolyte scan and check protein levels and every lab test available, including an EBT! I've got to find out what happened to cause this!"

"Shall I order electrolytes, magnesium, and calcium stat? And I figure you want her admitted to Medical ICU?" asked Susan.

"Yes, definitely. And don't leave her until she's hooked up in the MICU. I'm going to call her parents and Dr. Nash so he can alert Dr. Dorland in advance of the electrophysiologic studies they're planning."

"I'll stay with her for a few hours. I'll keep you posted if anything else happens."

"Thanks, Susan. I really appreciate your help."
"No problem."

* * *

Thompson retreated to his office to page Mike Naylor. He tapped his fingers nervously on the counter while waiting for the return call. He had to keep Wendy in good health until Dr. Nash and Dr. Dorland could figure out what was wrong. If Wendy died now, he knew he'd be in trouble. Too many people knew about his illicit study to keep quiet. If the authorities didn't get him, the Brey Agency would. Fortunately, Naylor answered promptly. Thompson told him what had occurred and reassured him that Wendy was stable and the arrhythmia only seemed to happen during exercise. He noted that he was keeping Wendy quiet in the Medical ICU until Dr. Dorland could examine her later tonight. He figured Dorland would not do any studies on Wendy tonight because of her extreme cardiac excitability, but that she would no doubt want to transfer Wendy to Jefferson Hospital in Philadelphia, where she could perform a cardiac catheterization tomorrow. There, she could also do extensive electrophysiologic studies. Mike was appreciative of the call and said he would be in to see Wendy very soon. He decided to call Ken Turner on his way to the MICU to see if Turner had any luck getting the autopsy report on Matt Madison.

As soon as Thompson hung up with Naylor, he called Kent Nash to update him. Nash said he would alert Dr. Dorland, who was expected around 7 PM. He would make sure she reserved her top team for a cardiac cath on Wendy tomorrow. She should be able to get operating room time on Saturday since Wendy's case was an emergency. Besides the electrophysiologic studies, Dr. Dorland wanted Wendy to have catheterization ultrasound readings of the coronary arteries and the entire myocardium. Her lab was one of only three in the United States testing the brand new state-of-the-art equipment. Nash had requested the ultrasound readings to see if the coronary arteries were thickened with fibrous tissue as he suspected. Thompson agreed; he wanted every test possible done to find out what was happening.

* * *

Mike was extremely glad to see Wendy looking OK after her recent ordeal. She was worried, though, and Mike had a hard time reassuring her since he wasn't convinced himself that all would be well. Mike was feeling extremely guilty for getting Wendy into this predicament. He spoke to her about the vast talent of Dr. Nash and his hope that he and Dr. Dorland would be sure to figure out what was happening. While Mike was sitting on Wendy's bed talking to her, a nurse brought him a fax.

"Dr. Naylor," said the ICU nurse, "this fax just came in here for you. It's marked urgent."

"Thank you, Dana. I was looking for this." Mike read the fax, which was the autopsy report on Matt Madison. He told Wendy that he'd be nearby at Kent's lab and would return very soon. He then told Dana to call him immediately if anything changed and quickly headed for Nash's lab.

Thirty-Five

Friday, May 16
Kent Nash's Lab, Kelly Hospital, Wilmington, Delaware

Mike barged into Kent Nash's office and thrust Matt Madison's autopsy report on the desk so he could read the crux of the report first. "Heavy particulate protein deposition throughout the myocardium and coronary arteries resulting in a 30% thickening of the ventricular and artery wall thickness. Deposition around the sinus and AV nodes is especially thick."

"That has to be the problem," said Kent. "I bet this protein accumulating is, in effect, a waste product of the enhanced myocardial cells that were stimulated by the gene therapy code, making the cells operate at a much higher capacity. This protein was designed to speed healing of ligaments in joints. It wasn't supposed to be used for longer than a few months. We didn't know what effect long-term use would have on the organ systems in the body. Now, thanks to Thompson, we're getting a good idea of what it does to the heart."

"Are you sure this is the problem?" asked Mike. "Could there be something else as well?"

"Of course," said Kent. "There can always be more. But since we're in a hurry here, let's deal with the most likely things first. We have heavy excess protein accumulation in the heart muscle and conducting system. We have cardiac irritability and easily induced ventricular tachycardia in Wendy. Matt and Kim both had sudden death, most likely from a dysrhythmia. Jennifer Fields had a life-threatening heart rhythm and is recovering from a small heart attack. She has had to stay on procainamide to keep her out of recurrent ventricular tachycardia. I'd say we've found the problem. If the ultrasound of Wendy's coronary arteries shows them to be thickened with a protein-like density, that will be enough to start working on figuring out a way to break down the excess protein without damaging the muscle cells of the heart."

"Do you have any idea how to do that?" asked Mike.

"Gebhart used another gene therapy code to stimulate the very same cells that made the excess protein to produce a low level of a collagenase substance that is specific for the new protein. It cleaves the new protein into three segments, which readily dissipate and are carried away by the lymphatic system. He actually refined the production of collagenase to make a type that didn't damage muscle cells. However, I'm not sure if he took it far enough to make sure the collagen holding blood vessels together wasn't affected. I wonder why these athletes are producing excess protein. There are no 17-sulfa side chains in my gene therapy codes. That's very curious. That's not important right now, though. I'll figure that out later. The protein accumulation shouldn't continue beyond 24 hours of the last dose Wendy received. I built in a self-limiting clock in the gene therapy stimulant just so I could stop the effects in a hurry if something untoward happened."

"What does that mean for Wendy?" asked Mike.

"It means the dangerous protein accumulation will stop within 24 hours of Wendy's last dose of 'nutrition' from Thompson's study. I know there is a way to dissolve the damaging protein away from the heart muscle and conducting system. I don't know what effect the antidote, so to speak, will have on the blood vessels feeding the heart, or the rest of the body for that matter. We must quickly confirm whether or not Wendy has this problem with the ultrasound cardiac catheterization tomorrow. And it means I have to talk to Gebhart as soon as possible. He is the one working on this problem, or at least he was."

"Did you speak to him yet?"

"No. Not yet. He was lecturing to medical students when I called. His secretary promised he would call as soon as he returned to his office."

"Was he definitely coming back to his office after the lecture?"

"That's a good question. His secretary said he would be back just as soon as the lecture was over. She said he was in the middle of an important experiment and his research fellows desperately needed his guidance. Besides, he lives in his lab. He's been divorced for 4 years and probably didn't even know it the first year because he never went home. He'll go back. Don't worry about that."

"Will he call, or will he get lost in his experiment and forget?"

"That's another very good question, especially since you don't know Gebhart. Yes, he could very easily lose track of time and forget to call. But that's where Sally, his secretary, comes in. We go way back, and in the interest of time, suffice it to say that she will make sure he calls. She owes me a few favors, and I told her how important it was that he call immediately. I considered having his lecture interrupted, but I'm glad I didn't now because of all this information we just learned. It's about 3 in the afternoon their time, so his lecture should end soon. Figure 10 to 15 minutes for questions from students after class, 5 minutes to his lab, and a few clever words from Sally. I figure he'll call in 23 minutes. If not, I'll check in with Sally at half past."

"Did Jennifer get cath'd?"

"Sure did," said Kent, "although she was catheterized here in Wilmington. That means there were no 360° ultrasound pictures from inside the coronary arteries. They're only available with Dorland at Jefferson, Williams in Boston, and Benton at UCLA. I heard the arteries were clean, by the conventional method. But I'm sure they don't know how thick they are or if there's excess protein deposition inside the artery wall."

"What should we do in the next 23 minutes while we're waiting for Gebhart's call?"

"You should make sure Wendy doesn't take any more 'nutrition.' And find out when her last dose was. You can reassure her she probably won't get any worse, and then you can call Dorland. Maybe she'll agree to cath Wendy tonight up in Philly."

"What do you mean, 'probably won't get worse'?"

"She won't accumulate any more protein, but if the protein already there is so thick it's hampering the capillary-level circulation, she could be infarcting tissue a few cells at a time. In that case, she could gradually get worse. But, I'm hopeful. Wendy is in such good shape, that's unlikely. But you asked."

"OK," said Mike. "Thanks for the information."

* * *

Mike smiled for the first time in days and headed off to see Wendy. He was feeling a little better and was amazed at the speed at which answers were coming. Now if only Gebhart had figured out how to safely get rid of this protein. He felt his pager vibrating. It was a message from his partner. Mike stopped at the nurse's station in the ICU to call Bill Owens back.

"Bill, what's up? It's Mike."

"Mike, please sit down. I don't know how to tell you this."

"OK, I'm sitting. Now tell me. What's up?"

"Mike, I just heard on the radio that Tom and Marsha Donovan were killed in an auto accident in Alaska."

"What?! Where did you hear this?"

"On WSRS. The local stations picked up the story from CNN. I was in my car on my way to make rounds, and I heard something about two local attorneys being killed in an auto accident. The announcer said they were on their way to the airport and their taxi ran off the road killing all three occupants. Two local attorneys, husband and wife, had to be the Donovans, and sure enough, the announcer said the victims were Tom and Marsha. Mike, what in the world is going on? I need to know."

"Bill, you know enough to help if Debbie or I get into trouble, and we call you. But I don't want to tell you more right now because I don't want you to risk becoming a target. If you don't know any names, you're not a liability. Just be sure to look over your shoulder, and don't ask me any questions. And no matter what, don't say anything to anybody. Not even to the police. You understand?"

"I don't like this. I don't like not knowing what's going on. It's not natural for a physician not to be trusted with the whole story."

"Bill, I have to ask you to trust me for awhile. I can't tell you what's going on right now."

"Are you doing something illegal?"

"That question is easy. No. But don't ask me any more questions. It's better right now that you don't know anything. You'll be safe that way."

"It's a good thing we've been together for 15 years, Mike. I wouldn't accept what you're saying right now if I didn't know you so well. I still don't like it. If I find out my family is in jeopardy, you will have to explain to me then. Will you agree to that?"

"Bill, your family is not involved. I would never put your family at risk."

"Good. Any idea how long you need me to cover the practice?"

"Possibly a couple of weeks. I need to know Wendy will be all right before I can concentrate on taking care of patients."

"And we'll still talk each day? You can at least tell me how Wendy is doing."

"That I can do."

"OK, take care of Wendy, Mike. I'll handle the practice."

"Thanks, Bill. I hope I never have to return the favor. But if I do, you know I will be there for you. And please, be careful."

Mike was stunned. He stared at the phone on the desk blankly. *How many tragedies would this involve? Was this truly an accident?* It was an awfully big coincidence. It couldn't be just an accident. Tom and Marsha had to have been killed. And it had to have been done by professionals to make it look so convincing. How did 'they' know the Donovans even knew about all this? How in the world could anyone know the Donovans knew anything? Wait a minute. Could Ken Turner be involved? He was the only person besides Debbie and Kent and the Donovans who knew what was going on. Mike sat back in the chair holding his forehead with his hands. He sat motionless with his hands on his head, thinking.

"Dr. Naylor, are you OK?" asked Dana.

"I'm all right, Dana." He dropped his arms heavily to his lap. "Ow!"

"What happened?" asked Dana. "Did you hit your arm?"

Mike looked down at his right arm as he turned it over to expose the underside that had felt the sudden pain. He saw bleeding and a knick in the skin. Dana saw the wound, too.

"Here, let me clean that for you," said Dana.

"Thanks," said Mike, still a little stunned. He looked in his lap and on his pants for what might have cut him. He leaned further back and stretched his pants and shirt apart looking, expecting to find nothing. He saw nothing that looked unusual.

Dana grabbed his arm, laid it on the counter, twisted it to the outside, and washed it with cold water and soap.

"Ow," said Mike. "What are you using? Hydrochloric acid?"

"Oh, you doctors are the worst patients. Only nurses are worse. I'm just cleaning it with soap and water. You know, basic first aid. The kind your mother invented. Look, your belt has blood on it. Is that where you cut yourself?"

Mike looked at his belt and saw a sharp piece of metal sticking out from his belt, hanging by a tiny hinge, with a small wire running into his belt. It was blood-stained. He didn't recognize the ornament on his belt.

"Oh, that. I guess so," said Mike, amazed he was able to answer at all. He was shocked. Why would a belt ornament have a tiny wire running into his belt fibers? What in the world . . . ?

"There. You're all cleaned up and the wound is dressed. When was your last tetanus shot?"

"Oh, thanks. My tetanus shot is up to date. Unfortunately, I cut myself often. My last shot was just two years ago. Thanks."

Mike studied the ornament and the wire. He stared at it as he moved it around in his fingers. The remaining rivet was firm, holding tightly to his belt. It wouldn't come off easily. He hesitated and stared at it for several minutes before deciding what to do. He checked the belt buckle. Yep, sure enough. It was his belt. The belt buckle was the same "TJU" for Thomas Jefferson University that his parents had given him the day of his medical school graduation. It was a little worn, but it was exactly the same. What was this strange ornament with a wire doing on his belt? Slowly, as he gazed at it, his eyes dilated. *A miniature microphone?* That's what it was! Yes, it had to be a "bug." He stared at the phone again while keeping his finger on the ornament/microphone. He had to think. Should he throw his belt away? He had to warn Debbie and Kent and Bill. But how? OK, if it was a transmitting device, it had to be from a very professional group. It was so small. How did it get there? And when? All he could think of for now was that he better not pull it off just yet. He grabbed a small piece of tape and secured the hinged ornament to his belt so that it wouldn't cut him again. He thought some more. For now, he'd better act normally and get on with helping Wendy. He got up and headed over to her bed. He stopped on the way to ask Dana to try to reach Dr. Dorland on her cell phone.

"Hi, Dad," said Wendy. "I was beginning to wonder if you were coming over here. You were at the nurses' desk for a long time."

"I just heard some bad news, Wendy. Tom and Marsha Donovan were killed in an auto accident."

"Oh no!" said Wendy. "What happened?"

"They were riding in a taxi to the airport in Alaska and were killed when their taxi ran off the road."

"They were such nice people," said Wendy. "I know you were good friends with them. Are you sure they were killed?"

"Bill Owens called me. I believe the report is probably accurate. He said he heard it on the radio."

"I'm so sorry, Dad."

"Thank you, Wendy." Mike paused. There was silence between them for several seconds. Then Mike spoke. "Now look, I came in here to give you a message from Dr. Nash. He thinks he's found out what's causing the irregular heart rhythms." Mike then remembered the bug. "Dr. Dorland should be here in a half hour. Dr. Nash wants her to cath you as soon as possible so he can get started on your treatment. Meanwhile, the procainamide should keep your heart rhythm stable. I called Dr. Dorland to update her."

"When will she cath me?"

"Hopefully either tonight, or first thing in the morning, up in Philly."

"Does that hurt?"

"Not very much. They numb your skin where they insert the catheter. It doesn't take long."

"OK, I'm ready. I'd sure like to get out of here."

"Soon, Wendy. Soon."

Thirty-Six

Saturday, May 17
Kent Nash's Lab, Kelly Hospital, Wilmington, Delaware

Mike left the ICU and went directly to Kent Nash's lab. He motioned for Kent to come into his office. After Kent went inside, Mike shut the door. Mike looked up at the ceiling and studied the tiles and then the door frame.

"What are you doing?" asked Kent.

Mike held his finger up to his lips and sat down. "I came to tell you about some bad news I just heard."

Kent wondered what was going on, but decided to honor Mike's request for quiet.

Mike continued, "Bill Owens called me to tell me he heard Tom and Marsha were killed in an auto accident in Alaska."

"What?! That's not possible!"

Mike held his finger to his lips again. "I know you must find it as hard to believe as I do since they were such good friends and we were just with them two days ago. But it was on the radio that two local attorneys were killed on their way to the airport. I'm sorry to have to tell you."

"I don't know what to say," said Kent.

"There isn't much to say," said Mike. "Words don't describe what we're feeling, and they don't seem to be much help right now." Mike continued his scan of the room looking for a hidden camera or wire. He focused on the desk lamp. He stood up and leaned over Kent's desk and grabbed a small tablet of paper. He wrote a short note and held it up against his chest for Kent to see. It read, "*We're being monitored.*"

Kent just stared blankly at Mike. "I don't know what to say. I can't believe this. What is happening to so many people I know?" Kent paused to think. "Are you OK, Mike?" Kent looked at his friend and waited for an answer.

Mike handed him a section of the newspaper on the chair next to him and said, "Kent, read this about Wendy. Let me know what you think."

Kent looked at the newspaper he was handed. It was the local section and the lead article was titled, "Local Church Group Selected for National Humanitarian Award." It wasn't about Wendy. Kent caught on that this was a way to give them time to sit quietly without raising the suspicion of anyone listening.

Mike wrote three more notes: "*My belt.*" "*Maybe my shoes and maybe your office.*" "*We should examine our clothes, our homes, and our offices.*"

Kent looked behind Mike, and once he was convinced there could be no camera there, he wrote, "*Just how are we supposed to speak to each other?*"

Mike wrote another note, folded it, and handed it to Kent. Then he motioned to Kent waving his hand gently and then pointed to the newspaper.

Kent was startled and then a little bothered that he understood his time was up and he was supposed to comment on Wendy's "report." He thought for a moment and said, "Mike, what do you make of this report?"

Mike chuckled to himself, realizing Kent just copped out by deferring to him. "It seems to me that the procainamide is controlling her rhythm. I placed a call to Dr. Dorland, and she's supposed to call us in your office. She's probably en route here right now, so we may actually see her before she calls back."

They sat in silence again. Kent looked uneasy and confused. He took the folded note Mike gave him and read it. "*We have to silently warn Debbie and Bill. I'm not sure we should trust Ken Turner yet. Can you think of anyone else?*"

Just then, Kent's phone rang. Kent jolted upright and stared at the phone. Mike noticed his friend was unsure what to do so he picked up the receiver.

"Mike Naylor."

"Hi, Mike. This is Brenda Dorland. I'll be there in 10 to 15 minutes. Can we talk then, or should we start now?"

"We can talk then, Brenda. That will be plenty of time."

"How's our patient?"

"Stable, and looking forward to meeting you."

"Fine. I'm in the car at the state line now. See you all soon."

Mike wrote another note. "*Leave her out of the loop for now, for her protection.*" Kent nodded. He wasn't adapting well as an actor yet. The phone rang again. Mike answered again.

"Mike Naylor."

"Dr. Naylor, this is Andy Gebhart. How are you? Is my fearless competitor there? For some reason, he's hot to speak to me."

"I'm fine, and Kent's right here." Mike handed the phone to Kent, who was still looking like a frightened kid forgetting his lines in the school play.

Kent rallied. "Hi, Andy. It's Kent."

"I know who it is. I called you back. What's happening in Delaware? You into dog studies yet?"

Andy's rascally tone loosened Kent up. "We're beyond dog studies. We don't believe in hurting man's best friend. We have a monkey study going, however, and I need some help from you."

"Be glad to help. You hit the last one right. Those 17-sulfa side chains fixed our problem pronto."

"That's what I need your help on. There must be something else laying down protein on a much slower basis. We have detected protein accumulations in the myocardium and conducting system after two years, even though we've eliminated all 17-sulfa side chains. How's your protein dissolution work coming along?"

"We're making progress. We have a gene therapy messenger that produces a collagenase protein that dissolves the artificial ligament protein accumulations in organs. It has to be given with a co-agent that stimulates endothelial repair in a ratio of 1:2.35 or the dog will bleed to death. If the ratio is greater than 1:2.67, a hypercoagulable state develops and the dog will start to get clots around the body and have a stroke or shut his kidneys down. If the ratio is less than 1:1.5, significant bleeding still occurs. We've calculated adjustments to these ratios for body mass, thyroid hormone, and baseline INR readings. We don't have calculations for body temperature, alterations in liver function, or any coagulation abnormalities. What's this all about? Do you have a favorite monkey you want to save? You know you're not supposed to get attached to your test animals."

"Can you fax me the adjustment ratio calculations? We'd like to save our whole group of monkeys. We'd like to study the effects of this protein accumulation over a long period of time, so we need to keep our monkeys alive."

"No problem. But the calculations won't be any good without the messenger protein. I suppose you want a year's supply of that, too."

"Six months will do. How about I send a plane to Washington to haul the stuff back here?"

"Well, OK. You must be really attached to these monkeys. I'll see if I can find someone to travel with the protein to be sure it's kept at the right temperature and remains stable. I'll try to get someone who can show you how we adjust the formulas."

"How about sending Bob Towson? Is he knowledgeable enough?"

"Yes, Bob can handle this. How did you know he's here? Did we recruit him away from you?"

"I met him a week or two ago on a plane trip to Alaska. He seemed very interested in helping."

"Bob's always up for a road trip. It is Saturday, but I'm sure he'll agree to go. I'll get him up to speed and get a load ready for you. When will your airplane be here?"

"I'll call you back. Maybe in 4 to 5 hours."

"We'll be ready. If Bob can't go, I'll recruit someone else."

"That's great. I really appreciate your help. You've probably saved us months. I'll be sure to send you my data as soon as I can."

"Anytime, my friend. We have to work together to beat Johnson in Chicago. He'll probably sell his breakthroughs to the highest bidder. Who knows what undesirable group his research will benefit."

Kent hung up and looked at Mike. Mike looked thoughtful.

"I'll call Ken Turner and get his jet to Washington. He said he'd keep his crew on standby."

Both men sat silently, planning their next move. After a few minutes, Mike said, "As soon as we get the protein here, we can adjust the ratios for humans and start treating Wendy within an hour or two of its arrival."

Kent wrinkled his forehead and tilted his head looking at Mike in a totally perplexed manner. Mike just held his finger to his lips for a brief moment and then said, "I'm going to head over to the ICU to be with Wendy. If Brenda Dorland comes there first, I'll call you. Otherwise, if you see her first, bring her right over to the ICU, and we'll take her to Thompson's lab." Mike wrote one more note, which read, "*Since we probably won't be able to get rid of every bug, we can at least try to use them to our advantage. Also, burn these notes.*"

Kent needed time to think about what Mike meant.

Mike left for the ICU, and while he was walking, he dialed Ken Turner on his cell phone. Ken agreed to send his plane to Washington. He said it would leave in 30 minutes and take approximately 4 hours to arrive. Mike then called Gebhart and told his secretary, Sally, when to expect the courier flight. Sally promised Mike that Bob Towson and the protein would be at the general aviation terminal waiting for the plane. Turnaround should take only as long as it took to fuel the plane.

In the ICU, Brenda Dorland listened carefully to every detail Kent described about Wendy and the similar results in the case histories of Jennifer, Matt, and Kim. It was clear to her that Kent was right. Wendy needed an ultrasound cardiac catheterization and any other testing should be deferred until the results of the catheterization were known. Electrophysiologic testing might precipitate another bout of ventricular tachycardia, and although it would probably be easily controlled, that was not guaranteed and was unnecessary if Wendy's catheterization demonstrated similar protein accumulation. Dorland said she could have a team ready to go at 6 AM at Jefferson and that they could accept Wendy in transfer immediately so she would be ready.

Mike took Debbie into the nurse's station ICU conference room to communicate with her using a note pad and a finger on his lips. She caught on readily and was able to provide background chitchat while Mike was fumbling with the notes. After hearing the whole story, Debbie decided she should go to Boston to check out Ken Turner and Mark McCormack. Mike didn't agree. He thought the police should handle that, but she thought it was too dangerous to wait. They didn't know when they could go to the police, and they had to know who they were up against to have a shot at saving their lives. She figured Mike should concentrate on saving Wendy, and meanwhile, she would start looking ahead to how they were going to survive once Wendy was safe. Mike protested, but Debbie just held her finger to her lips and waved goodbye. Then she hugged Mike, looked him in the eye, and placed her finger on his lips. He knew it was pointless to try to change her mind.

Thirty-Seven

Saturday, May 17
Mike & Debbie Naylor's Home, Wilmington, Delaware

Debbie stopped at home, booked a flight to Boston on her computer in her maiden name, quickly packed a light bag, and then took all the money they had in their safe—$4,000. She then called her friend Katie Wilson, who was a travel agent. She asked Katie to turn on instant messaging so they could talk in private with their computers. Debbie was hoping that whoever was monitoring them had not bugged her computer, although after hearing her refer Katie to her computer, that method of conversation would probably not be secure for very long. She told Katie she was having a problem with her phone and asked her what reasonably priced but decent hotel would be near the Boston Elite Sports Medicine Center. Debbie then reserved a room at the Embassy Suites on Forrest Street using her computer and her maiden name once again. She wrote a note to Mike, giving him the address and phone number for the Embassy Suites and telling him to use her maiden name if he needed to contact her, and sealed it in an envelope. She placed the envelope under his pillow, hoping no one else would find it if their home was being searched.

Debbie then went into Wendy's room and put on a pair of her daughter's underclothing and a baggy sweat suit. She inspected the clothing for anything hard or any wires and found nothing. She then left the bag she had packed in her closet and walked at least a mile, cutting through her neighbors' yards to a payphone to call for a taxi. She had the taxi meet her a block away at a busy intersection. Debbie ran into the busy street and hopped into the taxi. She had the taxi take her to the international terminal at the Philadelphia airport, and after cutting back and forth across the drive, she then caught the shuttle to the domestic terminal in an effort to avoid being followed. Shuttles were going to Boston every hour until 10 at night. She just had time to catch the last one.

While waiting for the plane, she figured that in order not to be traced, she had to use cash for all her expenses in Boston and she therefore had to conserve her limited supply. She realized that she should also carefully go through her purse and get rid of all her identification. She could leave identifying items in the hotel safe in her room. She figured she could cash a check for more money if necessary, but preferred not to take that risk in case she was being followed or tracked. Checks and credit cards can give away where a person is if someone has connections or a computer link with her bank. She very carefully looked around the gate area and kept changing where she stood to see if she could notice if anyone was watching her. No one seemed to stand out in the usual assortment of characters that fill up airports worldwide. She spent her time waiting for her plane at the gate across from hers. She did not check in at her gate; she went to the desk at the gate across from hers, where she was waiting, showed the gate attendant her ticket, and managed to talk to her about her flight without having her point to where she should go. She hoped that would convince anyone watching that she was waiting for the flight to Atlanta, not Boston. She decided to wait until the last boarding call to board the airplane to make it as difficult as possible for someone following her to get on her flight.

Her strategy seemed to work. The gate attendants were very accommodating. They were not fazed at her tardy request to board;

apparently they were quite used to late arrivals for the shuttle. The flight was full. Debbie was extremely confident that no unwanted passengers were traveling with her.

Once in the air, she thought about using the AirPhone. She thought that at least on the plane, no one could hear what she would say. But the only person she wanted to call was Mike, and his phones were likely tapped. Suddenly, it occurred to her to call Marshall Keller since he was a financial expert and might be able to help her figure out who was backing Wendy's study in Boston. But she finally decided cellular calls were too easy to trace. She knew she was on her own.

As she exited the airplane, she quickly ducked into the thick of the crowd and headed away from the baggage claim area. She remembered a trick Marshall had told her about how to get a taxi when the airport was extremely busy. She'd use the maneuver more to stay hidden than to get out more quickly. She headed to the taxi dispatch area and timed her sprint to catch the taxi driver just getting into his cab who was next to leave the staging area and get in line at the arriving passenger area. Picking up a taxi here normally was not permitted, but when successful it meant getting out of the airport much sooner and away from the crowds. Most drivers in this situation would justify their action by telling their dispatcher that the passenger initiated the pickup and was in a desperate hurry.

Debbie gave her driver a destination two blocks away from her hotel and then slid down low in the back seat. She asked the driver to watch for anyone following her. He replied without emotion, "No problem, ma'am." He looked rather unimpressed. Debbie was satisfied with that, and she kept her face down and hidden as much as possible so he might have a difficult time describing his passenger to an interested person. She thought about how many details she must attend to in order not to be followed or discovered. She was amazed at how difficult it was to adjust to traveling without the benefit of credit cards, checks, and a cellular phone. How did people survive just a few years ago?

She got out of the taxi after paying the driver and headed directly inside the first department store she saw. She figured the prices in center city Boston would be high and was pleased that she had wandered into a Sears. Debbie bought three outfits and a supply of underwear and then headed for the luggage department. She purchased the most unique, yet plain-colored suitcase she could find, trying to make it difficult for anyone to switch bags with her. She also did not want to stand out with a wild-colored bag. She paid for the bag in cash and then put her new clothes into the bag. Now she figured she could check into the Embassy Suites without attracting attention.

With her suitcase in hand, she headed out of the store and directly toward her hotel. She debated whether or not to tell the hotel clerk that she had lost her wallet and credit cards and had to pay with cash or just pay with cash and act naturally. She figured if she started making up stories, she might not remember everything she said and might end up looking suspicious. What the heck—some people still used cash. Why not use it and act like it's the natural thing to do? Next, she thought again about what name to use. She didn't have the energy to think about the possibilities and advantages of keeping her first name versus using a totally different name; she would just change the last name. That way, she would feel quite natural and was less likely to get confused. She would stay with Debbie Johnson, her maiden name. If someone were hot enough on her trail to check out her hotel, using a totally different name would be of no use at that point. She checked in, almost accepted the room assigned to her, and then at the last moment, asked to change the room, saying she wanted one on the other side of the building. If someone were bugging her room, they'd have to start over. She wasn't about to make it easy. She went to the mini mart in the lobby area and purchased some food for her dinner and breakfast. Then, she stopped at the pay phone bank. Fortunately, the Embassy Suites was prestigious enough to actually have phone books at their pay phones. She selected a relatively private phone station.

Her first call was to the Boston Elite Sports Medicine Center. She got the answering service, demanded to speak to the director, Mark McCormack, and said it was an emergency and that she would hold. The exchange offered to have him call back, but she declined, saying she was at a pay phone and that his call wouldn't get through. She would just stay on the line and wait. Debbie told the operator to page Dr. McCormack for a call holding, a great trick to get a physician to call back quickly. Besides, the operator's business charged at least triple for such service. The operator promptly figured she was dealing with someone in the know and she had better do what was asked or she may end up hearing about it.

"This is Dr. McCormack. Did someone page me to this number?"

"Yes, Dr. McCormack. I did. I'm sorry to interrupt you in the evening, but it's urgent I talk to you. My name is Debbie Johnson, and I have a 14-year-old son named Brad who's dying to be a professional football player. And I understand you are the only person I should talk to about that. I'm calling you at night because I want to keep my privacy, but I'd like to meet with you as soon as possible to work out any arrangements. I believe I can make it worth your while financially."

"Yes, Mrs. Johnson. Who referred you to me?"

"A Mr. Ken Turner told me about your program. He said you could get me in touch with the folks who would help me get my son into your conditioning program."

"And when would you like to meet?"

"Tonight, or anytime tomorrow would be fine. I see no point in waiting."

"OK, how about tomorrow afternoon at 2 PM at the Sports Medicine Center? I'll be there finishing up some paperwork."

"That's fine with me. Don't you have to confer with your backers?"

"No, not really. They will defer to me, if I believe your son is right for the study."

"Look, Dr. McCormack, I do wish to meet with you before I agree to have you work with my son. But I also need to meet the folks behind this enterprise if I'm going to be dropping substantial money into this venture."

"Are you saying you wish to be an investor?"

"With what Ken Turner told me it could cost, I would say so. I don't plan to invest that much money without a good possibility of a financial return along with some sort of guaranteed results for my son!"

"Well, Mrs. Johnson, I'll see what I can do. Where can I call you back?"

"I'm in town for the weekend, but I haven't checked into my hotel yet. How about I call you, say around 9 tomorrow morning? What number shall I call? I'd really like to avoid the delay and hassle with your answering service."

"Mrs. Johnson, I guarantee you they will know your name tomorrow and will give you outstanding service. Please let me know if they let you down at any time."

"Fine. Until then, goodbye, Dr. McCormack."

"Goodnight, Mrs. Johnson."

* * *

Debbie decided she should call Marshall Keller, from a different pay phone. First, she called her friend Katie Wilson, the travel agent, to ask another favor.

"Katie, this is Debbie. I need your help. I can't explain everything right now, but I will in a few days when I get home. I called you because I know I can trust you. I need you to call me back at this phone number and then make a three-way conference call for me. Can you please do that?"

"Debbie, is everything all right?"

"No, everything isn't all right. So far, things are holding on, but they aren't all right. Hopefully they will be. Mike and I are fine, but we're worried about Wendy and the study she's in. I can't go into any more detail right now. You have to trust me. I just need you to make a conference call for me so no one will know I'm in Boston."

"Debbie, you're scaring me."

"I'm frightened too, but I'm safe for now. Will you please make the call?"

"OK, Debbie. I'll call you right back."

Debbie figured that if Katie initiated the call, Marshall's caller ID would try to indicate Katie's phone number. Since Katie had that feature blocked, her number would not be disclosed. And Marshall would only know it was a local call. Therefore, he would think she was in Delaware and wouldn't let it slip to anyone that she was in Boston. Wilmington was such a small town; the word could easily get around to the wrong person that she was in Boston. She believed Katie could keep quiet and would not be traced. It should work, and it should be safe. Debbie answered on the first ring.

"Hello."

"Debbie, it's Katie. Now who do you want me to call? And am I supposed to listen?"

"It's OK to listen, but you have to keep everything you hear to yourself. Please do not say anything to anybody. Even your husband. I'll explain later. And I may have to call you again, if it's OK."

"Oh, don't worry about Fred. He could care less what I do. He won't even be interested, so I don't have to say a word to him."

"OK, but for both our safety, keep all this to yourself! Now, please look up Marshall Keller's phone number and let me do all the talking."

"Debbie, what is this about?"

"I'll explain later. Please just call Marshall for me. And don't say anything during the call. Don't say anything. Don't even breathe loud enough to be heard. You can call me back after the call is over if you want to."

"OK, Deb, I have the number. I'm dialing now."

After three rings, Marshall answered.

"Marshall Keller."

"Marshall, this is Debbie Naylor. How are you?"

"Debbie, it's good to hear from you. I'm fine. How about you?"

"I'm fine, but I'd appreciate your help. You said to call if I thought I ever needed your help."

"Absolutely. I'm glad you called. What can I do?"

"Marshall, I need you to figure out who is financially behind the medical study at Kelly Hospital that Wendy is in. Something may have gone wrong that could affect Wendy, and I need to know to talk with the sponsors."

"Debbie, I didn't even know a major study was going on inside your husband's hospital. How would I know who's backing such a deal?"

"Marshall, you know all the deals in Wilmington. You have so many connections. Please, Marshall. It's very important."

"Debbie, if it's that important, I'll find out something. But can you tell me a little more about what's going on?"

"At this point, it would be best if I don't, Marshall. I'll explain later. I just don't have the time right now."

"How soon do you have to know?"

"Yesterday."

"I see. It is the weekend, but I'll make some calls and call you back."

"That's great, Marshall. I knew I could count on you."

"I'll do my best, Debbie. I'll call as soon as I hear something."

"Thank you, Marshall. I really appreciate it."

"Bye, Debbie."

Katie waited a few seconds and then hung up her phone. She called Debbie back in Boston.

"Debbie, what's wrong with Wendy?"

"Katie, the study she's in may be dangerous. We're afraid her life may be in danger. Since you're helping me, I guess I should tell you some more, but you have to stay totally in the background because if I'm right, it would be dangerous for you to be involved."

"What kind of danger?"

"The mob may be running this."

"Oh, right!"

"OK, don't believe me. Have you ever seen me act like this before?"

"Go on."

"You know that two athletes have died and that Jennifer Fields almost died. They were in the same study. And Wendy is having an irregular heartbeat. There must be big money in whatever this study does to enhance athletic performance, because these folks are willing to risk the lives of young athletes just to make themselves rich. They don't seem to care what happens to them."

"So why do you want to know who's behind this? Why not just get Wendy out of the study?"

"You don't just walk away if it's the mob. They eradicate evidence and witnesses."

"What good will knowing it's the mob's doing, if it is the mob? How does that change what you do?"

"That depends on what we find out. If it's just a few key people, we may be able to get them all arrested at the same time. If it's a huge network of hired killers, we'd be stuck with the witness protection program. If it's not the mob, we may have a chance."

"Debbie, this can't be happening."

"I said the same thing myself, many times. Katie, just be careful. I'm taking great care to keep you in the background. I will only call you from a pay phone, and I know your phone blocks caller ID. If you don't do anything but make calls for me, you should be safe. And I really need your help with calling, so don't be a hero. I'll call you tomorrow so we can call Marshall back."

"Can I talk to Mike?"

"No. Don't call our home or our office. Our phones are bugged. And Mike's clothes are bugged. I'm not kidding. Don't say anything to anybody, including Mike. It's not safe, and I don't even know for sure what is safe. All I know right now is that as long as no one knows I'm in Boston and I call you from a pay phone, you and I should be OK. Once anyone associates you with me, you might be monitored or followed. So don't take any chances. I mean it!"

"OK. How can I call you?"

"You can't. Don't try."

"How will I know you're all right?"

"You won't. Not until I call you. If you never hear from me again, don't ever let on you were helping me. Not even to the police. You just don't know who you can trust, including some of the police. So if I'm found dead, stay out of it. You don't know enough to help anyway, so protect yourself and your family. Katie, I'm so sorry I involved you. I just didn't know any other way. I guess I took a chance that you'd help. But you can call our voice message service and check our messages. You'll have to call from a pay phone each time and move around. The number is 228-2424 and our password is 1200. I'll call you mid day tomorrow."

"Got it. I'll call tonight and late tomorrow morning. Debbie, how long have you known there was a problem?"

"Two or three days. If we had known about this from the start, we would never have let Wendy get involved. It was just supposed to be part of her training at an elite level. It was just one of the perks when you reach a national ranking."

"I'm glad you said you just found out. I don't believe I would be very happy helping you two and being drawn into this now if you had known about this dark venture from the start."

"We didn't know, but we have to deal with what's going on now. Thanks for helping. I'll you call tomorrow around noon."

"OK. Talk to you tomorrow some time. Goodbye, Debbie."

* * *

"Hugh, this is Marshall Keller. I just heard from Debbie Naylor. My caller ID gave me an unavailable local number, so I don't believe she called from home so your team may not have heard the call."

"What's up?"

"Debbie Naylor asked me to find out who was backing the study Wendy's in."

"She sure is a persistent cuss. What else did she want?"

"That's all she asked over the phone. How soon can you get me the answer I'm supposed to give her?"

"We can notify Mr. Carter tonight. We have a debriefing scheduled for 10 PM. I'm over at the hospital now monitoring Nash and Naylor. Why don't you come over here by 9:30 so we can talk live to Mt. Olympus in Boston?"

"Sounds good. I'll be there."

"Oh, Marshall, come in the private entrance. One of my workers asked me last week why you kept stopping by the maintenance department. Try to be a little more discreet if you can."

"Just tell him I'm on the Board of the damn hospital and I'm a hands-on boss. Quit worrying over trivial matters."

"Whoa, touchy tonight are we? Just be a little less noticeable. Board members don't usually come by the hospital on Saturday night. OK?"

"I'll be there by 9:30 with my top hat and trench coat."

Saturday, May 17, 10:12 PM
Maintenance Department, Kelly Hospital

"Hugh, in this day and age, why does it take so long to get a friggin' phone line to Boston?" snarled Marshall.

"For your information, it's not a simple fucking phone line," exclaimed Hugh. "It's 20 lines for the video and audio leads, and they're all secure. That takes time to complete all the checks and get them all running together. I thought you were so smart. And you're handling the finances for this venture?"

"You construction types are all alike. If it always takes this long, why don't you start a half hour before the meeting is supposed to start?"

"Because I've been busy. A lot has been happening around here. Nash and Naylor got back from Philadelphia, and we've been trying to figure out what they found out with Wendy. We would like to know what they plan to do. Wouldn't you?"

"Of course, but you have a staff. Let's get this thing going. Carter and Dellose don't like to wait."

"No, they don't. And it sure looks like you don't either. Hold your pants on. We'll be connected in a few minutes."

Hugh didn't like Marshall, and Marshall returned the favor. Hugh thought Marshall was arrogant and mildly incompetent. He wondered why the Brey Agency seemed to trust him with their finances. Maybe he was smart with investments and money laundering, but he wasn't very bright with practical matters. They had been sitting without speaking for a few minutes when the video image finally appeared.

"Hugh, what took you?" asked Dean Carter. "We've been waiting over 15 minutes. It's Saturday night in Boston. We've got things to do." Dean Carter was allowed to be firm and a little funny at the same time. He called all the shots.

"We had a little trouble with the video line. It sometimes takes an extra half hour or so to assure all the lines are secure."

"Are we secure?"

"Mr. Vinton says we are."

"Then we are secure. What's the story in Delaware?"

"Marshall is here. He'd like to tell you about a call he received off our radar screen."

"Shoot."

"Mr. Carter, Mrs. Naylor called me and asked me to find out who was behind Thompson's study. She said something may have gone wrong, and she wanted to talk to whoever was in charge."

"This was Mrs. Naylor, not Dr. Naylor?"

"That's right, Mrs. I guess Dr. Naylor is too busy looking for a cure to handle the undercover work."

"Why didn't we get the call on any of our monitoring equipment?"

"My caller ID showed a blocked local number," said Marshall. "I guess she wasn't home."

"Hugh, why did we miss the call? She's supposed to be wired."

"I don't know Mr. Carter. I'll check into that. Maybe she changed her clothes. How extensively did Mr. Vinton's crew wire her clothing?"

"Enough that she should have been picked up. Unless she found out she was wired and changed everything. You had better get a man inside her home to see what you can find. Is she in town?"

"Marshall said his caller ID read a local, blocked number. Doesn't that mean she's around?"

"Well, no one saw her leave her home, and she's calling from an unmonitored phone. I'd say she broke out. If she's smart enough to do that, she's smart enough to have a call forwarded. You better find her and find her fast."

"Mr. Carter, what would you like me to tell her? I'm supposed to call her back."

"First of all, see if you can get a hint where she is. I doubt you'll reach her at home. That means she will be checking her messages. Hugh, you'd better be ready to trace the call to her message center. Marshall, tell her Joe Reilly is the point man for the investor group and he'll meet with her Monday. He's flying in here tomorrow afternoon, and he can get to Wilmington on Monday. That could be our way to get her back under monitoring. Oh, and Hugh, do try to find her before Monday. I hope you and your staff can at least do that."

"We're on it, sir. And we're just getting Nash and Naylor's information from their day in Philadelphia sorted out. We'll have a summary faxed to you by midnight. I'll call if we discover something dramatic. Next video call tomorrow, same time?"

"Yes, 10 PM every night until we're back under control. And that better be soon."

Mike Naylor couldn't believe his ears. And he couldn't believe he was lucky enough to stumble on to the videoconference. He had changed into surgical scrubs to lose his wire so he could come ask Hugh for help getting into Thompson's files. In light of what Dr. Dorland discovered during ultrasound cath testing earlier, Kent figured he could plot a progression rate for Wendy's protein deposition and get a good estimate of how long he had to reverse Wendy's problem. Mike had seen Hugh in the hospital several minutes earlier and figured he was on the 3 to 11 shift. As Mike started down the long corridor to the maintenance control department where he figured Hugh would be, he saw Marshall Keller throw the door open and quickly head inside. He thought it peculiar that Marshall would be in the hospital at this hour on a Saturday evening, and it was doubly strange that he would be in this area of the hospital at any hour. Marshall did not fit in well with any type of maintenance or any activity, for that matter, that might get his hands greasy or dirty. Mike quietly trailed Marshall, and with Marshall's loud voice, he was easy to follow. Mike had no trouble staying far enough behind to remain out of sight. Mike could barely hear them once they went into the conference room and shut the door, but he quickly discovered the kitchenette at the head of the meeting room had an outside entrance that put him behind a thin, tambour-paneled sliding door that blocked very little sound.

Mike was now petrified. This group knew everything they had been doing. Both Hugh and Marshall were the enemy! He was almost glad Marshall was a crook, because he never really trusted him. But Hugh. Hugh! He had saved Hugh's mother, and he had saved Hugh from getting kicked out of school. And Hugh had just told him how much he owed him. Incredible. Mike knew he was really in over his head. At least he thought that he and Kent were still safe until they discovered a cure. He could easily warn Kent, who already knew he was being watched. But how was he going to get word to Debbie? It was time to ask for help.

Thirty-Eight

Sunday, May 18
Embassy Suites, Boston, Massachusetts

Debbie slept fitfully. She awoke with a start and sat up quickly. Her heart was racing. She then realized where she was and sat back against the headrest to think for a few moments. It was already 8:30. After finally falling asleep, she had slept later than she had planned. She remembered she told Dr. McCormack she would call around 9. She needed to plan the call. What if he refused to have her meet his backers? Why would he even consider doing that? Just for the money? His operation had to be more careful than to open up to a stranger just for a verbal promise of money. She figured he would probably agree to have someone come, but how could she know he was one of the top people and not an underling role player. She realized she wouldn't know. She had to get a name and demand to meet that person, or she wouldn't learn much about the operation. She had better get going with her research. After she talked to Dr. McCormack, she had to call the football coach of the relatively famous Lane School outside of Boston and figure out a way to come up with a credible name of a potential football player. His name didn't matter, but he had to be a real player with credentials, and a player who would stand up to a quick verification check by the Sports Medicine Center people. If the last name was different, McCormack and his gang would surely understand why she hadn't given her real name when she first called.

Debbie figured she should wait to call until a little after 9 so she wouldn't look too anxious. She decided to take a shower and then grab a donut and coffee downstairs before going to a pay phone to call McCormack. The pay phones weren't busy on a Sunday morning.

"This is Debbie Johnson. Please page Dr. McCormack for me. He is expecting my call."

"We'll get him for you right away, Mrs. Johnson. He told us he is expecting your call. He won't be long."

Debbie noticed the significant difference in their approach from yesterday. She had to hold for less than a minute.

"Dr. McCormack."

"Hi, Dr. McCormack. This is Debbie Johnson. Are we able to meet with someone from your group?"

"Yes, we can make that happen. Mr. Reilly can meet with us today. Unfortunately, he isn't available until this evening, around 8. He's out of town until late this afternoon. Mr. Reilly thought it would be good to meet with you because if your son is truly talented, he will need a sports agent, and better sooner than later."

"That will be fine. Are we meeting at your center?"

"We should have the whole facility to ourselves tonight. Security will let you in the main entrance, and I'll meet you in the main waiting area around 8, if that is all right with you."

"See you there."

So far, so good, thought Debbie. Now she had all day to research her son the football player and plan her approach. She picked up the receiver and dialed again.

"Hello, this is Paul Brady."

"Mr. Brady, this is Sally Smith. I'm a freelance reporter covering high school sports in Massachusetts, and I'd like to talk with you about your team, your players, and your coaching strategy. I trust the Lane School notified you that I would be calling?"

"No. I had no idea. What story are you doing?"

"I'm doing a story about the hidden talent in high school sports in Massachusetts, both players and coaches. I cleared this with your school over two weeks ago. I'm sorry they didn't tell you. They seemed quite excited. *Sports Illustrated* has bought several of my stories."

"No, no, that's OK. I can handle this. Did you say you wrote for *Sports Illustrated*?"

"Actually, I'm a freelance writer. *Sports Illustrated* has purchased several of my stories." Debbie was really glad she remembered the name of Sally Smith who really did write for *Sports Illustrated*. She decided she should start taking notes to remember all the roles she was having to play.

"OK, great. Hey, I've got to pick my kid up from Sunday school in a few minutes. Can I call you back, or would you like to meet later this morning? Are you in the area?"

"Let me check my schedule, just a sec. I guess I could meet you around 1 this afternoon for about an hour. Is that convenient?"

"How about 1:30 at Harry's Pub. It's a half-mile from the school on Township Road. That way if you need to stop by the school or see our facilities, we're there! Do you have a photographer with you?"

"No. Not on this part of the interview. If *Sports Illustrated* is interested and buys the story, they will send out their own photographer. I don't usually send photos with my stories. It's too much, and each magazine usually has its own ideas about which shots it wants anyway. Can you give me directions from center city? And, I just remembered, could you bring your roster with each player's home address and parents' names? I need to send each student I write about, and their parents, a release to be in the story."

Debbie thought the directions seemed easy. A rental car would beat taking a taxi, but she wasn't sure how she could handle the insurance coverage part of a rental car without leaving a trace on her location. And she would have to show her license. She thought for a few moments. Maybe she could use Katie's license number and insurance. She could say she lost her purse and have them check Katie's number on line. Brother, another story. Anyway, now her research could take on a higher level of credibility. She would have some authentic stories to tell about the real live coach of her "son." Thank goodness Coach Brady was anxious to get himself and his team in print.

Next, she had to call Marshall. Debbie called Katie who had checked Debbie's voice mail and discovered a message from Marshall. He had a name for her and asked her to please call him back and where was she anyway? Fortunately, his was the only message, leaving insufficient time for Katie's call to be traced. Katie made the conference call to Marshall.

"Marshall Keller."

"Marshall, it's Debbie. I got your message. What have you found out?"

"Debbie, where are you? Why aren't you home?"

Debbie was startled at the question. Why would Marshall be concerned that she was not home? And how did he know she wasn't home?

"What do you mean where am I, Marshall? Is there a problem?"
"Er, no." He hesitated. "I was just a little concerned after your phone call yesterday. You seemed so nervous. I was surprised not to catch you at home so early this morning."

"It's nice of you to be concerned, but I'm just downtown eating breakfast before I check on Wendy. I have a few errands to run. Things have been a little hectic with Wendy in the hospital. Now, what did you find out? Is there someone I can talk to?"

"Yes. Joe Reilly is the point man for the financial group. I took the liberty of calling him. He said he can meet with you on Monday. He'll be in Wilmington from mid morning on, so anytime after 10 AM is fine with him."

"How do I reach him?"

"You can call Dr. Thompson's office, and they will page him or give him a message."

"Marshall, what do you know about his investment firm?"

"He's with a group of independent capital investors. It's a very private group. They are not registered anywhere that I could find. I guess only the IRS knows anything about them. They haven't officially borrowed or loaned any money in Delaware, so I don't have access to anything on file on them."

"Do you know Joe Reilly?"

"I've never met the man. I guess you could ask Dr. Thompson. He should know something about him."

"I'm sure he does. But I'm not sure Dr. Thompson is going to tell me anything significant."

"I'll ask around some more today, Debbie. How about you and I meet later so I can update you on Reilly and you can tell me about your problem with Wendy? I'd really like to help."

"Marshall, I appreciate your offer. I really do. However, I still believe it's better that you don't get involved. If you find anything out about Reilly that I should know, please call. Otherwise, I'm asking you to be careful and don't do any snooping around about Wendy and the study. Asking questions about Reilly may be risky enough."

"Debbie, I . . ."

"Marshall, please don't. You've already helped a lot. I really appreciate what you've done. Now, I have to go. Goodbye."

Katie disconnected both lines, right on cue, but it was not soon enough. Frank Vinton had their trace. Now he had to check out the Wilson residence.

* * *

Katie called Debbie back. "What's next?"

"Time for you to lay low. I don't think I'll be calling Marshall back. I may need you to call Dr. Thompson for me later. Let me think . . . How about you call Thompson for me first thing tomorrow morning and set up a meeting for me with Joe Reilly for lunch tomorrow at the Melting Pot, say 1:30? The restaurant should be almost empty at that time of day. I think I'd rather have quiet when I talk to him. Oh yeah. Katie, what's your license number and who is your auto insurance agent?"

"Oh my God, Debbie. What now? What crime are you committing in my name in Boston?"

"You're just renting a car and paying cash up front. No problem. You won't even go to jail for this one."

"You know, Deb, you really have a way with words."

"I know. All the men say that!"

"Debbie, . . . never mind."

"Katie, just think of the book we can write when this is over."

"I'm sure I'll be too heavily sedated to write."

"Keep your sense of humor, Katie. I need you focused right now."

"Right, Commander. Over and out. Wilco. Goodbye."

* * *

Debbie met with Coach Brady at Harry's Pub and had no trouble interviewing him. The man loved to talk about himself, especially in the off-season. And yes, he had a top player with the last name of Johnson. How did she know? His mom was called Darlene, but Debbie could be a nickname. Close enough. Debbie got the address and phone number of Shawn Johnson's home and a dozen stories to make things seem authentic. Debbie took extensive notes and made Coach Brady promise to meet her in about two weeks for stage two of the interview when she would be back in the area. She promised to bring him some word of *Sports Illustrated*'s interest in the story by then.

It was now 4 o'clock. She had 4 hours to get ready for the meeting with Mr. Reilly at the Sports Medicine Complex. As she headed toward center city, her hotel, and the Sports Medicine Complex, she saw a quaint shopping center. She pulled in. This place ought to do. Debbie first stopped at a coiffure shop. She picked out a long-haired red wig. The shop owner said with her short blond hair, he could fit the wig so no one, even someone running his hands through the strands, could tell it was a wig. She could even take a shower with it on, but she could not go swimming without risk of giving her secret away.

Next, she stopped at Lens Crafters and picked out a set of librarian-looking glasses with the lowest magnification she could get. The wig and glasses probably modified her looks enough, but she might have to fool trained people and thought she had better go further. She picked out a set of bright green contact lenses without correction. They were meant for changing eye color only. They worked. Instead of pale blue, her eyes were now noticeably green. Her eyes had been attractive, but they did not stand out. Now they did.

After leaving the eyeglass store, she went into the Nantucket Department Store and headed straight for the cosmetic department. She could do wonders there, but she figured she should stay conservative. She thought most men preferred minimal makeup, especially during close-ups.

Next, the jewelry section of the department store. She picked out some bolder costume jewelry than she would normally wear. She was hoping her efforts at going incognito were effective. What worried her the most was that she had no one to double check her efforts. She was truly on her own.

Her shopping took the remainder of the afternoon and into the early evening. She figured she had time to eat a quick dinner and then go to the meeting with Reilly. She decided to skip returning to the hotel room until after she met with Reilly. As a result, she didn't get the phone message from her husband.

Debbie pulled into the parking lot of the Boston Elite Sports Medicine Center. The facility was larger than she imagined. It was built in the shape of a horseshoe, with the main entrance in the middle on the south side, at the top of the shoe. The inside area framed by the building was an immaculate courtyard with gardens, fountains, picnic tables, benches, and gazebos. She thought it hard to imagine that such a beautiful and serene place could be a focal point for such a draconian venture.

She walked through the doors of the main entrance, and after gazing up at the cathedral ceiling and glass walls, she noticed a security officer sitting at the information desk. He was turned to the side looking at a dozen TV monitors. He turned toward Debbie as she approached the desk.

"Mrs. Johnson, I presume?"

"Yes, Officer. I believe Dr. McCormack is expecting me." She did her best to add a touch of a New England accent to her voice. It didn't need to be original New England, it just had to show a New England influence so she could add to the illusion that she had lived in the area for at least a few years.

"Yes, he is. He asked me to take you to the Executive Conference Room in the West Wing. He and Mr. Reilly will be right with you. Shall we?"

The security officer motioned in the direction he wished Debbie to go, and as she started forward, he walked next to her.

"Is this your first trip to Boston?"

"No, I've lived outside of Boston for a few years. I get into the city once a month or so."

"The conference room is halfway down this hall on the right."

Debbie noticed the spacious hallway and the sports artwork in large drawings and photographs on the walls. Each door was labeled with the department, but no names of individuals were evident. Only a few offices or labs had windows; most were protected from view. She passed the swimming pool on the left, lined with windows along the hall and outside wall. Through both sets of windows, she could see there were several luxurious sports fields surrounding the building.

"How long has this center been around?"

"The sports medicine group has operated for almost 20 years. We've been in this building and grounds for the past 6 years. Here's the conference room. Please make yourself at home. There's coffee on the counter and cold refreshments in the kitchenette. Please feel free to help yourself. Dr. McCormack with be along soon. He's with Mr. Reilly. They're finishing up some center business and will be right in."

"Thank you."

"If you need anything, dial 0 for operator, 1 for security, and 5 for an outside line."

"Yes. Thank you again."

The security officer gave a friendly salute with the second and third fingers of his right hand and turned to go back to his desk in the entrance area.

Debbie sat down at the conference table and looked around the room. The table was rather long, capable of seating 32 people. The paneling was mahogany, and the carpet was plush. Several elegantly framed photographs of athletes competing in their sports were arranged around the large room. Four modern circular microphones were spaced evenly around the table, with wires running into the table. The chairs were high-backed, leather, multidirectional, mounted on large wheels, and extremely comfortable. The ceiling revealed a trap door blended into the tiles for a large motorized screen to be lowered at each end of the room. Debbie leaned back and closed her eyes for a moment. She had to remember why she was here. She had to find out as much about this organization as possible. And, she had to remember who she was pretending to be. The center conference room door opened, and two men walked in. The first was Joe Reilly, barely of medium height with dark hair cut to highlight the waves coursing to the back, and a wide pleasant grin on his face.

"Mrs. Johnson, I'm Joe Reilly. I hope you didn't have to wait long. It's a pleasure to meet you."

"Thank you. I haven't been waiting long. I'm glad to meet you, too."

"This is Dr. McCormack. I believe you two have spoken a few times lately."

"Yes, we have."

"Mrs. Johnson, please tell me about yourself and what you would like to accomplish here."

"Feel free to call me Debbie. Right now, I could best be described as a mother of a promising high school football player who truly loves the game and wants to end up in the pros. I know the odds of his making it there, and I'd like to do whatever I can to help him get there. What I need to know from you gentlemen is what you have to offer that can help him?"

Joe Reilly said, "Tell us about him. Where does he play, what position, and who's his coach?"

"He is a rising junior. He plays center linebacker, and Coach Brady at the Lane School is his coach."

"What's his name?"

"His name is Shawn. Some of his friends call him Brad."

"How do you get Brad out of Shawn."

"It's a long story. It goes back to when he was much younger and didn't like the name Shawn for a time."

"What is it you've heard that makes you think our center can help your son? Is he injured?"

"No, he's fine. I heard you are doing research here on conditioning and strengthening without using banned drugs. I hear the results have been amazing."

"How do you know about our results?"

"I've lived in the area for about 3 years, and I've read about several athletes from Dr. McCormack's program who seem to be doing quite well. It almost seems like those who get hurt and come here go back to their sport very much improved and significantly stronger. As long as your methods are safe and my son won't get banned from his sport from the use of illegal substances, I'd like to find out more. If it looks good, I'd be willing to invest as well."

"Mrs. Johnson, does Shawn have a verbal commitment with an agent yet? I guess first I should ask if he's presently good enough to think about having an agent."

"He's getting there in my estimation. He's got two more years left in high school, so I think it's a bit premature to actually ink a deal."

"Mrs. Johnson, er Debbie, I've been rude. I really should let Dr. McCormack talk some. He has to leave shortly, and I'm sure you have a few questions for him."

"Yes, I do. Tell me, Dr. McCormack, exactly what are you doing in this study and how safe is it?"

"Our research is designed to maximize conditioning and dietary nutrition. Nothing our athletes take involves a banned substance. Actually, everything the athletes ingest is considered a food supplement by the FDA. We've had excellent success in the preliminary phase of our study with the physical development of our athletes in that they have all achieved levels in their sport that far exceed both their expectations and those of their coaches. In addition, we have the finest sports medicine staff around, with board-certified sports medicine physicians, athletic trainers, and physical therapists. Our athletes get the best injury and preventive care possible. That way, we greatly minimize down time, and we optimize training, pushing it to a very safe limit."

"That's why I'm here. Word gets around. However, word also gets around about one of your athletes dying recently. Is that true?"
"One of our athletes did die recently. We are concerned that she may have had an occult primary congenital defect in her heart that did not show up in any of our tests. We are still investigating what happened. As far as we can tell, her problem did not come from us. We've had all our tests reviewed by an outside sports medicine group, and they have not found anything we might have missed. We do not give the athletes anything risky. In any case, none of the athletes in either location of our study had any difficulty in the first 2 years. And they all dramatically overachieved their goals. We are quite proud of that."

"What do you do to evaluate the athlete before accepting him or her?"

"We put them through an exhaustive examination that takes 3 full days. First, I personally obtain a complete history from you and your son and then examine him. He would already have undergone a complete battery of blood and urine tests. If he passed the first phase of my examination, he then has an exercise stress test, extensive aerobic capacity evaluations, and pulmonary function testing. Then I would examine him again and review the results of this first round of testing. Next, I would go through all his old medical records. Our trainers would then take him to an elite level of physiologic testing, including an extremely high level of aerobic capacity while his heart is being viewed by ultrasound. If there are any areas of concern or question, he would have further specific testing, say an MRI or CT scan. We did electrophysiologic testing in one athlete before we accepted him. He's fine today, 2 years and

2 months into our program. It is very unlikely that we would miss anything significant."

"Impressive. It looks like you do your homework."

"We most certainly do. And I'm sure your son would like our staff and the other athletes here in our program. They seem to become quite close to each other. The team spirit is valued greatly—so much so that we have declined to accept a few athletes whose coach questioned their attitude and drive to train."

"It sounds like you care about your athletes."

"Absolutely, Mrs. Johnson. We get to know them so well that we couldn't help but care. Besides, that's why most of us go into the medical field. We like helping people. It is a service business after all."

"Do you discuss your medical evaluation with the athlete's parents?"

"In most cases, yes. Occasionally, the parents ask us to tell them only if we find something of concern. It depends on the parents."

"How about an outside physician, say the family physician?"

"We would be happy to talk to the family physician or pediatrician. As a matter of fact, we would especially want to do that if anything in the history warranted clarification."

"Do you send the family physician all your medical records?"

"We send the basic test results. We do not send our original study testing results. That information is proprietary. We do need to make a living, Mrs. Johnson. If we need further evaluation, we consult outside physicians who will keep our testing confidential, but would alert the athlete and his or her family about any necessary medical attention that is needed."

"Sounds fair. I appreciate all your explanations, Dr. McCormack."

"Thank you. Now, if there are no further questions, I need to meet my wife and friends for dinner. I promised I would not miss this night out."

"And that would be my fault," said Joe Reilly. "I was out of town and could not meet you at 2 this afternoon as you two previously agreed. Dr. McCormack was gracious enough to meet us at 8 tonight and then catch up with his wife, who will forgive him as long as he gets there before long." Mark McCormack then left the room quietly, turning to wave goodbye to Debbie. After a few moments of silence, Debbie spoke.

"Thank you for seeing me today. I do want to move this along if it's appropriate for my son. I'm leaving in the morning for an extended trip abroad, and I didn't want to delay until my return."

"I understand. How about if we move to my office, where I have the preprinted agreements you may want to review."

"Does that mean I can't take them with me to look over?"

"That is our policy. We want to protect our study. There are many organizations out there that are quite interested in our success. We protect our unique program almost as much as our athletes. Besides, I thought you were anxious to speed this up."

They walked down the hall to a luxurious office with a comfortable meeting area away from the desk with a large leather couch and an elegant glass coffee table. On the wall was a large home theater screen flanked by huge, flat speakers. The lighting was set a bit low for reading contracts. Debbie sat at one end of the sofa, while Joe Reilly took the other.

"Debbie, what do you have in mind for your son?"

"I'd like to enroll him in this study, and if your results look promising, I'd like to invest as a partner. Surely you could use a few million dollars more to launch your program to a higher level. What's the first step?"

"First, we believe our athletes should be verbally committed to an agent. We've had such success in our study, that it's important to start early and make sure you develop a good relationship with someone you can trust. Our athletes are all national-level competitors by their second year, and depending on their sport, they are hounded by the press as well as unethical agents trying to lock you up in miserable deals with outlandish promises. It can be quite distracting, and our athletes have enough to deal with during their very rapid rise in success. Our agency has an exclusive deal with the athletes in this study. We attend to their studies and their psychological development and keep the vultures away. We don't get paid anything until a pro contract is signed, and we take the usual percentage, nothing more. We keep the relationship well within NCAA rules while the athlete is in college and protect each student from even getting close to breaking a rule. We chaperone them like pampered children of politicians who couldn't afford to have a kid of theirs get into any trouble. Most of our parents really love that feature."

"So, I first have to sign an agency deal with you and, I see here, the Brey Agency."

"That's correct. Then you would sign a conditioning contract and, of course, pay all fees. Our fees are significant, but they have to be to cover the cost of all we do. However, it doesn't sound like that would be a problem for you. All fees are here in this contract and are paid yearly in advance." "Then what?"

"That's about it as the parent of an athlete. We do ask that you come to quarterly review meetings. But that's it. We do the rest."

"And the partnership?"

"We do accept a very limited number of limited-liability investors. We do not accept partners. We do not wish to dilute the control, since we feel we are doing such a good job."

"And who are 'we'?"

"Any investors we accept would be with the Brey Agency. We are funding this study. Dr. McCormack and his group are doing such an excellent job with their athletes that we figure we will do very well with a high percentage of the athletes once they go pro. And it looks like most of them will be highly sought after."

"How do I get enough information to decide if I want to be an investor?"

"Since we are not presently in need of investors, that would only come after we get to know each other. If you decide to sign up your son, hopefully it won't take long for you to see results you like. If you're still interested then, you know how to find me, and I will take your request to our Board."

"Are you listed anywhere?"

"We are entirely private. We have no public stockholders. We report only to the IRS. We have been sports agents for years and do quite well. That is our only business, and we do it much better than any other agency in the world. Like I said, we protect our athletes. We guard our investment, and that works wonders for the athlete as well. So, Debbie, I am very interested in your offer, but we are very selective with our investors. We need to know each other well. No offense, but we don't take money from just anyone. Even though this study is extremely expensive to underwrite, we are already well funded."

Debbie noticed that Joe Reilly seemed very polished, very polite, and very smooth. No further information would be obtained tonight. The Brey Agency was private and apparently, at least on the surface, clean. At least she had the name of the backers. She figured their FBI friend may be able to find something out, especially since they were at least partially a legitimate business. She knew it was still too risky to involve the FBI or police, but once they had the medical answer for Wendy, the more information she and Mike could obtain, the quicker their FBI friend could advise them of their options and the likelihood they would not need to disappear.

"Well, Mr. Reilly, I am definitely interested. I'd like to read these documents before I leave, but I will not be able to sign them until I talk with my son. I guess a few weeks will not hamper his career development."

"I will leave you alone to read them here in my office. When you are done, please call security by dialing 1, and the officer will escort you out of the building. I look forward to meeting with you again soon."

Debbie stood up and walked over to Joe Reilly. She looked him directly in the eyes and said, "The same applies for me. I will call when I return from Europe and have talked with my son. Thank you for your frankness and all your time. I look forward to working very closely with you." Then she took his hand in both of hers, in a goodbye gesture, hoping to make an impression that could be of benefit sometime in the future. Joe smiled and looked appreciative.

"Until then. Just call Mark McCormack when you wish to talk." He turned and left the room, without looking back. The door closed with a loud, firm click, suggesting a heavy lock. Joe turned left and went in another office two doors down. He locked and bolted the door behind him and picked up the phone on the desk. He hit the speed dial.

"Did you get all that?"

"Yes, loud and clear," said Dean Carter. "We'll get Frank and his team checking out the Johnsons in a few days. Right now our priority is what's happening in Wilmington. You need to get back there tonight and do some checking around. Naylor's wife wants to meet you tomorrow at 1 or 1:30. Thompson and Hugh have the details."

"How did you read her?" asked Joe.

"Just another parent wanting to buy success for their kid," answered Dean. "There are tons of them out there."

"Did Ken Turner remember her?"

"No, but he refers dozens of parents to us. We'll have Frank show him her picture and see if he remembers. We got quite a few shots of her in the hall and in your office. We'll watch her in your office, but we aren't going to trail her just yet. We've got to stay focused on Nash and Naylor. And speaking of Naylor, find out why our men lost track of his wife back there. How can an amateur lose our men, especially if she doesn't know she's being followed?"

"Maybe she found out. And maybe our men didn't expect her to sneak around when she didn't know she was being followed."

"Maybe, maybe. Just find out. We do well when we're in control. Right now, we're a little shaky. We're going to have to start clearing house a little sooner if we don't get all the details accounted for very soon. We'll get another update on the video line at 10, but you'll miss that en route. Hugh can brief you in the morning. Now, Joe, I don't have to tell you what this means for you. This is really your baby. Find out what's really going on so we can be sure. I'd hate to terminate this project after so much time and money."

"No problem. It's not like we're fighting pros. We'll be fine. I'll talk to you tomorrow."

Thirty-Nine

Sunday, May 18
Kent Nash's Lab, Kelly Hospital, Wilmington, Delaware

Mike walked into Kent's office and saw him slumped over his desk. "Kent, are you all right?"

Kent awoke with a start and felt his heart race. He looked at Mike while he gathered his thoughts. Mike was relieved to see that Kent was apparently OK. "Why did you have to wake me so suddenly? You know it's not good for the heart."

"Sorry. I'm just a little stressed. I'm sure you understand. With the Donovans and two athletes dead and you, Patti, and another athlete almost dying, I'm a little on edge. Besides, I haven't heard . . ." Mike stopped in mid sentence. He forgot he was performing for a live audience. He thought about what he just said, and he was very glad he hadn't even started to get Debbie's name out. He started again, changing the sentence. "As I was saying, I haven't heard what progress you made overnight. Well?"

"The messenger protein and adjustment calculation ratios arrived just after midnight, and I've been going over them until a few minutes ago when I lapsed into blissful sleep. Then you jolted me back to my extremely sleep-deprived state. Anyway, it looks like the messenger protein should work. I just have to attach it to a carrier suitable for humans. We've done that many times before, so I don't anticipate that taking more than a few hours. The biggest concern, however, is the dose. If I give too much, Wendy will bleed to death. If I give too little, it won't improve the situation and might only slow the downward spiral. And we still have to keep giving more, not knowing exactly how much has worn off from the previous dose—which makes giving more very dangerous. The safest thing to do would be to guess the correct dose, give it, watch for a week or so, and measure the response. Then it would be safe to give another larger dose. That way, I could start low and gradually build up to the ideal dose, with very little risk of an overdose. That kind of approach would be very safe and probably get us the proper answer within 2 to 4 months.

"We might not have 2 days, we probably don't have 2 weeks, and we definitely don't have 2 to 4 months," said Mike.

"That's why I've been up all night. I'm trying to figure out how to factor in all the variables so I can get the dose right on the first try. I don't know how many tries we'll have, so I'm going for it on the first try."

"Would it be helpful to test a dose on me and measure the response?"

"Yes, I would feel much better for Wendy, but not for you."

"Why is that?"

"If I give a protein dissolution code to a normal individual, it will dissolve protein out of the arteries that is at an optimal level. That could mean disaster. It probably would give me a better idea, compared with the dog data, of how much to give Wendy, but then I'd be trying to estimate the reverse dose for you to save your life. Believe me, I don't need two patients in critical condition going in opposite directions. I'd like to get some sleep sometime in the next month or so."

"What if I take a very small dose? Would that be relatively safe and give you any indication of adjustment reaction speed?"

"No and, at best, maybe. It's just not worth it. Mike, I don't need two patients, so don't even think about it any more. There's enough literature on dog-to-human comparisons in protein metabolism that I should be able to get close enough to the right dose. If I get close, Wendy should improve dramatically in a rather short time."

"And if you don't?"

"Then we have to adjust the dose as best we can."

"What if we give too much?"

"You're so kind to say 'we'. I'm taking responsibility for this, Mike. Not you. I don't want you blaming yourself if anything goes wrong. I don't need an emotional assistant either. If I give too much, I replace fluids and blood as fast as I can and I try to create a mild hypercoagulable state and ride it out. If I give too little, I get to guess again for the second dose. I'll take into account what the first dose did and get it right the second time. We will need Dr. Dorland's cath lab if that occurs so I can measure the protein dissolution we achieved, if any, with the first dose. The biggest risk is a bleed into the brain. The other bleeding sites are more manageable."

"When will you be ready?"

"In another 12 hours or so. I have to go through these adjustment calculation ratios and look up the dog-to-human protein metabolism ratios to calculate the dose. I need some sleep soon, so I figure 6 to 8 hours of work and 4 hours of sleep."

"Why don't you go to an on-call room and I'll wake you in 4 hours?"

"That's a deal, as long as you come to breakfast with me now."

"Always food first. Are you sure you need sleep? Maybe if you just eat a big breakfast you could go on for another 2 or 3 days."

"Yeah, yeah. Let's go. By the way, how's Wendy?"

"She's only had a few ectopic ventricular beats, about double normal. That's not bad. There have been no runs of V tach and nothing like Torsades or any tachydysrhythmias. We've started tapering the Pronestyl to see if she still needs it."

"Are you sure you want to do that?"

"Dorland suggested it. She couldn't believe it was making that much difference. As long as Wendy's being monitored, she thought it might be better for her to be off."

"I'd be nervous doing that. We don't know how much more protein deposition Wendy will get until we turn her exogenous gene therapy code off."

"I'll go check her right after I watch you pig out. If there is any sign of increased ectopy, I'll resume the Pronestyl."

"Good idea. After I eat, I'll call Dorland and discuss the Pronestyl with her. I think Wendy should stay on it until I can get some of this protein dissolved away."

"I'm sure she'll accept your recommendation. I'll restart the Pronestyl right after breakfast if you think it's best. A few more days on that drug shouldn't hurt her."

During breakfast in the hospital cafeteria, Mike and Kent mindlessly chatted about the Phillies and Orioles while they traded notes. They felt secure from being watched because they were in the physician area of the dining room and rather secluded. They were sure they were on audio, though. Mike wrote, "*Assuming you give the right dose, shouldn't you act like it's not the answer so we'll have time to figure out what we need to do with these guys watching us?*" Kent answered, "*Already planned that. I'll even act concerned if necessary and give a few placebo doses, acting like they are possibly lifesaving. That could give us time to get the authorities in while we plan our escape. We may have to stay hidden for months until enough of them are rounded up.*"

"*And where, besides Alaska, would you like to hide?*" wrote Mike.

"*Wherever the Witness Protection Program can safely hide us.*" "*And where do you think the US government can hide the world's expert on gene therapy, and keep him busy enough to be happy?*"

"*They're bound to have an underground lab somewhere out West. You could be my lab co-director. I'd teach you all about research and gene therapy. We could make superhumans together.*"

"*I really like patients, not memorizing formulas and calculations.*"

"*It would only be for a few years.*"

"*Right!*"

Kent suddenly got serious. He wrote quickly, "*Before we continue with this pipe dream, you have to make a safe connection with the police. We just don't know who they have hidden in the police force. I figure you will have to use your friend the FBI agent. You can trust him, can't you? Can he make this an FBI matter and bypass the local police?"*

"*Good question. I'm going to have to break cover to talk to him. That won't be easy. We didn't have any espionage courses in medical school.*"

"*Just ask Debbie. Even you don't know where she is right now.*"

"*You must be tired. You're not usually this sarcastic.*"

"*You're right. I'm tired and afraid. I don't mean to be rude. I know you're worried about Wendy and about Debbie. I was just trying to lighten things up. You're probably in more jeopardy than I am. They might settle for bribing me with Patti's life so I keep silent and continue to develop gene therapy techniques. And I'd agree to that.*"

"*I wouldn't trust them one bit. Let's get Wendy out of the woods and then get us out of Dodge.*" Both men sat in silence and stopped writing notes. Mike started tearing up their messages to each other into tiny bits of paper. He mixed them up in the huge serving of hash browns that neither one had touched. That should insure that the pieces of paper were dumped directly into a food-and-beverage garbage pail when their trays arrived in the kitchen. The silence continued. Mike and Kent seemed to need the few minutes of peace together, allowing them to think about what the next few days would entail. After a bit, Mike figured he should resume talking about baseball to prevent someone from getting the urge to breeze by to check on them.

"Did you see the Phillies blew another 5-run lead in the 9th inning . . ." Mike was interrupted by the loudspeaker.

"Code Blue, ICU. Code Blue, ICU."

Mike and Kent looked at each other for a brief moment, and they both realized it could be Wendy. They bolted from the table together and headed for the stairs. Kent stopped just before the door and said, "Go. I'll get the trays." Mike paused, then nodded with relief, and took off running up the stairs. Kent put the breakfast trays on the conveyor belt so the paper scraps would not be discovered and then ran for the ICU.

As Mike burst into the ICU, he saw the nurse with the defibrillation paddles on Wendy's chest. She shouted, "Shock is indicated. Stand clear!" She looked around to make sure no one was touching Wendy and that she was not moving. Then she hit the shock button on each paddle. Wendy stiffened and arched her back for a moment and then dropped down on the bed. "Analyzing rhythm. Stand clear. Still V fib. Shock indicated, charge to 360. Stand clear!" Wendy once again stiffened and arched her back before she collapsed limp on the bed. "Analyzing rhythm. Stand clear. Shock indicated, charge the unit. Stand clear!" Another shock was delivered leaving Wendy looking lifeless on the bed. "Analyzing rhythm. Stand clear! Wait . . . sinus rhythm returning. Hold CPR. Check the pulse."

Mike by now was standing near the bed, but offset to the Code Blue team. Tears had welled up in his eyes. His heart was racing. He felt totally helpless. Why had he put Wendy in this situation. She didn't deserve this. She didn't deserve to die. She could be brain-damaged by now, even if she lived. He felt like kicking in Thompson's door and beating him lifeless. He should die before Wendy does. He started thinking about how and when he should perform this act of revenge when he felt someone reach around and hold him from the side.

"Mike, don't think what you're thinking," said Kent quietly.

"We'll make this work. I know she'll be all right. We'll do what we have to do later. Stay with me. Don't lose it now." Kent didn't care if the mob heard what he was saying. They were probably a little nervous right now as well.

Mike let his head hang down. The tears were flowing. He just had to think for a few moments. Kent was right. He could beat up on himself and others later. He had to stay strong for Wendy. He had to help Kent. That was all he had to do right now.

Mike finally spoke to the charge nurse. "Let's restart the Pronestyl, same dosing."

She answered, "Right now, or should I stay with the lidocaine for a little while longer."

Kent responded. "You're right. Stay with the lidocaine for now. Give another bolus, and then hang a drip. We can titrate the Pronestyl in after 2 hours."

"Sounds good. Do you want me to write it?"

"I would very much appreciate your doing so."

"No problem. Be glad to. Don't worry so much, Dr. Naylor. She'll be OK. She's too young not to get through this."

"Thank you, Dana. I hope you're right." Mike listened to Wendy's lungs and heart. He felt her pulses and pushed on her abdomen. He checked her legs for swelling and then held her eyelids up one at a time. Her pupils were responding to light. There was hope. She was out for the time being, however. Mike went to the physicians' desk to examine the chart and sit down. Kent was there waiting.

"Kent, we don't have two days, do we?"

"Probably not. I'll get figuring right away. I'm not tired now. We'll give her a dose this evening."

"Take your nap. You need the rest so you don't make a mistake."

"Maybe in an hour or so. I'm not tired now. I have enough adrenaline in me to last a few hours. Come check on me in two hours."

"I'll be there soon. I just want to watch Wendy for a little while and make sure the lidocaine and Pronestyl doses are correct. I'll call Dorland and update her and let her determine the Pronestyl dose."

"Good idea. We're all tired and a little too emotional right now. See you in the lab."

Forty

Monday, May 19, 9 AM
Maintenance Department, Kelly Hospital, Wilmington, Delaware

"All lines secure?" asked Dean Carter.

"They all check out," answered Hugh. "We're ready to begin." Hugh Wheeler and Marshall Keller were in the Maintenance Department of Kelly Hospital for their "add-on" videoconference. Last night's meeting was to be continued at 9 this morning for several reasons. The heads of the Brey Agency needed to make some executive decisions overnight, and the team needed to be put on the same page by morning to make things happen in a well-timed, coordinated fashion. Joe Reilly wasn't available last night, en route to Wilmington from Boston, and he needed current assignments to straighten things out in Delaware—especially with regard to monitoring. This was his project, so he needed a full update and a clear charge to get control back. In Boston, Dean Carter, Dan Dellose, Frank Vinton, and Ken Turner were seated around the conference table in Carter's private office. Jessica Miller, in Georgia, and Ted Duffy and Rob Glenn were patched in on audio lines.

Dean Carter spoke first. He wasn't happy. "Operation Olympic Sacrifice represents a golden opportunity for the Brey Agency to gain a monopoly control as *the* agency for professional sports. We can't and we won't let this opportunity pass us by. We're invested beyond money, so we now have no choice. We've lost some control, and that is not acceptable. We are the professionals at this game. We have no business allowing amateurs to outsmart us, even for a short period of time. I will not accept further failures."

"I'm quite disappointed that our physicians, Thompson and McCormack, were unable to warn us in advance of the complications we are facing. However, we're close to getting back on track. Dr. Nash appears ready to reverse the problem that has endangered our athletes' development. We've just signed a lucrative and life-bound contract with Dr. Jason Jeffreys in Chicago. Dr. Jeffreys is a world leader in gene therapy and can take over where Nash leaves off. Gentlemen and Ms. Miller, Nash is soon to be expendable. Once he proves that his protein mixture reverses the side effect that 2 years of superathletic development gene therapy has produced, he and his wife are to be put to sleep. Mr. Vinton, they are to be considered collateral damage at that point. Their being made permanently quiet is part one of our four-part plan to regain total control. I will confirm directly with you when you are to proceed. Do not proceed with any of these plans until I say so. Am I clear?"

Frank Vinton nodded in the affirmative.

"Nash's wife is about ready to leave the hospital. The ride home may be an ideal time to have a convenient accident. The Assistant Medical Examiner on our payroll has arranged to be on call for the next 2 weeks, so he will be on the watch when we act. He should be able to paint a picture of a tragic, simple auto accident, involving a world-renowned researcher. I don't know how I can make it any easier. Do not let me down." Dean looked directly at Frank Vinton, who nodded in agreement. He then said, "Hugh, understood?"

"Got it," replied a very nervous Hugh.

"Part two is the silencing of Dr. Naylor and his wife Debbie. It will be a little messy to get rid of them as well, but total control mandates that we do so. Naylor and his wife will be in the hospital often visiting with their daughter, and Dr. Naylor seems to be especially curious, snooping around and trying to discover what we're doing. Hugh, you will arrange to meet both him and his wife at the appropriate time on interfloor 2B when no one will be around. They will be made unconscious and transported to the Smoke House Bar in the projects, downtown. There they will both die from a drug overdose while partying together. Their reputation and their credibility will be ruined. This is not an uncommon event for doctors, and newspapers love to dramatize the scandal." Dean again looked at Frank. "Any questions?"

Frank responded for both, "None."

"Good. Part three is taking charge of Wendy. It is best for our operation that she lives and thrives as an athlete. We will tolerate no more complications in our study group. Once her parents are dead, Thompson will keep her sedated until he can arrange to transfer her to Chicago, where Dr. Jeffreys will personally handle her rehabilitation and reconditioning. Once in the Windy City, Jeffreys will have her brainwashed so she will understand how her parents almost killed her and how they tragically died while abusing drugs."

"Part four involves the remaining 14 athletes in the first phase of our study and the 50 new athletes lined up to start phase two. Dr. Jeffreys will oversee Thompson and McCormack in correcting the protein overgrowth of the phase-one athletes, making sure they remain very healthy. He will handle the protocols for both the Wilmington and Boston arms of phase two, and he will remain alert for any new potential complications and stop them before they interfere with Mr. Reilly's project. Mr. Reilly and Ms. Miller will directly handle all 64 contracts. They will each have a staff of 6 subagents and 5 private investigators to keep total control of each of their athletes, who must be treated as the children they are and watched over during everything they do. They will be given 'parental advice' whenever needed, and they will not be allowed to even get close to trouble. They will have as many 'chaperones' as appropriate, and they will all remain in top physical condition, or they will be forced to retire to a remote country, never to return to the United States."

"Gentlemen, we expect to have 64 athletes under a lucrative professional contract within the next 4 years. The return on our investment will be billions of dollars within the next 10 years. I will accept nothing less than a total regain of control of this operation. We must immediately clean up the leaks that have occurred. I will tolerate no less. Mr. Dellose and I have spent considerable effort planning our exit from the difficult, but correctable situation in which we currently find ourselves. I expect there will be no failures in anyone's assignments. You have each been given ample resources and a clear directive, so I expect each of you to complete your assignments within the parameters specified and on time. Are there any questions?" Silence captured the rooms. After a few moments, Hugh responded.

"Thompson told me he received a phone call on his recorder from a woman who said her name was Mrs. Naylor asking for a meeting with Joe Reilly in his office this afternoon at 1:30. I understand that Marshall set up that meeting, but I asked the monitor boys to check the tape to verify the voice. It did not match Mrs. Naylor's. Do you know why that would be?"

"No. That sounds curious," said Dean. "Have the monitor team do a cross match on all the voices we are monitoring. If she's a new player, find out what she knows. She may have to be eliminated. And I want Mrs. Naylor found! Is that clear? Frank, how did a rank amateur give your men the slip? You have never let us down before."

"My men were not expecting her to run. They did not believe she knew she was being monitored. However, the team member who let her get away has been relieved of duty. He will fail no one again—ever. Not in this world. My team now knows first hand not to make assumptions."

"I'm glad you perceived the importance of discipline with your men. You will all play this as if your life depends on it. Because it does. Anything else?"

There was silence in both conference rooms for a long few seconds.

"Yes," a nervous Marshall Keller answered. "What happens if we do not find Mrs. Naylor in the next few days?"

"It is not a question of not finding her, Mr. Keller," answered Dean. "It is only a question of when she is found. For now, her husband is to remain alive until she is located. If we dispose of him and she happens to be hiding in another state, she may go to the authorities where we do not have control. Once she's in town, and Wendy is on the mend, we will take care of her with her husband. For now, they both must be kept alive. The monitoring of both continues until I give the OK to terminate them together as planned."

"Don't you think she would agree to remain silent if her husband is dead in order to protect her daughter?" asked Marshall gathering his courage.

"No, I do not. It's too risky. I don't care to spend the next several years watching my back because we have protection-for-silence agreements out there just waiting for someone to get a conscience. Nor do I want to watch her for the next 20 years to keep her from going to the police if Wendy should die for any reason—related or not."

"OK. Assignments are clear. I expect results, or heads will roll. I personally will initiate the timing for the silencing of the Nashes and Naylors. Now get busy finding Debbie Naylor. Joe, call me after your meeting with her today. I'll listen in live, but I want an immediate debriefing."

"Yes, sir."

"And, Frank, I expect your men to keep her under close surveillance once she shows up for the meeting."

"Understood."

"All right. Our meeting is over. You will be notified of the next. Now, get busy, everyone!"

* * *

Debbie Naylor kept her disguise on and caught the 6 AM shuttle flight from Boston to Philadelphia. She flew under her maiden name and paid cash for the ticket, enabling her to slip through the computer monitoring Frank Vinton set up for the

Philadelphia and Baltimore airports, the train stations in both cities, and the limousine and bus services. Frank Vinton's men were quite good, but they did not have the numbers to personally watch all the possibilities of travel if she did not use her real name or a credit card. Debbie caught a taxi and got off 3 blocks from Kelly Hospital. Since Vinton's men had not yet found her, she had no trouble walking right in the main entrance and heading for a back corridor. She went into the Hematology lab, picked up a phone, and dialed Kent Nash's office private line. Debbie did her best to change her voice. Kent picked up the receiver. "Kent Nash."

"Dr. Nash," Debbie squeaked. "This is Wanda from Hematology. The protein coating assay on the leukotriones you ordered is coming out all screwy. When you get a chance, will you stop down here to look at the slides yourself?"

Nash knew everyone in Hematology. He also knew this test description was as bogus as they came. He didn't recognize the voice, but it did sound like he should. He was sure no one from Hematology sounded like that. He figured he should find out who was trying to meet him. "I'll be down shortly. Run the test again from the beginning to see if you get the same erroneous result." Finally. He had come up with a reasonably good answer speaking in code!

"I already ran it three times, but I'll try again. You should look at it."

Debbie then went to the rear section of the convoluted Hematology lab office. She could see anyone coming and could hide reasonably well. No one was working in that section of the lab on Monday mornings. It was reserved for the infrequently ordered tests that were usually run on Tuesdays and Thursdays. She started writing a note for Kent to take to Mike. She wrote that she would meet him in the very noisy laundry around 11 AM. After 20 minutes, Kent appeared in Hematology and slowly walked around the lab tables. He eventually noticed Debbie in the back, looking busy. Debbie waited for him to look her way and held the note against her chest and then placed it down on a table with an obvious gesture. Kent looked around and seeing no one paying any attention, he slowly worked his way back to Debbie's section. Debbie turned her back and walked two rows away. Kent picked up the note and headed for the men's room. He sat down in a closed stall, read the note, and quietly tore it up into tiny pieces. He flushed the toilet three times, wondering if the monitoring agents were laughing, thinking he had diarrhea.

Kent wrote his own version of Debbie's note advising Mike to meet her at 11. He stopped by the ICU, ostensibly to check on Wendy. Mike was standing by Wendy's bed talking to her, although she had not awakened from her problems the day before. The Pronestyl had kept her out of V tach and she was mumbling at times, but she did not respond to verbal commands. Kent stood next to Mike and leaned into him. He stuffed his note into Mike's pants pocket and asked, "How is Wendy this morning?"

"She's lighter, responds to pain, but not to verbal stimuli."

"I want to get a high-resolution echo on her early this afternoon. Is that set up yet?"

"I'll bring her to Ultrasound myself," answered Mike. "The nurses know we want to move her then."

"OK. Call me if anything changes. I'm going to get a few follow-up doses ready in case we need them. Any sign of bleeding?"

"Nope. Not even microscopic hematuria."

"That's what I wanted to hear. See you soon."

Kent left the ICU to return to his office. Mike listened to Wendy's heart and lungs and then went to the men's room. He removed the note in the privacy of a bathroom stall, ripped up the note, and then flushed the paper so it wouldn't be discovered. He returned to sit with Wendy until about 10:30. He then told the ICU nurses he was going to take a nap and would be back in a few hours. He went to the OR locker room, took off all his clothes, and dressed in OR scrubs and slippers. He felt a little risqué not wearing any underwear or shoes, but realized that was his only hope of not being monitored. He slipped out the back door of the locker room, which exited directly into the stairwell. When he got to the laundry, he saw a row of countertops with piles of towels, surgical scrubs, sheets, and blankets in various states of disarray.

He noticed in three long rows only two people seemed to be working on sorting these piles while the other workers were operating the large washers and dryers in the huge rear section.

Mike walked by Debbie without realizing who she was. She was sitting at the counter apparently deep in concentration over requisition slips. She was wearing a red wig with a hair net and a baggy lab coat. He rounded the front aisle and walked back between the second and third to scope out the staff working on the heavy machines in the rear. As Mike walked by an aisle away near Debbie, she smacked her clipboard down on the counter to get his attention. When he looked her way, Debbie silently motioned to him. He came closer to see who wanted him. Mike barely recognized Debbie, looking straight into her eyes. Once he knew who she was, he looked carefully at her disguise. It was hard to not say anything. She turned her clipboard around so he could see the note.

It read, "*Are you clean*?"

He wrote, "*I think so. These are surgical garbs with none of my clothes on.*" He underlined the word 'none,' wondering if Debbie understood he had even thought to remove his underwear. Debbie rolled her eyes. He realized she would expect him to remove everything, including all clothes and shoes, his pen and pager, and even his watch. He had.

She said, "Well, we should be able to talk. It's so noisy here, they would have trouble understanding what we say even if they still have a monitor on us."

"Thank God you're safe. What did you find out?"

Debbie motioned for Mike to come with her around the corner into a secluded area so they would not be seen by anyone passing by.

"The Brey Agency in Boston is the organization behind this project. But I don't know if that is just a front or if the directors of the Agency are the real bosses. Joe Reilly is the point person both here in Wilmington and in Boston. I met him. He sent chills up and down my spine. He's smooth. I'm supposed to have a meeting with him today at 1:30 in the privacy of a restaurant. Marshall set it up."

"You're meeting him again?"

"I have to decide what to do. Right now I don't believe I should. I wore a disguise and pretended to be the mother of a football player in Massachusetts, but I'm afraid he will probably recognize me if I show up for the meeting as Debbie Naylor. Then we'll really be in trouble. And I'm not sure I'd learn anything else new from him. He's so polished and cold."

"Debbie, I overheard Hugh talking to Marshall. They're both in on this! You can't trust Marshall either."

"Oh, my God. No. They can't be!"

"They are. I overheard them talking to their bosses in Boston. They were quite concerned that they didn't know where you were. Marshall said you called him from an unknown number and he couldn't tell if you were in or out of town. They want to pick up your trail when you meet with Reilly today."

"Well, that decides it then. I'm standing him up. I need to find Jason Burke. We can't wait any longer. Once they think Wendy is safe, our immunity disappears as far as the mafia is concerned—especially before we can explain it all to Wendy. I guess I'll have to be the one to recruit him since I'm the only one off monitoring at the moment. He'll be able to arrange getting us into the Witness Protection Program."

"Oh, Debbie," Mike cried, "how did I get from arranging a miracle for Wendy's training to trying to save her life and then running away from all we know just to save all our lives?"

"We can hash this out later, but at least your intentions were good. Besides, didn't you say we shouldn't ever look back?"

"The path to hell is paved with good intentions."

"I'd say we're already in hell. And we've got to get out. Let's not beat ourselves up about this right now. We don't have time. We just have to get Wendy healthy and then take off. I don't see any other way. Do you? These guys obviously mean business. They're deadly."

"Not now I don't. There seems to be too many of 'them' for us to overpower or have arrested. And that's the only way we can stay in town. And marketing superhuman athletes with pro contracts is far too lucrative for them to give up without a fight unless their whole operation is destroyed. That means we end up teaching kindergarten in North Dakota—even if we end up taking some of them down."

"Right now, all I can think about is saving Wendy and keeping us from being assassinated. How about if I arrange to meet you here tomorrow at the same time? And I'll come up with a different meeting place after that. OK?"

"11 is good. The surgical locker room is usually empty then—the surgeons are all busy in the operating room so I can easily sneak in and change into unmonitored surgical scrubs for our meeting. I can tell the nurses I'm taking my morning nap again after watching Wendy all night, so the monitor folks will think I'm sleeping."

"See you then. Just take care of Wendy!"

"Good luck with Jason."

Mike, half dazed and exhausted, went back into the surgical locker room to change into his 'monitored' clothes. He didn't want to be unmonitored for very long, or he might arouse suspicion. He carefully put his clothes back on without ruffling them for the microphones. He saw a surgical friend and mumbled something to him about how surgeons got by on so little sleep. He then left for the ICU to check on Wendy.

* * *

Joe Reilly timed his arrival at the Melting Pot Restaurant to be a few minutes late. He figured his tardy arrival would create a little tension in his surprisingly crafty rival. He figured her wrong again. Frank Vinton's team was in place. A male/female couple were seated next to the table Joe had reserved, and both tables were wired. Two men were in control points at each door of the restaurant, well hidden or disguised. Frank himself was in the parking lot, parked in a solid dark blue Acura, backed in a corner with a great panoramic view of the entire lot and restaurant. There was only one way in or out of the medium-sized mall parking lot, so it would be difficult for anyone to scope out the area thoroughly without being seen by his crew. They would not lose her this time. Frank was very interested in what Joe Reilly could get out of her about where she had been for the past 2 days.

At 2:30 Frank pulled his men. He sent them back to relieve his other monitoring teams watching the Naylors' and Nashes' homes and all the happenings in the hospital. He knew Debbie Naylor now represented a major risk to the entire operation. He would contact Dean Carter and recommend immediate termination as soon as they found her. Joe Reilly couldn't believe she didn't come. She had to talk to him. He was in control of her daughter's life. He was in control of their whole family's life. She had no other choice!

Forty-One

Monday, May 19
ICU, Kelly Hospital, Wilmington, Delaware

As Mike entered the ICU, he saw quite a bit of activity around Wendy's bed. Kent Nash was there and so was the entire ICU staff. The chief medical resident was reading ECG strips, and a respiratory therapist was hand bagging her breathing. Kent noticed Mike as he approached.

"What's going on?" asked Mike.

"Wendy keeps having runs of V tach and ventricular fibrillation. We have to shock her every few minutes. Fortunately, we're only needing 200 joules and she goes right back to sinus."

"Why is she doing this? Is there any bleeding?"

"None. She's just having these pulseless runs of rapid heartbeats. Her conducting system must be affected by the dissolution of the protein. Everything else looks fine. Her lytes are normal, there's no enzyme elevation, and her blood gases are fine. The Pronestyl just isn't holding her anymore."

"How about bretylium?"

"I just discussed that with the chief resident here. The intensivist is on his way. She thought it might be time for bretylium as well—unless you want to go with the anticipated changes in the recommendations for V tach."

"Let's let the intensivist make a recommendation first. Is Wendy awake at all?"

"No, Mike. She doesn't know we're having to shock her so often. Thank God."

Mike picked up the chart. He searched for another answer. He had to be sure nothing was being missed. He studied all the lab work and the ECG strips. He listened to her lungs and heart sounds. "How about the ultrasound. Can we cath her like this?"

"We can, and we will. We may even have to pace her, so a cath is a good way to start. Dorland said she'd bring one of the cath ultrasound units here for a few days so we can test her as often we need to in our cath lab. Mike, it's starting to look like I may have to take a real chance and give her another big dose. We can't allow her to keep having these runs of V tach and V fib. It's only a matter of time before she sustains some neurologic damage. If the cath ultrasound shows some improvement, I'm going to have to give another dose. If it shows no reduction in protein deposition, I'll have to give a whole lot more. That will be risky, but we can't wait any longer. We don't have the option of slowly and carefully sneaking up on the correct dose. We have to get in range soon. It's getting harder and harder to keep her heart rhythm under control."

Both men thought for a few minutes, searching for ideas, searching for ways to make their decision easier. Kent spoke again.

"Dorland will be here soon. We'll take Wendy to the cath lab. Dorland can cath her faster than anyone around. Once I see what's going on, I'll give Wendy another dose. I don't see any other way."

The resident who was squeezing the Ambu bag helping Wendy to breathe stopped for a few moments. Wendy started breathing on her own. The effort was not optimal, but she was taking care of her own respiratory needs. Kent and Mike watched carefully. Mike spoke after only a minute.

"That's not going to be enough. You had better start bagging her again. She's going to get hypoxic soon, and that will probably start another run."

As he finished his sentence, Wendy started with ventricular fibrillation. The resident took back over control of her breathing, and the chief resident said, "Charge the paddles. I'm not getting a pulse."

This time, a 200-joule jolt did not restart her normal rhythm. "Recharging to 360. Stand clear." He pushed the charge button on the defibrillator. The unit charged rapidly. Wendy did not change her rhythm. "OK, I'm going to shock on three. One, I'm clear. Two, you're clear. Three, everybody's clear." He hit the shock buttons, and Wendy arched her back and tightened her muscles for a second. She dropped back onto the bed. The monitor showed a flat line, and then, in just a few seconds, normal sinus rhythm returned.

As Mike was feeling for Wendy's pulse, he felt someone standing very close to him. He turned to see Dr. Dorland. He was relieved to see her and said, "Kent wants you to cath her as soon as possible. He needs to see what the first messenger protein dose is doing before deciding how much more to give. With this recurrent V fib, he doesn't believe we can wait any longer before giving her more. But he needs to see what effect, if any, has occurred with the first dose before he can accurately estimate the next dose."

"No problem. I brought my ultrasound unit. I'm ready when your cath team is. I'll get you some good pictures in just a few minutes."

"They're ready," said Kent. "I already put them on the alert."

"Let's go then. Let's move her."

Mike liked Dorland's approach. She was confident, but not cocky. She seemed to be a natural team player. She understood the difficulty and the uniqueness of Wendy's case. Mike was glad he and Kent had recruited her early on.

The chief resident picked up his cue without hesitation and nodded to the head ICU nurse. She immediately started disconnecting the monitor wires and placed the defibrillator unit on battery power. She unplugged the bed power source, and her team started wheeling Wendy out of the ICU toward the catheterization lab. Fortunately, the lab was on the same floor. The team whisked her into the main cardiac catheterization unit and immediately went to work. A flurry of activity got all the wires connected, the site prepared and scrubbed, and the ultrasound cardiac catheter connected and ready to insert. Dr. Dorland quickly injected a local anesthetic and gave Wendy a small dose of Versed for conscious sedation, even though she hadn't been awake for several hours. Dr. Dorland effortlessly inserted the catheter and quickly reached the coronary sinus. She pushed the thin ultrasound probe into the left main descending coronary artery and injected dye to confirm her location and document the patency of the vessel. Satisfied that the coronary artery was normal, she activated the ultrasound unit and slowly advanced the probe. A clear picture of the lumen and wall of the vessel appeared on the screen. The artery was twice as thick as it should be, and the muscular wall had a slightly moth-eaten appearance. She finished probing the left main coronary artery and withdrew the catheter to the coronary sinus. She turned up the gain on the probe and mapped out the appearance of the AV node area. Compared with the previous films, the area was only 10% to 15% less congested with protein collections. Little protein dissolution had occurred.

"There's your answer," said Brenda Dorland. "Your protein dissolution is working, it just thinks it's getting paid by the hour. Not more than 15% has been cleaned up. You're going to have to increase the dose."

"Any sign of an effect on the internal lining of the coronary vessels?"

"No, the vessels still look clean and intact. You know, I just wonder how fast this amyloidal protein can be cleared, even if it has been broken up. There isn't much of a lymph system in the heart muscle itself. But, on the other hand, the muscle is so active, it should effectively massage any debris clear in rapid fashion."

"Are you trying to confuse me more?" asked Kent. "I don't look forward to guessing the next dose. And at this rate, I'm going to have to give quite a bit larger dose and pray it doesn't dissolve the intimal lining of the coronaries. I did confirm with Dr. Gebhart in Seattle that the protein dissolved by the messenger protein is small enough to diffuse through the vessels, allowing it to be easily removed without causing a backlog of sludge. So at least that shouldn't be too big a confounding factor. I suppose he agrees with you that congestion from accumulated protein debris should not be significant. That means the first dose hardly touched her. I'll have to at least double the dose. I gave her 300 mg last night; I'll probably have to give her around 700 to 800 mg for the next dose. Do either of you have any suggestions about what we should do if Wendy starts bleeding excessively?"

"Other than giving her some more gene therapy, what is there?" asked Mike. "She's not anticoagulated. She would only be leaking blood from breakdown of the lining of the vessels."

"That would be like driving a car with one foot on the brake and one on the accelerator," said Brenda. "But you're right, we'll have to do it. I guess the only other choice that might be of some help some would be giving platelets and clotting factors intravenously. They would be of ancillary help; they wouldn't correct this type of massive bleeding by themselves."

"Let's hope we don't need to do either," said Kent. "I'm figuring if 300 mg produced a 10% to 15% improvement, then a total dose of 1 gm should still be safe. We could expect up to a 50% resolution, which should correct the overstimulation of the conducting system. Giving 700 more mg will keep us under 1 gm. That's my final answer. Let's hope we don't get an exponential response." Kent looked up from his calculations and winked at Mike. He continued, "Then, I'll calculate the next dose twelve hours later. She'll need adjustments over the next 3 to 4 days before I'll be able to safely predict how to treat the other athletes."

Mike understood Kent was telling him the next dose should do it for Wendy and that he was adding the comment about multiple doses over the next 3 to 4 days for the benefit of the Brey Agency folks who were likely listening to their conversation. Kent was finally getting the hang of double innuendo and actually was starting to believe he was misleading those listening in. The stress must be getting to him. He was probably buying a few days' time, though. Mike hoped the follow-up doses would be placebo and not lifesaving guesses at more medication. Kent's comments about 3 to 4 days' time made him think about Debbie and her efforts to contact their FBI friend. He knew Debbie couldn't come home, and he was starting to think she should not come back to the hospital to contact him until she had completed arrangements for their getaway. Then, it just occurred to him that if he were completely out of his clothes and in surgical scrubs, she should be able to call the ICU and speak to him without risking coming into the hospital. His predators couldn't possibly tap every hospital line. They couldn't possibly have enough men or connections to do that. Could they? He had to keep thinking logically. He had to control his fear and make rational judgments. That plan would certainly be safer than having Debbie sneak into the hospital on a daily basis. And she certainly had to know how well Wendy was doing so that they could time their escape. He thought for a moment. He could get into surgical scrubs at 11 AM, and 11 PM would probably be a second good time. That way Debbie could contact him twice a day if necessary. He could use a nap as the reason to go dark at 11 AM and a shower for 11 PM. Now, he had to figure out a way to get Kelly when they headed for cover. That could come later. He had too much to deal with now. Wendy was still in a coma, and he was planning like she was definitely going to be OK in a day or two or it would mess up their schedule. What was he thinking? No, he was on the right track. He had to be ready whenever she started to recover. It would be easier to delay action than to be unprepared for early action. He decided to stay with Wendy and not contact Kelly or Debbie's sister. It would be better if her sister were left out of the loop. It might save her life. He'd figure out a way to get a note to Kelly through one of her friends. They wouldn't be watching Kelly's friends. And Kelly would love the challenge of sneaking out of school and hiding in Rollins Park until their FBI friend picked her up. He'd figure out the details while sitting with Wendy. It looked like he'd have quite a few hours in which to formulate a plan.

Forty-Two

Tuesday, May 20
Wilmington, Delaware

Wendy's monitor was chugging along with a steady, comforting, evenly spaced beep, beep, beep. Mike sat by her bed with his head and shoulders slouched over the side so he was half on/half off Wendy's bed like a schoolboy on his desk. He was deep in thought, lulled into a half-conscious state by the steady rhythmical beating of the cardiac monitor. Mike thought to himself that even though Wendy was still unconscious, he was incredibly reassured by the hypnotic trance of the monitor. He thought only medical people could ever appreciate what that sound meant. Probably most people just tuned it out and never realized just how important it could be for the monitor to carry on beat after beat in a steady, regular rhythm. But, then again, maybe a nonmedical parent sitting by a child for days or a spouse waiting for a loved one to awaken could learn to appreciate its meaning. Anyway, he was thinking how much it meant to him and how it made it easy to believe his daughter would wake up soon and be normal. Normal! For two years he wanted to give her a special edge so she could be better than normal. He believed she was special enough to deserve that boost. Now, he just wanted her to be normal. He prayed that she would recover and that she could forgive him. She couldn't die. She didn't even know what he had done to put her in this horrible situation. She didn't know what a sacrifice she was making under her father's guidance for a chance at the Olympics. She believed she just had to dedicate years of hard work and training for a shot at the Olympics. Now, he thought, she may be sacrificing her health or even her life.

"Hey, wake up, old buddy," said Kent. "It looks like the 700-mg second dose may be working. She hasn't had a run of V tach for over 8 hours now. Her blood pressure is steady, and she hasn't had one PVC or any bradycardia!"

Mike slowly picked his head up off the bed to regard Kent. He listened without a word and then looked at Wendy. He didn't know what to say.

"Mike," said Kent, "you need some rest. Go. I'll stay here until you get back. I just slept for 5 hours, and it really helped. You try it. You won't be so depressed. Go. Don't argue. We need you sharp—and you ain't right now. Go."

"OK, I'll go—under one condition."

Kent looked at Mike knowing Mike would verbalize the condition without having to ask.

"You call me immediately if she wakes up or if she starts with V tach again."

"That's two conditions," said Kent.

"No, it's not. It's one compound condition."

"Fine. Just go. Trust me. I can loom over the nurses here just as well as you can."

"OK. I'll go. But just remember, I'm doing this for you. You owe me."

"Don't worry, Mike. Your sense of humor will improve with sleep."

Mike sat back in his chair for a moment wondering if he could summon the energy to get up. "Hey, what time is it!?"

"It's quarter of 11. Why, what difference does it make?"

Mike started to answer Kent, but then ran out of ICU without saying a word. He was supposed to meet Debbie at 11, and he almost forgot. He had to hurry to get to the surgical locker room to change while he was pretending to take a nap. If someone was in the locker area, he would have to wait to change or he would have to take a few extra minutes to take a shower to make his listeners believe he was preparing for a nap. Fortunately, no one was there. He changed out of all his clothes and put on clean surgical scrubs—again no underwear or shoes. He put shoe covers on his feet and quietly but quickly headed toward the laundry. Debbie was waiting, acting like she was waiting for a load of laundry to carry somewhere.

"I like your threads today," Debbie said to Mike. "Pink is definitely your color. They go well with the bags under your eyes."

"It's good to see you, too. Do you have any news for me?" asked Mike.

"Yes, I do. But first, tell me about Wendy!"

"Wendy has now gone 8 hours with no irregular rhythm after her second dose of protein dissolution. She's still not awake, but her vitals are all good. I think she's going to make it, I really do."

"Thank God. I believe you. She has to make it."

"Now my news?"

"Oh, yes. I've arranged a meeting with Jason at 2 this afternoon. I said I was a close friend of his son and had to talk privately with him today on a life-and-death matter. I told him he could bring any trustworthy friends he wanted, but he had to be sure he wasn't wired or followed. He didn't seem too interested so I told him I was beautiful and he finally agreed to come. I didn't use my name, and I tried to camouflage my voice. Am I getting too paranoid?"

"Subterfuge 101 from my medical school days says you can never be too careful, so no. I wish we did have courses like that in medical school. Debbie, I don't think it's safe for you to come here any more. Your wig and make-up and weird clothing won't fool them long. They're getting desperate. I figure that I can pretend I'm taking a nap and call you every day at 11 AM and PM. They can't tap all the hospital lines. I'll call from a different spot each time, and each time you give me a new pay phone number to use for the next call. Here, take this number. It's Sean's work number at Colony South Restaurant. He's expecting you tonight. Be sure to get me a pay phone number for tomorrow morning's call. What do you think?"

"Good idea. And if we get out of sync, I'll return to Colony South for a message. Now we need a way I can get a message to you, just in case."

"How about you call Kent's office and say you're a patient of mine named Pam Patterson and you need to talk to me. If I'm there, I'll just tell you I can't talk and refer you to my partner. Then I'll call Colony South within a half hour to get your message. If I'm not there, I'll know to call the restaurant when I get the message."

"Did you have to pick an old girlfriend's name?"

"Yes, because you will be sure to remember."

"Right."

"OK, that's settled. What else?"

"How long do I tell Jason he has before we have to run? How long before Wendy is able to travel?"

"That's why we need to keep in touch. In the best scenario, she'll be able to travel in 2 days. And if she does well, that's all the time we'll have, because the Brey Agency will not fall for our stalling any longer. If she doesn't do well, we'll have longer, but how long I have no idea."

"I see. Could you be any more specific?"

"No, not really. It sounds clear to me. Two days at the least, many days at the most. How long does it take the government to print up fake IDs and book travel? Two days should be plenty."

"Let's hope Jason agrees to all this."

"Debbie, I'm sure you can be very persuasive. Now you'd better get going. Just do me one favor, please."

"What's that?"

"Once we're in Hawaii, lose the wig."

"Right. You need some sleep."

"OK, I'll call. We'll do lunch soon."

Mike headed back to the surgical lounge to change back into his bugged clothing. Then he changed his mind. It was only 11:30.

He really should get some sleep. And he probably should do it in his surgical scrubs. He turned around and headed toward the residents' sleeping quarters. He should have a choice of rooms during the day.

* * *

Debbie went to the main lobby of the hospital and waited, hiding behind a newspaper. After 15 minutes, she finally saw what she wanted. She walked in stride with a middle-aged gentleman walking toward the main doors to leave the hospital. She hooked her arm in his, looked him in the eye while they were walking, and said in the best Southern accent she could muster, "I'm so glad you happened by. I need an escort to the parking garage. I just hate to walk alone."

The unsuspecting man was flattered and felt obligated to honor her request. Debbie was already planning how she would ask him to drop her off a few blocks away. How nice of this man to help her sneak around.

Her escort dropped her off three blocks from the Acura dealership where she planned to meet Jason. Perfect. She walked immediately into a jewelry store to browse. She studied every person around her and stayed in the store for close to an hour. She had been in this store many times and knew there was a rear exit for those who parked in the garage behind the row of stores. When no one was around, she headed toward the exit and into the parking garage. She walked around the garage for a half hour, changing floors, taking the elevator, then the stairs, and then finally leaving by the rear exit. Next she headed for the dealership. She could wait in the Service Department waiting room for an hour to get a feel for the place until Jason arrived. ***He*** could plan future meeting places; ***he*** was the expert at undercover work. She had just plumb run out of ideas.

At exactly 2:00, Jason Burke walked up to Debbie and asked, "Are you Molly?"

Debbie looked carefully at him, thought for a moment while looking around and answered, "Yes. Are you Mr. Burke?"

"I am. How long have you been here? I've been watching you for half an hour, and you haven't moved."

"I've been here for an hour. I wanted to be careful. Who is with you?"

"Just my dog in the car. You didn't sound too dangerous."

"Mr. Burke, do you know who I am?"

"No. Should I?"

"Yes."

"Are you going to tell me?"

Debbie looked around. She saw no one and hadn't for over an hour. Folks generally didn't pick up their cars until closer to 5 PM—that's why she picked the place. And after all, now she was with Jason Burke. He was a trusted friend and an FBI agent. If anyone could protect her, Jason could. She took off her wig, brushed her hair back, and looked up at Jason.

Jason looked at her for a moment and then said, "Debbie?"

"Yes, Jason." Debbie put her wig back on. "I was hoping I could leave the wig off, but I had better keep it on. I've got a lot to tell you, and my family desperately needs your help. You have to trust me. I've not gone mad—although I may soon. Where can we talk so no one will hear?"

"I'll take you to my club. It should be deserted this time of day. Let's go. You've got a lot of explaining to do."

Debbie and Jason walked together out of the dealership and got into Jason's car—a government-issued Plymouth. Debbie spoke first.

"Are you sure you haven't been followed?"

"Yes. That's why you beat me to the Acura dealership. I took the long way."

"And how about being wired?"

"FBI agents usually aren't wired. I'm not on any supersensitive cases right now."

"You are now," said Debbie. "Could your car be wired?"

"If so, it would cost more than the car. Actually, our cars are swept clean at least once a week on a random basis—without telling us. Debbie, what have you gotten into?"

"Jason, Wendy's in trouble. Right now she's in the ICU fighting for her life. She's been in a sports medicine study at Kelly Hospital for the last two years, and it's gone terribly wrong. The Brey Agency, whom I believe has mob ties, is in control of the study to make superathletes bound to them for life, so they can cash in on agent fees when the athletes go big time."

"Debbie, there aren't any big-time contracts for gymnasts. What could they possibly want with Wendy?"

"You're right there, Jason. They won't get big bucks by using Wendy, although they could make decent money off her for a year or two if she wins an Olympic medal. They're using her as a guinea pig to perfect their gene therapy treatments to make superhumans out of good athletes. And she's paying the price of being in the first batch. It's gone wrong. Two athletes have died, another had a heart attack, and who knows what's happening to the others."

"How about if you start from the beginning as soon as we get inside the club. We'll be safe and alone there. I'll get a private meeting room if necessary."

"Jason, you have to believe me. We don't have much time."

"Debbie, I've already decided you're not crazy. I believe you. I've known you and Mike a long time. Mike gave my dad 5 extra years of life, and I'll never forget that. You've always been there for me. So let's get to the crux of the matter. You don't have time to worry about what I'm thinking. I'll help you.

Debbie followed Jason through the main entrance of the Stony Creek Country Club. He headed straight for a private conference room, looking like he was supposed to be there. As they entered the room, Debbie immediately felt the warmth of the room and admired the plush carpeting, the paneled walls, and the living room seating in an oval in front of an expansive fireplace. Jason motioned for her to sit down as he took a small electronic device out of his coat pocket. He passed the device over the lamps, tables, fireplace, chairs, and walls. Debbie watched intently, but quietly. He then spoke.

"There should be no reason for this room to be bugged. My device is supposed to be extremely accurate, and it's showing no active surveillance equipment. We should be OK here. There's not even a phone—by design. They have to bring in a portable if we get a call. Now, why don't you start at the beginning—whatever that is?"

Debbie recounted the story about how she and Mike enrolled Wendy in Dr. Thompson's study and how well she did. She went over the deaths and near deaths of some of the athletes in the study group and how they went to Alaska to get Kent Nash back. She told him of Tom and Marsha's recent deaths and how they were definitely not accidental. She even suspected that there might be something behind the Nashes' plane wreck. She told of her undercover travel to Boston and the Elite Sports Medicine Center and her meeting with Joe Reilly. She told him about Mike's discovery of Hugh Winston and Marshall Keller's involvement. She went into detail about gene therapy, its potential, and what Mike and Kent were doing with Dr. Dorland to save Wendy's life. She told Jason about Mike's estimate of 2 days if Wendy did well to several days if she didn't before they would have to disappear or miraculously do in all the bad guys or their days were numbered with very small numbers.

"Mike thinks that there are too many of them and that we'll have to go into protective custody with the Nashes," said Debbie. "Can you arrange that in two days?"

"I've been with the agency long enough that I can arrange protection immediately and custody to follow soon if necessary," said Jason in an effort to calm Debbie. "But let's not jump the gun here, Debbie."

"That's not a good pun, your 'jumping the gun' choice of words," said Debbie.

"So, you still have a sense of humor. That means we have a chance. What proof do you have of all this covert activity?"

"Enough to know we're close to death. Not enough to convict anyone of anything. That's your job."

"So, if I can get them to try to kill you, I'll have my proof. Of course, I'll be sure to stop them just in time."

"How courteous of you. However, unless you can get the

hired killers to turn evidence on the people who hired them, you'll have nothing on the Brey Agency. I suspect the chosen few selected to kill us won't even know those in power. Who knows, do they still hire hit men with planted tape recorders that self-destruct?"

"Haven't found any yet, but I'll let you know."

"Hey, why don't you go to one of the 11 PM conference calls at Kelly Hospital? You should be able to learn something important there."

"Now that's a good idea. But I can't take any recording devices. Their equipment would pick it up."

"Good, I'll come with you."

"Bad idea. I can't be stealthy with a novice sneak."

"Well, I've eluded them for several days. Maybe I could teach you a few things."

"Maybe you could, but not while under fire. I need you safe and hidden. If you're caught, it could accelerate killings. If you're alive and safely out of their reach, you could even be a bargaining tool."

"You mean witness."

"That, too. But I do mean bargaining chip as well. Let's go. I'm taking you to our office and getting two agents assigned to you around the clock. We'll put you up in a secluded motel."

"Make it near the Colony South Restaurant. That's where I send and receive messages from Mike. Oh, and make it clean will you. I hate roaches."

"You've seen too many movies. Your accommodations will be quite comfortable."

"I guess this means you believe me."

"Unfortunately, I do. Now what else do I need to know to get into this meeting tonight?"

"They meet in the Maintenance Department conference room. Apparently there's a kitchen area you can hide in to listen without being seen."

"I'll check it out. Page me if you hear from Mike or if anything of significance happens."

"I will. Just please remember, we may have to skip town in two days if Wendy does well. And we won't have much longer if she doesn't."

"Not to worry. I've done this before. I'll talk to you tonight."

"Godspeed."

Forty-Three

Tuesday, May 20
Wilmington, Delaware

Mike walked into the ICU to a welcome sight. Wendy was sitting up! He rushed over to her bed, where Kent was leaning over Wendy talking quietly to her.

"Wendy!" exclaimed Mike. "How do you feel? How long have you been awake?"

Wendy turned toward her father and smiled. "Hi, Dad. I don't know. I just woke up and noticed Dr. Nash. He told me you've been here for days and that I'm finally getting better. What happened?"

"Oh, thank God!" exclaimed Mike. "Your heart rhythm has been out of control, but thanks to Dr. Nash, it looks like it's OK now. It's so great to talk with you again. Thank God you're awake."

Tears formed in Wendy's eyes, matched by her father's. Mike held her hand and alternately studied her face and her monitor.

Kent said, "Today appears to be a good day. Patti is cleared to go home. She's fully alert and can walk without any problem. I'm taking her home after dinner. Her sister can stay with her starting tonight."

"Dad, what day is it?"

"It's Tuesday, Wendy."

"How long have I been out?"

"Two days."

"Oh, my. Am I going to be all right?"

"It sure looks that way. And since you're talking so clearly already, you should be just fine."

Wendy dozed off during Mike's answer. Mike turned to look at Kent, winked, and said, "Good job, Kent. Now how much longer before she stays awake and how many more doses does she need before she's out of the woods?"

Kent smiled. He figured Mike wanted him to speak for the hidden microphones and that Mike was assuming no more protein dissolution injections would be necessary. Mike was an eternal optimist.

"Wendy will need 4 or 5 decreasing incremental doses spread out over the next 3 to 4 days. I'll give her one more dose tonight and arrange for a cath/ultrasound tomorrow morning with Dr. Dorland. That she has had no dysrhythmias now for 12 hours is a good sign, but protein deposition continues as we speak. The reversal medication will still be needed until all protein deposition stops. It should wind to a close over the next 4 days by my calculations." Kent hoped Mike wouldn't want more than 4 days to plan their escape. He believed Patti was ready now, and hopefully Wendy would be able to travel safely in two days. That would give them a buffer, albeit a small one, in case any complications arose.

"That sounds great. When will you give her tonight's dose?"

"Right after dinner. Then I'm leaving with Patti. You can stay and watch Wendy for me. I'll come back if there's any problem. I just want to get Patti home safe and sound. Her sister will watch her for me. She's a nurse practitioner, not that she'll need any medical care. I'll be back in the morning in time for the cath."

"Have you called Dorland?"

"The resident was with me when Wendy woke up. He asked the nurses to page her. I was going to find you myself in a couple of minutes to tell you in person. I wanted to see your face when I told you the news."

"OK, I'll be here with Wendy and talk to Dorland when she calls. Why don't you go calculate the next dose and then go see your wife. She'll want to know the news."

"Fine, and you should take a nap before I leave. If you're not here when I come back at 6, I'll wake you up before I give her the next shot. See you then."

Kent left Mike sitting on Wendy's bed. Wendy looked comfortable for the first time in days, and the monitor continued in perfect sinus rhythm. Mike thought about what he should do next. He figured he should put in a message for Debbie about Wendy and that she would need to plan their escape by Thursday, less than two days away.

"Mr. Carter, this is Frank Vinton. I'm on a secure line. I have good news."

"It's about time. I was beginning to question your efficiency. I was wondering if you were getting old."

"One of my men found Mrs. Naylor. He's trailed her to FBI headquarters in Wilmington. It looks like they will keep her in protective custody."

"Can you get to her?"

"Shouldn't be much of a problem. Tonight would be good since they believe she's still hidden. They won't be expecting anything so soon."

"Excellent. I'll get back to you. Tonight may be appropriate. Make sure you don't lose her. I'll page you. Be sure you're on a secure line when you call back."

"Always."

"Oh, Frank. Where was she?"

"The Stony Creek Country Club. One of my men was eating lunch there. Just luck that he saw a strange woman with another member who is an FBI agent. He stayed to check them out. They went to a private conference room for 20 minutes and then left together. As they were leaving, he heard the FBI guy call the woman Debbie. He got a good look at her and noticed she was wearing a wig that wasn't on too well. She matched the picture perfectly."

"Is he sure?"

"Yes. He's good."

"Well, put another man on her just in case."

"I already did. Another man and another woman. It's tough for men to trail women into women's rooms."

"Good. I'll get back to you within the hour."

"Dr. Jeffreys, Dean Carter here. Our patient is awake and talking coherently. Nash thinks she'll need 4 or 5 more incremental doses of protein dissolution injections and will be OK in 4 to 5 days. She's been in a normal rhythm for over 12 hours now. I need to know when you can take over for Nash, and the sooner the better."

"How long has it been since she received any of Thompson's drugs?"

"Over 4 days now."

"Then she's fine. That stuff is very short-acting. I can take over now. When do you want me there."

"Next plane. Report to Hugh Winston tonight. He'll get you into the ICU, and you can study the chart and the patient. You've got her effective immediately, so don't waste any time. I'll have a driver pick you up in 15 minutes."

"My bag is packed, and my associate knows I may have to leave in a hurry. It's all arranged."

"OK, you're on. Don't mess up."

"Frank Vinton."

"Frank, line secure?" asked Dean.

"Confirm yes."

"Tonight for the Nashes. As they're leaving the hospital, as we planned. The road home is full of curves through the woods out in the country."

"The location has been identified, and the Assistant Medical Examiner is on alert. I already talked to him, and he's ready for tonight's accident."

"Oh, and Frank, are you really busy?"

"I'm fine. Why?"

"Can you handle phase two tonight also?"

"I will supervise that one myself. Hugh is overseeing the accident. That's easy."

"OK, confirm termination of Mike and Debbie Naylor as planned, tonight."

"Confirmed."

"Report back when appropriate and when each phase is complete."

"Roger."

Forty-Four

Tuesday evening, May 20, 5:00 PM
Wilmington, Delaware

***B**rian Taggart was sitting on the floor of the reception arcade for floor 2B arranging supplies in the bottom drawer when he heard two men rush by the entrance.* He started to get up to check on the people passing by, but just before he spoke he recognized Hugh, his boss, escorting another man toward Dr. Thompson's office. Not knowing why, he decided not to say anything as he observed them pass by in a very serious mood. Instinctively, he turned on Dr. Thompson's intercom just as they opened Thompson's door. The noise from the door drowned out the initial 'on' signal from the intercom. Brian figured he could pretend he didn't know it was on if they ever discovered it was. Frank Vinton spoke first.

"Where's Thompson? Is it secure in here?"

"Dr. Thompson is speaking at a dinner tonight, trying to increase his sports medicine presence in the community. This office is secure. It is one of 14 we sweep at least once a day. We've been doing that for over two years and never found a hint of any espionage in any of the 14 locations."

"Don't get complacent. Now is the time for something like that to happen. Things have heated up. When there's controversy we must be most careful."

"Right. I agree. My staff of two will be very careful. Now, what's on your mind?" Hugh was getting tired of his "bosses" believing no one could think beside themselves.

"Tonight is confirmed for both phase one and two. The Nashes rest tonight. You've rehearsed this numerous times. Location 2 is a go. The road near the Nashes' home is virtually deserted, is very winding, and the cliff overhang at location 2 is ready. My men have artfully sabotaged the guardrail so the Nashes' car will easily go over the 200-foot drop. The rail will not look altered."

"OK, so far, everything as planned."

"Right. My men will have the road blocked off above and below the accident scene right after the Nashes' car passes checkpoint alpha. We already have a wide-mouth dump truck waiting at location 2, ready to block the Nashes and then push their car over the rail once it's on fire. The road where they will have to stop has a natural bowl-like dip that will hold sufficient gasoline to ignite their car. We have a spark wire in place to start the fire under their car, which will very quickly cause an explosion. Your man will remove the wire as soon as the fire is lit."

"What if they get out of their car when they see the fire?"

"Good question. The position of the dump truck will obscure an obstruction preventing them from going forward until the dump truck passes them on the side. Once on the side before there is enough room to pass, the fire will start and the dump truck will immediately turn to push them over the cliff. They will have no chance of getting out, assuming they were still physically able to move after the fire and explosion. The police officer who will happen by at the right time and who just happens to be an accident investigation specialist and be on our payroll, along with the Assistant Medical Examiner, will see to it that the appropriate skid marks (which have already been placed) are recorded in the accident report. He'll be waiting above the accident scene, out of sight around the second curve."

"What if they don't go right home?"

"We wait. But they plan to; remember Nash is bugged, so we know exactly where he is and what he's doing at all times. His wife's sister is already at their home waiting for them to arrive, so I doubt they will delay going home."

"Can she see where the accident will be?"

"No, and she isn't likely to be watching anyway."

"What else could go wrong?"

"Nothing. Unless your dump truck guy is too slow or out of position."

"That won't happen," said Hugh.

"Tell me why not. I could use some reassurance."

"Because I'm driving the dump truck, and I've operated heavy machinery for 8 years. I even competed in truck derbies for 5 years. I was the demolition derby champion in the eastern region for 3 years in a row." Hugh wanted to say more, but knew better. He couldn't wait until this gene therapy crap was perfected so he could turn it over to his cell of patriots. He was getting tired of being patient. He wanted to show these assholes what real leadership was. This game of camouflaging the killing of those who got in your way was for wimps and fraught with a heavy amount of unnecessary risk. Americans and their police were too weak anyway. They spent so much time on investigations and being politically correct, they cut their efficiency more than half. If he had his way, he'd just put a bullet in both of them and let the police spend a fortune and a year or two trying to figure out what happened. By then, his men would have moved on and left a path of many more righteous acts of retribution for them to investigate.

"Then this should be easy. Just don't mess up. Mr. Carter is on edge. That Naylor lady had him shook up real bad. He was entirely too grumpy, and that clouds his thinking. It's a good thing we finally found her."

"Just tell me when Nash is supposed to leave the hospital with his wife?" Hugh thought it was funny and arrogant that Vinton actually said his men found Mrs. Naylor. One of his men was goofing off eating and stumbled on to her. It was just pure luck. And he was supposed to be so good. Right.

"Sometime before 7 tonight. You had better get going. We'll use band 17 Charlie. No one uses that one around here. We've monitored it for 6 months, and no one has used it yet."

Brian couldn't believe what he was hearing. His heart started racing. Why in the world would anyone want to kill the Nashes? All these athletes dying, and now a hit was being planned on Dr. Nash and his wife! He had to warn him. But how? Nash was bugged. He couldn't tell him by talking to him. And would Dr. Nash even believe him if he could speak to him, let alone give him a note with a crazy message? Brian had the intercom on a handheld receiver so noise from the reception area wouldn't be transmitted to Thompson's room. But if he hung up, it would make a clicking noise in Thompson's office, alerting Hugh and the other man that the intercom had been on. If he left it on, they might see the receiver off the hook when they left or more likely hear some background noise after Brian left and then realize he had listened in. Either way, Brian now feared for his life, too. What should he do? What could he do? All he could think of was turn the intercom off and then immediately on and make up a message for Hugh. It had to work.

Brian paused for another moment. He couldn't think of anything better and he had to act quickly. He turned the intercom off and then immediately on, waited for the paging signal to end and then spoke. "Mr. Winston. This is Brian Taggart. I have to leave the floor to get some supplies. Do you need anything while I'm gone?"

"No, Brian, I'm fine. How did you know I was here?"

"I heard you come in. I was on the floor filing when you and your guest arrived."

"And who monitors the floor while you're gone?"

"The head physical therapist. I lock the entrance when I leave, and no one without a key can get in without buzzing since he's with patients and not able to watch the entrance. He lets them in after they sign in."

"OK. We're fine. Go."

Brian hung up and breathed a sigh of relief. He grabbed a small note pad and headed to Patti Nash's room. As he got on the elevator, he thought. Now he couldn't have Dr. Nash saying hello to him since he was monitored. Then Hugh would know he had lied about where he was going. So, he would get a nurse to call Dr. Nash to the nurses' station and he could present him with notes telling him not to speak. He was hoping Dr. Nash would respond correctly to a simple finger over his lips. After all, they did know each other and were friends. He'd motion for Nash to follow him into the small conference room next to the nurses' station and then write his message in front of Nash. If only Dr. Nash had enough patience not to speak.

Brian knew almost everyone in Kelly Hospital. He approached the nurses' station and saw Rachael Preston standing at the counter charting medications.

"Rachael! Hi."

"Oh hi, Brian. What brings you up here tonight?"

"I need to see Dr. Nash. Is he here?"

"Yes, he's in his wife's room, 312."

"Thanks!"

Brian sat down at the receptionist's desk. He was familiar with all the equipment and layout. He was still for a moment and looked toward Rachael. She was engrossed in her charting. He looked up and down the hallway and saw no activity. He then looked toward room 312. He positioned himself so anyone coming out of the room would not be able to see him until rounding the corner of the nurses' station and standing right next to where he was sitting. He then clicked on the intercom to 312. He spoke in a husky, formal voice.

"Dr. Nash, you're needed at the nurses' station as soon as possible. Dr. Nash to the nurses' station." He then clicked off the intercom and lowered his head, further hiding from view. Rachael had disappeared into a patient's room. Soon, Dr. Nash came out of 312, headed for the entrance to the nurses' station, and turned the corner entering the reception area. At that moment, Brian turned around in his chair holding his left hand up in a 'stop' position and his right pointer finger over his lips. It worked. Dr. Nash was too startled to say a word. He regarded Brian carefully, wondering what in the world this young student was doing. He honored the silence, waiting for an explanation.

As soon as Brian knew Dr. Nash was willing to play along, at least for now, he motioned for Dr. Nash to follow him into the conference room. He wanted to be alone for their silent communication. Kent Nash looked around and hesitantly followed Brian into the room. Brian motioned for him to sit down, and after looking around, he did. Brian sat across from him, looked him in the eye, and again held his right index finger over his lips. Kent gestured 'OK' with his hand and head and waited. Brian wrote a short message and passed it across the conference table.

"Please trust me."

Kent wrote back, *"OK. Why the silence?"*

"I understand you are bugged."

"How did you know?"

"I heard Hugh Winston talking to another man."

"Did they see you?"

"No, I don't believe so."

"Unfortunately, I am. What did you hear?"

"They're going to kill you."

"Did you hear when or how?"

"Yes, tonight. They're going to burn your car and push it over the cliff near your home."

"Did you hear anything else?"

"No."

"Thanks. I hope you've saved my life."

"What can I do to help?"

"Nothing. It's too dangerous."

"I think I should stay with you. I could drive you and your wife to the police."

"No. It's too dangerous for you."

"It's too late. I'm already involved."

Kent Nash looked at Brian carefully. He didn't quite know what that meant, and he realized he didn't have much time. Apparently his stall with Wendy wasn't working. He didn't know if he could trust the police, but he thought Brian was right that it was probably his best option at the moment. He thought for a minute more and couldn't come up with any other ideas. He tried to think what was the best way for Brian to help that would be the safest. He wrote another note and passed it across the table.

"Can you get word to Dr. Naylor?"

"Yes."

"He needs to know as soon as possible. I'm going to leave the hospital with Patti now. Tell them I'll be right back, so they don't try to stop us for the paperwork. Then tell Dr. Naylor we've gone to the police and to be careful. They will try to kill him also."

"I understand. I'll tell the nurses I'm taking you two downstairs for a moment, and we'll be right back. Then I'll get you to your car and then tell Dr. Naylor. I presume he's bugged, too."

"Yes. Be careful."

The two men sat still for a moment looking at each other. Neither knew what else to say. Dr. Nash slowly got up and started toward his wife's room. Brian followed. Once inside the room Kent spoke to Patti.

"Patti, let's go downstairs for a quick bite to eat while the nurses are doing your paperwork. They'll be ready for us to go in about an hour."

"Does paperwork take that long, just to leave?"

"An hour is for physician and staff families. Consider yourself lucky you're not a regular patient. It could take 2 or 3 hours. Oh, I saw Brian at the nurses' station. He said he'd walk us down."

Bingo! That didn't make sense to Ted Duffy who was manning Nash's monitoring live since it was so close to the planned hit. Something was missing from that conversation. After being called to the nurses' station, there was a long unexplained silence and sometime during that silence Brian Taggart supposedly 'spoke' to

Dr. Nash and told him he'd escort him downstairs. I don't think so, he thought. That sounded like Nash and Taggart were up to something. Ted looked at Rob Glenn and said, "Get your men on Nash and Taggart immediately. I bet they're making a run. Make sure they're contained—however necessary. Nash's wife, too."

Rob sprinted in the hospital entrance from their monitoring station just outside. He sent two men up the stairs, one getting off the second floor and the other going to the third floor nurses' station. They were dressed in maintenance worker overalls, and once outside the stairwell, their speed slowed to an inconspicuous walk. The man on the third floor soon picked them up. He radioed the others and blended in the background. Ted Duffy called Dean Carter to inform him of the apparent run.

"Mr. Carter. Ted Duffy here. This line is secure. Dr. Nash and his wife and a hospital worker are apparently fleeing the hospital. They're getting off the elevator at the parking garage level as we speak. What are your instructions."

"Abduct them and kill them quietly so we can make them disappear. But regardless, kill them. If they're running, they will probably go to the police. They don't have children we can go after, so kill them immediately if necessary. Send your men to pick up the Naylors' other kid, but don't hurt her. And Ted, one more thing. Don't screw this up. We've got a billion-dollar opportunity here, and all we've got to do now is eliminate a few people. Now go!"

* * *

Brian and Kent helped Patti out of her wheelchair into the Nashes' car. Brian quickly turned to take the wheelchair back to the elevator area and then head back inside the hospital to find Mike Naylor. Dominic and Chip pulled along side the Nashes' car as Kent was walking around the car to get into the driver's seat. A well-placed blow from behind to Kent's neck dropped him into the arms of the attacker who hauled him into the waiting car. They then went to Patti's door, threw it open, grabbed her, and started to pull her out of the car. She screamed before Chip could get the duct tape over her mouth. Hearing the scream, Brian turned around, saw the commotion, and started running toward the Nashes' car. Dominic heard the footsteps, turned, and shot Brian in the chest with his silenced automatic. Brian fell sideways, hit the railing, and fell over the second floor ledge. Dominic ran to the ledge to see his victim lying unconscious between bushes on the ground, one floor below. Blood was oozing out of the right side of his chest and his neck was twisted in an awkward manner.

"He's dead," Dominic said to Chip, who had just finished forcing Patti into their Durango SUV. "Let's get out of here!"

Chip hopped into the driver's seat, and Dominic got in the back with Kent and Patti. He seat belted Kent in the back seat behind the driver and covered Patti with a blanket so no one could see she was gagged. He then leaned her over into his lap so he could pretend he was comforting her as Chip drove through the cashier's line. Chip stopped to pay the cashier with a sudden jolt that jerked Kent forward and caused him to hit the inside door control. He started to wake up, but somehow managed to realize that he should stay very still until he figured out where he was and what he should do. Dominic's attention was focused on the cashier to decide whether or not she would become suspicious.

Kent gradually came around. He glanced over at Dominic and up to Chip, who were paying attention to the cashier and trying to get out of the garage without causing a major stir. Kent glanced to his side and saw a stairwell and passageway into the hospital. He looked ahead and saw two police cars and an ambulance parked outside the Emergency Room. Two police officers were leaning against their cars talking. He saw a high chain-link gate on rollers that, when slid open, would allow cars in the checkout line to leave the garage. If he moved quickly, he could do it. He had no time to waste. Kent grabbed the door lever, opened it, and quickly rolled out onto the ground. He got to his hands and feet and ran as low as he could to the gate. He rolled outside the garage and reached back to grab the gate door and pulled to close it. He closed it enough to partially block the SUV. He quickly ran to the end of the 10-foot high sliding door and threw his weight against the metal frame and pumped his legs gradually closing the gate further. He screamed to the police, "Help! Help! They're trying to kill my wife!"

Kent heard a shot and felt a burning in his neck. He slumped to the ground. The police ran toward Kent with drawn weapons and looked for cover. Chip pulled the SUV forward to test the chain link door blocking their way. He splintered the wooden banner that had not yet been raised and yelled at Dominic to get in. The parking garage cashier, a former lineman for a local high school football team, grabbed a crow bar he always kept for self defense, ran out of his booth, and smashed the side window by the driver knocking Chip unconscious. Dominic shot the attendant, hitting him in the shoulder, and then turned to shoot Patti, to quiet one witness. The time for a convenient accident was over. He then bolted from the SUV and looked around for Kent. He couldn't see Kent well since he was slumped over behind the concrete guardrail. It looked to Dominic like both Kent and Patti were dead. The police were now headed his way, so he turned to run. He headed into the hospital to lose his chasers. The police radioed for help and stopped to attend to Kent and the parking lot attendant.

Mike entered the ICU after a 3-hour nap, feeling significantly stronger. He was happy to see Wendy sitting up talking to her nurse.

"Hi, Wendy," said Mike. "How do you feel?"

"I feel great. I'm ready to go home."

"Now Wendy, don't get your hopes up that high," said Sally, the ICU nurse. "The doctors want you monitored for another couple of days."

"But it sure is great hearing you talk like that," said Mike. "It's wonderful that you're improving so quickly now. I might be able to get you out of here in a day or so."

"Do you mean the ICU, or the hospital?" asked Wendy.

"Both. Just keep getting better. Don't forget, you still need some tricky doses of medication." Mike was hoping those listening would allow him to stall 2 more days. "Now, please rest. I'm going to take a nap for 2 to 3 hours and then I'll be back to talk some more."

"OK, Dad."

"Wendy."

"Yes, Dad."

"I love you."

"I love you, too, Dad. Now go before you get all mushy. I'll see you soon. I'm not going anywhere."

Mike was planning to change into surgical scrubs to have a private conversation with Wendy. He turned to leave and noticed a large man duck out the ICU entrance door just as he turned. Was somebody following him? He decided he would be very careful and he'd take the long, circuitous route to the surgical locker room.

As he exited the ICU, he opened the door slowly. He looked up and down the hall and saw no one. He went out into the hall and turned left, figuring anyone tailing him would guess the other direction. Not much of interest was left. He rounded the next corner and looked back to see if anyone might be following. He saw no one. As he turned back around, he felt a pain in his head and neck just before passing out. Two men quickly lifted him to an erect position supporting him. One rolled up his right sleeve and injected 15 mg of Versed in his triceps area. They then took off in the direction Mike had chosen toward the deserted section of the hospital, supporting their catch. They took the stairs down to the basement. The Assistant Medical Examiner had given them a key to the morgue, and they went inside without anyone seeing them. They put Mike in a body bag, made several air holes in the bag, and loaded him into the hearse waiting at the loading dock.

The Sheraton Suites Wilmington was a nice hotel convenient to center city Wilmington, and very close to the Colony South

Restaurant, as Debbie had requested. It wasn't lavish or plush, but it was definitely clean and very comfortable. It even had a bellman on the weekends, and its parking garage was actually roomy, with a direct connection to the hotel.

The two FBI agents, Jim Thomas and Jeff Richards, walked with Debbie into the main lobby area. Jim went with Debbie to register while Jeff cased the lobby and observed people, including hotel staff who passed through. Jim Thomas registered them as husband and wife and took a second room next door for Jeff, "their friend from out of town." Debbie's room was on the corner so no one would have a room on either side. Jim and Debbie went over to Jeff after registering. Jim handed Jeff his keys.

"Why don't you get our things out of the car and meet us in the room?" suggested Jim.

"OK, good buddy. I'll be right along. Room 720, right?"

"That's the one. And try to get there directly. We need to stay together and report in as soon as you get to the room."

"Be there in a flash," said Jeff.

The woman jabbering rapidly on her cell phone turned her head telling her listener, "Seventh floor, Room 720. Heading up now." She quickly turned back around and carried on about her wild daughter and the school dance last night.

Jim and Debbie were alone on the elevator. It stopped on the fourth floor, allowing three men with brief cases to get on. Debbie moved close to Jim, holding his arm, trying to look like a loving wife. As the elevator door opened, Jim and Debbie started to get off. An electronic device suddenly sounded a distinct five-note melody, repeating itself. Both Jim and Debbie were struck hard on the head at the same time. Two more similarly dressed men appeared, and with an assist under the arms got them up to standing position. The two with Debbie headed for the stairs. The two with Jim took the room key, unlocked room 720, dragged Jim into the bathroom and snapped his neck. They shut the door and left the room with the key on the bed. The two assailants helping Debbie exited the stairs on the sixth floor and silently and slowly walked up and down the hallway until they got the signal that the second

FBI agent had been subdued. They didn't want to accidentally run into him on the stairwell. Sixty seconds later, their pagers went off with a different catchy signal, telling them it was now safe for them to go back to the stairwell with Debbie.

Leaving the stairwell into the parking garage, they passed three people in business attire coming into the hotel, so they feigned talking about their "co-worker" getting drunk so early in the day. The passersby seemed to buy the appearance and chuckled to themselves wondering how people ever had the luxury of drinking so much during the daytime. Frank Vinton's team number 4 loaded Debbie into their minivan, where one of them injected 12 mg of Versed into her thigh. The driver then drove toward south Wilmington and the Smoke House Bar.

Forty-Five

Tuesday, May 20
Wilmington, Delaware

The Smoke House Bar was a popular spot for the harder element in the south side of Wilmington. It had been around for many years, and over time the place had come to an arrangement with the local police. The drug trade was impossible to control in this section of Wilmington, but the clientele of the Smoke House Bar kept their drug utilization discreet and understood that they would not carry out major drug deals on site. They were free to negotiate and plan such deals, but the actual transactions were banned within the bar by an understanding spread by the locals. Most regulars were tough neighborhood folks who made their living on the street or by migrating between minimum-wage jobs. The temptation to score big with illegal drugs was very much in the minds of most of the customers. However, no one would violate the well-known restrictions on the premises. Thus, the bar served as a business center for many to make their plans to supplement their minimal and sporadic job income.

Frank Vinton's men knew the atmosphere of the Smoke House rather well. They had spent hours there getting to know the place, confirming that it was an appropriate location for overdosing a chosen victim. They also knew that they would get only one opportunity, for if they returned to the scene of their planned crime, the locals would not forgive them for bringing police attention to their sanctuary.

The black Lincoln pulled up to the side door of the bar, which opened to an alleyway. Two men got out with Mike, placed his arms around their shoulders, and literally carried him inside to a table in the back. The smoke-filled bar was rather large, but haphazard passageways led to several mostly secluded sections, where privacy was easily obtained. They propped Mike up on a bench seat against the wall between the two men who brought him inside. Two minutes later, another man appeared holding onto a passed-out Debbie. She was positioned in the corner of the bench seat, next to her husband's threesome. The three men ordered five drinks, with no intention of drinking them. Mike and Debbie were very heavily sedated and having great difficulty waking up. As soon as the waitress left to get the drinks, one of the men made radio contact with another associate outside of the bar.

"Bob, Burns and Allen are in place. Over."

"Any problems?"

"None. How long before delivery?"

"Fifteen minutes. Call if anything develops."

"Roger. Out."

Hugh Winston heard the gunshot that sent a bullet into and through Nash's neck. He looked outside through the small window in the thick maintenance area door, adjacent to the parking garage. He saw the police talking to Nash and radioing for an ambulance to take him around the corner to the Emergency Room. Just then, Dominic burst through the Maintenance Entrance door.

"Hugh, where can I hide? Quick."

"What the fuck did you do to blow this assignment? You can't leave now, you have to finish these two off!" Hugh was disgusted. He couldn't believe Dominic and Chip had screwed up such an easy set-up. Typical lazy American soldiers. Americans were incapable of being real fighters. Al-Qaeda loyalists would never run away from their mission.

"Don't worry your wimpy ass. They're both dead. I shot Nash's wife in the SUV before I got out, and Nash got a bullet in the neck. He's done. Now where can I hide? Vinton told us you would hide us if we needed it."

"Look again, Mr. Incompetent. Nash looks very much alive. Now who's the asshole? What are you going to do about it? If Nash lives, the agency will come after you and you've got no chance of living. You've just fucked this whole operation up for everyone."

"Don't you call me incompetent, you fucking wimp!" Dominic came at Hugh who had his switchblade ready. Hugh imbedded the blade deep into Dominic's abdomen and ripped the blade sideways sheering the aorta instantly, dropping his assailant to his knees and then face down on the concrete maintenance floor. Hugh pulled his knife out and wiped it on Dominic's shirt. He pocketed the blade and took off his surgical gloves and shoe covers. He put them in the incinerator.

Hugh had to think fast. He didn't have long before the police would come in. He carefully looked out the window. The officers were still kneeling beside Nash and one had a radio to his ear. He couldn't let Nash survive. If he got into police protection and lived to tell what he knew, Nash could cause serious problems for the Brey Agency and ruin everything Hugh had worked so hard to have at Kelly Hospital. All he was planning for his cell would be ruined. He wouldn't be able to deliver the gene therapy to make the true soldiers of the world invincible. If Nash lived, he figured he would become a rapid casualty. Pawns were often sacrificed to save the leaders. And he realized he couldn't run out and escape; the Agency would hunt him down. They would not let him leave under these circumstances. Their team had orders. Kill Kent and Patti Nash at all costs, and do it now. His choice was clear. He really had no choice. If he terminated Nash and got away, he had everything to gain. If he did nothing and Nash lived, he would be caught or terminated by his own team. Hugh decided if he acted quickly enough, he could get away. He knew the intricacies of his hospital so well that no one could find him. He would kill Nash with a sniper shot and then disappear to an interfloor, reappearing minutes later in a place totally separated from the shooting. He put on another pair of surgical gloves and uncovered his already loaded 927 Remington special rifle hidden behind the kick plate of a storage counter. He removed the rifle, replaced the kick plate, and slid the boxes back in place, covering up the hiding place. He then opened one of the maintenance area doors a few inches, enough to give him a view of Nash lying on the ground next to the two policemen talking into their radios 50 yards away.

Hugh couldn't believe his luck. He had a perfect, hidden view of Nash. He laid down on the floor and aimed the rifle. He positioned Nash's head in his telescopic sight, figuring one shot to the head would keep Nash from telling what he knew. He took a breath in slowly and let part of it out before holding his breath. He then slowly squeezed the trigger just as a paramedic squatted down beside Nash and took the bullet meant for Nash. Nearby, Brian Taggart had just come to. He heard the shot and looked in the direction of the rifle fire. He saw Hugh's face, staring at the scene, looking stunned. Hugh then dropped the rifle and got up to run as planned. Brian called out, "It's Hugh Winston! He going inside." The two policemen pulled their guns, took protective stances over their injured charge, and immediately motioned for people to get out of the way while scanning the area for danger.

Hugh heard his name just before the maintenance door closed. He figured he needed to change his plan. He'd better disappear and escape from the hospital fast, then leave town and head for Canada. Al-Qaeda would take care of him there. Fortunately, he was prepared in case he had to leave town in a hurry. He grabbed his emergency knapsack and ran to the utility closet with the stairs for interfloor 2B.

The three men in the Smoke House Bar placed tourniquets on Mike and Debbie's arms. Their Special Forces training made it easy for them to slip a butterfly needle into a vein in their healthy prisoners' arms. They taped the needles in place and then secured the 4-inch plastic tubing further down the arms. Their victims were ready. Once the deadly supply of injectable cocaine arrived, it would only be a matter of minutes before the Naylors died of a drug overdose. They would leave them huddled together and would be long gone before anyone bothered to notice. One of the men removed his surgical gloves so he could show his hands above the table when the waitress returned. He knew sterile surgical technique so he could do so and still flawlessly avoid leaving any fingerprints. He felt for the hanky in each side pocket making sure they were in place in case he had to use his hands. The men already had five twenty-dollar bills on the table, showing the waitress they wanted to run a tab.

After 10 minutes, their associate arrived with prefilled syringes. He removed the syringes from his coat pocket, allowing them to gently fall out of a cloth wrapper. He remained standing to block the only view a curious onlooker might have. The two men with gloves on each took a syringe and prepared to inject their contents into Mike and Debbie.

Jason Burke put a Magnum 45 into the standing man's back and said, "I wouldn't do that if I were you."

The standing man wheeled around to strike Jason while pulling a gun from his waist. Jason fired into the man's abdomen, pushed him aside, pulled a second gun out of his belt, and pointed both guns at the two who started to stand also. Jason spoke with quiet but deadly force.

"Put the syringes on the table and raise both hands slowly. My men are behind you with orders to shoot to kill if they see any more quick movements. Drop the syringes now!"

The two men slowly looked behind them. They saw three men with guns pointed at their heads. They slowly turned back, dropping the syringes on the table.

Dean Carter and Dan Dellose were in Dean's office in the

Brey Agency in Boston talking to Frank Vinton over their secure line, when the office door suddenly burst open and four men jumped inside with high-powered rifles aimed at their heads. Their leader spoke.

"FBI! Arms up on your heads. NOW! Do it!"

Dean Carter and Dan Dellose looked at each other, wondering what was going on. They immediately complied. Frank remained silent on the speakerphone.

"Now, slowly stand up. Slowly!"

Dean and Dan carefully stood up with no panic. They had been arrested before and had faith that their lawyers would get them off. Dean spoke first.

"What's this all about? Why are you breaking into my office?"

"You're under arrest for murder, attempted murder, and conspiracy to commit murder. Now, you first, Mr. Carter. Move over here so we can cuff you and read you your rights."

Forty-Six

Wednesday, May 21
Wilmington, Delaware

The tables were turned. This time Wendy was standing beside her father's bed, rubbing his arm. Mike slowly came to and realized where he was. He looked over to Wendy, who grinned from ear to ear to see her father waking up.

"Dad, you're all right! Everything's going to be OK. The FBI caught the guys trying to kill you!"

"What are you saying, Wendy? What's going on?"

Jason Burke stood up and walked around to the other side of his bed.

"How do you feel, Mike?"

"Jason, it's good to see you. I feel hung over. What's going on?"

"Well, with help from someone who believes in family, we got to the Smoke House Bar just before you were going to take one hell of a trip. Mike, you really shouldn't hang out in that place."

"Jason, I didn't know I was there. How's Debbie? Where is she?"

"She's sleeping across the hall. I've got three agents watching her. The doctors say she'll be all right. They say you'll be fine, too, and they were actually right. You woke up first."

"Jason, I don't know what you did, but thank you so much. And Wendy, you look great. How do you feel?

"I'm fine, Daddy. This lady told Mr. Burke these guys were going to kill you so he could save you. And they caught the ringleaders, too."

"Jason, what is she talking about?"

"Are you sure you're going to remember if I tell you? You know you're still somewhat drugged."

"I'll remember this. Just tell me, will you?"

"OK. Jessica Miller, who said she was from the Southern Sports Agency in Atlanta, walked into my office right after my men took Debbie into hiding. She told me she wanted no part of any family massacre and that I'd better act fast. She explained how the Brey Agency intended to use gene therapy to create superathletes that she and others would manage so everyone involved could become rich. She had no problem with the gene therapy part of the scheme, especially since it technically wasn't illegal, at least not yet. She said her whole goal was to be able to provide well for her father, but she knew he wouldn't want her to be part of any intentional killing. She decided she had to prevent that. She couldn't stand that her bosses intended to make an orphan out of Wendy."

Jason continued, "So while listening to this story and trying to decide if I should believe her, I then radioed Jim and Jeff. When they didn't answer, I figured I had better listen very carefully. She told me of the plan to take you and Debbie to the Smoke House Bar and kill you both with an overdose, making it look like you did it yourselves."

"How about Kent and Patti?"

"Patti is fine. She had a metal brace across her chest that deflected the bullet meant for her heart. She's resting now. Her doctor gave her something to put her to sleep for a few hours. She's been through quite a lot. And Kent is going to be OK, I'm told. He's in ICU recovering from a gunshot wound to his neck and a concussion. The bullet missed his spinal cord and carotid artery. It just ripped a bunch of muscle. He's already complaining that he wants to see his wife and you."

"Do you have any other news for me? Is Kelly OK?"

"Kelly is fine. She's at your sister's now. She was taken from your home to a hideaway not too far from the Smoke House Bar. Her captors just left her alone, and she walked to the corner newsstand and talked the owner into calling the police. They knew to call me since we were working together, and I had her taken to your sister's. Kelly suggested that. She said she had some homework to do and seemed quite undaunted by the whole affair. She did say she wanted to talk to you and Debbie as soon as you woke up. She's an amazing kid."

"I'm surprised she didn't talk her captors into giving up."

"Maybe she would have. She didn't have much time. She said they only kept her there about a half hour and then they suddenly left."

"Well, go on. I'm sure there's more."

"As a matter of fact, there is. Brian Taggart saved Kent's life twice, and he's in the ICU, also in critical condition, with a bullet wound to the chest, pneumothorax, non-displaced neck fracture, and concussion. He's supposed to have a good chance of being OK, too."

"My God, did we have a war around here?"

"Close. A paramedic took a bullet for Kent, too. He died an hour ago. Two FBI agents died trying to protect Debbie. A parking garage attendant was shot in the shoulder trying to save Patti and protect Kent, but he should be OK. I don't know about his shoulder though."

"What about Hugh Winston and Ken Turner?"

"We haven't found Hugh Winston yet. Brian identified him as trying to shoot Kent. He took off and disappeared into the hospital. We have the hospital cordoned off. If he's in there, he won't escape. And who's Ken Turner? Is he a bad guy, too?"

"I'm not sure. He's in Boston, and he's very wealthy, so he should be easy to find. I'll tell you about him later."

"How about Dr. Thompson?"

"We arrested him a few hours ago. He broke down crying. He wasn't too stable."

"What about the guys in Boston?"

"You mean a Mr. Carter and a Mr. Dellose?"

"Yes, among others."

"Well, Carter and Dellose appear to be the ringleaders and are being 'interviewed' as we speak by FBI in Boston. I understand they are pretty polished and aren't saying anything. We're trying to break them down, but it may take some time. They're probably too smart to talk. At least we have enough to keep them for a very long time without bail and convict them for a protracted jail sentence without parole."

Mike thought for a few moments, taking in all that Jason had said. He looked at Wendy, who squeezed his hand. Mike started to cry.

"Wendy, I'm so sorry. I only wanted the best for you. I should have told you there might be some risk. I had no idea all this would happen."

"Dad, it's OK. I know you do everything you can for me. And I know how hard you've worked to help me when things went wrong. Jason told me all about Alaska and what you and Dr. Nash did when I was in ICU."

"I wonder what I did to deserve you, Wendy."

"Oh, Dad. Don't get all weepy now. There are other people here."

Mike turned to Jason. "Does my partner know what happened?"

"He knows you're going to be all right. And that you're now safe. He wanted me to call him when you woke up, and he wanted to know when you'd be ready to take call. Shall I call him now?"

"What time is it?"

"It's 7:15 in the morning."

"Then call him. He can stop by on rounds, or if he's already gone, I can see him tonight. Do you think it's really safe for us? Will we be able to stay here in Wilmington and lead normal lives?"

"It sure seems that way. We've arrested enough of the ringleaders and conspirators that the agency is completely broken up. Jessica Miller saw to that."

"What's going to happen to her?"

"She'll probably get off. She hasn't actually broken any law that I know. I could see some overzealous assistant DA charging her with conspiracy, but coming forth like she did, not even asking for immunity, she probably saved many lives. She has quite a few supporters on my team. I believe most judges would realize the good in her and dismiss any charges."

"Hey, how about you getting me out of here, and I'll take you and Wendy out for all the pancakes you can eat?"

"You doctors are all alike. Both you and Nash are the worst patients. You ask your doctors when it's safe for you to leave. I'm not going to sneak you out against doctors' orders. When you get released, then we'll talk."

Epilogue

Wilmington, Delaware

Jason Burke was right. The ring was effectively destroyed. Hugh Winston, however, was not found. Frank Vinton, Ted Duffy, and Rob Glenn disappeared as well, and the FBI did not have their names because Dean Carter and Dan Dellose remained silent. Both Carter and Dellose were convicted of first-degree murder, among other charges, and are presently on death row pending the usual appeals.

Wendy recovered without further incident under the watchful eyes of her father and Dr. Nash. Debbie woke up 3 hours after Mike, experiencing the same headache he had. Bill Owens was quite happy to get his partner back to work, so he could have some time off and a month or two without taking night call.

Katie Wilson was found tied up and gagged in her home, essentially unharmed. Apparently, Frank Vinton's men had kept her alive as a prisoner in case they had to use her to contact Debbie. She was thrilled to learn she had played an important part in defeating the Brey Agency and mentioned she might take some espionage courses at the University of Delaware. Jason didn't have the heart to tell her she'd have to attend a military or police academy to be able to take such a course.

One week after Jason Burke, with Jessica Miller's help, cracked the Brey Agency ring, a representative of the National Institutes of Health called on Dr. Naylor and Dr. Nash. He insisted on meeting them together. He brought them both a job offer from the NIH, which wanted them, as a team, to oversee the national government effort to ethically control gene therapy research. They would report directly to the Director of the NIH, and they would both be paid a half million dollars per year, plus benefits, for a minimum of 10 years. The money for their salaries was already financed and was guaranteed, even if they resigned early, as long as they worked for at least 1 year. A 'private benefactor' named Ken Turner had learned of their efforts and wanted to be sure no other young athletes ever had their lives put in jeopardy because of gene therapy.

Gene therapy is currently under study for many of the things discussed in this book. Gene therapy is already being used clinically in sports medicine to aid with the healing of partially torn ligaments, including torn anterior cruciate ligaments. The potential is vast, but currently, the control is yet to be defined. Everything that happened in this fictional story relative to gene therapy is theoretically possible. We need to be sure the appropriate authoritative power is overseeing, and supporting, the research being done in this area.

BVG